" u'd rath "

He nind rebell   er
so some strang   ple
th didn't know. But wasn't that what she'd
do anyway? Dalton Hale was little more than a
str ger to them. And his house was like no place
sh Logan had ever lived before.

Bu he felt safe there, she realized. She had
no rticular reason to feel that way, but she
did gardless.

"N she said, not intending to say so aloud but
not ally regretting it when she heard the word
slip ver her tongue.

Sh lt his gaze on her again, a caress of scrutiny
tha nt a little shiver of awareness darting down
he ine. He released a soft breath, as if he'd been
hol g it.

"I 't regret asking you to stay with me."

"I 't regret staying." She slanted a quick look
tow d him. "We'll have to take pains to keep it
tha ay, won't we?"

THE LEGEND OF SMUGGLER'S CAVE

BY
PAULA GRAVES

Published in Great Britain 2014
by Mills & Boon, an imprint of Harlequin (UK) Limited,
Eton House, 18-24 Paradise Road, Richmond, Surrey, TW9 1SR

© 2014 Paula Graves

ISBN: 978 0 263 91355 2

46-0414

Alabama native **Paula Graves** wrote her first book, a mystery starring herself and her neighborhood friends, at the age of six. A voracious reader, Paula loves books that pair tantalizing mystery with compelling romance. When she's not reading or writing, she works as a creative director for a Birmingham advertising agency and spends time with her family and friends. She is a member of Southern Magic Romance Writers, Heart of Dixie Romance Writers and Romance Writers of America.

Paula invites readers to visit her website, www.paulagraves.com.

For my niece Melissa,
who has added unexpected joy to my life
in some of the most surprising ways.
I love you, Missy.

Now go do your homework.

Chapter One

The front door was unlocked. Jenny never left it unlocked.

Hair rising on her neck and arms, Briar Blackwood took a careful step backward on the porch and drew her Glock 27. Not her weapon of choice; her Mossberg 835 shotgun was locked in the cabinet inside the cabin. But the Glock would do.

She stayed still for a breathless moment, listening for movement within the cabin. Was she overreacting? Maybe her aunt had fallen asleep on the sofa without locking up.

No. The break-in a month earlier had rattled Aunt Jenny's nerves. She hadn't been comfortable staying at Briar's place with Logan alone at night since. She always locked all the doors and windows the second Briar left and wouldn't even answer the door unless she knew the voice on the other side.

So why was the door unlocked now?

Everyone who mattered to Briar was behind that unlocked door. And she could stand here holding her breath, or she could go in there to see what was what.

But not through the front door.

Briar edged to the corner of the porch, making herself a harder target if someone inside started shooting. Tightening her grip on the Glock, she pulled her cell phone from her jacket pocket and dialed the cabin landline. She heard the phone ringing through the cabin walls.

No answer.

Now she knew for sure something was wrong. Aunt Jenny was a light sleeper. She never slept through a ringing phone.

Shoving her cell phone back in her pocket, Briar slid between the wood slabs of the porch railing and dropped three feet to the ground below. Stopping below the big kitchen window, she peered up at the jars of fruits and vegetables stacked in three tight rows in front of the window. The colorful jars took the place of curtains, both as a dash of brightness in the small kitchen and as a privacy screen, keeping out the unwanted gazes of strangers who might be lurking outside the mountain cabin.

They were still intact. Last time someone had broken in, they'd shattered the jars and left a huge mess in her kitchen.

What could they want? She was poor as a church mouse. Her new job as a Bitterwood police officer would do little more than pay the bills and allow her to put aside a little bit for her son Logan's college fund.

Could it be her job that had drawn the intruders to her door?

She edged her way around to the root cellar door and eased it open, wincing at the low creaks of the hinges. Six concrete steps took her down into the tightly packed cellar, where shelves full of canned goods filled one side of the room, and bins of root vegetables filled the other. She used the flashlight app on her cell phone to illuminate the narrow path between shelves and bins, but she still managed to stumble into the shelves near the stairs. With a muttered curse, she barely caught a jar of tomatoes as it started to topple off the shelf above.

Setting it right, she shined the cell-phone light up the

stairs. The door to the cabin was closed. She crept up the stairs and tried the doorknob. Locked, as expected. She eased her keys from her pocket and inserted the right one. The doorknob turned smoothly, and she carefully slipped into the hallway, shutting off the phone light.

She went very still, just listening. There was no sound at all, she realized. Not even the hum of the refrigerator or the whir of heated air blowing from the wall heater nearby.

The power must be out. Had someone cut it?

Glad for the rubber soles of her work shoes, she went silently into the living room and took a quick scan of the situation. Her eyes had begun to adjust to the low light, allowing her to see that the living room was a mess. Sofa cushions had been pulled from the sofa and ripped open, the stuffing lying all over everything. The intruders may have spared her jars of fruits and vegetables this time, but most of the contents of her refrigerator lay scattered across the floor and counters of the tiny kitchen, going to ruin.

She stepped back into the hallway, her heart pounding with equal parts adrenaline and dread.

Please, God, let Logan and Jenny be okay. Please, please, please....

The door to her own bedroom was closest. That was where Jenny slept when Briar was working a night shift, as she'd done during her stint as a dispatcher, and as she'd be doing for the first few months on the job as a police officer. But when Briar tried to push the door open, something was blocking it. She peered through the narrow space between the door and the frame and saw a pale white hand outstretched.

Jenny!

A noise in the next room down made her freeze. That was Logan's room.

Someone was moving within.

She reached through the narrow crack in the door and touched her fingertips to Jenny's wrist. Relief rattled through her when she found a strong, steady pulse.

Pulling back, she pushed to her feet and fell back on her police-academy training, so recently finished. She led with her pistol, moving as quietly and quickly as she could. The thumping sound she'd heard earlier repeated. A drawer closing, she recognized.

She touched the door and found that it wasn't latched. It swung open slowly and silently—thank God she'd oiled the hinges recently. It used to creak like crazy.

A tall dark-clad figure stood silhouetted by the faint moonlight coming through Logan's window. He had his back to her, allowing her to spare a quick glance toward the bed to reassure herself that Logan was still there, his face turned toward his pillow and his little chest rising slowly and steadily.

"Freeze—police!"

The dark silhouette whirled not toward her but toward Logan's bed.

She couldn't fire at him, not with her son so close, so she shoved the gun in her jacket pocket and ran, hitting the intruder solidly. They both bounced off the bed and hit the floor.

"Mama!" Logan's soft, frightened wail tore at Briar's heart, but she couldn't let go of the man punching and kicking at her in an attempt to escape.

He eluded her grasp and started toward the door. She scrambled up after him, tackling him as he darted into the hall.

Suddenly, strong, cruel fingers bit into her arm at the same time she was yanked back by her hair, allowing the man she'd brought down to scurry out of reach.

She grabbed the Glock from her jacket and twisted around, shoving the barrel at her captor. "Let me go!"

He dropped her with a hard shove, slamming her back into the floor. Her head hit the hardwood with a jarring thud, and for a second the whole world seemed to explode into colorful confetti.

Then her vision cleared, and she swung the Glock in a semicircle, looking for any sign of the intruders.

The front door was open, barely visible from her position on the hallway floor. She pushed to her feet, wincing at the pain in her shoulder, and edged her way into the living room.

She took a quick peek outside. There was no sound of a motor, but she thought she made out the rustle of leaves in the woods just beyond her property. Even with a three-quarter moon in the sky, she couldn't detect any movement in the gloom of the woods, just the fading rustles of the two intruders running away.

She shoved the door closed and engaged the lock, her heart pounding and her head aching.

"Mama!" Logan's wail drew her back to the hallway. Pocketing her weapon, she pulled out her cell phone and turned on the flashlight app, shining it into the darkness.

Logan stood in the middle of the hall, his blue T-shirt riding up his little round belly and his pajama pants sagging to reveal his big-boy underwear.

She ran and scooped him up, pressing her face against his little chest, breathing in the beautiful smell of sleepy little boy. "Mama's right here," she assured him, patting his back in soothing circles.

Mama's got you.

HE SHOULD HAVE known Doyle Massey would be at the hospital. The Bitterwood chief of police seemed to show up everywhere Dalton Hale went these days, like a particularly hard-to-kill weed in a flower garden. And, as luck would have it, tonight the sister was there, as well, her auburn hair, green eyes and prominent cheekbones a persistent, visible reminder of what a mess his own life had become in the last month.

Dalton had finally reached the point, however, where the sight of Doyle and Dana Massey didn't send him into a seething rage. At least, not on the outside. He was still boiling a little inside, but he set that emotion aside and entered the Maryville Mercy Hospital waiting room with his head high and his own green eyes clear and focused.

He bumped gazes with Laney Hanvey, who sat next to Massey. She was about to marry the chief, which had strained their formerly collegial relationship, but she was still the friendliest face in the room. She murmured something to her fiancé and crossed the room to meet him.

"Is something wrong?" she asked quietly.

He realized she didn't know he was there for the same reason she was. "Not on my end of things. I'm here to talk to the victim."

Her gaze narrowed. "Jenny Franklin is still undergoing tests."

"I meant the widow. The Blackwood woman." He realized, as Laney's expression darkened, that he sounded cold and officious. Not the sort of man he'd ever been, not before now. He'd been the prosecutor who went the extra mile, tried to get to know the people for whom he sought justice. He still received Christmas cards from people he'd helped. He never used to call people things like *victim* or *the widow.*

He was doing a lot of things now that he'd never done before.

"Her name is Briar," Laney said quietly. "Do you have to do this tonight?"

"Was she injured?"

"Just roughed up a little. Didn't even let the paramedics check her."

Dalton looked past Laney until his gaze snagged on the dark-haired woman sitting with a small boy sleeping in her arms. She sat apart from the others, though most of them threw concerned glances toward her now and then.

"That's her, isn't it?" He nodded toward the woman with the child.

Laney followed his gaze. "Yes. You know the police already have her statement, right? She's a cop herself. She was thorough."

That was news to him, actually. "I thought she was a dispatcher."

"She graduated from the academy back in December, and a slot opened on the police force last week, so she finally got her badge."

Laney was answering all his questions with details, he realized, because she wanted to keep him from bothering Briar Blackwood. And hell, maybe if he were in her position, he'd be doing the same. He hadn't exactly covered himself with glory over the past few weeks as he'd dealt with finding out his whole bloody life had been a lie.

Matter of fact, he'd been a complete ass about it.

"I just want to ask her a few questions about the break-in." He intentionally added a gentle tone to his voice, though he was feeling anything but gentle at the moment.

Laney's eyes narrowed again, as if she saw through the pretense. But after a moment, her expression cleared. "I'll introduce you."

He'd have preferred to approach the woman alone, away

from all her friends, but he couldn't exactly make any demands, could he? It wasn't as if she were the culprit here.

At least, not that he could prove.

He followed Laney across the waiting room floor, ignoring the watchful gazes of the others, though he did spare the slightest glance at Dana Massey, as if his eyes couldn't resist one more quick look to make sure he hadn't been mistaken about the resemblance.

No, still there, the faint but unmistakable traits that had convinced her, on the day of their first meeting, that he was the long-lost half brother she'd only recently learned about.

He dragged his gaze forward, grinding his teeth.

"Briar?"

The dark-haired woman looked up at Laney, then let her gaze slide slowly to Dalton's face, her clear gray eyes darkening with recognition. So she already knew who he was. Probably not good news, given the tumble his reputation had taken around the Bitterwood Police Department in the past few weeks.

"Mrs. Blackwood, I'd like to ask you a few questions about the break-in this evening," he said, not waiting for the unnecessary introduction.

Beside him, Laney released a soft sigh. "Briar, this is assistant county prosecutor Dalton Hale."

"I know who he is," she said quietly, still holding his gaze. "I've given a statement to the Bitterwood Police Department. Detective Nix is the lead detective." She nodded toward the dark-haired man sitting next to Dana Massey. Walker Nix. Bitterwood detective and Dana's significant other. Nix stared back at him, as if daring him to cause a ruckus.

In Briar's lap the dark-haired little boy stirred and made a low mewling noise that sounded like a puppy whining. He tightened his little arms around his mother's neck, clinging like a monkey as she rubbed his back and murmured soothing nonsense to him until he settled down.

A painful sensation wriggled in the pit of his stomach. He killed it with ruthless dispatch. "I understand that. But I have some questions about the incident that the detective may not have known to ask."

Something shifted in those gunmetal eyes, a flicker of flame warming their wintry depths. "Such as?"

Ah, he thought, *she's curious.* That was good. Curiosity was exactly the sort of trait he needed from this woman if he was going to get the answers he sought. "Such as, do you believe this most recent break-in could be related to the one that happened a few weeks ago?"

Her eyes went from molten steel to flinty ice in a split second. "What makes you think Nix wouldn't have asked such an obvious question? Do you have such a low opinion of the police?"

Dalton gave himself a mental kick. Once more he was letting his anger at Massey taint everything and everyone connected to him. Of course Nix would have asked the obvious question. "Fair enough."

Briar glanced up at Laney. Some communication moved silently between them, for Laney patted Briar's arm and walked away, leaving him alone with her.

He sat in the empty chair beside her. "You like handling things on your own. Don't you?"

She didn't answer.

"You're sitting off here by yourself, away from your friends. You sent Laney away so you could handle my questions alone."

"You seem to know something, or think you know something, about the break-in. So spill it." She kept her voice low, her hand still drawing soothing circles around her son's back.

"I know your husband died seven months ago."

"He was *murdered* seven months ago," she corrected quietly. Her voice had an oddly detached tone, making him wonder about the state of the relationship at the time of Johnny Blackwood's murder.

"You weren't a suspect?"

Her gaze flicked toward him. "I had an alibi."

"Work?" She'd still been the emergency services night-shift dispatcher at the time of Johnny's death.

She nodded. "Plenty of security video to establish my whereabouts."

"But you had a motive?"

She took a quick, sharp breath through her nose. "Is there a point to this line of questioning?"

He supposed there wasn't, other than curiosity. He knew the basics about Johnny Blackwood's goings and comings during the months leading up to his murder. It was how he'd latched on to Johnny in the first place—reading through the case notes and seeing signs of a potential connection to another case he was looking into. But the personal details in the case file were scarce, perhaps because Briar was part of the Bitterwood P.D. family. Personal matters not pertaining to the case would have been minimized and even left out to protect her privacy.

Like the state of the marriage at the time of his death. The cops would have wanted to know if there had been trouble in her relationship with her husband. And Dalton knew that on Johnny's side, at least, there had been trouble to spare.

But did his wife know what Dalton knew?

As he puzzled through how best to ask her such a delicate question, a doctor in a white jacket over green scrubs entered the waiting room. "Mrs. Franklin's family?"

Briar's whole body seemed to snap to tautness at the

sound of the doctor's voice. She stood, clutching her small son more tightly to her, and crossed to meet the doctor halfway.

Dalton trailed behind her, catching up in time to hear the doctor say, "We'll want to keep her until tomorrow because she lost consciousness, but she's not showing any continuing mental confusion, which is a very good sign. She did sustain a fracture of both bones in her lower right arm, however. We've reset the bones and applied a fiberglass cast to just above the elbow. She'll need to wear the cast for at least four weeks."

"Can I see her?" Briar asked.

"Check with the nurse at the front desk in the E.R.— she'll tell you what room she'll be in." The doctor smiled, gave Briar a comforting pat on her shoulder and left the waiting room, moving at a clip.

"Good news," Dalton murmured.

Briar turned her gaze toward him, her eyes narrowing. "You're still here."

"Yes, I am," he said, not taking offense. He knew he was making a nuisance of himself by coming here at this hour of night to bother her, but it couldn't be helped. She might hold the key to his uncertain future without even realizing it.

"I have to go check on my aunt." She turned away from him and crossed to where Laney sat, murmuring something before she handed off her son to the other woman.

Dalton watched her straighten her back and leave the waiting room with her shoulders squared and her chin up, like a soldier readied for battle. It struck him, in that brief glimpse of her steel core, that Briar Blackwood was a woman who thrived on challenges that made other people collapse.

Could that trait of hers be useful to him?

As Dalton started out the door after her, Doyle Massey rose from his chair and moved into his path. He was smiling as he did so, in that charming snake-oil salesman way of his, all teeth and beach tan and ulterior motives.

"Where are you going?" Doyle asked.

"That's none of your business." Dalton tried to take a step around him, but Doyle shifted, staying in his path.

"I don't know what you're up to or why you've suddenly taken an interest in my newest recruit, but don't drag our bad blood into it."

Dalton couldn't help smiling at the chief's choice of words. "Bad blood, huh?"

"Dana and I get that you don't want to be part of our family, and you know, we can live with that. But don't think that means we'll let you screw with our lives and the lives of people around us."

"Your faith in my integrity is touching."

"I have no faith in you at all," Doyle snapped back, dropping all pretense of friendly civility. "What brought you here tonight?"

"A case." Dalton lifted his chin, daring the chief to start a fight.

"Which case is that?"

Dalton glanced to his right as Walker Nix rose from his seat and headed for the waiting room door. Off to see after the Blackwood widow and her aunt, he guessed. Maybe take the older woman's statement.

He'd wanted to be there for that statement himself, but clearly the chief had other ideas.

"Why don't you both try being straight with each other?" Laney rose from her chair and moved to turn their tense twosome into a threesome.

They both looked at her, and she lifted her eyebrows in response.

Doyle looked back at Dalton, his eyebrows mimicking his fiancée's. "Well? What case are we talking about?"

Dalton was tempted to just leave without answering. But with so much on the line—not just his own ambitions but the safety of all the people he'd sworn justice for— he couldn't afford to let his emotions muck up the works.

"I've been trying to piece together a conspiracy case against the people we suspect were involved in the Wayne Cortland crime network," he said finally, lowering his voice by habit. "You know that Blake Culpepper has been fingered as one of the people involved."

"And you come here in the middle of the night to a hospital waiting room to ask Blake's distant cousin questions about his criminal activity?" Doyle sound unconvinced.

"Not about Culpepper." Dalton tamped down a smile at the thought that he actually knew something his know-it-all half brother didn't. "I came here to ask her questions about her late husband."

"You have questions about Johnny? Why?"

"Because odds are good he was part of Cortland's organization."

Chapter Two

Briar had never liked hospitals, even before her mother's death from breast cancer. The antiseptic smells, the dim artificial lights, the rhythms of machines that beat like the pulse of some giant predatory beast—they were alien to the life she knew, a life of fresh air, changing seasons, the loamy essence of earth and trees and the feel of wind in her hair.

In the white-sheeted hospital bed, her aunt looked like a thin, sickly child instead of a strong, wiry woman in her late fifties. Her shiny silver-streaked black hair looked dull and brittle beneath the single light shining over her bed, and when Jenny turned her tired gaze to Briar, she looked as if she'd aged a decade overnight.

The cast on her right arm was bulky and the color of old paper, not quite white, not quite yellow. "Does it hurt?" Briar asked, resting her hand on the rough-textured surface of the cast.

"Not at the moment."

There was a knock on the door behind her. Then it inched open and Walker Nix's face appeared in the opening. "Is it okay to come in?"

Briar looked at her aunt. "I think Walker wants to ask you some questions about what happened."

"Of course." Jenny flashed the detective a wan smile as he entered and came to stand at the foot of her bed.

"How're you feeling?" he asked Jenny, briefly squeezing Briar's shoulder before dropping his hand to his pocket to pull out a notebook.

"I'm not feeling much of anything at the moment," Jenny admitted, making Briar smile. "I guess you want to know what I remember."

"As much as you can."

Briar's aunt lifted her left hand to her brow. "I'd just put Logan to bed when there was a knock on the door." Jenny's gaze slanted to meet Briar's. "I know you say never to answer the door at night, but the person on the other side said he was Doyle Massey, and you know that light on the porch went out night before last."

Briar gave herself a mental kick. "I meant to put a new bulb in before I left tonight."

"You can imagine what I was thinking." Jenny reached out to Briar, clasping her hand when she offered it. "It was your second week on the police force, and here was the chief of police knocking at the door in the middle of the night...."

It had been a ruse guaranteed to get Jenny to open the door, which meant the intruders were familiar enough with her life to know it would work, Briar realized with a shudder of dismay.

"Did you get a good look at the intruders?" Nix asked.

"They wore face paint and dark camouflage. One of them had a skull cap kind of hat—black, I think. It was dark and it all happened so fast. His hair was up under the cap, so I couldn't tell you what color it was. I think his eyes were dark—they didn't really give me much time to look at them, to be honest. Just pushed me inside, turned out the lights and started throwing me around."

Anger built like a fire in the pit of Briar's gut. "Did you fight them?"

Jenny shook her head, looking stricken. "First blow, they broke my arm. Felt like they'd torn it clear off. Then I guess I hit my head on the hearth, because the next thing I remember is waking up when you came into the bedroom to check on me. I don't even know how I got there."

The intruders had probably dragged her there so they wouldn't have to step over her body while they ransacked the place, Briar thought. "The hospital has her clothes. They've bagged them up for evidence," she told Nix.

He nodded, his dark eyes reflecting the fire she felt roiling in her gut. "Miss Jenny, is there anything else you can remember? Did the men say anything when they were pushing you around?"

Jenny reached up and dashed away tears that had welled in her eyes. "I'm not sure—it was all such a blur...."

Briar squeezed her aunt's hand. "You never know what might make sense to someone else."

Jenny gave her hand a little squeeze back. "The other man said something about books."

Nix and Briar exchanged glances. "What books?" Nix asked.

"I don't know." Jenny shook her head, wincing as the motion apparently made her headache flare up. "He just said something like 'The books could be anywhere.'"

"What kind of books do you have?" Nix asked Briar curiously.

"Nothing valuable," she assured him. "Some of Logan's picture books, all my books from community college, some novels. Johnny didn't do a lot of reading for pleasure, so I don't even know if I have any of his books left. But none of them would be worth breaking into a cabin and beating up a woman for. Believe me."

Jenny's eyelids were drooping, Briar noticed, though she was trying not to show her weariness. Turning to Nix, Briar gave a little nod of her head toward the door.

"Miss Jenny, thank you for the information. I'm going to head out now and let you get some rest." Nix closed up his notebook and put it back in his pocket. "You just let me know if you remember anything else."

"I don't know how much help I've been," Jenny said with a sigh.

"You've been a big help," Briar assured her. "Now I want you to concentrate on feeling better. Okay?"

"Who's going to keep Logan for you while I'm all trussed up in this thing?" Jenny feebly lifted the heavy cast on her broken arm.

Briar hadn't had time to think that far ahead. "I'll figure it out, Aunt Jenny. You know I always do."

"I'm sorry. I shouldn't have opened the door."

As Nix headed for the door, Briar bent and kissed her aunt's furrowed brow. "You didn't do anything wrong. Don't fret yourself about it, okay?"

She waited by her aunt's bedside until the older woman had drifted back to sleep. Then she tiptoed out of the room.

Nix was waiting outside the door, leaning against the wall. "She's lucky to be alive."

"I know." Briar pushed back the springy curls that had slipped the bonds of her ponytail holder to fall in her face. She'd already had a rougher night off duty than she'd had on patrol. "What are the odds this break-in isn't related to the previous one?"

Nix fell into step with her as she started down the hallway toward the waiting room. "I don't know. We thought the last break-in was related to Dana's visit, remember?"

"The Cumberland curse," she murmured. Shortly after

Dana had made a visit to Briar's cabin, someone had broken in and trashed the place. Briar had assumed the break-in might have been an act of malice, to punish her for letting Tallie Cumberland's daughter into her home.

The people of her small community, Cherokee Cove, had come to blame the Cumberlands for almost everything that went wrong in their world. Dana Massey's mother, Tallie Cumberland, had become the target of a ruthless wealthy family after she'd accused them of stealing her child.

Dalton Hale's family, in fact.

It didn't matter that Tallie had told the truth. Subtly but unmistakably, Sutherlands and Hales had let it be known that any friend of a Cumberland was an enemy. And their influence in Bitterwood was far and wide. Nobody defied them without consequences. Tallie had left Bitterwood before the age of twenty, driven from town along with her family.

When Dana Massey had come to Bitterwood a couple of months ago, looking so much like her mother, a new round of Cumberland-curse fever had commenced. At the time of the last break-in, Briar and Nix had assumed one of her Cherokee Cove neighbors had been leaving her a message about mixing with Cumberlands.

Now she wasn't so sure.

"Is Dalton Hale still here?" she asked Nix.

"He was still in the waiting room when I left."

Great, she thought. *Just great.*

What the hell did he want with her, anyway? Why had he been asking questions about Johnny's murder? That mystery had been languishing in cold-case territory for months now.

Why was the Ridge County prosecutor's office suddenly interested in the murder again?

DALTON HALE HAD never seen himself as an angry man. Passionate, yes. Forceful in the pursuit of justice. But not one who possessed the kind of bitter rage that destroyed the lives and families of those who passed through his world.

But he was angry now. Fury burned in his gut like acid, eating away at every vestige of the man he'd once believed himself to be. It had poisoned his relationship with his father and grandfather until he'd found himself struggling to speak to them with any semblance of civility. It had ripped holes in the solid foundation of his career, taking him overnight from golden boy to uncertain risk in the eyes of the men and women who could make or break his future.

And for what? For a lie told years ago and a truth buried for over three decades. The vindication of a woman long dead and the total destruction of a man whose name had once meant something, not just here in Tennessee but all the way to the steps of the United States Capitol.

In a world where very little in life was fair, Dalton had spent his own life trying to even the odds for people without power or privilege.

People like the woman who had given birth to him.

And now he was angry at her, too. For having existed. For having come back here nearly fifteen years ago for one last look at the son she'd left behind. For becoming, with her husband, a victim of his grandfather's steely will and his father's emotional weakness.

And for giving birth to another son and a daughter who had invaded his well-planned world and asked inconvenient questions about a truth that should have remained buried.

They had made him into a man he didn't recognize anymore.

And he was angry at himself, most of all, for letting them.

Maybe if he'd been brought up by earthy, straight-talking mountain folk like his birth mother, he could have vented all this rage in one rip-roaring, glass-smashing, fist-flying explosion. Gone on a tear and let the fury have reign. Got it out of his system and been done with it.

But he'd been raised by Nina Hale, not Tallie Cumberland. And Hales didn't throw angry fits. They kept their emotions under control, functioning on reason and behaving at all times with civility and good manners.

Except when they were killing inconvenient people, he reminded himself as he faced his half brother with clenched fists and fought the urge to take a swing.

"What evidence do you have to support your theory about Johnny Blackwood?" Doyle's calm tone was deceptive. Dalton didn't miss the dangerous gleam of anger in the chief's green eyes, eyes so like his own that he'd all but given up hoping the past couple of months had all been one nightmarish mistake.

"I'm not prepared to try my case before you, chief."

"In other words, you're talking out your—"

Laney put her hand on Doyle's arm, stopping him midsentence. "Dalton's been looking into the Wayne Cortland case," she told her fiancé. "He's been trying to unravel the Tennessee side of the organization, see if he can build criminal cases against everyone involved."

Doyle's expression took on a slight grudging hint of admiration that caught Dalton by surprise. Even worse, he felt an answering flutter of something that might be satisfaction deep in the pit of his gut, as if the chief's approval actually mattered. He beat back the sensation with ruthless determination.

"I have to confess, I don't know a lot about Johnny Blackwood," Doyle said in a less confrontational tone. "I know he was murdered several months ago, and the case went cold pretty quickly."

"It's not his murder that interests me," Dalton answered before he remembered he didn't want to share any information with the chief. He sighed, knowing what he'd said would only make Massey more, not less, interested in Johnny Blackwood's possible connection to Cortland.

Fortunately, Briar Blackwood chose that moment to return to the waiting room. She looked tired and angry, her black curls spilling into her face from her untidy ponytail as she strode into the room. Her storm-cloud eyes locked with his, and she gave a curt backward nod of her head, a silent invitation to join her outside. She murmured something to Nix and then walked out of the waiting room again.

"I have to go," Dalton murmured, already moving toward the door.

"Be careful. She's tougher than she looks." Doyle's words sounded more like a taunt than a warning.

His back stiffening, Dalton left the waiting room and looked up and down the corridor for the Blackwood woman.

She stood at the window at the far end of the hall, her back to him. She had a neat, slim figure accentuated by snug jeans and a curve-hugging long-sleeved T-shirt. The messy ponytail had almost given up, gathering only a small clump of curls at the back of her neck while the rest of her hair spilled free across her shoulders. As he walked toward her, she reached back and pulled the elastic band free, letting the rest of her hair loose to tangle and coil around her neck.

An unexpected tug in his groin caught Dalton by surprise. His steps faltered before he caught himself.

Not an option, Hale. Not even close to an option.

Unfortunately, the more he tried not to think about Briar Blackwood as a woman, the more of her feminine features he noticed. Like the perfect size of her breasts, neither too large nor too small for her compact frame. Or the flare of her hips and curvy contours of her bottom.

She had a fine face, too—more interesting than conventionally pretty, with lightly tanned skin splashed with small cinnamon freckles and large black-fringed eyes currently the color of antique pewter.

Fire flashed in those gray eyes as she turned to look at him. "Mr. Hale, I don't know what you think you know about my husband or his murder, but if you think it's a way to get back at your brother and sister—"

"Don't call them that."

Her dark eyebrows notched slightly upward. "You don't get to tell me what to do. I don't sugarcoat the truth. You and the chief share a mother. You don't have to like it. I don't reckon he likes it much himself, but there you are anyway. And if you're messing around in my life because you think it'll piss off your brother, you can just move along and find somebody else to use. I won't be party to it."

He wanted to be angry at her for her bluntness, but in truth, he found it something of a relief. Everybody else he knew, friends and colleagues he'd known for years, seemed to walk around on eggshells around him, as if they feared speaking plainly about the train wreck his life had become. He might not like what Briar Blackwood had to say, but at least she was saying it aloud and without apology.

"Understood," he said with similar bluntness. "But my interest in your husband's murder has nothing to do with Massey."

"Then why are you suddenly interested in what happened to Johnny?"

He studied her, wondering if her straightforward style

and "call a spade a spade" philosophy extended to her own life. "Why aren't you *more* interested, Mrs. Blackwood?"

His question hit the mark. He saw her eyes widen slightly, and her pink lips flattened with annoyance. "What makes you think I'm not?"

"Most people who lose a loved one to murder don't move on with their lives so easily."

The fire returned to those gunmetal eyes. "What would you have me do? Bury myself with him? Turn the cabin into a shrine and worship his memory? I have a small son. I have bills to pay and debts to honor. I don't have time to haunt the police station begging them to solve his case. I was there for the whole thing. I knew how hard they tried to follow leads. But there weren't any leads to follow. Not here in Ridge County."

"Where, then, if not here in Ridge County?" he asked softly.

Up flickered those eyes again, changing tone with quicksilver speed. Now they were hard edged and cold as hoarfrost. "What made you come to Maryville at this time of night to ask me questions about my husband? Why to-night, smack in the middle of all this uproar?"

She wasn't going to tell him what he needed to know, he saw, unless he gave her something in return. The chief was right—she *was* tougher than she looked. But how much could he tell her without driving her further away?

"I'm investigating the Wayne Cortland crime organization. I assume, as a police officer, you have at least a passing knowledge of the case."

She nodded quickly. "I do."

Much of the information he'd gathered over the past few months was highly confidential, but he had a feeling he wouldn't get far with this woman if he didn't cough up a little new information. But the newest revelation of his ongoing investigation, the lead that had brought him to Maryville Mercy Hospital in the middle of the night, was something he didn't think Johnny Blackwood's widow wanted to hear.

"I'm trying to connect the dots between Cortland and some of the Tennessee groups that may have been working for him."

"I know. My cousin Blake is part of the Blue Ridge Infantry. Tennessee division." She spoke in a dry, humorless drawl liberally spiced with disdain. Clearly not a fan of either her cousin or his pretense of patriotism. Good. That made his work here marginally less difficult.

But only marginally.

He paused a moment to size her up again, telling himself it wasn't an excuse to appreciate once more her tempting curves. But his body's heated reaction demolished that lie in a few accelerated heartbeats.

He forced his focus back to the problem of her husband's potential involvement in Cortland's organization. "How much did you know about your husband's job?"

She hadn't been expecting that question, he saw. Her brows furrowed and she cocked her head slightly to one side, countering with a question of her own. "What do *you* know about my husband's job?"

"He was a driver with Davenport Trucking."

Her eyes narrowed. "And because Wayne Cortland was trying to take control of Davenport Trucking through a proxy, you're wondering if Johnny might have been on Cortland's payroll."

"Yes," he answered, though it wasn't the entire truth. He hadn't made the connection between Johnny and Cortland because of Davenport Trucking, but if she bought that reason for his questions, he'd go with it.

"That's thin gruel," she said with a shake of her head.

"There are dozens of people driving trucks for Davenport Trucking. You have another reason for targeting Johnny."

"He was murdered."

"And you think it's connected to Cortland because...?"

She wasn't going to be mollified by half truths, he saw with dismay. Not only was she tougher than she looked; she was smarter than he'd reckoned.

Still, he gave it one more shot, not so much out of concern for her feelings as from his own bone-deep weariness of scandal and acts of betrayal. "Can you accept that I have my reasons and I'm not inclined to share them?"

The look she gave him was uncomfortably penetrating. He felt himself closing up in defense, not ready to have her poking around in his brain.

She turned suddenly and started walking away.

"Wait." He trailed after her.

She stopped and whirled around so quickly he almost barreled into her. "I want the truth. I don't need you to protect my feelings or try to handle me. If you can't play fair, you can count me out of your game."

"It's not a game."

"What drew your attention to my late husband? What makes you think he's connected to Wayne Cortland?"

There was steel in her voice but also a hint of a tremor, as if she knew whatever he had to say would be bad. So she hadn't been naive about Johnny Blackwood's personal failings, he thought. It wouldn't make the truth any less sordid, but she might be less injured by the blow.

"I'll make it easier for you," she said quietly, her gaze dropping to the collar of his shirt. "The day Johnny's body showed up on Smoky Ridge, I'd spoken to a lawyer about filing for divorce."

The words were spoken flatly, but Dalton didn't miss the

tremble of vulnerability that underlay them. Not a broken heart, he assessed silently, but a deeply shattered pride.

"I didn't know. I'm sorry."

She gave an impatient toss of her dark curls. "Just tell me why you think Johnny was involved with Cortland."

"Because he was involved with Cortland's secretary," Dalton answered. "They were having an affair. And she thinks he was using her to get closer to Wayne Cortland."

Chapter Three

Briar didn't flinch. She didn't tremble or cry or do anything that Dalton Hale was clearly bracing himself to deal with as he lowered the boom.

But inside she died a little, another tiny piece of herself ripping away to join the other little scraps of soul shrapnel that had come unmoored during the slow unraveling of her marriage.

"How long?" she asked, pleased at the uninflected tone of her voice.

"She says about three months."

That was about right, she thought, remembering the growing distance between Johnny and her in the months before his murder. In fact, she'd long suspected he might have been unfaithful during her early pregnancy, when her normally sturdy body had betrayed her with dizzy spells and five months of near-constant nausea before she'd regained her strength for the last four months.

Johnny had liked the idea of having a baby, but the process had left him feeling peevish and neglected. As if the whole thing should have been about him and not the baby she was desperately trying to carry to a healthy birth.

In fact, he'd reacted like an overgrown baby himself. It had marked the beginning of the long, tortuous end of their twelve-year romance.

"Mrs. Blackwood?"

She realized she hadn't responded to him, hadn't even moved a muscle, her body and mind focused inward to her own unexpected pain. She gathered the tatters of her wits to ask, "What makes her think he was using her to get to Cortland?"

"Do you really want that much detail?" he asked, not unkindly.

She supposed not. At least, not right now, when she was still processing another ugly piece of truth about the only man she'd ever loved. "Did she offer any proof other than her own feelings?" The question came out with a hint of cold disdain. Not an attractive sound, but she couldn't unsay it.

"I'm not at liberty—"

"Get back to me when you are." She turned and started walking away once more, this time not stopping when he called her name.

She entered the waiting room, where only Nix and Logan remained. Logan lay curled up in the chair beside Nix, fast asleep.

"Everybody else had to go," Nix said quietly, rising as he spotted her. "Work comes bright and early in the morning."

"For you, too," she said with a faint smile, hoping her inner turmoil wasn't showing. Nix was the closest thing she had to a brother, and if he thought for a moment that Dalton Hale had upset her, he might go looking to mete out a little Smoky Mountain justice on her behalf.

"This *is* my work."

He opened his arms and she slipped into his brotherly embrace, glad that his deepening relationship with the chief's sister hadn't changed the warmth of their own long-standing friendship. Right now she needed a friend

in her corner, someone who'd back her up without asking
any hard questions. "Aunt Jenny's probably not going to
be up for any more questions tonight. You can go home
and get some sleep."

He rubbed her back. "You and Logan are coming home
with me."

She looked up at him. "Dana's okay with that?"

"She's making up the sofa bed as we speak."

"Don't screw up and let that one go," she said. "I like
her."

"Yeah, I kind of like her, too," Nix murmured.

As she started to pull away from his embrace, movement in the doorway caught her eye. Dalton Hale stood
there, watching her and Nix through narrowed eyes. She
let go of Nix and turned to face him, lifting her chin.
"Later, Mr. Hale."

He gave a short nod and walked away.

"You sure he's not giving you trouble?"

"No trouble," she lied, turning to ease her sleeping son
out of the chair and into her arms.

DALTON TRIED TO stretch his legs, but the cab of the Chevy
S-10 pickup truck was too small to allow for much motion. He'd wanted to buy a big, spacious luxury car—he
had money, damn it, and it wasn't a sin to spend it on comfort sometimes. But his campaign manager, Bill Murphy,
had pointed out that he was running for office in a county
where many people still fed themselves and their families
with wild game and the fruits of their homestead gardens.
An American-made pickup truck said Dalton was one of
them, just another homegrown Smoky Mountain boy. The
smaller, more fuel-efficient S-10 said he was environmen-
tally conscious and a protector of the land they all loved.

But the Infiniti M35 he'd wanted to buy instead of the

S-10 would have said he was a tall man with a good income who could afford not to have cramps in his legs to appear as if he were something he wasn't.

Serving the people of his county shouldn't have been so damned hard. Whatever people like Doyle Massey and Briar Blackwood thought, his motives for wanting the job of head county prosecutor weren't entirely self-serving. He supposed it might be seen as a stepping-stone to state office and maybe national office one day, but if that were his only reason for wanting the job, he would have given up a long time ago. He wasn't a politician by nature. He supposed, in a sense, that trait was one he and Briar Blackwood shared in common.

Sugarcoating things had never come naturally to him.

Her house was dark and quiet. She wasn't there, of course; she worked the five-to-midnight shift at the police station—rookie hours, his clerk had called it with a laugh when he'd asked the man to learn her work hours.

Her absence was why he had come here at night to keep watch over her cabin, to see if the people who'd broken in the night before were of a mind to give it another try. He wasn't even sure she was staying here tonight; she'd stayed the previous night with Walker Nix at his Cherokee Cove cabin about a mile up the mountain. He assumed, though he couldn't know for sure, that Dana Massey had stayed there, as well, marking her territory.

That's unfair, a small voice in the back of his head admonished him. His mother's voice, he recognized—not the troubled girl who'd apparently given birth to him but the sweet-natured, softhearted woman named Nina Hale who'd raised him from infancy. *She* was his mother. Tallie Cumberland was an inconvenient fact of biology.

He hadn't talked to his mother in a couple of days. He needed to remedy that fact, because of all the people involved in the Tallie Cumberland scandal, she was the most fragile and innocent of all. She'd lost as much as Dalton had—her husband and father were in jail, looking at spending years behind bars, and she'd learned that the son she'd loved even before his birth had died in his hospital bassinet thirty-seven years ago.

He checked his watch. Only a little after nine. She'd probably be awake still, all alone in that big rambling house in Edgewood. He pulled out his cell phone and hit the speed dial for her number.

His mother answered on the second ring. "Dalton?"

"Hi, Mom."

"I've been meaning to call you all day," she said, her voice soft with badly veiled anxiety. "Your father's lawyer called this morning. He wants me to talk to Paul about taking the plea deal. Your father doesn't want to do it. You know how he can be when he sets his mind on something."

Like covering up a fifteen-year-old murder and taking potshots at a woman asking inconvenient questions, he thought. He'd never speak those thoughts aloud, of course. He loved his mother dearly, but she was no Briar Blackwood, able to take emotional body blows without batting an eye.

"I know you want him out of prison as early as possible," he said gently. "But I respect that he feels the need to pay for what he did."

"He was just trying to protect us," she said softly. "You know that's all he cared about. Tell me you know that, Dalton."

"I know that," he said, and hoped she didn't hear the doubt.

"Please talk to him. He won't let me visit him at the jail, but he'll talk to you. I know he really wants to talk to you."

Guilt sliced another piece out of his conscience. He

hadn't gone to see his father or his grandfather in a month, ever since the truth about what they'd done had finally gotten past his denial. Outrage at Doyle and Dana Massey destroying his family hadn't gone away; he'd just added fury at his father and grandfather to the toxic mix.

It wasn't healthy, feeling so angry all the time. He just hadn't yet figured out how to let go of the anger. He was beginning to wonder if he ever would.

"I'll think about it," he said, because he didn't think he could sell a lie on that particular topic, not even to his mother, who wanted to believe they could somehow patch up their shattered lives and move forward as if none of it had ever happened.

"I wouldn't mind seeing you soon, too," she added softly.

"I'll come by soon," he promised. "We'll have dinner."

"I'll make shrimp creole. Your favorite."

It hadn't been his favorite since he was eight years old and discovered the joy of Italian-sausage pizza, but he kept that fact to himself. "Can't wait."

"I love you, Dalton."

He closed his eyes, swallowing the ache in his throat. "Love you, too, Mom. I'll call you tomorrow and we'll figure out when I can make it for dinner." He slid his phone back in his pocket and settled down to watch Briar Blackwood's darkened cabin.

BY THE TIME her patrol shift ended at midnight, Briar had begun to wish she'd taken up the chief's offer of a night off to recover from the previous evening's excitement. Despite the recent rise in crime in the county, the Bitterwood P.D. night shift wasn't exactly a date with danger.

She'd answered exactly two calls during her seven-hour shift, and one of them had been a false alarm. The other had been a car crash on Old Purgatory Road near the bridge, but even that had turned out to be more paperwork than a daring rescue. Two patrons at Smoky Joe's Tavern had tried to turn out of the parking lot at the same time, crashing fenders. Neither had registered as high as .08 on the Breathalyzer, so she'd written up a report and left it to them to sort out the insurance issues.

When she dropped by Nix's cabin to pick up her son and the bag of clothes she'd packed for the overnight stay, Nix was waiting up for her. "You can stay here another night," he said when he opened the door for her.

"No, I can't." She squeezed his arm and smiled. "Got to get back on the horse again."

"A cabin break-in isn't exactly the same thing as getting tossed from a pony. Plus, you'll have to wake up the little man."

"Too late to worry about that," she murmured as she heard her son calling her name from down the hall. She followed the sound to the spare room, where Nix had set up the sofa bed for Logan, piling pillows around him to keep him from rolling too close to the edge. Logan looked sleepy and cranky, but the watery smile he flashed when he caught sight of her face made her heart melt into a sticky little pool of motherly love in the center of her chest. "Mama."

"You ready to sleep in your own bed tonight?" She plucked him from the tangle of sheets and buried her nose in his neck, reveling in the soft baby smell of him.

"Yep," he answered with an exaggerated nod that banged his little forehead against her chin. "Ow!" He giggled as he rubbed his forehead.

"Watch where you put that noggin, mister," she answered with a laugh of her own, pressing a kiss against his fingers. "Let's go home, okay?"

"I'll get his things." Nix picked up the scattered toys she'd packed for Logan while she carried him out to the front room. Nix carried the two small backpacks for her and put them in the front seat of the Jeep while she strapped Logan into his car seat in the back.

"If you decide you'd rather come back here, no matter what time it is, you pack up the little fellow and come on back. I'll keep the sofa bed ready." Nix reached through the open back door and gave Logan a head ruffle. Logan grinned up at him and patted his curls back down.

"I'll keep that in mind," she said, although nothing short of a full-on assault was going to drive her out of her own house. She wasn't going to play the damsel in distress, not even for someone like Nix, who had only her best interests at heart.

She'd made too many decisions in her life already based on what other people wanted her to do. She wasn't going to ignore her own instincts any longer.

Still, her steely resolve took a hit when Logan's sleepy voice piped up from the backseat as she turned onto the winding road to her cabin. "Mama, are the mean men gonna be there tonight? I don't like them."

She put the brakes on, slowing the Jeep to a standstill in the middle of the deserted road. "I don't like them either," she admitted, beginning to question her motives for taking her son back to the cabin so soon after the break-in. Was she willfully putting him in danger just to bolster her own desire to stand on her own two feet?

But she couldn't tuck her tail and run away from their home. It was one of the few things she could call her own in the whole world. Her great-grandfather had built the cabin over a hundred years ago with wood he'd chopped himself and the sweat of his own brow. Her grandfather had added to it over the years—indoor plumbing, extra rooms as the family had expanded. When he had died, he'd left the place to Briar's mother, who'd deeded it to Briar as a wedding gift.

It was one of the few things she had left now of her mother. That cabin and twenty-four years of good memories.

She couldn't let fear drive her away from that legacy. For her own sake and especially for Logan's.

"I won't let the bad men scare you anymore," she said firmly, hoping she was telling the truth. Because as much as she'd tried to hide it the night before at the hospital, Dalton Hale's words had weighed heavily on her. Not the thought of Johnny's infidelity—she may have been dismayed by the information, but she hadn't been surprised. But the idea that he might have gotten himself tangled up in Wayne Cortland's criminal activities—that was the notion that had nagged her every waking hour since Hale first brought up the subject.

Johnny hadn't turned out to be the strong, solid man of honor she'd thought he would be. They'd married too young, she supposed, right out of high school. They'd started trying to have a family before either of them had reached their twenties, and the lack of success for the first few years had been an unexpected strain on their bond.

She'd given up before Johnny had, figuring a child of her own just wasn't going to happen, but he'd seen the failure as a personal affront, a challenge to his masculinity. His inability to get her pregnant had turned out to be one of those moments in life where adversity led to unpleasant revelations about a person's character.

She hadn't been happy with what she'd seen in Johnny during those months when he'd fought against the tide of reality. She hadn't realized how much his sense of self had been tangled up with his notion of sexual virility, maybe because she'd made him wait until marriage before they slept together. She'd seen his patience and willingness to deny himself for her as a sign of his strength.

She'd begun to wonder, as he grew angrier and more resentful with each negative pregnancy test, if she'd read him right. What if he hadn't denied himself at all? What if he'd been sleeping with other girls the whole time she was making him wait?

Then, almost as soon as they stopped trying, she'd gotten pregnant with Logan, and for a while Johnny had seemed to be his former self: happy, good-natured and loving. Until the nausea had started, and the doctor had started warning her about the possibility of not carrying the pregnancy to term.

"Mama?"

Logan's voice held a hint of worry, making her realize how long she'd been sitting still in the middle of the road, trying to make a decision.

They were almost home. And it *was* home, after all. Two invasions of her sanctuary made her only that much more determined to reclaim its sense of peace and safety.

"We're almost home," she said firmly, shifting the rear-view mirror until she could see her son's sleepy face. He met her gaze in the mirror and grinned, melting her heart all over again.

She reached the cabin within a couple of minutes and parked in the gravel drive that ended at the utility shed at the side of the house. She paused for a moment, taking a thorough look around for any sign of intruders. But the night was dark, the moon fully obscured by lowering clouds that promised rain by morning. She still hadn't changed the front-porch light bulb, she realized with dismay. The only light that pierced the gloom was from the

Jeep's headlights, their narrow beams ending in twin circles on the flat face of the shed wall.

Don't borrow trouble, Briar Rose. The voice in her head was her mother's, from back when she'd been as strong and immovable as the rocky face of Hangman's Bald near the top of Smoky Ridge. *Don't borrow trouble—it'll come in its own sweet time, and more than soon enough.*

She cut the Jeep's engine and walked around to the passenger side to get Logan out of his seat. He lifted his arms with eagerness, despite his sleepy yawn, and she unlatched him as quickly as she could, wanting to get inside the cabin before the Jeep's headlight delay ran out.

She had just pulled him free of the car-seat belts when the headlights extinguished, plunging them into inky darkness.

Without the moon and the stars overhead, the darkness was nearly complete. The town center lay two miles to the south; her closest neighbor was a half mile up the mountain, invisible to her through the thicket of evergreens and hardwoods that grew between them.

Tucking Logan more firmly against her side, she reached in her pocket for her cell phone. Her fingers had just brushed against the smooth casing of the phone when she heard a crunch of gravel just behind her.

She let go of the phone and brought her hand up to the pancake holster she'd clipped behind her back before leaving work. But she didn't reach it before hands clawed at her face, jerking her head back until it slammed against a solid wall of heat. She heard Logan's cry and felt him being pulled from her grasp.

Clutching him more tightly, she tried to get her hand between the body that held her captive and the Glock nestled in the small of her back, but her captor's grasp was brutally strong. His fingers dug into her throat, cutting off her air for a long, scary moment.

Then the air shattered with the unmistakable crack of rifle fire, and the world around her turned upside down.

Chapter Four

The rifle kicked in Dalton's hands, nearly knocking him from his feet, but he tightened his grip and fired another warning shot into the ground, his pulse stuttering in his ears like a snare drum.

He'd had little hope that his desperate intervention would work, but to his relief, the two figures tugging at Briar Blackwood dived for cover at the second bark of the Remington.

The darkness of the night was near total, but he'd been dozing in the car for hours, his eyes adjusting to the gloom enough for him to make out the shadowy shapes of the two men escaping into the woods. Definitely both men—he had quickly discerned that fact as soon as he'd seen them gliding out of the woods in the wake of Briar's arrival.

He'd had no time to warn her, only enough time to un-strap the Remington 700 rifle that hung on a rack in the back window of the S-10's cab, another gift from his campaign manager. He knew enough about rifles to check that it was loaded and to point the barrel where it would make a loud noise but have no chance of causing injury, but in truth, he was damned lucky his ruse had worked, and he was praying like crazy as he raced toward Briar's still fig-ure on the ground by the Jeep that the men didn't figure out he'd been bluffing.

She stirred as he came closer, putting her son between her body and the Jeep as she rose to her knees and turned a pistol toward him.

"Don't shoot! It's Dalton Hale."

She held her shooting stance for a heart-stopping moment while he froze in place. Fear flooded him, roared in his ears like a storm-tossed sea and made his hands shake as he held the rifle away in a show of surrender.

"Cover me until we reach the cabin," she rasped, shoving her weapon behind her back and turning to scoop up her son.

He hurried behind her, keeping his eyes on the woods, looking for any sign of the intruders returning, but the gloom was absolute. He heard no sounds of movement in the underbrush, however, as they hurried up the cabin steps. With a rattle of keys, Briar unlocked the door one-handed and shoved her way inside, growling for him to hurry and come in behind her.

Once he was inside, she turned the deadbolt and slumped hard against the front door, her chest rising and falling in quick, harsh gasps.

"Are you okay?" he asked, setting the rifle aside and reaching for the little boy, who was wobbling precariously in her faltering grasp.

She tried to pull her son away from him, but her knees buckled, and he grabbed the boy quickly, keeping him from falling. With alarm, he watched her slide to a sitting position in front of the door, her breath labored.

"Mama!" The child started crying, wriggling against Dalton's grasp.

"It's okay, little man. Your mama's going to be okay." He lowered the boy to the floor, and he raced away on stubby little legs, throwing himself at his mother.

She lifted her arms and hugged him close, her face

buried in his neck. "Call 911," she said, her voice muffled against her son's body.

Pulling out his cell phone, he reached for the light switch on the wall by the door. Golden light flooded the front room, making him squint as he punched in the numbers and crouched in front of Briar. A female voice came through the phone speaker. "911. What's your emergency?"

He summarized the situation quickly, putting his hand on Briar's shoulder. "I can't tell if she's injured—"

"I'm okay." Briar pulled her face away from her son's neck and met Dalton's gaze. She was pale, and her eyes were red-rimmed and damp, but her voice sounded a little less tortured, and color was coming back into her cheeks. "Tell her to call Walker Nix."

Dalton gave the instruction. "Do you want paramedics?" he asked.

Briar held her crying son away from her, looking him over for injuries. "Logan, are you okay? Do you have any boo-boos?"

"Mama!" he wailed, tightening his grip on her neck like a baby monkey.

She hugged him close and looked up at Dalton. "I think we're both okay. No paramedics."

He wasn't so sure. Dark bruises had begun to form along the curve of her throat. "You're injured," he murmured, reaching out to touch the purple spots before he realized what he was doing.

She stared up at him with wide stormy eyes, a dark flush spreading up her neck into her cheeks. "I'm fine," she said again, forcing her gaze back to her son's tearstained face. "Just get Nix here."

"Just get the police here," Dalton told the dispatcher. "I'm going to hang up now." He pocketed the phone and tried not to tumble backward out of his crouch. His knees were starting to feel like jelly.

"Can you help me up?" She reached out one hand.

He took her hand and pushed to his feet. Her fingers tightened around his as he helped her up, and she didn't let go right away, as if afraid that she might topple over again if she let go of his grasp. She had a warm, firm grip, even in her present distress, he noticed. She apparently came from what his grandfather would have called "hardy stock," for already she looked close to full recovery, save for the mottled contusions on her throat.

"Did you hit either of them?" she asked, rocking slightly from side to side as she rubbed her whimpering son's back.

He shook his head. "Didn't aim for them. I'm not a great shot, and I wasn't going to risk hitting you or the kid."

"Logan," she said with a hint of a smile. "His name is Logan."

The little boy had settled down to a series of soft hitching sniffles. "Can I get something for him?" Dalton asked, trying to remember what he'd found comforting as a little boy. "A cookie or a toy or something?"

"There's ice cream in the freezer. Strawberry—it's his favorite."

Dalton headed for the kitchen. He noticed, in passing, that she'd cleaned the place up sometime between the night before and now. Even the torn sofa cushions had been mended.

As he reached for the refrigerator's freezer compartment, Briar said, "No, not that one. The one in the corner."

He spotted a chest freezer nearby and pulled open the top. Inside, instead of the brand-name carton he was expecting, he found a large plastic tub labeled Strawberry Ice Cream in neat, clear handwriting. He pulled out the tub, uncovering what looked to be stacks and stacks of vacuum-packed cuts of some sort of meat. Looking closer, he saw that, like the ice cream, they were labeled in the same strong handwriting. Venison Shoulder, read one of the packages, with a date—December of the previous year—inscribed below. Another nearby contained pork—wild pig, to be exact—apparently put in the freezer only four weeks ago.

He closed the freezer and set the container of ice cream on the small kitchen table. "Hey, Logan, how about some ice cream?"

The little clinging monkey turned his tearstained face toward Dalton, his big gray eyes wide with a mixture of caution and curiosity.

Dalton tried again. "Ice cream, Logan. You want some?"

Logan looked up at his mother as if to seek her permission. She lowered him to the floor. "It's okay," she said. "You can have some."

Logan crossed the distance to the kitchen with small cautious steps, still watching Dalton with a healthy dose of distrust.

But when Dalton plopped a hearty scoop of homemade strawberry ice cream into the bowl in front of his chair, he climbed up and grabbed the spoon, ready to dig in. By the time Dalton put away the ice-cream container and turned back to the kitchen, Logan was half-bathed in the sticky sweet stuff.

His mother stood at one of the front windows, peering out through a narrow gap in the curtains.

"Do you see anything?" Dalton asked, walking toward her.

She let the curtains fall closed and turned to look at him. "It's dark out."

Not quite the question he'd asked, but he let it go. "How's your throat?"

"Why are you here?"

Yeah, he'd figured that question would occur to her sooner or later. "I don't suppose you'd buy it if I said I was just driving by?"

Her dark eyebrows twitched in reply.

"I was staking out the place. In case the intruders returned."

The tiniest hint of a smile curved one corner of her mouth. "And what did you plan to do if they did?"

"Call the cops."

She nodded toward the Remington 700 propped by the door. "Where'd you get the rifle?"

"It's mine."

"You hunt a lot, do you?"

He took a stab at changing the subject. "Somebody around here does. Freezer's full of game."

"I bag as much as I can during the hunting seasons. We'll live off that meat for the rest of the year." She waved her hand toward the rifle. "May I?"

He nodded, and she picked up the weapon, first checking for ammunition. "I heard two rounds. Where did you aim?"

"At the ground."

She looked up at him. "You have the rest of your ammo on you?"

He didn't know if there was any other ammunition for the rifle at all, he realized. He'd been lucky it had been loaded—he wasn't sure what he'd have done if he'd pulled the trigger and nothing had happened.

"Have you ever shot this rifle before?" She sounded as if she knew the answer.

"No."

"Why do you have it, then?"

"Emergencies," he answered, the truth too humiliating to admit.

From the look on her face, she saw through his answer anyway. She set the empty rifle against the wall. "If you'd like shooting lessons, I can help you out with that."

"For a fee?"

Her gaze snapped up to meet his. "You saved us tonight. I reckon I could let you have a lesson for free." Her voice tightened. "One, at least."

Great. He'd insulted her. "I didn't mean—"

"What do you think you're going to find here?" She leaned her back against the front wall and crossed her arms, looking at him through narrowed eyes. "Or maybe you're here because those men were working for you?"

He stared at her a moment, wondering if she was joking. The look on her face suggested otherwise. "You think I would put you and your son at risk? For what possible reason?"

"To play hero? To worm your way into my life so you could use me for whatever it is you're up to."

"What do you think I'm up to?"

She shrugged. "Hell if I know. Maybe you just want to punish your brother for existing."

He wouldn't mind knocking the smug smile off Doyle's face now and then, but he wouldn't use someone else to do it. He'd knock it off himself.

"I told you the truth last night at the hospital. I think your husband's involvement with Wayne Cortland may have gone beyond sleeping with the man's bookkeeper. I even think his murder wasn't as random as the police believe."

She was silent for a long moment, as if letting that thought sink in. Finally, she pushed herself away from the wall, rubbing her eyes with both hands. "What do you want from me? What do you think I can give you?"

It was a good question, and until just a few minutes ago, he'd have said all he wanted was a few minutes of her time, a chance to pick her brain for anything in her husband's last few months of life that might offer a new lead in the Cortland case. But two attacks on the woman in a row went far beyond coincidence. Apparently he wasn't the only person who thought Briar Blackwood could aid in the investigation, and unlike Dalton, the others didn't care who got hurt in the process.

"I think the more pressing question is, why did someone break into your house last night? And why did someone attack you again tonight?"

The sound of a truck engine began to filter through from outside the cabin, and a moment later, headlights flashed through the window, bouncing off the walls. Briar turned to the window. "It's Nix and Dana."

Dalton's heart sank. Dana. Of course she'd be with Nix. They were practically inseparable these days. Walker Nix was one of the reasons she'd decided to stick around Bitterwood instead of heading back to Atlanta.

"If you want to go without seeing your sister," Briar said quietly, "you can always go out the back."

Was his dismay so obvious? "I'm not sneaking out like a criminal."

She shrugged and opened the door at the first sound of footsteps on the front porch. Dana Massey entered first, her eyes widening a notch at the sight of Dalton. Walker Nix followed on her heels, the look he shot at Dalton tinged less with surprise and more with suspicion.

"What are you doing here?" Nix asked.

"He came to my rescue," Briar answered, locking the

door behind them. "Don't ask why. He doesn't seem inclined to share his secrets."

She made him sound like a foot-stomping adolescent, Dalton thought. Hell, maybe that's what he'd been acting like for the past few months. He'd be the first to admit he hadn't taken well the earthshaking change in his life history.

"I saw what transpired," Dalton said. "I'll tell you what I remember, though I'm afraid it was too dark for me to have seen anything I could testify to in a court of law."

Nix looked him up and down once, then nodded toward the sofa. "Well, we'll start with what you can tell us and worry about prosecution later. How about that?"

As Dalton followed the detective to the sofa, he spared one last look at Briar Blackwood standing by the door, her arms crossed defensively over her breasts, her thundercloud gaze following him relentlessly across the room.

"WHAT DO YOU think he wants with you?" Dana's voice was little more than a whisper as she walked with Briar into the kitchen.

"He thinks Johnny was part of Cortland's crew," Briar answered just as quietly, moving past the now-sticky kitchen table to grab a clean dishcloth. She drenched the cloth with water from the tap and headed for the table to clean up the mess, starting with Logan's hands and face.

He was grinning now, a strawberry-stained show of little-boy joy that made her heart swell with love. If he was traumatized by what had nearly happened outside only a short while ago, the ice cream had sent it into remission for the time being.

But she couldn't forget as easily. The men who'd accosted her outside her Jeep had tried to pull Logan away from her. In fact, the more she went over events in her mind, the more convinced she was that this attack, at least, had been all about taking Logan.

But why? She wasn't in the middle of a custody battle. Johnny's family saw Logan as much as they cared to, which wasn't that often, and none of them had shown any sign of wanting to change the custody situation. She certainly had no money or possessions to offer as ransom, and anyone who could sneak through the woods quietly enough that she hadn't heard them coming would surely know that much about her financial situation.

Yet she couldn't change the facts of what had happened outside tonight. She couldn't forget the way one of the men had tugged so ferociously at Logan that she'd been terrified, for a heart-stopping moment before the shots rang out, that she would lose her grip on her son and he'd be spirited away, lost from her forever.

"Do you think Johnny could have been working for Cortland?" Dana asked.

Briar had been pondering that question ever since Dalton had raised it at the hospital. Was it possible? She knew Johnny's truck route included Travisville, Virginia, where Cortland Lumber had been located before an explosion destroyed the place not long after Johnny's murder. It was obviously how Johnny had met the woman Dalton Hale believed Johnny had been sleeping with.

But could the man she'd married, the man she'd loved since she was fifteen years old, have gotten involved in the kind of violence and murder Wayne Cortland and his crew of drug dealers, gunrunners and anarchists had spread through the hills for the past couple of years?

The last few years of their marriage had left Briar with few illusions about her childhood sweetheart. He was a better liar than she'd ever credited him to be, and, sadly, she suspected Dalton was probably right about the affair. There'd been other infidelities, as well.

But crossing the line into extortion and murder? Could she really picture Johnny doing such a thing?

She didn't want to believe it. But something had driven a couple of ruthless intruders to her home for two nights in a row.

"I don't know," she answered finally. "But I mean to find out."

"So, why are you here, anyway?"

Dalton turned his gaze from the head-to-head huddle between Briar Blackwood and Walker Nix, meeting Dana Massey's wary gaze. He shrugged. "Just passing by."

"Convenient timing," she murmured.

"Do you have something you want to say to me? Spit it out."

Dana's lips pressed to a tight line. "I know you hate me right now."

"*Hate* is far too loaded a word," he said quietly. "I don't hate you. I don't know you well enough to feel anything that strong for you."

"And you don't want to."

He shrugged. "Biology isn't destiny."

"Clearly." She pinned him with a long, cool look and moved away.

With a sigh, Dalton looked back at the two cops locked in low conversation on the sofa. From what little he'd over-heard of their discussion, Nix seemed to be asking Briar most of the same questions he'd asked Dalton. He hoped Briar was able to fill in more blanks for the detective than he had.

The noise of Briar's Jeep passing close by had jarred him from a doze, but it had taken him several seconds more to drag himself to full consciousness. Several seconds more to see the hulking shadows slinking into the clearing from the woods nearby, and more seconds still to realize that he was watching an ambush unfold. He'd looked away for several seconds to retrieve the rifle and set himself up to fire a warning shot.

In truth, he'd seen little of what had gone on between Briar and her assailants. The one thing he remembered, the one element of the attack that had stuck in his head after the rest had faded into chaos, was how desperately she'd held on to her little boy when one of the attackers had tried to wrest him away.

Clearly, Logan meant everything to her.

The boy was asleep on the sofa beside Briar, curled up under a crocheted throw. Dana had offered to take him to his bed, but Briar hadn't wanted to let him out of her sight. Dalton wondered how she would handle it the next evening when she had to leave him with someone so she could work her patrol shift.

He could solve that problem for her, he realized, the solution weaving itself into place in his sleep-deprived mind. Staying here at this cabin, in the middle of nowhere, only made her and her son more vulnerable to further attacks. Attempts, he corrected himself silently. Tonight hadn't been an attack so much as an attempt to steal Logan away from her.

The question was, why?

Chapter Five

The front door opened without a knock, and Doyle Massey walked in, his eyes widening as he spotted Dalton. Briar watched warily, prepared to jump in if crisis prevention was needed, but Doyle simply let his gaze slide past his half brother and crossed to where Nix and Briar sat. Dana moved from her standing position by the fireplace to join them.

"What's he doing here?" Doyle asked quietly.

"He witnessed the attack," Briar answered in a tone that didn't invite further questions.

Doyle tipped her chin up with his forefinger to get a good look at the bruises on her throat. "Are you and Logan okay?"

"We're fine."

He gave a little wave of his hand toward her injury. "Anybody look at that?"

"I did. In the mirror," she answered flatly. "Just bruises."

Doyle glanced at Nix, as if seeking a second opinion. Nix gave a shrug. Doyle looked back at Briar, his eyes hooded in thought. Then he looked at Dalton Hale across the room and gestured with his head for Dalton to join them. He moved aside to make room for Dalton to join the circle.

Briar glanced up at the county prosecutor, curious to

see his reaction to Doyle's silent command. His gaze met hers briefly, then turned toward the chief, who had begun to speak.

"It's too dark for a search party to do us any good." Doyle's voice lost its earlier gentleness. This was his police-business voice. "Neither of you recognized the two men. No soft ground to allow for footprints. Briar said both men wore gloves, so looking for prints is pointless."

"Are you saying there's nothing you can do to find those guys?" Dalton looked frustrated. "You don't think for a second they'll stop trying, do you?"

"What do you think they want?" Doyle asked him.

"I wasn't here last night, so I can't be sure about what motivated those particular intruders," he answered, his tone measured. "But tonight what I saw was two men trying to take Mrs. Blackwood's son out of her arms. They came here for the boy."

Briar couldn't stop a soft groan from escaping her sore throat at Dalton's confirmation of her worst fear. She'd known the truth the second the man outside her Jeep tried to pull Logan from her arms.

They had come here tonight to take her son.

"I wish I could say I had enough officers available to post a twenty-four-hour guard here," Doyle told her.

She looked up at him. "I know you can't."

"You can move in with me," Nix said.

"No." Dalton shook his head. "Don't you live in a shack in the woods? You think it'll be any safer than this place?"

"It's not a shack," Nix said defensively, but Briar could see that Dalton's words had hit a nerve.

"Do you have a better idea?" Dana asked.

"I do." Dalton took a deep breath, then spoke in a rush, as if he was afraid he wouldn't make it all the way through. "Mrs. Blackwood and her son should come stay with me."

AFTER THE BRIEFEST of stunned pauses, a chorus of *nos* greeted Dalton's offer. From Nix, from Doyle, even from Dana.

But not, Dalton noted with surprise, from Briar.

She just looked at him thoughtfully, her head slightly cocked, as if by changing her perspective she might be able to discern some hidden aspect of his character that had eluded her to this point.

"Before yesterday at the hospital, I doubt you could have pointed out Briar in a crowd." Nix's tone was barely civil. "And now you want to take her and Logan home with you? What's your game?"

"Nix." Briar put her hand on his arm, stepping between him and Dalton. She looked up at Dalton, that same speculative look in her eyes. "Could the rest of you leave us alone a minute?"

"Briar, this isn't a good idea," Doyle said.

"I'm not going to hurt her." Dalton winced inwardly at the hint of injury in his voice. As if Doyle's distrust actually meant anything to him. Which was ridiculous, of course. He owed these people nothing, and he sure as hell didn't care what either of the Massey siblings thought of him.

"Come on." It was Dana who stepped forward and tugged the other two men with her toward the front door. She led them out onto the front porch, shooting Dalton a considering look before closing the door behind them.

"What are you up to?" Briar asked.

"I'm trying to keep you and your son alive."

"Nix is right. Two days ago you didn't have a clue who I was."

"Not entirely true," he disagreed. "For nearly a month now, I've learned almost everything there is to know about you, on paper, at least."

She looked faintly horrified by his answer. "You've been checking up on me? Do you realize how invasive that is?"

"It's my job. You were a person of interest in a case I'm trying to put together against a multistate criminal enterprise."

Her chin stabbed the air between them. "I have nothing to do with Wayne Cortland or anyone who worked for him."

"Your cousin Blake worked for him."

"And I haven't had anything to do with Blake since we were both kids."

"Which I now know because of the background check," he pointed out in what he thought was a perfectly reasonable tone.

But she looked anything but mollified. "I haven't had the opportunity to return the favor." Acid burned the edges of her voice. "I don't know anything about you but what I've read in the newspapers and heard from some very good folks you've treated like garbage for the past few weeks. And you want me to move my son out of the only home he's ever known and into yours? What's in it for you, Mr. Hale?"

"A chance at salvaging what little there is left of my life," he answered before he could stop the bitter words. He stared at her in consternation for a moment before he turned away, raking his fingers through his hair.

After a long silent moment, he felt her hand close over his arm. "I know you've been kicked in the teeth with this whole mess. And I'm real sorry about that. You didn't deserve to be lied to that way all your life. Your daddy and especially your granddaddy let you down something awful. And I can't hold it against you that you want to punch a hole in the world for the wrong it's done you."

He wanted to shake her hand off, to disconnect himself from the warm, gentle weight of her touch. But God help him, nobody had touched him with such compassion in what felt like forever.

His mother was barely holding herself together. His father couldn't bear to look at him anymore, so ashamed was he of his part in the lies and crimes. His grandfather refused to admit to his guilt, choosing self-preserving silence over justice and truth.

All the trouble his grandfather had gone to in order to keep his mother from learning that the son she'd prayed so long to have had died—what good had it done? The truth always came out. Pete Sutherland had been the man who'd taught Dalton that truth years ago as a child.

Had he really thought he could keep this particular truth buried forever?

Dalton hadn't been in his grandfather's position that day at Maryville Mercy Hospital. He hadn't walked into his daughter's room to find his grandson dead in his crib. Maybe the times, the situation, the emotions had all conspired to push Pete Sutherland into the choice he'd made.

But Dalton just couldn't imagine himself taking another woman's baby in order to protect his daughter from pain, regardless of the circumstances, because at best, it was a stalling tactic.

Old Pete hadn't saved his daughter any pain. He'd just pushed it thirty-seven years into the future, after years of lies and schemes and even crimes that made the truth exponentially uglier than it had been that day on the maternity ward at Maryville Mercy. Dalton couldn't turn to Doyle or Dana, even though they'd both indicated, at the beginning, at least, that they would welcome the chance to know him. They couldn't understand what it was like to look at them and see not family but the source of his pain, the strangers who'd blown into town and blown up his world.

It wasn't fair or right. He knew it wasn't. But he couldn't figure out how to stop thinking of them as the enemy.

"What do you want from me?" Briar asked quietly, turning him toward her until he had no choice but to look at her.

There wasn't pity in her gaze, as he'd feared. She looked at him with a mixture of curiosity and, strangely, a hint of understanding.

"I want to bury the Cortland organization once and for all," he answered after gathering his wits. "I want them gone from these hills for good."

"Because you think it's the only thing that will make folks around here forget your family scandal and pull the lever for you in the voting booth."

He shook her hand from his arm and turned away in anger. Not because she'd insulted him but because she was partially right. It might not be his only motive for wanting to see justice done, but it was a big part of it. Maybe too big a part of it.

"I'm not sayin' I won't help you," she said as the silence filling the space between them threatened to smother him. "I just want to be clear on our motives. You want to be elected County Prosecutor. I want to protect my son, and if you're right about Johnny, I want to make right what he did. And I wouldn't mind solving his murder so my son won't have to wonder about all that in years to come."

"I don't think it will be enough to save my ambitions," he said quietly. "But I want the job anyway."

"You could make more money in private practice," she murmured.

He shot her a baleful look, unable to stop his reaction. "I don't care about the money."

"Everybody cares about the money. I know I do." She

waved her hand around the cabin. "You think I live here because I like a drafty cabin with a sometimes-leaky roof? You think I can my own food and kill my own game because I'm part of some organic whole-food locavore movement?" She shook her head. "I live here because it's paid for. I grow and kill my own food because it's cheaper that way, and it allows me to put money away so Logan can go to college and get the hell out of these mountains if that's what he wants. Money matters."

He rubbed his jaw, wondering how many different ways he could make this woman despise him in one short night. "I have all the money I need. You must know that. I have the luxury of choosing a job because it satisfies something more than my bank account."

"Lucky you." She turned away, crossing to the sofa and sitting next to her sleeping son. She gently circled her palm over his back, lowering her voice. "I don't have that luxury. I have to work so we can eat. And I can't afford to put him in day care. Aunt Jenny won't be able to watch him for a while, so you see, I'm in a really desperate situation at the moment."

He waited, realizing she was on the verge of making a decision. Anything he said at this point would probably hurt his chances of getting what he wanted. And though she might not believe it, one of the things he wanted more than anything in the world was to protect her and her son from going through another night like tonight.

She looked up at him. "I would do anything to protect Logan."

"I know."

"I know you know. That's why you're offering to take us in. You know I'd never even consider it otherwise."

He waited, keeping silent. The moment stretched to the breaking point.

"I'll do it." She looked down at her little boy. "But I have some conditions of my own."

He moved slowly toward her, settling on the end of the scuffed pine coffee table in front of the sofa. "What conditions?"

"You let me pay rent."

"It's not necessary."

"I'm not doing it for you. I'm doing it for me."

Pride, he thought, not without admiration. "I need your cooperation, not your money. It's far more valuable to me."

Her gaze snapped up to meet his. "You'll have my cooperation. Matter of fact, I insist on being part of your investigation."

"You already have a job."

"I have time off, too. And I'll spend what I can of that helping you with your investigation. But I get to see everything in your files."

He wasn't sure that condition was even possible to meet. "It's an open investigation—"

"And I'm a Bitterwood police officer. It's a condition of my agreement. I get to see all the files. I might recognize a clue you wouldn't."

He released a sigh. "Okay. But you have to tell me everything you can remember about your late husband's time with Davenport Trucking."

He could see the idea made her uncomfortable, but she finally gave a swift nod and extended her hand toward him. "Agreed."

He took her outstretched hand, closing his fingers over hers. Her handshake was firm and businesslike, her palm dry and callused. He felt a sudden unexpected surge of anger at the feel of that small tough hand rasping against his. God only knew how hard a life she'd lived, trying to make a future for her son. How many more years of struggling and saving still lay ahead of her. The thought of those sons of bitches out there trying to rip her son away from her for who knew what reason—

He caught himself before his rage reached full throttle. There was a lot about her life he couldn't change. But he could do this one thing. He could make the next few weeks of her life as comfortable and secure as he could.

"Let me tell the others," she suggested, releasing his hand and pushing to her feet. "Watch Logan for me?"

He stared after her as she stepped out to the porch and closed the door behind her, realizing what an honor she'd just bestowed on him by trusting him to watch her child alone, even for a few moments with her so close by.

He looked down at the sleeping boy, carefully flattening his hand against his warm, flannel-clad back. He was so tiny, so breakable, Dalton thought, holding his breath as he felt the child's rib cage expand and contract with his slow, deep respirations. And tonight someone had tried to rip him out of his mother's arms, for reasons they still hadn't quite figured out.

"Nobody's going to take you away from your mama," he whispered, his own breathing falling into rhythm with the boy's. "Not on my watch."

POKE, POKE, POKE.

Briar opened one eye and found herself looking up at her son's bright, wide eyes. He poked her again in the ribs and laughed.

"Hey there, mister." She pushed herself up on her elbows and looked around the borrowed bedroom, so unlike her bedroom at home, and wondered how on earth she'd let Dalton Hale convince her to come here to stay.

"I'm hungwy," Logan informed her, patting her cheeks with his little hands. He bounced, too, foot to foot, the springy mattress too great a temptation for an energetic boy his age.

"I bet you are." She hugged him to her, dipping her nose into the curve of his neck for a nice long smell. "Did you find the potty okay?" The guest room had a bathroom of its own, and somehow in the chaos of the previous night, she'd managed to remember his step stool for the bathroom.

Poor Dalton Hale, she remembered with a little smile as she followed Logan to the bathroom. His eyes had grown so huge watching her gather up the necessities of life with a three-year-old, she'd half expected that he'd rescind his offer of a place to stay.

Her watch read nine in the morning. She wondered if Dalton had left for the office already without waking them. He'd given her the grand tour of the place the night before so she'd know where everything was and how to work the security system. But by the time he'd shown her the guest bedroom where she and Logan would sleep, she'd been riding the last fumes of her adrenaline rush. He'd cut the tour short, told her to get some sleep and escaped to his own room before she'd been able to ask about his plans for the next morning.

Holding Logan's hand, she helped him down the long flight of stairs down to the first floor, trying not to gape like a hillbilly on her first trip to town. It wasn't so much that the house was grand and ostentatious—it wasn't, really. It was large and roomy, yes, but it didn't have priceless paintings on the wall or rare sculptures displayed under glass.

But almost everywhere she looked, she saw things that were nothing but luxuries, things that had no purpose beyond looking pretty or drawing the eye to something else. Things that Dalton Hale had bought, not because he needed them or could make use of them but because they'd caught his eye and pleased his tastes.

That's what I want for Logan, she thought. *I want him to be able to have things he likes just because he likes them. And not worry about whether they're taking money away from the things he needs.*

To her surprise, Dalton was still there, perched on one of the breakfast bar stools in the kitchen reading the Knoxville morning newspaper. He looked up and smiled, the expression softening the stern lines of his face.

"Did you sleep okay?" he asked.

"Better than expected. I thought you'd be off to work by now."

"I took the day off." He folded the paper and set it aside, sliding off the stool to crouch in front of Logan, who was half hiding behind Briar. "What would you like for cereal, little man?"

Logan leaned his head around Briar's leg. "Ice cream."

Dalton grinned and looked up at Briar, who shook her head firmly. "I think we'd better have something a little more nutritious."

"He likes peanut butter with sliced bananas on toast," she suggested, trying to think of something even a bachelor might have in his kitchen.

"I can handle that." Logan rose and crossed to the large pantry by the refrigerator. His kitchen, like the rest of his house, was built for convenience and ease of use, with plenty of cabinets and miles of counter space. The breakfast bar doubled as a butcher block, but despite its large size, it barely seemed to make a dent in the spacious room.

"I know folks who'd kill to have a kitchen like this," she said as he brought a jar of peanut butter, a couple of ripe bananas and a bag of sliced bread to the counter. "And no jury in this part of Tennessee would convict them."

"It's too big for one person," he admitted. "But it comes in handy when I entertain."

"Do you do much of that? Entertaining?"

He put four slices of toast in the oversize toaster on the counter nearby. "More than I want to. The price of politics."

She set Logan on one of the stools and perched on the one beside him. "I'll do some shopping for Logan and me sometime today. So we don't eat you out of house and home."

He paused in the middle of twisting the top off the peanut butter jar. "No. You're here as my guests."

"No, we're not." She lifted her chin. "We're here so you can pick my brain about Johnny. And I'm here because you live in a gated community and you have a real nice alarm system. We're not friends."

He looked at her for a long moment, and for a second she thought she saw something that looked suspiciously like hurt in his green eyes. Then he looked down at the open jar of peanut butter and shrugged. "As you wish." He sounded indifferent, not insulted, and she shook off the guilt that had fluttered for a moment in the center of her chest.

"Speaking of that," she added a moment later, "how soon can you get me those files we talked about last night?"

The toast popped up and he gingerly removed the hot bread from the toaster and set it on a paper towel spread across the counter. "I'll have to go into Barrowville to retrieve them, but I think today would be better spent figuring out the logistics of your stay here."

"I work the five-to-midnight shift at the station," she said, reaching for the bananas sitting next to the jar of peanut butter. While Dalton spread peanut butter on the bread, she peeled the bananas and started slicing them into thin rounds and putting them atop the peanut butter and toast. "My aunt has been watching Logan while I'm at work, but she can't deal with him with her arm broken the way it is."

"I took the liberty of calling Laney this morning to discuss the options." He left the counter and walked over to the refrigerator.

"Yeah?"

He pulled a jug of milk from the refrigerator and looked at the expiration date. Wincing, he put it back into the refrigerator and turned to look at her, his expression apologetic. "Will water be okay?"

"Water's fine," she answered, hiding a smile. "What did Laney have to say?"

"My work keeps me in the office until six most nights. It's a ten-minute commute from Barrowville to here, so I can be home by six-fifteen or six-twenty at the latest. I assume you'd need to leave for work around four-thirty in order to have time to change into your uniform and gear, so we're talking about less than a two-hour window of time we need to cover, correct?"

"I suppose so."

"How well behaved is Logan? In general?"

"He's a three-year-old boy. He's impatient and rowdy, but he's not particularly disobedient. It helps if he likes you."

Dalton set a small cup of water in front of Logan and bent to look him in the eye. "You like me pretty well, don't you, Logan?"

Logan looked up at him as if considering the question. "Ice cream?"

"Cupboard love," Briar murmured.

"What I'm thinking is you could leave a little early and drive him by my office when you're ready to go to work.

Laney and I can take turns watching him until it's time to leave the office."

"I don't know about that—" Briar began.

"I can set up a place for him to play. I'll buy him some coloring books and picture books—is he starting to learn to read?"

She nodded. "He has a few favorite books. I brought them with me."

"I can buy duplicates for the office, then. So he'll have the things that are familiar to him."

"You don't have to do that. I can pack them in his little backpack to take with him. But are you sure you want to do this? I don't want him to interfere with your work."

"I'm sure. It's the only thing that makes any sense. The point of bringing him here is to protect him from the people trying to use him against you. Hiring a babysitter neither of us knows isn't going to work, is it?"

She shook her head quickly. "No."

"Do you trust me with him, Briar?" His green eyes were darkly intense as he met her troubled gaze. "Do you trust that I will protect him for you?"

There was no good reason why she should, she knew. He was little more than a stranger to her, and his motives were anything but unselfish. He was bitter and angry at his life at the moment, and even when he wasn't, he possessed the sort of driving ambition that could make a man grow self-focused and myopic.

But for some reason, she found herself nodding in answer to his question. "I do. I trust you to protect him."

"Then it's settled? At least until we try the system and find it wanting?"

"Yes," she said. "But I have a condition."

His eyes narrowed warily. "Another one?"

"Yes. You need to learn how to shoot a gun the right

way. No more of that aiming at the ground and hoping nothing bad happens." She allowed herself a little smile at his expense. "If you're going to try to look like a good ol' boy to win an election, the least you owe your constituents is to walk the walk as well as you talk the talk."

Chapter Six

"How long have you been shooting?" Dalton asked a couple of hours later as he peered at the rather sad results of his first target-practice round. He'd hoped to acquit himself better, but he wasn't surprised to see how badly he'd failed.

Briar tucked an errant curl behind her ear and cocked her head as she studied the holes in the target. "My uncle Corey gave me my cousin Dan's .22 when I turned eight. Dan was getting a bigger one, and Uncle Corey knew I'd been wanting a gun of my own. Of course, my daddy taught me to use a rifle earlier, I guess when I was six or so."

"That young?"

She shot him a look that made him feel like an idiot. "If you're going to have guns in the house with kids around, you need to teach them young that they're not to be toyed with. I've already introduced Logan to my pistol and my shotgun. He knows not to touch them, even if they're not loaded. When he's a little older, I'll teach him how to shoot."

"My father wasn't much of a gun person." Almost as soon as the words escaped his lips, he felt a hot wave of embarrassment flush through him. He felt Briar's gaze on him but he couldn't quite meet her gaze. "Lucky for Dana Massey, huh?"

Not too long ago, his father had taken a few potshots at Dana when she'd started nosing around in her mother's past. Apparently, his father and grandfather had feared she was getting too close to the truth about Dalton's parentage, and they'd decided to take dire steps to stop her. But it had been his father who'd ended up with a bullet in his shoulder and a future in jail stretching out in front of him. "Dana thinks your father didn't really want his shots to hit her. That's why he missed so badly."

Dalton handed her the borrowed rifle and walked a few steps away. "I think he was just a bad shot."

When she didn't say anything else, he ventured a quick look at her. She was just looking at him, a thoughtful expression on her face.

It struck him, not for the first time over the past couple of days, that Briar Blackwood was a pretty woman. It wasn't the kind of polished beauty he met in his work or even the corn-fed cuteness of small-town beauty queens who rode parade floats or won the local pageant crowns. She wasn't wearing a stitch of makeup, and her hair was a mess, but he found he liked looking at her anyway. She had a natural sort of prettiness that came from good health, good genes and, he was beginning to believe, a good soul.

He had seen earlier at his house that she felt out of place there. She'd tried not to let it show, but her poker face wasn't nearly as good as she'd probably like to believe. She didn't enjoy feeling obligated to him, like some poor mountain girl he'd taken pity on.

He didn't pity her, though. She was, in many ways, a remarkable woman. A strong woman, with discipline, integrity and guts.

Dalton had done his homework on Briar Blackwood before he'd ever approached her, looking into the basics of who she was and what kind of life she'd lived before and after marrying Johnny Blackwood. She had been born a Culpepper, and a person didn't grow up in Bitterwood, Tennessee, without knowing a Culpepper was more likely than not to break the law. How she'd dodged that family tradition he didn't know, but her record was clean, and now she was that most rare of creatures, a Ridge County Culpepper who wore a badge.

She'd married Johnny Blackwood when she turned eighteen and remained his wife until Johnny's death nine years later. She'd worked as an emergency services dispatcher while going to community college part-time to get her criminal justice degree. She'd gone through the Bitterwood Police Academy and graduated with honors back in December.

By all accounts, she was a good-hearted, hardworking woman liked by one and all. He certainly couldn't claim such a thing about himself, not since his life had gone so askew. There were plenty of people who didn't care much for him at all, starting with the Bitterwood chief of police.

Doyle had arrived at the rifle range about fifteen minutes ago. Dalton had spotted the chief about the time Briar finished her brief primer on shooting a rifle. Doyle must have seen Logan with Detective Nix, who had agreed to watch the boy at the police station while Briar gave Dalton shooting lessons. No doubt the prospect of watching Dalton make a fool of himself on the range had been too tempting for the chief to resist.

"Doyle's here," he told Briar.

"I know. I saw him earlier." She switched out the target to a new one. "Come on. Let's give it another try."

She'd showed him how to load the rifle earlier, and fortunately, he was a quick study. Her nod of approval when he had finished reloading felt like lavish praise.

"Remember, you're not pulling the trigger. You're pressing it. You want as little movement in the rifle as possible. Don't close your eyes when it fires. You want to keep looking at the target. Guide it in."

He slanted a look at her, and she grinned a little sheepishly.

"I know it sounds like hokum, but the thing is, if you're focusing on getting that round into the target, your whole body is aligned toward that goal and you're just going to make a better shot."

He settled the rifle barrel on the bench rest and sighted the target through the scope.

"And breathe," she added. "Just breathe."

He focused on the target and tried to rid his mind of everything but that one center spot he wanted to hit. But clearing his mind seemed to be something he could no longer do at will.

So he did the next best thing. He focused his thoughts on Briar and Logan. He'd promised to help her protect her son, and if he had to spend hours every day on this range, shooting this bloody rifle and suffering the scrutiny of Doyle Massey, he'd do it. He'd given himself this task, inserted himself into their world for his own purposes.

Competence was the least he owed them.

He pressed the trigger. The rifle kicked but he held it as steady as he could, keeping his eye on the target.

The bullet didn't hit center, but it was close.

"Nice," Briar said softly from her position a few feet away.

He couldn't hold back a satisfied grin.

He took his time and fired the next three rounds into the target. None of the three got as close as the first round, but his aim was considerably improved over his earlier effort.

"Not bad at all," Briar told him as they studied the target more closely. "You're pulling a little to the right with your shots, though. You'll need to figure out how to compensate for that."

Dalton started to answer when he saw Doyle walking toward them behind Briar's back. He tried not to react, but he couldn't seem to keep his lips from pressing into a thin line of annoyance.

"How long are you going to keep hating him for being your mother's son?" Briar asked softly without turning around.

"I don't hate him."

Her eyebrow twitched upward a notch, but she didn't comment.

"Second try was pretty respectable," Doyle commented when he got close. "Pulling a little to the right, but not bad at all."

Dalton wanted to snap out some brilliant cutting remark, but he didn't want to do it in front of Briar. He settled for something milder if not entirely friendly. "Town not keeping you busy, chief?"

"Overseeing the shooting range is part of my job description." Doyle turned his gaze to Briar. "Logan's got my entire station wrapped around his little finger. I'm pretty sure we're about to make him an honorary police officer."

She flashed the chief a toothy grin that made Dalton's breath catch. Damn, but when she smiled, she just lit up everything around her. It made him want to make her smile more often. God knew, she'd had little enough to smile about in her life.

"I'll go take him off Nix's hands," she said, glancing at Dalton. "Chief, would you sign Mr. Hale out of the range for me?"

Dalton opened his mouth to protest, but she was already well down the firing range. He clamped his mouth shut and looked at Doyle.

"How's she doing?" Doyle asked, ignoring the glare Dalton couldn't keep in check.

He sighed. "She's remarkably resilient."

Doyle smiled a little at the description. "She is that." He gestured with his head for Dalton to follow him.

They walked down to the range master's kiosk, where Dalton handed over his visitor's badge and signed out of the range. From there Doyle kept stride with him as they crossed the grassy no-man's-land between the police station and the firing range.

"You've lived here all your life," Doyle said after a few moments of silence. "Has there always been this much trouble with the bad elements around these parts? Or is this something new?"

Dalton was surprised by the question. Not so much by the content as the fact that Doyle spoke as if he actually wanted Dalton's opinion. "It's both, I guess. They were always around—the drug dealers, the militias, even the anarchists. But recently, thanks to Wayne Cortland, they've coalesced. And they're a hell of a lot meaner and more effective now that they've joined forces."

"It's an odd coalition," Doyle mused. "Although I guess maybe it's the anarchy element that's holding them together."

"That and the money. They get to wreak havoc on civilization and make obscene amounts of cash doing it."

"But what do they do with that cash? The elements we're after are still out there in the hills, living like they always did."

Dalton thought about the question for a moment, realizing it was an angle to his investigation he hadn't really given proper thought before. "I don't know. I guess that's something we should find the answer to."

Doyle nodded. "I guess it is."

Dalton stopped as they reached the back entrance of the police station. "I'm investigating what's left of the Cortland crime organization."

Doyle nodded. "I know. I'm engaged to your colleague, remember."

Dalton managed a smile. "I hope you realize how lucky you are to be marrying her."

"I do."

"I don't hate you." Dalton bit his bottom lip as the words spilled from his mouth and hung in the warm air between them. He hadn't meant to blurt them aloud, but he found he wasn't that sorry he had.

Doyle's eyes narrowed slightly, but his lips curved at the corners. "Duly noted."

"I'm not ready to be part of your family, either."

"Nobody expects you to."

He looked away from Doyle's understanding gaze, not willing to go past this declaration of a truce.

"Have you talked to your father recently?" Doyle asked.

The muscles of Dalton's neck and shoulders tightened until they ached. "That's none of your business."

"You're right." Doyle nodded toward the door. "After you."

They walked in silence to the stairs. Once there, Doyle paused, his jaw tightening as he looked up the flight of stairs.

His leg, Dalton thought. The chief had broken his leg a little over a month ago in a car crash.

A car crash Dalton's grandfather had engineered.

Doyle hadn't been out of the cast long. "Take the elevator," Dalton suggested.

Doyle glanced at him. "I need the exercise." He started up the stairs, clearly favoring the bad leg.

"You're a stubborn fool," Dalton called up after him.

Doyle turned at the landing, grinning at him. "Takes one to know one."

Dalton took the steps two at a time, blasting past Doyle before they reached the top.

"Show-off," Doyle muttered.

To Dalton's surprise, he felt a grin creeping over his face in response.

He didn't wait for Doyle, striding quickly down the corridor to the detectives' office, where he found Briar sitting on the edge of Walker Nix's desk, her jean-clad legs dangling as she watched Nix reading one of Logan's books to him while the little boy blinked to stop himself from nodding off. Dalton paused in the doorway, suddenly feeling like an interloper.

Doyle limped up behind him, stopping beside him in the doorway. He looked at the homey little scene for a moment before murmuring, "Nix is like family to Briar."

She thinks the world of him, Dalton thought, watching the smile play across her face. What would he have to do to make her smile at him that way?

And why did it matter?

"What do you really want from them?" Doyle asked softly. His tone wasn't accusatory, Dalton realized. Just curious.

"I want to keep them safe."

"Why?"

Dalton closed his eyes. "I don't know."

Doyle gave him a light thump on his chest as he hobbled past him. "Maybe you should give that some thought."

Briar looked up at the chief's approach, her gaze sliding past Doyle to lock with Dalton's. He felt a shimmery sensation in the center of his chest as those solemn gray eyes held his and a faint smile played across her full lips.

Why did he want so badly to keep them safe, badly

enough to upend his orderly life to bring them into the heart of it?

Doyle was right, as much as Dalton loathed to admit it. He needed to figure out his motives, and quickly. Because he'd worked too hard for too many years to let his plans be derailed by another reckless decision.

DALTON HALE'S GAZE was so focused and relentless that Briar imagined she could feel it brushing across her cheek like a gust of wind. He'd come in with his half brother—had something happened between them on the walk to the station from the firing range? Neither looked any worse for the trip, so she assumed they'd avoided getting into a tangle. But Dalton's silent scrutiny was really starting to wear on her nerves.

"What?" she asked finally after she'd strapped her sleeping son in his car seat in the back of the Jeep.

"What what?" he countered drily.

She opened her own door. "You've been lookin' at me for an hour. Do I have spinach in my teeth?"

"Did you eat spinach today?"

"Don't be so literal." She slid behind the steering wheel.

Dalton's mouth curved as he settled in the passenger seat beside her. "You don't have spinach in your teeth."

"Then what?"

"I heard the chief offer you the night off. Why didn't you take it?"

It wasn't an answer to her question; Dalton's sudden scrutiny had started a while before Doyle had made the offer. But she supposed a question was better than another few minutes of unadulterated appraisal. "I believe in carrying my weight. I don't want special treatment."

"I don't think the chief or anyone else would think otherwise."

"Why don't you call him Doyle?" she asked, even though she knew the question was none of her business. Still, if he could unnerve her by staring at her all afternoon, she supposed she could dig under his skin a bit with an impertinent question. "I know you don't see him as your brother, but he has a name besides *the chief.*"

Dalton's mouth tightened. "I don't know. I suppose it's a way not to think of him as a person."

"That's a lovely sentiment," she drawled.

"You don't know what it's like to learn your whole life is a lie. So you don't have standing to judge how I handle it."

She felt the sting of his quiet rebuke. "I'm sorry. You're right. I don't." She pulled the Jeep out of the police department parking lot.

After a long silence, Dalton spoke, his tone softening. "No, I'm sorry. I know you and everybody else want things to be easier for all of us. I just don't think easy is in the cards."

"My mama always said that nothing worth doin' is easy." She shot him a grin, surprised when he returned it.

"Everybody's mama says that."

"Doesn't mean it's not true." She looked away from that toothy, surprising grin, pressing her hand to her chest as if she could calm the sudden acceleration of her pulse.

"I don't know why I'm doing this," he said a few minutes later, after a steady silence had fallen between them.

She looked away from the road briefly, tightening her grip on the steering wheel. "Letting Logan and me stay at your place?"

"I could have put you in a safe house if I wanted to. I have access to those, you know."

She hadn't realized. "Do you want us to go to one? It's okay if you do. It would probably be better."

"You'd rather go to a safe house?"

Her mind rebelled at the notion of taking her son to some strange place, surrounded by people they didn't know. But wasn't that what she'd done anyway? Dalton Hale was little more than a stranger to them. And his house was like no place she or Logan had ever lived before.

But she felt safe there, she realized. She had no particular reason to feel that way, but she did regardless.

"No," she said, not intending to say so aloud but not really regretting it when she heard the word slip over her tongue.

She felt his gaze on her again, a caress of scrutiny that sent a little shiver of awareness darting down her spine. He released a soft breath, as if he'd been holding it.

"I don't regret asking you to stay with me."

"I don't regret staying." She slanted a quick look toward him. "We'll have to take pains to keep it that way, won't we?"

His only answer was a steady, thoughtful stare.

She turned her attention back to the road, blowing out a tense little breath of her own.

She left Logan with Dalton around four, explaining that she had an errand to run before she reported for her evening shift at the police station. What she didn't tell him, because she knew he'd object, was that her errand involved returning to her cabin to have a look around.

Nix, who'd driven past her place that morning before he went to the station, had assured her the place had looked untouched. But she couldn't believe intruders who'd invaded her home two nights in a row would give up simply because she'd packed up her son and escaped to a well-secured house in a gated community.

Whatever they'd been looking for, they clearly believed it was located at her house. The attempted kidnapping of her son, she'd come to believe, was to give them leverage against her in case she found what they were hunting before they did.

But what were they looking for? And how could it be so important that they'd rip a child from his mother in order to get their hands on it?

The cabin looked undisturbed as she pulled the Jeep into the gravel drive. She parked and stepped from behind the steering wheel, listening carefully for any unexpected sounds.

A light breeze flowed through the trees, rustling the new leaves and rattling the desiccated limbs of the dead Fraser firs dotting the mountainside. Sunset was still a couple of hours away, but here at the foot of Smoky Ridge, shadows had already begun to creep across the landscape, creating an early, false twilight. Though the temperature was mild even in the shade, Briar tugged the collar of her lightweight jacket closer to her neck and wrestled back a shiver.

You're armed and you're resourceful, she reminded herself as she started a slow circuit of the cabin, her watchful gaze taking in each window, looking for anything out of place.

As she neared the back corner of the cabin, she heard a soft keening noise that stood out from the whisper of the wind through the trees. The low animalistic tone set the hairs on her neck prickling with alarm.

Reaching behind her, she tugged the Glock from its holster and edged toward the corner. She took a fast peek and sucked in a silent breath.

Tommy Barnett, her neighbor down the hollow, lay in her backyard in a sticky pool of his own blood, his pale face staring up at the cloudless sky.

She scanned the area quickly, looking for any sign of

movement that might indicate someone had set a trap for her. She saw nothing but the flutter of leaves in the wind.

Tightening her grip on the Glock, she hurried to Tommy's side, taking a quick assessing look at his injuries. Blood had drenched his blue plaid shirt in the front, pouring from five puncture wounds in his chest and abdomen. By the sheer volume of blood seeping out beneath him, she suspected there might be other wounds she couldn't see.

She pulled out her cell phone and called 911, reporting the situation with the terse, detailed skill of someone who'd once made her living on the other end of the line. "I have to try to stop the bleeding," she told Karen Allen, the dispatcher. "I'm going to have to hang up."

"EMT and police are on the way," Karen assured her.

Briar shoved the phone back into her pocket and assessed the wounds more closely, her heart sinking as she took in the full measure of damage done to her neighbor. There was little she could do at this point, but she tried direct pressure on the wounds in hopes that she could stanch the bleeding long enough for the EMTs to arrive and take over. "Tommy? It's Briar. Can you hear me?"

Tommy's face had turned to a ghastly gray that Briar could barely make herself look at, since she knew what it meant. Death was coming, sure and swift, and she feared there was nothing she could do to stop it.

"Tommy, please hang on. The ambulance is on the way."

His lips moved faintly, a soft gurgling noise spilling from his bloodstained lips. She leaned closer, trying to make out words in the rattle of sound escaping his throat.

"He won't stop," Tommy rasped.

"Who won't stop?" she asked, pressing her fingers to his throat, seeking a pulse that was already growing too weak to discern.

"Blake," he said. "Blake won't stop."

She closed her eyes, not surprised to hear her cousin's name on a dying man's lips. But pained nevertheless, as if she carried the poison of his crimes in her own blood. "Did Blake do this to you?"

Tommy's hand, sticky with blood, closed over her wrist, his grip surprisingly strong. "You can't run far enough."

His grip loosened. His fingers slid away, leaving a streak of blood across her skin. She heard the guttural growl of death laying claim to his prey, then still, hollow silence, as if the man's departing soul had taken with it all the music of life.

She sat back on her heels, tears burning her eyes. A prickling sensation raced through her body, raising the hairs on her arms and legs and setting off tremors low in her belly. She rose slowly to her feet and turned a slow circle, her breath quick and shallow as the woods closed in around her like a tomb.

You can't run far enough.

She was beginning to fear those words were true.

Chapter Seven

"You should have called." Dalton's heart was still racing from the surprise of finding a pale, bloodstained Briar Blackwood standing at his door when he opened it shortly after dinner. She'd calmed his initial fear by assuring him the blood wasn't her own, but the story she'd relayed as he'd helped her out of her jacket had done little to steady his rattling nerves.

"I'm sorry. I didn't want to worry you, and then the chief ordered me home."

He felt a rippling sensation shoot through his chest at her use of the word *home* to describe his house. She seemed to realize her mistake, flashing him a brief humorless smile. "Here, I mean."

"Go get cleaned up," he said gently. "Do you want a drink?" He didn't have much in the house; he hadn't entertained in weeks, thanks to the turmoil in his family, and he wasn't much of a drinker himself. But he could probably find some brandy or something stronger if she needed it.

"Do you have any hot chocolate?" she asked.

He smiled. "Going for the strong stuff, are you?"

She smiled then, a genuine one, not that bleak flash of teeth she'd sent his way earlier. "I like to live on the edge."

He couldn't smile back, realizing how close she'd come to walking into an ambush that evening. Her cousin and his minions couldn't have been gone long if Tommy Barnett had still been alive when she'd found him. From her description of his wounds, the blood loss would have been massive and death quick. "Use my bathroom. Logan's asleep in your room. I don't think he should see you like that."

Her smile faded. "No, you're right. Thank you for thinking of him."

He watched her climb the stairs to her room, feeling the weight of her grief in each weary step she took. When she'd disappeared from view, he turned to the phone to call his office. But it rang before he reached it.

"Dalton Hale," he answered.

"It's Doyle."

The sound of the chief's voice in his ear was, unexpectedly, a relief. "She's here. She's safe."

"I know. I had Nix follow her there."

Of course, Dalton thought. The Bitterwood P.D. took care of their own. Depending on the circumstances, it could be a very good thing. Or a very bad one. He'd seen both situations during his tenure at the Ridge County prosecutor's office. "She's upstairs cleaning up. Do you want to leave a message for her?"

"No, I just wanted to make sure you knew what was going on."

"She told me."

"Did she tell you what Tommy told her before he died?"

"She mentioned he'd implicated her cousin Blake."

"He told her Blake wouldn't stop until he got what he wanted. That she couldn't run far enough."

Dalton felt a flutter of unease run through him. "You think they'll come after her here?"

"I think it's possible. Maybe even likely. Maybe we

should rethink the situation. Put her and Logan under guard."

"I already told her I could put her and Logan in a safe house."

"Really?" Doyle sounded surprised.

"I want her safe."

"Yes, I believe we've established that." Doyle's tone was dry as dust.

"She said she doesn't want to go to a safe house. I haven't asked her tonight, though."

"We mentioned it to her earlier. Maybe you should back out of this setup, Hale."

"Give her no other option?" He recoiled at the idea of abandoning her. "I don't think I can do that."

"Yeah, I didn't really figure you could." Doyle's sigh sounded like a roar through the phone. "I don't suppose you have the funds to hire security?"

"I have the funds," he said.

"Then I'd suggest you contact Sutton Calhoun at The Gates, that new detective agency over in Purgatory. He's married to one of my detectives. He'll set something up for you."

"I know Calhoun," Dalton said quietly. He'd heard of The Gates, as well. They were starting to make waves in the area, mostly for the good. However, some of the people the detective agency was hiring seemed, to Dalton, at least, to be questionable risks. Calhoun was one. The son of Ridge County's most infamous grifter, Calhoun had only recently returned to Bitterwood after years away. He seemed decent enough, Dalton supposed, though it was hard to imagine how Cleve Calhoun's son could be so very far removed from his incorrigible father's criminal ways.

And he'd also heard the agency had recently hired Seth Hammond, Cleve Calhoun's longtime apprentice at the confidence game. Admittedly, the man seemed to have cleaned up his act, even marrying Rachel Davenport, a woman from a well-respected Bitterwood family. But risk was risk, and The Gates seemed a bit reckless about taking more than its share.

"I'll give you his number," Doyle added as the silence between them stretched across the phone line.

"I have it," Dalton answered. "I'll talk to Briar and see what she says."

"Tell her to call if she needs anything."

"Will do." He hung up the phone, leaving his hand on the receiver as he considered whether there was any point in calling his office at this late hour. Some of the other lawyers worked late, but it was nearly eight o'clock now. It wasn't likely that anyone was still around.

And what could anyone do at this point? There was no suspect in custody, and Blake Culpepper was already on the BOLO list; every lawman in the state of Tennessee was already on the lookout for the man.

He dropped his hand away from the phone and went into the kitchen to start making the hot chocolate.

From the floor above, he heard the muted sounds of the shower running, and the image of Briar's body, naked and slick from the soap and water, filled his head so thoroughly he nearly dropped the cocoa mix. He set the can on the counter, his heart pounding like a timpani.

What the hell was he doing? She had just escaped death by moments, had fought and failed to save a friend from death and was even now upstairs washing the man's blood from her skin, and he was thinking of naked breasts and the soap-slick curve of her hips and thighs?

Get a grip, Hale.

He concentrated on the hot chocolate, bypassing the ease of the microwave for the old-fashioned but longer task of boiling water on the stove. By the time he stirred steaming water into two mugs of cocoa mix, the sound of the shower had subsided. In fact, everything upstairs seemed silent and still. He waited several minutes for her to return from upstairs, but she remained wherever she was.

Crossing to the stairs, he gazed upward and listened for sounds of movement from the second floor. But all he heard was the soft hum of electricity coursing through the walls. He had a sudden throat-gripping notion that Blake Culpepper had crept through a window upstairs and spirited Briar and her son away while Dalton remained downstairs, oblivious to the danger.

Before he realized he meant to do it, he had ascended the stairs two at a time and burst into the second-floor hallway.

He strode to the guest room, not bothering to knock on the door before throwing it open to look inside, his pulse throbbing in his ears. Logan lay asleep in the bed, his face cherubic in slumber. Relief swamping him, Dalton crossed to the bed and crouched beside the sleeping child. He touched the little boy's soft hair, pulling back as Logan snuffled softly in his sleep.

As he rose to go, he stopped short at the sight of Briar standing in the open doorway, watching him.

Her eyes were the murky gray of a storm-tossed ocean, hinting at endless depths beneath the reflective surface. Her damp curls framed her scrubbed-clean face, dark against fair. Water drips had left darkened streaks on the heather-gray tank top skimming her curves, including a blotch on her left breast that seemed to cling to the small peak of her nipple, a blatant if inadvertent announcement that she wore no bra beneath the thin cotton.

Below the hem of the tank top peeked a pair of black running shorts that bared the toned perfection of her thighs, the rounded muscles of her calves, a pair of shapely ankles and small slender feet. Her neat toenails, he saw, were painted a bright neon blue.

Heat like a furnace blasted through him and settled, languid and heavy, in his groin. "I thought—" He stopped short, unsure what he'd meant to say.

She stepped back, her head giving a little backward nod, a silent invitation to join her outside. He closed the door behind him, his heart still racing in his chest like a rabbit chased by a fox.

She gazed at him, her lips slightly parted, her breath coming in soft, rapid respirations. In a little blue vein in her temple, her pulse throbbed visibly. Rapidly.

He didn't know how to breathe anymore. His lungs burned for air, but he couldn't draw in enough oxygen to fill them.

Her fathomless gaze drew him closer. He lifted one hand to her face, his fingers brushing aside a tangle of curls to bare the curve of her cheek to his gaze. "I couldn't hear any sounds from up here, and for a minute I thought—"

Her eyes fluttered closed as his fingers skimmed the edge of her jaw.

She was, in so many ways, a hard woman. Tough as the hills that had shaped her from infancy, hard as the rocky soil she tilled to grow the food that fed her and her son. But her skin was silky soft, as if spun from the gossamer mists that shrouded the mountains at sunrise.

The crisp scent of his own shower gel heated by her clean skin filled his lungs, transformed into a heady feminine essence.

Curling his hands into fists, he forced himself to step back from her. One step, then another, until his back flattened against the opposite wall. "I was worried."

Slowly, she slid down the wall and ended up sitting on

the hallway floor, her knees tucked up to her chest. He lowered himself to the floor across from her, grimacing a little as his knees creaked, reminding him he wasn't getting any younger.

"I didn't find Johnny's body when he died." Her gaze settled somewhere around the middle of his chest. "But I made them let me see him afterward. In the morgue."

He knew. He'd read the case file already. More than once. He'd read transcripts of interviews, the autopsy report, the detective's report, the coroner's inquest. "Did tonight bring it back?"

She rubbed her chin with her thumb, her gaze slowly lifting to his. "I won't be surprised if they prove the same knife that killed Johnny killed Tommy, as well."

He wouldn't be, either.

"Why did they kill Tommy, though? Did he surprise them in the middle of something?"

"What do you think?" he asked.

She shook her head. "I don't know. I think maybe I'm afraid to know."

A thought occurred to him suddenly. "You don't blame yourself for this, do you?"

She looked down at her feet.

"Don't. You're not to blame here."

She looked up slowly. "They want something they think I have. But I don't know what it is. Or why it's worth killing for."

Dalton wasn't sure, either. "It would have to be big. Dangerous to more than just one person."

"Why dangerous to more than just one person?"

"You've already told us that you don't think the two men who tried to take Logan were the same men who broke into your house the night before, right?"

She nodded thoughtfully.

"And none of them was your cousin Blake."

"Definitely not."

"But tonight your neighbor mentioned Blake by name, right?"

"Yes." She looked down at her feet again, as if studying those brightly painted toenails. "So either Blake was there or he sent more people in his stead. Maybe the same people as before. Maybe not."

Dalton watched the play of emotions across her downcast face. "That's at least five people involved, right? The four we know about for sure plus Blake. Maybe more."

"That's a lot of people."

"They're protecting something corporate. Not private."

"But what?" She looked up at him suddenly, her gaze so intense it sent a little rattle skittering down his spine.

"Something they fear enough to take big chances," he answered after a moment of thought. "Something that's worth walking into the home of a cop and taking a look around."

"Something worth trying to steal a child from the arms of that same cop. A cop they knew would be armed." Her eyes narrowed. "Something they think I have or know how to get."

"Any ideas?" he asked.

"Only theories," she answered.

"Care to share?"

She moved suddenly, sliding back up the wall almost as quickly as she'd sat. He levered himself to his feet with much less grace, the twinges in his limbs an unmistakable reminder that he was on the downhill slide to forty these days. Almost a decade older than his nimble hallway companion.

With a slight nod of her head the only invitation to follow, she started down the stairs to the first floor.

He followed her into the kitchen, watching as she picked up one of the cups of hot chocolate, took a sip and grimaced.

"Cold," she said. She put both mugs in the microwave, set the timer and turned to face him, leaning back against the counter. Her eyes followed his movements with an almost feral wariness, and he wondered if she was remembering their electric encounter in the hallway.

To ease her tension—and his own—he took a seat at the breakfast bar, putting a layer of granite countertop and polished oak between them. "You have theories?" he prompted.

"I've been thinking about what you've told me about your investigation. How you think Johnny fit in. And I keep going back to the Davenport Trucking connection. Has anyone ever established how a lumber-yard owner in Travisville, Virginia, even got interested in a Tennessee trucking company in the first place?"

"We're pretty sure what caught Wayne Cortland's attention was the fact that Davenport had contracts with the Oak Ridge National Laboratory," Dalton said. "It's guesswork at this point, now that Cortland's dead, but we think he was planning to cause a scare at the nuclear research facility in hopes that it would stop or at least delay oil-shale exploration and production in the area."

He could tell by the look on her face that this information was new to her. "He wanted to stop oil-shale production? Why?"

"He controlled a lot of people in a lot of areas that can be charitably called wilderness. He liked it that way—fewer eyes mean fewer chances to be caught doing something illegal. His network thrived on isolation and people who live on the fringes of society and like it that way."

"And oil-shale production means less wilderness and more people."

He nodded. "More eyes. Exactly."

"He wanted to use a Davenport truck to deliver something to Oak Ridge that would pose a threat, then. Something that might cause a nuclear incident."

"We don't think he was planning to do anything horribly damaging." The microwave dinged and Dalton retrieved the two cups of hot chocolate. He gave her the cup she'd sipped from, keeping the other for himself. "Careful. It's pretty hot."

She looked up at him, her expression curious. "Do you think they were planning to use Johnny to drive the truck that would get into Oak Ridge and cause the trouble?"

"I'm not sure. I just know Johnny seemed to be asking a lot of questions at Cortland. Questions that even that pretty little bookkeeper noticed. If she noticed, other people might have, as well."

"You think that's why he was killed."

"I think it's possible."

She sipped her hot chocolate, her expression hard to read.

"Were you and Johnny happy?" he asked, regretting the words the second they spilled from his lips.

She looked up sharply. "Does it matter?"

He shook his head.

She set the cup of hot chocolate on the breakfast bar counter. "I told you, the same day he died, I started divorce proceedings."

"I know."

She cupped her hands around the mug. "I did love him. He was my first everything. You know? But he never grew up. The woman in Virginia—I know she wasn't the first one. And I couldn't keep myself and Logan in that kind of situation. So I started looking into my options."

"And then he was murdered."

She looked up at him. "I was lucky I had an alibi, huh?"

The urge to reach out and smooth those little frown lines from her face was so overwhelming he had to curl his hands around his hot-chocolate mug to control it. "Why don't you try to catch up on a little sleep, since you have the night off?"

She shook her head, turning to pour out the remains of her hot chocolate into the sink. "I'm okay now. There's no reason why I can't go back to the station and put in some hours."

"I thought they ordered you home."

She shrugged. "I'm ordering myself back." She started toward the stairs, then suddenly stopped, turning to look at him. "If Logan wakes up, he may want you to read him a story. Is that okay? His books are in a bag in the guest room closet."

Dalton smiled. "I can do that."

The faint smile she offered in return made his chest ache a little. She turned and continued upstairs.

As he was pouring the rest of his own hot chocolate down the drain, his cell phone rang. He dug it from his pocket and checked the display. With a sigh, he answered. "Hi, Mom."

"You didn't call me about lunch today."

He closed his eyes, grimacing. "I'm sorry. Things have gotten real crazy around here all of a sudden. Rain check?"

"How about tomorrow? I can meet you at the Sequoyah House Tea Room around noon."

He could tell from her tone that she wouldn't take no for an answer. "Okay. Sequoyah House tomorrow, noon. How're you doing, Mom? Everything okay?"

"I'm well," she answered sparely. "I'll see you at noon."

He hung up and shoved his phone in his pocket, both wishing he could get out of lunch with his mother and hating himself for feeling that way.

His father and grandfather had hurt a lot of people with their lies and machinations.

Including the people they were supposed to be protecting.

Chapter Eight

The doorbell chime startled Briar from a light doze on the sofa. Curled up on the cushion beside her, Logan was still napping, but that wouldn't last long if whoever was leaning on the doorbell didn't give it a rest.

She put down the book she'd been reading and grabbed the Glock from her waistband holster, standing on tiptoe to reach the security lens set high into the solid oak of Dalton Hale's front door. The fish-eye lens revealed Walker Nix's face, to her relief. She holstered the Glock, twisted open the deadbolt and unlatched the security chain to let him in. "Aren't you on duty?" she asked, keeping her voice low.

"Good morning to you, too," he whispered, stepping inside.

"Logan's asleep." She locked the door and led him into the kitchen.

He sat, looking around. "Nice digs. Never been here before."

She grinned at him. "What, you're not on the Sutherland/Hale society guest list? I thought you Nixes were one of the oldest families in the hills."

"Oh, we are. That might be the problem."

Chuckling, she perched next to him. "What are you doing here?"

"Just checking on you. Seeing how Hale's treating y'all."

"Very kindly, actually," she answered with a smile.

"You sound like you actually like the guy."

She shrugged, thinking about that brief tension-strung moment she and Dalton had shared in the upstairs hall the night before. She'd put it from her mind, filed it away under Things That Don't Need to Be Repeated, but the memory seemed to have a rebellious streak. So she'd found the man more attractive than she'd expected. That didn't mean she needed to act on it.

"He's nice," she said when it became clear that Nix was waiting for something more than a shrug. "Logan seems to really like him, too."

Nix nudged her with his shoulder. "What makes you say that?"

She slanted a look at him. "Jealous? Afraid Logan may end up liking him more than he likes you?"

"He *can* afford better toys."

"Logan adores you. But you're never going to be his daddy." As soon as the words came out of her mouth, she realized how they sounded. "Not that Dalton can— I mean—"

"Don't get any ideas about him, Briar." Nix's smile faded.

"I haven't."

"He'd be damned lucky to have you, of course."

"Of course." She smiled, though beneath the humor was a little sting.

"I just think there's a reason why he's thirty-seven and still single."

She blinked. "You think he's gay?"

Nix shot her a look of amusement. "Should I?"

She thought about that moment in the hall again and shook her head. She hadn't imagined the way his eyes had darkened when he touched her or the tremble in his fingers. "No, I don't think so."

"He was engaged once. A long time ago. Her name was Calinda Morgan." Nix smiled a distant smile. "Prettiest girl at Ridge County High School. Everybody wanted her, but Dalton Hale was the one she wanted. Everybody thought they'd marry. Then his granddaddy sent him to Harvard Law, while Calinda stayed behind. A couple of years later, she met another guy, broke it off with Hale and got married."

"Old Pete sent him to Harvard after college? Right about the time Tallie Cumberland and her husband came to town looking for him...."

"I hadn't thought about it before, but yeah. It would have been right about that time." Nix shook his head. "All I know is, when Calinda ended things with him, Dalton took it pretty hard."

"And he's never been serious with another woman since?"

"Not really. I mean, he dates all the time. He's forever getting his picture in the paper, and there's usually some pretty blonde on his arm."

"Blondes, huh?" She said it lightly, to cover the disconcerting quiver in the pit of her stomach.

Nix tugged one of her dark curls. "Tough luck, Briar Rose. You'll just have to find some other rich bachelor now."

She was relieved when they moved on to the topic of Nix's relationship with Dana Massey. "Things still going well with you two?" she asked.

"Gotta show you something." He reached into his coat pocket and brought out a small, velvet ring box.

"Oh, my God," Briar said, her heart rate jumping as she

realized what it was. "You're going to do it, aren't you? You're gettin' hitched!"

"If she says yes." He flipped open the box to reveal a square-cut diamond set in a simple white-gold band. "It's small, I know—"

"It's beautiful. It's perfect. She's going to love it!" Briar threw her arms around Nix and gave him a tight hug. "Look at you, steppin' up!"

He laughed, the happiness transforming his dark face. She realized with quiet wonder that her old friend had become a brand-new man since he met and fell in love with Dana Massey. *That's how it's supposed to be,* she thought. *That's what love's supposed to do to you.*

After almost a decade of marriage, Johnny had still been the same overgrown teenager she'd married. And had she really changed, either?

Maybe their relationship had been doomed from the start.

"When was the last time you talked to your father?"

It had taken his mother almost twenty minutes of small talk to get around to her real point for meeting him for lunch, Dalton thought, laying his fork on the table by his plate. "I'm not sure. A few weeks."

"Four weeks," she corrected mildly. "He thought you wanted to help him."

"I did."

Nina Hale's eyebrows lifted slightly at his use of the past tense. "I know he hurt you. He hurt me, too. And I can't even think about what my father did without wanting to cry my eyes out."

He reached across the restaurant table and touched his mother's hand. Just a light touch, nothing too maudlin. Not in a public place like the Sequoyah House Tea Room.

Sutherlands and Hales didn't perform for an audience. "I'm sorry, Mom. I'm not a defense attorney. I prosecute law-breakers. I can't defend them."

"He's your father."

He almost snapped out a denial but stopped short, curling his fist around the napkin in his lap. "I secured a very good attorney out of Knoxville. He's getting the best defense available to him."

"He doesn't need the best defense available. He needs his son."

"Mom—"

"He doesn't deserve to be cut off from you. He did what he did for you."

Dalton shook his head. "He did it for himself. For you. Probably for Pete, as well. But he covered up the murder of two people who did nothing wrong. He tried to shoot my—" He stopped short, shocked by the word still lingering in his mind unspoken. "He tried to shoot a deputy U.S. marshal."

"He didn't get close to hitting her."

Dalton stared at his mother. "You don't fire a gun at a person unless you're willing to risk hitting them. He may have been relieved she wasn't hurt, in the end, but he was willing to take the risk that she might be. Don't defend what he did."

"He didn't want to lose you."

"Mother, I was twenty-one years old when he learned the truth. I was a college graduate, living on my own. How could he lose me at that point?"

"Apparently by making a wrong choice," she murmured, her voice controlled but the expression in her eyes bleak.

Dalton sighed. "He hasn't lost me. I will forgive him. I just need time to deal with the betrayal."

"Betrayal?"

"I trusted him to tell the truth when it was important. And he didn't." A cavern-dark bubble of bleak emotion burned his throat. He'd fought so hard to keep from admitting, in front of Doyle or Dana, at least, that he gave any real credence to the story of his origins. All for show, of course. He'd known the first time he'd laid eyes on Dana Massey that his world was already changing. He'd seen the resemblance. Wondered what it meant.

Ultimately, his father's confession had been a release. An answer to doubts that had played in his head over and over from the first time he looked into a stranger's eyes and saw his own.

"Did you know I had another brother?" he asked aloud. "Three siblings. After growing up an only child. Lucky me."

"I would have given you brothers and sisters if I could," Nina said.

"I know. But I had another brother." One he'd never met and never would.

"I spoke to Doyle Massey," Nina said.

Dalton looked at her. "Why?"

"I ran into him in town. He introduced himself."

"I'll tell him to leave you alone."

"I don't need you to protect me from him. He was polite. And kind." Nina took a long slow sip of tea and replaced the china cup carefully on its saucer before she continued. "I liked him, actually. He smiles a lot."

A tearing sensation rippled through his chest. He buried it deep, though he knew it could stay contained only so long. "Why are you telling me this?"

"I understand you've brought a woman to your house to live with you."

Small-town gossip was more efficient than a CIA operation. "She's a potential witness in a case I'm investigating."

"She's a police officer, they say. Is she pretty?"

"It's business."

"Is she pretty?" Nina repeated, emphasizing each word.

"Yes."

"Does that pose a problem for you? Living in the same house?"

"I don't want to have this conversation."

"No, I don't suppose you do." She took another sip of tea. "It could affect your campaign. Having her there."

Ah. His campaign manager, Matt Merrick, had run an end around and spoken to his mother. "Did Merry give you any other helpful suggestions to pass along?"

To his surprise, his mother's lips curved upward around the rim of her teacup. "No, just the one."

"I'm not sleeping with her," he said, trying to ignore the memory of Briar's long toned legs, perfect round breasts and the smell of his bath gel on her warm skin. "She has a three-year-old son, staying there with us. I couldn't ask for a more efficient chaperone."

"Her husband died a few months ago. Murdered?"

"Mother."

"I hate when you call me Mother. It means I've disappointed you."

He closed his eyes briefly. "You told me gossip is an evil. Remember?"

"Well, apparently it's the only way I get to find out what's going on with my son these days."

"Fine." He pushed away his plate, the food mostly untouched. "I'll go see Dad."

"Is she in danger?" she asked, ignoring his offer.

He released a long breath. "Yes. Her son even more so."

"Are you prepared to protect them? Your last Tae Kwon Do lesson was a while ago."

He laughed. "She's a much better shot than I am. In fact, she took me to the firing range for lessons yesterday."

"You *do* like her," Nina said with a hint of a smile. "Don't you?"

"Mom...."

"She's a Culpepper. I guess by now you've heard a few things about the Culpeppers from these parts."

"Don't be a snob, Mother."

She didn't hide her smile behind her cup that time. "Sweetheart, I'm not the snob of the family. Besides, the Cumberlands had a far worse reputation. Yet I love you beyond distraction."

He stared across the table at her, surprised both by the stark declaration of his true maternal origins and by her placid delivery of that painful fact. "Did you ever meet my— Did you meet Tallie?"

"I met her in the park one day when you were about a year old. I didn't know who she was then, of course. I had no idea what your father and grandfather had done. And we'd never seen her before, you see. She'd been a juvenile when she gave birth to you, so they didn't identify her in the papers or show a photo. But I know it was her. She looked a great deal like your sister, Dana, you know. But younger then. She couldn't have been more than eighteen at the time." Nina's gaze seemed to recede from the present, as if she could see that moment in the past playing out before her eyes. "She was so taken with you. Of course, I was mad about you myself, so it didn't seem strange that another person would have found you just as captivating."

"Dana told me that moment was when Tallie decided to stop trying to convince people I was her son," he said quietly. "She saw how much you loved me. And how much I loved you. *Love,* sweetheart. How much I *love* you. How much you love me."

"Always."

To his surprise, she reached over the table and clasped both his hands, squeezing tightly. "Your police officer friend loves her son just as much?"

He nodded. "Every bit as much."

"Then tell Merry to mind his own business."

He walked her to her car after lunch, giving her a swift impulsive hug as she started to unlock the door. "Thanks for lunch. I needed it."

She smiled up at him. "I don't care what that DNA test says. You're my son. And I'll say that to anyone who asks." Her smile drifted away, her blue eyes growing suddenly serious. "But I would never make you choose between me and your brother and sister. They seem like good people, and they're no more at fault for what happened than you or I."

He kissed the top of her head, breathing in deeply the rosewater scent of her, the light floral essence that could take him back to his earliest childhood memories. "I'll keep that in mind."

The rest of his afternoon seemed to drag, dedicated as it was to catching up on outstanding paperwork before running back through his compiled files on the Wayne Cortland crime organization one more time. He'd promised Briar access to these files, he remembered. He called his secretary, Janet, into his office and asked her to make copies of everything before the end of the day. Janet gave him an odd look but took the files and headed off to do what he'd asked.

Around three-thirty his phone rang. It was Briar. "I thought I'd check to make sure it's okay to bring Logan by before my shift starts."

"I'll be waiting. Be sure to bring plenty of things for him to play with in case I can't get out of here early."

"Will do. See you in a bit." She hung up before he could ask her how her day had been.

He leaned back in his chair and gazed out the large picture window that took up a large portion of his eastern wall. From his third-floor office, he had a stunning view of the Smoky Mountains. Sunlight bathed them in a warm golden glow, though it wouldn't be long until twilight painted them in cool hues of blue and purple.

His grandfather hadn't wanted him to stay in Tennessee after college, he remembered. He'd wanted him to go see the world, or at least, that's what he'd said at the time.

Now Dalton wondered if he'd been determined to keep him away from Tennessee until he figured out what to do about Tallie Cumberland.

The office door opened and Janet looked in. "You have a visitor."

Briar had made good time, he thought. But it wasn't Briar who walked through the door. Instead, a willowy blonde entered, dressed impeccably in a flattering navy skirt and jacket, four-inch heels and a crocodile purse that had probably cost a fortune.

"Lydia." He rose as she strode toward his desk, her hair swinging in shimmery golden waves.

"You didn't return my calls." She walked around to perch on his desk, looking up at him with a mixture of irritation and affection.

She'd called twice that morning while he was catching up on the work he'd missed the day before. He'd sent her calls straight to voice mail, meaning to get back to her after lunch. He'd forgotten all about it. "I'm sorry. I took the day off yesterday and I've had to race to catch up."

"Well, I hope you have, because I managed reservations at Chez Berubi in town. Seven-thirty sharp."

He looked at her in dismay. "Seven-thirty tonight?"

Her smile collapsed. "Yes, tonight. We planned this last week."

He looked at her in consternation. She was right, of course. He'd put her off for a week because his caseload had been busy; this week was supposed to have been free of any court appearances.

But that was before Briar and Logan had crashed into his life.

"Lydia, I can't make it tonight. Something's come up—"

Her eyebrows lifted. "I beg your pardon?"

A quick knock on the door interrupted, and Janet stuck her head through the opening again. "Two visitors this time."

Before he could speak, Briar walked in with Logan on her left hip and a fuzzy turtle-shaped backpack slung over her shoulder. She stopped short at the sight of Lydia perched on his desk. "Sorry. Didn't mean to interrupt."

Lydia took one look at Briar and Logan and turned her chilly blue gaze toward Dalton. "Something came up?"

He looked at Briar, who was watching him through narrowed eyes. She shifted Logan's weight to tuck him more securely against her side. "I can find someone else to watch him," she said, already turning toward the door.

"No," he said quickly, moving around the desk, past Lydia, to stop her.

She paused, looking down at his hand on her arm. "It's okay. You've gone above and beyond already. I can probably catch Nix before he leaves."

"It's not necessary." He smiled at Logan, who was watching him shyly from his mother's shoulder. "Logan and I had plans for tonight, didn't we?"

"You and Logan weren't the only ones," Lydia muttered.

He turned to look at her. "Lydia, I'm sorry. I forgot

about our plans. I didn't realize they were set in stone, and you didn't follow up—"

"I left messages that you never returned." Lydia's voice was as sharp as jagged glass.

He felt like a heel, mostly because it seemed he'd just driven the final nail in yet another relationship—and he wasn't particularly upset by it. "I'm sorry."

"What, not even a request for a rain check?"

He hesitated, acutely aware of Briar's watchful gaze. "Lydia, I'm sorry. I just don't think I'm going to have the time to be a proper escort—"

She actually flinched at his choice of words. "Escort? That certainly clarifies things, doesn't it?" Grabbing her purse, she rose and walked to the door, pausing for a moment to look down at Briar and Logan. "Hope you don't have any expectations where he's concerned," she said. "He's not exactly reliable."

She gave the door a sharp jerk, slamming it closed behind her.

Dalton dropped heavily in his chair. "Sorry about that."

"You should go after her. I really can find someone else to watch Logan tonight—"

"The problem is," he said wearily, "I don't want to go after her."

"Oh."

He rubbed his gritty eyes. "You may have picked the wrong person to keep you and Logan safe. Clearly, my life is falling apart these days."

She sat in the chair across from his desk, waiting silently for him to look at her. When he did, she shot him a brief smile. "First, I didn't pick you for anything. You picked us. And second, I don't know anyone in this world whose life doesn't fall apart now and then. Now's just your turn. So quit kickin' yourself about it." She set Logan down on the floor and gave him the turtle backpack. "Logan, why don't you go over there in the corner and get your trucks out to play with?"

Logan looked up at her warily but took the pack in his arms and toddled off to the corner to start unpacking his toys.

"I left his car seat with your secretary. If you'll go sit down with him and play trucks for a little bit, I'll slip out and he probably won't even notice I'm gone," she said, nodding toward her son. "I need to head out soon."

She looked uncertain, as if she doubted he could keep her son from fretting when she left. He took it as a challenge, levering himself down to a cross-legged position on the floor beside Logan. "Can I play?"

Logan looked up at him soberly for a moment, then picked up a little blue police car and handed it to him. "Mama police."

Dalton glanced at Briar, who had edged toward the door. "That's right. Mama's a police officer." When he looked up again, she was gone.

Logan didn't notice her departure for several minutes, and by the time he did, Dalton had given up all pretense that he'd be able to get any work done for the rest of the day. "Why don't we pack up and head home, Logan?"

"Okeydokey," Logan said with a lopsided grin that made Dalton's heart do strange flip-floppy things in his chest. He helped Dalton pack his toys and reached up one small hand to be held. "Go now?"

Dalton let Logan wrap his hand around his index finger. "Sure thing."

The parking lot was still full of cars, as the county-courthouse workday was still at least an hour away from coming to an end. As Logan's short legs struggled to keep up with Dalton's longer strides, Dalton coaxed the boy onto his hip, looping the car seat and backpack over his free hand.

Logan held himself at arm's length at first, but after a few steps, he melted into Dalton's grasp, pressing his forehead into the curve of Dalton's neck. The flip-floppy sensation in Dalton's chest rushed back with a vengeance, and by the time he reached his car, he was grinning like an idiot.

Briar had explained how the car seat worked earlier that morning before he left for the office, and fortunately, he was pretty good at following directions. The seat fit snugly on the bench seat of the pickup truck, and Logan didn't whine too much about being strapped in once Dalton handed over the backpack full of toys.

The drive from Barrowville went quickly since they were ahead of rush hour. As they neared Edgewood, Dalton made a spur-of-the-moment decision to stop at the convenience store about a block from the subdivision to pick up milk and cereal for Logan's breakfast the next morning.

Logan actually reached for him this time when he went to unbuckle him from the car seat. Dalton gave him a quick hug and lowered him to the ground. "You like cereal, Logan, my man?"

"Cheerios!"

Of course. Dalton held out his hand, and Logan curled his fingers around his index finger again. They entered the convenience store and went straight back to the coolers for a half gallon of milk.

"How are you doing with your reading, Logan? Think you can help me find the Cheerios?"

Logan applied himself to the task, grinning brightly when he located the box in the dry-goods aisle. "Cheerios," he announced.

Logan picked up a box and added it to the basket with the milk. They headed to the front to pay.

The clerk was a weary-faced girl in her twenties with lanky blond hair and makeup slightly smeared by a day's work. But she grinned brightly at Logan. "Ain't you a cutie?"

Dalton paid for the milk and cereal, smiled at the clerk and nudged Logan out the door, trying not to think too hard about how much he was enjoying playing Daddy for a little while.

"You and I are going to have a fun time tonight, Logan, my man."

Logan grinned up at him, making Dalton smile in return.

But his smile faded quickly when a dark-clad figure rose from a crouch beside his truck. He wore a camouflage hat low on his head and his face was masked with smears of sooty camouflage face paint. His hulking appearance out of nowhere was such a shock to Dalton that he froze for a moment, half certain he'd conjured the man from his anxiety-fueled imagination.

Then the sinking sun sparked off the large-bladed hunting knife the man brandished in his right hand, and Dalton knew all the wishing in the world wouldn't drive this vision away.

The man in black spoke with a low mountain twang, full of bridled violence, that sent a shudder down Dalton's spine. "If you want to live, give me the kid and get the hell out of here."

Chapter Nine

Dalton had prosecuted his share of violent-crime cases over the ten years he'd worked for the Ridge County prosecutor's office. He'd comforted witnesses and helped them prepare for testimony. And the one thing they'd told him that had always seemed strange was how tunnel-visioned they became when confronted with violence.

"All you see is the gun in your face," one woman had told him after she and her husband had been robbed at gunpoint. "You don't even let yourself look at the person holding it. You just keep looking at the gun. It's like you think as long as you look at the gun, it won't do anything to you."

He understood now. All he could do was stare at the enormous glittering blade of the hunting knife waving in front of his face, to the point that he almost lost his grip on Logan's tiny hand.

Logan had started crying, his little body wrapping around Dalton's leg as if he were trying to hide there. The sound of his soft cries was like a spur in Dalton's side, prodding him to action.

His rifle was in the truck, locked up. He didn't even have a pocketknife on him, but it would have been no match for the enormous blade in the other man's hand anyway.

But he had a half gallon of milk dangling in a bag clutched in his right hand. Five pounds' worth of bludgeon.

He feinted to the left, drawing the knife and the man behind it in that direction. His other hand he swung in an arc, slamming the jug of milk against the man's hand.

The black-clad man didn't lose hold of the knife, but the blow knocked him sideways into the car parked next to Dalton's truck. Dalton hoped it would be enough. Grabbing up Logan, he started running back toward the convenience store.

Sharp stabbing pain raced through his side, and he almost lost his grip on Logan. He felt a tearing sensation, heard the rip of fabric, but he didn't stop running, even as footsteps pounded after him.

There was another customer coming out of the convenience store as he reached the door, a young man in his mid-twenties with shaggy hair and a patchy beard. His eyes widening, he reached out and grabbed Dalton by the arm, his grip amazingly strong. For a moment Dalton tried to shake him off, until he realized the man was dragging him into the store. As Dalton stumbled forward, the younger man threw the deadbolt on the door, locking them both in.

Dalton regained his balance and turned to look at the storefront windows. Standing in the full-glass doorway, knife raised, the dark-clad man with the face paint glared back at him through the glass, his pale eyes blazing with fury. He pounded the butt of his knife against the door, making the glass rattle.

"Call the police," Dalton gasped, turning his body to shield Logan from the man outside.

"They're on the way," the woman behind the counter told him. He looked up to find that she was holding a shotgun gripped tightly in her hands, her gaze on the door.

"Hey, mister, you're bleeding." The young man who'd

pulled him into the store put his hand on Dalton's arm, setting his nerves jangling again. A faint ringing started in his ears and he grabbed for the cashier's desk as the world started to spin around him.

The man tried to pull Logan from his arms, but Dalton held on tightly, pressing the crying baby against his chest as he slid to the floor.

THE CALL HAD come over the radio around five-fifteen. 10-52—armed robbery—with a 10-39, injured person. Briar and her patrol partner, Thurman Gowdy, were the closest unit and responded within minutes. A fire-and-rescue unit had responded, as well, flashing cherry lights strobing the convenience store parking lot as Gowdy pulled the patrol unit into an open parking space.

They made their watchful way into the convenience store, where the action seemed to be focused. Several people stood in a semicircle around two paramedics crouched in front of the cashier's desk. One of the two men, speaking in a low, soothing voice, said, "It's okay now. You can let him go. We'll take good care of him."

"No," a pain-filled voice gritted out. "He stays with me."

Briar's heart jumped in her chest. That was Dalton Hale's voice.

"Police," she announced, moving past Gowdy and pushing her way through the gathered crowd. Dalton Hale sat slumped on the floor in front of the cashier's counter, his arms curled around her son's body. Logan had been crying, but at the moment he was silent, just blinking with confusion at the people standing in a ring around him.

Dalton looked up at the sound of her voice, his green eyes melting with relief. "He's okay," he said.

Logan spotted her and started wriggling to get loose. Dalton let him go, his arms dropping to his side.

Briar scooped her son into her arms, staring at Dalton. He was bleeding from his right side, she could see now. Not a lot, but enough that blood had begun to pool on the floor beside him.

The paramedics moved in quickly, coaxing him onto his back.

"I didn't let him take Logan," Dalton said, his gaze still locked with hers.

Briar looked at Thurman Gowdy. He stared back, then thumbed the shoulder radio and called for backup.

She carried Logan over to the checkout stand and set him on the glass-top counter, quickly looking him over for any signs of injury. He was still making soft hiccupping sounds, and his nose was running from his earlier tears, but she didn't find any sign of injury. "How you doing, buddy?" she asked, pressing a fervent kiss to the top of his head.

"Dallen?" Logan craned his head for a look at Dalton, who was being poked and prodded by the EMTs trying to assess his condition.

"Dalton's going to be fine." *Please be fine,* she added silently.

Gowdy caught up with her a few minutes later. A thin balding man in his late fifties, Gowdy had been a fixture in Bitterwood P.D.'s patrol unit since he joined the force almost forty years earlier. He'd turned down dozens of promotions over the years, preferring to ride patrol, and now he was the go-to officer when there was a rookie cop in need of a senior partner. "I'm not detective material," he'd told Briar on their first day together on the job. "But if you listen to me, you'll learn a hell of a lot about police work in a short amount of time."

Right now he gave her a quick update on what had happened. "Bearded white male, mid-twenties, wearing a dark

shirt, dark pants, camo cap and camo face paint. Carrying a hunting knife. Witnesses say he confronted the vic
there on the floor. The vic swung his groceries at the guy,
grabbed up the little fella here and ran for the store. Someone inside let him in and locked the door before the perp
with the knife could get in." Thurman put his hand on her
shoulder. "This is your baby, ain't it?"

Briar stroked Logan's mussed hair off his damp forehead. "Yes. The vic is Dalton Hale."

Thurman's eyebrows lifted. "The prosecutor?"

She nodded, struggling not to cry. The paramedics were
taking a scary length of time tending to Dalton, and while
she didn't want to get in the way, she needed to talk to him,
find out exactly what had happened.

Her cell phone rang, jarring her so sharply that she
nearly jumped. She checked the display. Walker Nix.
"Hello?"

"I just got a call about a knife attack in Edgewood.
Someone said Dalton Hale was the victim—did he have
Logan?"

"He did, but Logan's fine. I'm on scene."

"What about Hale?"

"He's hurt. I don't know how bad, but it doesn't seem
immediately life threatening."

"We're on the way. Hang tight." Nix hung up.

Briar put her hand to her head, willing the pounding
pulse in her ears to settle down to something approaching
normal. "Thurman, I can't leave Logan—"

"No hurry now." His tone was kindly. Soothing. "You
worry about your little fella. Backup's on the way."

One of the paramedics moved away from Dalton and
approached her. She knew him from her time as a dispatcher—Clark Emerson. Nice guy. Doting father of three.
He bent to look her in the eyes. "You two okay over here?"

"I think so. I didn't see any signs of injuries." She looked over at Dalton. "How's he?"

"It looks worse than it is. The wound is mostly superficial, though it cut through some muscle, so he's probably hurting a little. He needs stitches, but he doesn't want an ambulance. He wants to talk to you."

Briar glanced at her son. His sleepy-eyed gaze was on Dalton, who had pushed into a sitting position and was watching them as the other paramedic checked his vitals. "Come on, kiddo. Let's go talk to Mr. Hale." She scooped Logan up and carried him over to Dalton.

"How's he doing?" Dalton asked, lifting a hand toward Logan.

She crouched next to him, lowering Logan to his feet beside Dalton. Logan looked with interest at the blood-pressure cuff on Dalton's arm, peering more closely as the cuff began to expand.

"He's fine," she answered. "How about you?"

"I'm okay. Feeling a little embarrassed about nearly fainting from a little nick in the side."

The paramedic shushed them, forcing them to wait until he was finished with the blood-pressure check. "One-thirty over eighty," he murmured as he wrote it down.

"Is that good or bad?" Dalton asked.

"Not bad," the paramedic said with a smile.

Briar put her hand on Dalton's knee. "What happened?"

He looked down at her hand, then back at her. "I stopped for milk and cereal. Thought the little tiger here should have a decent breakfast in the morning. He picked Cheerios."

"His favorite." She managed a weak smile.

"We paid and went back out to the truck. Suddenly, the guy was just there. Dressed in dark clothes and he had this camouflage paint stuff on his face. And he had a knife."

"Do you know what kind of knife?"

"An enormous one." He shot her an apologetic look. "I'm useless as a witness, aren't I?"

"Maybe." Her smile was a little stronger this time. "But you faced down a man with a knife and kept my boy safe. So you're not going to hear any complaints from me."

"I'm sorry, Briar." He reached out and touched her hand where it lay on his knee. "I shouldn't have stopped for milk. I just didn't expect someone to strike in broad daylight, in public like this."

She hadn't, either. And the fact that the knife-wielding man had taken such a risky chance scared the hell out of her.

"WHY AREN'T YOU in an ambulance right now?"

Dalton dropped his hand from his aching head and turned at the sound of Doyle Massey's voice. Doyle had apparently come in on the heels of the detectives, who had pulled Briar aside for an update.

Dalton sighed. "I'm okay. I can drive myself to get stitched up."

"We'll need your shirt in case we can match the rip mark to a weapon."

"I know how evidence works," Dalton answered defensively.

Briar walked up, Logan on her hip, in time to hear his last words. "Then you know there's a chain of evidence that has to be maintained."

Doyle looked away from Dalton and frowned down at Briar. "Blackwood, you're on paid administrative leave until further notice."

Her brow furrowed as her eyes widened. "Sir?"

"What happened here isn't her fault," Dalton protested, reaching out to grab Doyle's arm. "This is my mistake.

I'll make sure it doesn't happen again. Please don't punish Briar for it."

Doyle's scowl disappeared and his gaze softened. "It's not punishment." He turned his gaze to Briar, his voice gentling. "You have a son to protect. You don't need to be leaving him with other people while you try to work. It'll be too much of a distraction."

Briar's chin came up, pride blazing in her cool gray eyes. "I don't want special treatment."

"I'm not giving you special treatment. Your son needs protection. So I'm assigning you to protect your son. This is your new job until we can figure out what's going on."

"Don't argue with him, Briar," Dalton murmured. "He's always right. Haven't you figured that out yet?"

Doyle snapped his head around to look at Dalton. "Not always. Sometimes people still manage to disappoint me no matter how low my expectations." He moved away to confer with Nix and Delilah Brand, the other Bitterwood detective who'd responded to the call.

"Don't you just love these family meetings?" Dalton murmured.

"You both seem to like gettin' a rise out of each other." Briar pressed her nose against Logan's hair and breathed deeply, as if breathing in the sweet, clean scent of him. "Dalton, I don't think I've said this properly—"

He jerked his head up, meeting her gaze with alarm. "Don't." He didn't want her to say thank you. He was damned lucky to have gotten away from the man with the knife. If the slightest thing had happened differently—he couldn't bear to think about what might have happened.

"You knocked the guy into a car with a half gallon of milk." Despite the haunted look in her eyes, her lips curved a bit at the sheer absurdity of his method of self-defense. "You got Logan to safety. While a guy was sticking an enormous knife in your side. If that's not heroic, I don't know what is."

"Technically, he swiped the knife. He didn't stick it," he corrected. "I'm not a hero, Briar. Anyone else would have done the same thing."

"You'd be surprised how few people would have done the same thing." She bent her head toward her son's soft curls again. "I hear he told you he'd let you go if you gave him Logan."

"I would never do that."

"I know. That's why I entrusted him to you in the first place." She looked up at him with shining eyes. The almost violent urge to wrap her and Logan up in his arms and never let them go caught him utterly flat-footed.

Nix's arrival kept him from doing something stupid. The detective looked at Briar with obvious affection, reaching out to palm the back of Logan's head. "The chief says if you want a ride back to the station, he's got room in his car." He looked at Dalton. "And if you'd like a ride to the hospital, he's offering that, as well. He'll stay with you and drop you back home when you're done."

Dalton looked past Nix and found Doyle leaning against the window near the door. His gaze met Dalton's and he gave a slight nod.

Oh, hell, Dalton thought. *Why not?* He needed a ride, and whether he liked it or not, the man was his brother. If the situation were reversed…

If the situation were reversed, he realized with some surprise, he'd do the same thing.

"I'll need your keys, Hale. To get Logan's car seat out of the truck."

Dalton handed off his keys. "Tell him I'll take the ride to the hospital."

Nix shot him an exasperated look. "For God's sake,

you're adults. Tell him yourself." He headed out to the parking lot.

"Are you sure you'll be okay going to the hospital alone with the chief?" Briar asked.

He slanted a look at her. "I'm a big boy."

"Remember to tell Doyle thank you."

Dalton laughed. "I'll try. It's a toss-up whether or not we'll make it to the hospital without killing each other."

"Do your best." She laid her hand on his arm, letting her fingers slide slowly down to his wrist before she let go. He barely controlled a shiver as her light touch sent tremors up and down his arm.

"Ready to go?" Doyle pushed away from the wall as they approached. He looked pointedly at Dalton. "Am I carting your butt to the hospital or what?"

"Your brotherly devotion is touching," Dalton murmured.

Doyle shot him a smart-alecky look, and Dalton realized he was getting to the point that he could predict the chief's reaction to his words.

Almost like a real brother.

IT WAS WELL after nine when Dalton finally called Briar to tell her he was coming up the front walkway. She hurried to unlock the door and let him in. She waved to Doyle, who waited in his police cruiser until Dalton was safely inside. "All stitched up?"

He nodded. "Want to see my wound?"

Smiling, she shook her head. "You hungry? Logan and I had chicken soup for dinner. I can heat some up for you."

He caught her hand as she moved toward the kitchen, his fingers warm and firm around hers. "Doyle and I grabbed a burger on the way home."

"How'd that go?" She waited for him to let go of her

hand, but he twined his fingers with hers instead, leading her over to the sofa. He sat heavily, tugging her down beside him.

"It went...better than I expected. He wasn't a complete smart-ass, and I tried not to be a defensive jerk. So...progress." He gave her hand a light squeeze. "Logan asleep?"

She looked down at their twined hands, her gaze drawn by the intersection of her fair skin and his tanned fingers. "About thirty minutes ago. We had to read a couple of extra stories, and he was worried that you weren't home yet, but I explained you had to go somewhere with your brother. I also promised you'd look in on him before you go to bed. You don't have to, though. Once he falls asleep, it takes a bulldozer to wake him. He wouldn't know you were there."

"I'll know," he said, turning his head toward her.

She met his gaze, a ripple of pure feminine awareness rolling through her, setting off a dozen tingles along her spine. Despite the weariness in his eyes, the faint pallor beneath his healthy tan, he was still one of the most attractive men she'd ever seen.

Man *being the operative word,* she thought as she drowned a little in his warm green gaze. He was a man, flaws and all, in a way Johnny never had been. Though she was still in her twenties, giving birth to Logan had changed her from a girl to a woman almost overnight.

But was she woman enough to deal with a man like Dalton? A man who'd lived a life of privilege she couldn't even begin to imagine, much less understand? A man with his own demons that made her day-to-day struggles seem like bumps in the road in comparison?

She'd worked hard over the past few months to simplify her life, to focus her attention completely on her son and his future. Letting herself get involved with another person had never figured into her plans.

But she knew, with a certainty that sent heat blazing into the center of her sex, if he dipped his head closer, she would close the distance between them and take whatever he chose to offer.

"Last night," he murmured, "I wanted to kiss you."

She closed her eyes, overwhelmed by his raw honesty. "I know."

"I still do."

She opened her eyes and leaned closer, even as her self-protective instincts screamed at her to get up and walk away. "It's a bad idea."

"It really is."

She brushed her fingertips against his chest, tracing the contours of his muscles. He was well built for a man who worked in an office, with lean, defined muscles. He kept himself fit.

"Do you know why I never called Lydia back today?" he asked, his gaze dropping to her mouth.

"Because you're a heel?" she asked, her own gaze sliding over his mouth, noting—not for the first time—the tempting fullness of his lower lip.

That lower lip curved upward at the corners in response to her remark. "I suppose I can't deny it, can I? You saw the whole scene play out."

"You should have told her the truth."

His eyes flickered up away from her mouth, and his gaze leveled with hers. "I don't think she'd have liked the truth all that much."

"Which was?" she prodded, knowing she was playing with wildfire.

"That I forgot all about her the minute I saw you that first night at the hospital." He dipped his head toward her. "You're all I seem to think about. How to keep you safe. How to protect Logan. Whether I can do it or not."

He always seemed so confident and controlled. To hear him express uncertainty was a sobering experience. "What a messy situation you've gotten yourself into."

His lips twitched upward again. "I have a knack for it these days."

"How was lunch with your mother?"

He lifted one dark eyebrow. "How'd you hear about that?"

"I tried to call you around lunchtime but you were out. Your secretary mentioned you were having lunch with your mother." She couldn't stop herself from snuggling a little closer. "How is she holding up?"

"Better than I thought she would." He sighed, leaning away from her and laying his head back on the sofa cushions. "They were so wrong about her, you know. My father and grandfather. They claim they were protecting her, but she's so much stronger than either of them gave her credit for."

"How long has it been since you spoke to your dad?" Briar asked.

He rolled his head toward her. "Why?"

"I lost my daddy when I was ten. I wish I could talk to him now."

He reached out to touch her cheek, grimacing as the movement apparently pulled on his stitches. He fell back, gazing up at the ceiling.

If she'd been thinking more clearly, she probably would have gotten up right then and headed up to bed. But the night had been nearly as harrowing for her as it had been for him. And she wasn't quite ready for it to end.

Slowly, she lifted her hand to his face, cupping the curve of his jaw. His gaze slid down to meet hers, the green of his eyes warm and liquid, like a mossy mountain pool.

"I'm going to kiss you," she whispered. "It doesn't have to mean anything you don't want it to mean."

His hand sliding up her back to tangle in her hair, he pulled her toward him, his breath hot against her cheek. She angled her lips across his, a light exploratory touch. Dry, warm, closed-mouth. Almost chaste.

Almost.

His lips parted under hers, the slick heat of his tongue brushing over her bottom lip, teasing it lightly at first, then with a demanding intensity that shook her to her suddenly burning core.

And any thought of chastity went right out the window.

Chapter Ten

Briar straddled Dalton's thighs, sliding forward until he felt the soft heat of her sex settle flush against his growing hardness, flesh separated from flesh by a couple of layers of clothing. The sensation rocketed straight to his brain, exploding like fireworks and spreading molten pleasure to every part of his body. Convulsively tightening his trembling fingers in her tangle of curls, he flattened his other hand against the small of her back, urging her hips forward to increase the delicious friction building between their bodies.

He nuzzled his way down the curve of her throat, his lips brushing lightly over her skin. He kissed the skin beneath her jaw, the delicate curve of her chin, then lightly nipped his way back up to her mouth.

Her lips parting beneath the pressure of his own, she surged toward him, flattening her breasts against his chest. Her fingers skimmed his rib cage through his shirt, exploring the ridges as if seeking to map every contour. Her actions sparked a fresh surge of heat through his blood and fire along the path her fingers traveled, until his whole body felt on the verge of combustion. He didn't even care when her gentle touches tugged the still-tender skin of his wounded side.

Somewhere in the depths of his desire-addled brain, he

knew what they were doing was a mistake. But he couldn't seem to quell the primal urge to bury his hardness in her soft heat, and her sweet, fierce response to his touch drove out what remained of his good sense.

So easy, he thought. So easy to bury himself inside her and forget about everything else. Forget the tatters of his life. The danger gathering like a firestorm outside the walls of their sensual cocoon.

So easy to drop his guard.

Just as he'd dropped it earlier tonight in the parking lot.

With another groan, he dragged his mouth from hers, his breath coming in harsh, rapid gasps. He caught her hips in both hands and moved her carefully away from his own hips. "Briar, this isn't a good idea."

She dropped her head forward, let it fall against his shoulder. Her curls whispered against his cheeks. "I know."

For a long moment, they just breathed together, hitching, syncopated gasps that slowly ebbed into gentle sighs. Finally, she rolled away from his lap, slumping back against the sofa cushions. "I'm sorry," she said.

Her words surprised him so much that he couldn't stop a soft huff of laughter. "For what?"

"For…that."

He couldn't quite stop himself from teasing her a little. "For riding me like a cowgirl in a rodeo?"

She flashed him a look that made him laugh a little harder.

"Come on, Briar. We're adults. No harm done, right?"

Except he wasn't so sure about that, was he? He wasn't a man prone to indulging his body's urges without consideration and thought. His control, in fact, was damned near legendary, leading more than one woman he'd dated to accuse him of having ice in his veins instead of blood.

But no ice could have survived the flood of fire that

had swamped his body at Briar's touch. He didn't know why she had evoked such an uncharacteristic response in him, but he couldn't deny it had happened. And he had a bad feeling that if he gave it too much more thought, he wouldn't find the answer reassuring.

But whatever his reason for losing control, he was certain of one thing: he would be a fool to let it happen again.

"I wasn't expecting that," she ventured after another moment of silence. "I don't— This isn't something I do. You know?"

"I wasn't expecting it, either," he admitted.

"I know it's the twenty-first century and women are free to embrace their sexuality, but…" Her gaze lifted, finally, and settled on his face. "I just don't do this."

"Believe it or not, neither do I. Not out of the blue this way." He hadn't meant to admit that fact to her. He could have shrugged it off with jaded humor, as if he went about seducing women every day. Better than admit that her touch had damned near unraveled him.

"So we agree?" she asked.

He gave her a wary look. "About what?"

"That we don't need to do this again."

What he needed, he thought, barely tamping down a shudder of raw need, was to strip off those snug little jeans of hers and sink into the softness hidden between her sleek thighs. That's what he needed.

Aloud, however, he said, "Agreed." He pushed himself up from the sofa and looked down at her. "I need some sleep. I bet you do, too."

She stared up at him, her eyes dark and liquid. The urge to seduce her all over again, to take her up to his bedroom and finish what they'd started, damned near overwhelmed him once more.

But she rose to her feet with steady, unhurried dignity

and took a step away from him. "If you'll make sure the alarm is set, I'll check all the locks."

Working in silent accord, they kept their distance from each other as they fortified their defenses against the danger outside. But as Dalton found his gaze straying toward Briar's slim figure over and over, he realized there might be no way to defend himself against the unexpected danger of Briar Blackwood living under his roof.

Twilight cast a deep indigo gloom over the convenience store parking lot, broken only by the flash of cherry lights spinning atop the fire department emergency bus. A crowd had gathered, vultures circling a fresh kill. They stood in a writhing knot of anticipation near a pickup truck parked not far from the store entrance.

Briar made her way through the throbbing mass of onlookers, her pulse racing so frantically that she couldn't make out individual beats, just a cacophony of terror building to incessant white noise in her ears.

The crowd seemed to go on for miles, rolling around her like waves in the ocean, prolonging the dread. But finally, she reached the center of the throng to look upon the spectacle that had drawn them.

He lay facedown on the dirty parking lot pavement, utterly still. Beneath him a river of red spread in lightly undulating waves, the ripples slowly dying away to nothing, the memory of his life pulse fading into stillness.

She tore her gaze away and looked at the ground beside him. A torn bag lay next to him, spilling its contents on the edge of his pooling blood. A jug of milk. A box of cereal. Both stained red.

And beside the torn shopping bag, a turtle-shaped backpack, straps severed, as if someone had ripped it off the little boy who'd worn it.

"No," she moaned, but the words felt as if they stuck in her aching throat. She crouched beside the fallen warrior, heedless of the blood staining her hands. "Please, please—" She lifted a shaking hand to his pale face, touched his cold cheek.

His eyes snapped open. "Briar?"

She jarred awake, her heart rat-a-tatting against her breastbone. It was still dark outside, the only light coming from the open doorway.

In the rectangle of light from the hall, Dalton's tall muscular silhouette stood over her. "I'm sorry to wake you," he said quietly, glancing at the sleeping little boy by her side. "I have to leave for a while."

She squinted at the travel alarm she'd set on the bedside table. Not even six yet. "What's wrong?"

"It's my father," he answered. "He had some sort of attack. He's in the hospital in Maryville."

She pushed her tangled hair out of her face, the jangling sensation in her sleep-addled brain finally subsiding. "How bad?"

"He's stable, but nobody's been able to give me any information beyond that. I just didn't want you to wake up and wonder where I'd gone. And maybe we should call Nix or someone to come stay with you?"

"No need to bother Nix. Those hillbillies can't get to me here the way they can out in the woods. And if they try, well, I'm armed and lookin' for a little payback." She pushed off the covers and rolled to a sitting position on the edge of the bed, relieved she'd decided to wear sweats to bed the night before. Of course, considering how close they'd come to getting naked together the night before, her attack of modesty was a little tardy. "Have you eaten anything?"

"No, but—"

She stood and wrapped her hand firmly around his arm, nudging him toward the door. "You can't go to Maryville hungry. Not in your condition."

He didn't protest as she led him downstairs to the kitchen. He even sat quietly at the breakfast bar and let her take over. She darted a look at him as she searched the cabinets for his cookware, seeing in the glare of the kitchen light what the shadows of his bedroom had hidden.

He was in emotional shock.

She put down the frying pan she'd just retrieved and crossed to the bar, reaching for his hands. They were cool to the touch.

His haunted green eyes rose to meet hers. "I told him I was ashamed I'd ever called him my father. That's the last thing I said to him."

She tightened her grip on his hands. "So tell him you made a mistake."

"What if he's—"

"You just said he's stable."

"That could change. It could change before I get there." He looked down at their clasped hands. "Briar, he could die before I get there."

She wished she could go with him. Give him the moral support her friends had given her that night as she waited for word on her aunt's condition. But she had to stay with Logan.

"Let me call somebody to go with you," she suggested.

His gaze snapped up to meet hers. "There's no one. Mother can't—I don't want her there until I know more."

"There's your brother. Or your sister."

He closed his eyes. "I haven't exactly given them any reason to want to hold my hand through this mess."

"Family doesn't need a reason."

The vulnerability in his eyes when they met hers made her heart ache. "I can't ask them."

Maybe not, she thought.

But she could.

"IT WASN'T A HEART ATTACK." The E.R. doctor had introduced himself as Dr. Treadway. He was a short stocky man in his early forties with thinning hair and a kind smile. "His blood pressure was elevated when he came into the E.R. and his heart rate was up. He was hyperventilating a bit, but we were able to get that under control with a sedative. We're doing more tests to be sure, but the signs are pointing to an anxiety attack."

Dalton covered his eyes with his hand for a moment, his body tingling with relief. "Can I see him?"

"There's a guard posted outside his room. You'll have to clear it with him."

Of course. His father was still a prisoner. The judge in Barrowville had refused to set bail, considering Paul Hale a flight risk and a potential danger to Dana Massey.

But he didn't look like a dangerous man, lying pale and groggy in the hospital bed. The guard turned out to be a man Dalton had met several times in his job as a prosecutor. He'd allowed Dalton into the room without protest.

Paul Hale turned his head at the sound of Dalton's footsteps approaching the bed. Color flushed through his cheeks, driving out the pallor. "I didn't expect to see you."

Dalton pulled up a nearby chair. "I didn't expect to be here."

"They say I'll live."

"I'm glad."

Paul's gaze narrowed. "Are you?"

"I'm sorry about what I said to you before."

"Which thing? You said a lot of things."

Dalton felt a flurry of anger beating in his chest like bats flushed out of the dark bowels of a cavern. "You tried to shoot my sister."

His father's gaze snapped up to meet his. "Your sister."

"That's what she is." The words flowed easily over his tongue, surprising him. But he felt a glimmer of freedom in saying the words aloud.

"I've never heard you call her that."

"I haven't called her that before."

His father's expression shifted to curiosity. "Why now?"

"I guess because I've had enough time to accept the truth of it. She's my sister. Doyle Massey is my brother. Tallie Cumberland gave birth to me." *And your father-in-law stole me from her and gave me to you and your wife. And then made sure Tallie didn't live to tell me the truth.*

"Tallie Cumberland wasn't your mother."

"She wasn't given the chance to be."

Paul shifted restlessly in the hospital bed, the movement rattling the cuff chaining him to the bed. "That was your grandfather's doing."

"I'm aware of that."

"Have you talked to the old man?"

Dalton shook his head. "I don't expect to. He's not talking to anyone but his lawyer."

"How's your mother? Does she know?"

"About your being here? No. I'll call her later this morning to let her know."

"Don't let her come here. I don't want her to see me this way."

"She knows you're in jail. Seeing you shackled to the bed won't come as a surprise."

"She trusted me to be her protector. Her rock."

And he'd failed her, Dalton thought, trying not to think of his own near failure the night before. Trying not to remember how close he'd come to letting the man with the knife rip Briar Blackwood's life into shreds.

"I can't stay here long," he said, reaching out to straighten the rumpled edge of the sheet covering his father.

"Late for work?" His father's tone wavered between self-pity and a hint of admiration. Paul Hale had been enormously proud of Dalton's work as a prosecutor. Ironic, really, given his current state of legal woes.

"I'm working from home today." He didn't elaborate. He didn't quite trust his father enough to share Briar's problems with him, or his own part in trying to keep her and her son alive. "But I have things to attend to."

"I see." His father's chin lifted, vestiges of the old Hale pride evident in the set of his jaw and the steely coolness of his eyes.

"I'll visit you when you're out of here."

"Back in jail, you mean."

Dalton sighed, more disappointed than angry at his father. Progress, he supposed. "You did a terrible thing. Regardless of your motives, you could have killed Dana. She didn't do a damned thing to deserve it."

"She was going to rip us apart. She *has* ripped us apart."

"Grandfather ripped us apart. With your help." Dalton rose to his feet, needing to leave this room, to breathe something besides the poison of his father's self-pity. "I'll see you soon. I hope you continue feeling better."

"I love you." Paul's voice followed him to the door.

Dalton paused in the doorway, turning slowly. "I love you, too. Dad," he said.

And meant it.

In the hall, two people were waiting. They looked up at him warily through green eyes very like his own.

"Briar called us," Dana Massey said, breaking the tense silence. "She said to tell you she was sorry for interfering."

"But not sorry enough not to do it?" He wasn't angry with her, he realized. He was actually rather glad to see his brother and sister waiting for him. Otherwise, he might be feeling pretty damned alone about now.

"If you want us to go, we'll go," Doyle said. "But we thought you should at least have the option of having someone here with you for this."

"I don't want you to go," Dalton admitted.

Dana lifted one hand to his arm, her touch tentative. "There's a good coffee shop down the street from here. I discovered it when Doyle was in the hospital after his truck flipped."

The accident his grandfather had caused, Dalton thought with grim dismay. But neither Doyle nor his sister seemed inclined to hold him responsible for his family's crimes.

They had treated him far more kindly than he'd treated them.

He covered her hand with his, giving it a light squeeze before he let go. It wasn't much, he supposed, as far as brotherly affection went. But it wasn't nothing, either.

"You'll pay, right?" Doyle asked, shooting him a grin.

Dalton couldn't stop a laugh.

"Younger brothers," Dana murmured as they fell in step, heading for the elevators. "Such mooches."

Brothers and sisters, Dalton thought as he followed them into the elevator alcove. He guessed he had to get used to having them.

Chapter Eleven

Waiting for Dalton to return had proved a more nerve-racking experience than Briar had expected. She'd been afraid he'd changed his mind about working from home and had gone to the office to get as far from her as he could. But a call to his secretary had established that he hadn't gone in to the office.

Neither had he called, not once in the four hours since he'd left the house. The drive to Maryville took twenty minutes. Had he stayed with his father the rest of the time?

Had his father's condition deteriorated?

She had tried to fill the hours with the business of Johnny's murder and how it might tie into the recent threats against her and her son. He'd died months ago. So why had it taken Blake and his cohort this long to make a move? Had something changed?

Dalton had changed, she realized with a flash of insight. The upheaval in his personal life had led him to attack the Cortland crime organization investigation with additional zeal. She wasn't certain of the timeline, but he'd spoken of the lumber yard bookkeeper he'd interrogated as if she was a recent contact. A new lead in the investigation.

Dalton had been the catalyst.

It was possible, even likely, that Blake had learned of the new lead, as well. She knew Wayne Cortland's band of rogues had included people with access to the Bitter-wood P.D. Probably the county sheriff's department, as well. Maybe even the Ridge County prosecutor's office. If Dalton suspected Johnny had stolen something valuable from Wayne Cortland by way of his affair with Cortland's bookkeeper, then her cousin probably suspected it, too.

The rattle of the front-door knob sent a corresponding echo through her taut nerves. Her hand closed around the butt of her Glock, relaxing only when she saw Dalton walk through the open doorway.

He paused midstride when his gaze met hers.

"Are you angry at me?" she blurted, though it hadn't been the question she'd planned.

He shook his head. "I had coffee with my brother and sister." A fleeting look of wonder crossed his face. "Never thought I'd say that." He locked the door behind him and crossed to the sofa, dropping heavily onto the soft cushions. He looked so tired, Briar thought, her own muscles aching with sympathy. "Where's Logan?"

"He's napping."

Dalton looked at his watch. "At ten-thirty?"

She sat in the chair across from him, not quite trusting herself to sit beside him again so soon after their loss of control the night before. "Last night was a lot of excitement for a little boy. He didn't sleep well." She hadn't even had to try hard to coax him into taking an early nap. "How's your father?"

"He's going to be fine. The doctor is pretty sure it was a panic attack."

"I'm glad to hear it." She let herself breathe again. "Did you see him?"

"I saw him." He passed his hand over his face, as if he could wipe away the weariness lining his face. "I don't suppose I've ever actually thought about my father in terms of strength or weakness. I think we assume our parents are either saints or demons, you know?"

"We see what we want to," she murmured.

"Or what we need to."

"I think that's probably true of most people in our lives." She thought about Johnny, about the lies she'd fed herself with the willingness of a young girl in love for the first time. "We look past the flaws and oversell the good parts."

His green eyes met hers, understanding passing across the space between them through that electric clash of gazes. "My father feels sorry for himself. He can't quite let himself come to terms with his failures. He needs to blame someone else."

"That's pretty human," she said gently.

"It is." He gave a brief nod. "But it's not particularly admirable."

"Have you always done the admirable thing since learning the truth about your birth?"

He looked down at his hands, his brow folding into a grim scowl. "God, no."

"The truth can be a real cold bitch," she murmured.

"You said you knew Johnny had been cheating on you," he said after a few moments of awkward silence. "When did it start?"

"The cheating?" She thought about it, even though the stark truth was painful even now. "I don't know. I had made him wait until we were married to have sex. And he seemed so patient about it, even though I knew he wanted me. But now I wonder…"

"You think he wasn't really being patient at all?"

"I grew up with Johnny. I'd been crazy about him since I was old enough to realize just what the difference between boys and girls really meant. When we started dating, I was utterly determined that he was the man I'd marry someday. And I was right." She couldn't stop a little smile at the memory of her happiness when Johnny had asked her to marry him. She had seen that moment as the beginning of her future. And it had been, though not quite in the way she'd foreseen.

She gripped her knees to keep her restless hands still. "We were both eighteen when we married. Young, though not so young compared to our parents' generation. Johnny already had a good job driving trucks for a mining company, and I had started as a dispatcher with Bitterwood Emergency Services. We thought we had our lives all figured out. We wanted babies. Lots of babies. But that didn't work out so well, either."

He looked at her oddly. "But Logan—is he adopted?"

"No, he's my biological son," she said quickly. "Johnny wouldn't consider adoption. And we probably couldn't have afforded it even if he'd thought differently. I think he wanted a child to prove something."

"Prove what?"

"I don't know. You're a man. You tell me."

"Some men see it as proof of virility," he said after a moment. "Like they're real men if they can plant their seed somewhere." Dalton didn't sound as if he agreed. "I wonder if my father felt that way. If that's why he covered up the truth about me."

"He saw you as his son. For a lot of years, he didn't know you weren't. Biologically, I mean."

"Biology," he murmured. "Just a bunch of nucleotides on a double helix, and yet it seems to rule our destinies."

"God, I hope not," she said. "I'm a Culpepper by birth, remember."

He looked up with a smile. "Not all Culpeppers are bad, are they?"

She gave a rueful laugh. "Depends on who you ask, I reckon."

"I guess Johnny was thrilled when you got pregnant with Logan?"

"Over the moon," she admitted, smiling at first until she remembered the months and years leading up to that brief moment of sheer joy. "I thought everything was going to be better then."

"Better than what?"

She realized that she was spilling her deepest, darkest secrets to a man she'd barely known by sight just a few days earlier. How had she let herself become so vulnerable?

And why did the thought not scare her more than it did?

"I'm sorry," he said a moment later as she continued to hesitate. "I'm asking a lot of personal questions that are none of my business."

"Johnny's personality seemed to change when we kept trying to have a baby and couldn't," she said, making herself ignore his tacit offer to change the subject. She'd kept Johnny's secrets for years, preventing his friends, his family and especially her own family from seeing the growing cracks in their young marriage.

But there was no marriage to protect any longer. And Johnny had been dead for a while now. The secrets burned in her gut like acid, and maybe it was time to get them out of her system before they destroyed her.

"At first we just thought it was bad luck. Bad timing. We started reading books about things like ovulation and biological timetables. It was a lark at first. We laughed about it a lot. Johnny had never been a big reader, but he tackled those books like they were instructional manuals." She laughed aloud at the memory. "We'd make naughty jokes about screws and nails and putting the right tabs into the right slots."

Dalton's smile almost made it to his eyes.

"But when all the reading and all the jokes and all the sex never produced a baby, he stopped smiling about it." The mood change had been palpable, she remembered. Joy had become dread. Sex had ceased to be communication and became instead an act of desperation. "We couldn't afford fertility treatments or expensive tests, and I sometimes wonder if he didn't prefer it that way. Easier to blame me than himself. And if we couldn't test to see who was really to blame—"

"Then he could keep believing it wasn't his fault."

"It wasn't anyone's fault. That's not how it works. Nature gives us what it gives us, and assigning blame about it is stupid and cruel."

"My parents tried forever to have a baby, without luck. When they had me—" Dalton stopped, a rueful grimace of a smile touching his lips as he started again. "When they had their son, they considered it a miracle."

"I guess your grandfather didn't want to rip that miracle away from them," she said. "When the baby died."

"I guess so. But his motives don't excuse his actions."

"No."

He looked up at her, raw emotion burning in his green eyes. "I don't know how to feel about any of it. It's like I woke up one day, looked in the mirror and saw a stranger."

"You're the same person," she said quietly, wanting desperately to cross the space between them and take him in her arms. Comfort the lost little boy that stared out from those pain-filled eyes. But she didn't trust herself to stop with comfort. "It's the world around you that's changed."

"Then maybe I need to quit whining and just get on with changing myself to adapt?"

She smiled. "I think I'd have put it more delicately."

He laughed. "You're a lot of things, Briar Blackwood,

but delicate is not one of them." After a moment, when she didn't join in the laughter, he added, "That's a good thing, you know. Delicate things end up trampled to dust sooner or later. In my line of work, I've seen it happen too often."

"You can't afford to be soft living in the mountains," she said. "You have to be tough, or the hills will eat you alive."

He gave her a thoughtful look. "I guess this would be a bad time, then, to suggest you and Logan should leave Bitterwood."

She stared at him, her mind rebelling against the thought. Life in these mountains had been hard, just as she'd said. Painful at times. But the mountains were her home. She'd carved a life out of these rocks and trees and smoky hills, and she didn't want to leave this place in fear.

"I have a friend who lives in Colorado. In the mountains. It's beautiful there, especially during the snowy season. You and Logan could learn to ski. Or snowboard. No one would find you there."

"You think we should run away? Leave everyone we know?"

He looked down at his hands for a long moment before his gaze snapped up, blazing with raw energy. "I could go with you. You're right about the world around me being different. So maybe it's the perfect time to change my world on purpose. Go somewhere, start fresh."

"With me?" She couldn't believe that was what he was suggesting.

"I don't know," he admitted, finally looking away. She felt a strange sort of relief not having those burning eyes gazing into her as if he could read the secrets of her soul. At the same time, she felt as if a cord connecting them for a brief electric moment had snapped, leaving her floating in some cold and lonely void. Her head ached with confusion.

"I'm not finished fighting," she said when it was clear

he'd say nothing more. "Not yet. We don't even know what we're looking for, do we? Blake seems determined to get some sort of leverage over me before he even tells me what he wants."

"That reminds me. I stopped by the office on the way home to pick up some files I had copied for you, but I left them in the car. Be right back." He went outside and came back in a minute with a large manila file folder stuffed with papers. "Come over here and I'll go through them with you," he suggested, laying the folder on the coffee table and sitting on the sofa, making room for her to join him.

She settled beside him on the sofa, allowing herself the small pleasure of his solid warmth against her side, even though their bodies didn't quite touch. "This is a lot of information," she said, unable to contain her surprise. It was certainly more information than the Bitterwood P.D. seemed to have on the Cortland organization.

"I have access to a lot of jurisdictions, even outside Tennessee," Dalton told her. "I've tried to organize things into the groups we think are working together." Within the file folder, she saw, he'd divided the papers into sections. One section was labeled Police Agencies. Another bore the label Anarchists/Antigovernment Radicals. A third was called Meth/Pot/Oxy. That, Briar supposed, would be all they'd gathered on the hodgepodge of drug cookers, pot growers and narcotics dealers Cortland had used as informants and sometimes hired killers to do his dirty work.

The fourth section, labeled Militias, was thinner than the others, Briar saw with some dismay. Even calling it Militias in the plural was clearly a bit of wish casting, for everything inside that section of Dalton's notes was about one particular militia—the Blue Ridge Infantry.

"What do you know about the BRI?" Dalton asked.

"It started with a little moonshine and a whole lot of bitterness," she answered slowly, thinking back on the stories she'd heard from her mother, a woman with little love for any Culpeppers beyond her own husband and children. "I don't know how well versed in mountain genealogy you folks here on the Edgewood side of town are, but there are Culpeppers up and down these hills from Alabama to the Maryland state line. And about thirty-five years ago, some of the Culpeppers got sucked into the militia movement. Now, some of them had fairly honorable reasons for it. They thought the government was getting too big for its britches, and it was up to regular folks to remind the government just who served who."

"That's not the Blue Ridge Infantry's goal at the moment," Dalton countered.

"No, it's not. And that's why you'll find a whole lot of folks round here who'd just as soon spit on the ground the BRI walks on as anything. Some of the militia members left started using the whole 'government is the devil' excuse to run moonshine, cook meth, grow pot—anything they could call government overreach, they made it into a BRI cause."

"How did Blake Culpepper get involved?"

"He's like a lot of folks in these hills. Chip on his shoulder the size of Chimney Rock. Thinks the world owes him something better than he has, but he's not willing to work for it." She shook her head, pressing her mouth flat as if to suppress the anger rising in her chest. "Or maybe he just likes hurtin' people. Seems like he works hard enough doin' bad when he's looking to make life miserable for somebody else."

"Did he and Johnny ever have reason to cross paths?"

"Sure. Johnny grew up here. On our side of the tracks, you don't get to pick and choose your neighbors. Or lock yourself up inside some gate."

He gave her a thoughtful look that made her feel churlish for having said what she had. Maybe Blake wasn't the only one with a chip on his shoulder.

"Johnny liked everybody, and he wasn't one to judge. He once told me that if he had to cut people out of his life for breaking the law, he wouldn't have any friends left." She flipped through the list of names Dalton had compiled, names of men and women the prosecutor's office believed were connected, either directly or indirectly, to the BRI.

"We went to school with half the people on this list. Went to church with some of 'em. Johnny probably played football with several." With a sigh, she pushed the folder away, feeling tired and out of sync with the world around her, as if there was no place that felt like home anymore.

"What could Johnny have taken that would be worth terrorizing you to get?" Dalton asked.

"I've been thinking about that all morning, ever since you left. And the only thing that seems clear is that you're the catalyst that set everything into motion."

Dalton's dark eyebrow rose. "I'm the catalyst?"

"Johnny died months ago. But nobody gave me a minute's worry until just a few days ago. Why? What happened a few days ago to make Blake and his crew think Johnny had given me something incriminating?"

Dalton's brow furrowed.

"Why did you come to the hospital that night? Why would you do that?" she asked.

"Because I thought—" He stopped short, looking down at the file, the creases in his forehead deepening.

"You thought I might know something about what Johnny took from Wayne Cortland."

His gaze snapped up to meet hers.

"Why did you think that?" she asked. "Because you

found out Johnny had been having an affair with Cortland's former bookkeeper?"

"That was part of it," he admitted.

"But there was more?"

He looked down at the file again, a pained look on his face as if he knew something he didn't want to tell her.

"For God's sake, Dalton. I'm not going to crumble if you tell me something unpleasant about Johnny."

He took a long deep breath and slowly met her gaze. "She said he liked to take risks."

A finger of dread scraped its way down her spine, trailing cold tremors. "What kind of risks?"

"Like sneaking her into Cortland's office for sex."

She looked at Dalton through narrowed eyes, almost feeling sorry for him. She could see how much he disliked having to say such things to her, his regret etched in fine lines and dark shadows all over his face. "They had sex in Cortland's office? With Cortland there in the building?"

"I don't know. I didn't ask for details."

"Maybe you should have." An idea began to form, one she didn't particularly want to have. One, in fact, that she dreaded intensely.

But it made a grim sort of sense. And it just might give them the answers they were looking for.

"Tell me where I can find the Cortland bookkeeper," she said after a long, tense silence. "I want to meet her."

Chapter Twelve

Working as a bookkeeper for a now-notorious crime boss couldn't have given Leanne Dawson much of a career boost, Briar thought as she walked across the gravel parking lot in front of Pinter Construction in Wytheville, Virginia. The building housing the offices was a small cinder-block structure once painted a sunny yellow that had long since faded into a dusty dun color. The name Pinter Construction was barely legible in peeling blue paint over the front door.

Inside, there were no cubicles, only a central desk at the front and a handful of desks lining the walls. Most of those were unoccupied, save for one near the back, occupied by a dark-haired man in his forties who was typing something in a series of painfully slow pecks, and another on the right-hand wall where a slim blonde was writing something onto a notepad from time to time as she consulted a book lying open on her desk.

At the front desk, a pretty dark-haired girl in her early twenties had her cell phone perched on her very pregnant stomach and didn't even acknowledge Briar's entrance.

Briar stepped up to the reception desk. "Is Leanne Dawson here?"

The pregnant girl looked up in surprise. "I'm sorry, what?"

"I need to speak to Leanne Dawson. Is she here?" For a brief dizzying moment, it occurred to her that this girl could be Leanne. And if she was pregnant—

But to her relief, the dark-haired girl just waved a hand in the general direction of the slim blonde on the right. "She's over there."

No offer to let her know Briar was coming. Which, she supposed, might work in her favor.

She crossed to the desk where the blonde continued jotting down notes, her hair covering her face like a curtain. Briar cleared her throat, making the woman jump.

"Leanne Dawson?" she asked.

The woman swept the shiny blond curtain away from her face, giving Briar a good look at the woman her husband had been sleeping with.

She was a pretty woman and, to Briar's bemusement, at least five years older than Briar herself, with clear blue eyes and lightly tanned skin that contrasted pleasantly with her straight wheat-colored hair. She was slim but well proportioned, with full breasts and long legs, displayed modestly enough by her tailored blouse and well-cut slacks.

"I'm Leanne Dawson. May I help you?"

Her accent was Southern but light and well modulated. An educated woman who hadn't lived in the hills her whole life, Briar thought. Had that been part of the attraction for Johnny, beyond Leanne's position as Cortland's bookkeeper? Had he enjoyed being with someone so obviously different from the little hillbilly girl back home?

Stop it, she scolded herself silently.

"My name is Briar Culpepper." She wondered as she gave her maiden name whether or not Johnny had told Leanne Dawson anything about the wife back home. If he had, Leanne showed no sign of recognition. "I'm a police officer in Bitterwood, Tennessee, looking into the murder of John Blackwood."

Leanne's expression shifted at the mention of Johnny's name. Bleakness darkened the blue of her eyes, and her lower lip trembled slightly as she waved at an empty folding chair on the other side of her desk. As Briar took a seat, Leanne said quietly, "I don't know anything about his death."

"But you knew John Blackwood."

"We were...friends."

"You were a little more than friends," Briar pressed, feeling pretty terrible for pushing the other woman this way without revealing the truth about herself. And if Logan's life hadn't been at stake, she probably would have come clean and asked for the woman's forbearance. But she couldn't afford to alienate Leanne Dawson until she asked the questions she wanted answered.

"Officer—"

"Call me Briar."

"Pretty name." Leanne smiled slightly before the expression faded into gloom again. "I've talked to so many people about him. I don't know what more to say. I made a really awful mistake. Not just where Johnny was concerned, either."

"I understand from your earlier statement to Ridge County prosecutor Dalton Hale that you and Johnny engaged in your liaisons in Wayne Cortland's office."

Beneath her tan, Leanne blushed deep pink, making Briar feel like a complete creep. "Only a few times."

"Did you go into the office together always? Or was Johnny ever alone there without you?"

Leanne's gaze darted up to meet Briar's. "Why?"

"We're trying to establish if Mr. Blackwood ever had access to Cortland's office unattended."

Leanne licked her lips, looking down at the open ledger that lay on the desk in front of her. As if suddenly realizing the company's books were laid bare to Briar if she wanted to look, she snapped the book closed and folded her hands on top of the book. "I made the mistake of giving Johnny liberties I shouldn't have."

"Including allowing him to go into Wayne Cortland's office unescorted? Maybe to wait until you could safely sneak away?"

Leanne lowered her face to her hands. "He made it seem so exciting. Fun and dangerous." She dropped her hands and looked at Briar, her expression stiff with embarrassment. "I don't attract exciting, dangerous men. He made me feel so alive."

Briar felt a hard, hot ache in the center of her chest, but to her surprise, it had less to do with her own feeling of betrayal and more to do with her sympathy for Leanne Dawson's obvious sense of shame and regret.

"So he made a game of your relationship. And part of that game was doing something crazy and dangerous. Like having sex in your boss's office?"

She nodded, a tear sliding down her cheek. "Sometimes it would take a half hour to get away. I was so afraid Mr. Cortland would go in there and find Johnny, my heart would be beating a mile a minute by the time—" She stopped, dashing the tear from her face with an angry stab of her knuckle. "All that time, he had a wife and I didn't know it. I guess that's what made it feel dangerous for him, huh?"

Briar looked down at her own hands, at the faint ring of pale skin on her left ring finger where the ring had been until Johnny's death. "Did Mr. Cortland have a safe? Or a drawer or file cabinet nobody else was allowed to access?" she asked.

"You know, that prosecutor asked me the same question, but I didn't remember—" Leanne paused, then started again. "It might not have meant anything. But there was a drawer in Mr. Cortland's desk that he used to always keep locked. Not that unusual—he might have kept personal items there. People do, you know. But just the other day, I remembered that he stopped locking the drawer a few months before the explosion."

The explosion that had blown Wayne Cortland to his eternal reward, Briar thought, along with several other people, some of whom may have been innocent pawns in Cortland's games. Leanne was damned lucky she hadn't been one of them. "Was that before or after Johnny's death?"

"After," Leanne answered after a moment of thought.

If it was right after Johnny's murder, Briar realized, it was possible that Cortland had figured out what Johnny was up to. Had he sent someone to kill Johnny and retrieve what her husband had stolen?

Whoever he'd sent after Johnny clearly hadn't found what he'd been looking for, or Blake and his boys wouldn't be trying to kidnap Logan as leverage to get their hands on what Johnny had stolen.

So where, exactly, had Johnny hidden his bloody secrets?

"How soon after Johnny's death did he stop locking that drawer?" Briar asked.

"I don't remember." Leanne gave Briar a troubled look. "Do you think Johnny took something from Mr. Cortland's office?"

"Do you?"

The other woman looked down at her hands, her brow crinkled with thought. She had neat, well-manicured hands, Briar thought, darting a quick look at her own work-worn hands with their short, uneven nails and the occasional ragged cuticle. Johnny must have looked at this woman and seen everything Briar wasn't.

Maybe she'd been wrong. Maybe their marriage had failed not because Johnny wouldn't grow up but because they'd grown in different directions.

"I wondered if he took something," Leanne said quietly after another moment of silence. "The last time I saw Johnny, he told me I should look for another job. When I asked him why, he said he had a feeling something bad would be going down at the sawmill. He wouldn't tell me what. Wouldn't even tell me why he thought so." She shook her head slowly, tears glistening on the rims of her lower eyelids. "The day of the explosion, I'd taken a day off work to go for a job interview. This job, as a matter of fact."

No wonder Dalton had focused on Leanne Dawson as a person of interest. The coincidence of her being off work that day, and looking for a new job, at that, would have raised his suspicions.

"You were very lucky," Briar said.

"I know. I still can't believe it sometimes. Any of it. Mr. Cortland always seemed so nice and…ordinary."

"That's how it works sometimes." Briar couldn't stop herself from asking one final question. "Do you think Johnny loved you?"

Leanne's sharp blue eyes snapped up to meet Briar's. "That's a strange question from a police officer."

"I know. Forget I asked it."

The other woman's eyes narrowed. "What did you say your name was?"

"Briar Culpepper."

"Oh, my God." Leanne's eyes widened with horror. "You're his wife. Aren't you?"

Briar tried not to react, but her skin was already crawling with regret. She shouldn't have come here and pretended she was just another police officer.

"What, did you want to see what I looked like? See how I compare?" Leanne was crying now, soft silent tears spilling down her cheeks. "Do you want an apology? Because I'll give you one. God knows, I owe it to you."

"I don't want an apology. I believe you when you say you didn't know he was married. I sometimes think Johnny didn't really understand that fact himself." Briar made herself meet the other woman's red-rimmed eyes. "I'm sorry to have come here like this. I'm sorry I wasn't up-front about who I am. But you have to understand—there are people who believe Johnny took something potentially incriminating from Wayne Cortland. Very dangerous people who are willing to go after my son to get that information back."

Leanne's tears kept falling, but her expression shifted from despair to horror. "Someone's gone after your son?"

"Twice, at least. And I don't know what Johnny took, if he took anything at all. Or where he would have hidden it if he did."

"And you think *I* know?"

"I don't know. I was hoping, I guess."

Leanne pulled a box of tissues from her desk drawer and blotted her cheeks. "You're putting a lot more importance on my relationship with Johnny than either he or I did." She took a deep breath and lifted her chin, meeting Briar's gaze. "I knew it was a fling. I knew it was reckless, but he made me feel good, you know? Desirable and maybe a little dangerous myself." Her mouth curved in a self-conscious smile. "I know, me? Dangerous? But that's how he made me feel. Like I could take on the world single-handed. It was an addictive feeling."

Briar's stomach squirmed with sympathy. That had been

Johnny's most potent attraction for her, too, at least when she'd been younger. He'd had the verve and style of a bad boy without really being very dangerous at all. The most harm he'd ever done to anyone was all emotional, and even then, Briar thought, he'd never meant for it to happen.

He hadn't meant to break her heart. Or Leanne Dawson's. And if she was honest, her heart wasn't nearly as affected as her pride.

"You never had any suspicions about Wayne Cortland?" she asked Leanne. "That his business might be a front for something illegal?"

"Of course not. I wouldn't have worked for him if I had."

She sounded honest, Briar thought. There was nothing in her tone to even hint at deception. Wayne Cortland had played the part of the honest businessman very, very well. It was why he'd gotten away with his crimes so long in the first place.

"Thank you for your time, Ms. Dawson. I appreciate it. And again, I'm sorry for not telling you who I was up front."

Leanne shook her head. "I'm sorry I couldn't be more help."

Briar had gotten halfway to the doorway when she heard footsteps coming up behind her in a rush. She turned on her heel so quickly that Leanne nearly rammed into her headfirst.

The other woman took a quick step back, wobbling for balance. "Sorry," she said. "I just thought of something. I don't know if it means anything to you—it didn't to me. But that day Johnny told me to look for another job, I'd made a joke about stocking my pantry while I could in case the winter turned out to be a lean one. And he said he never had to worry about stocking his pantry. He had so much stored away folks were starting to think he was a doomsday prepper."

Briar released a soft huff of laughter. "If he'd had to stock things away for himself, he'd have starved."

"I never thought him one for gardening," Leanne admitted. "I was just sitting here thinking about that conversation and it struck me you must have been the one who stocked that pantry he was talking about."

Briar nodded. "Is that the strange thing you remembered?"

"No, it's what he said after that. He said, 'It's amazing how many different things you can store in a Mason jar.' And then he winked at me and headed off on his truck route."

Briar felt a little tremor run up her spine.

"Do you think that means anything?" Leanne asked.

Briar kept her expression neutral. "I doubt it. He's right—there are all kinds of things you can put away in a Mason jar. He was probably just trying to sound naughty and secretive."

Leanne's curious expression shifted to a mixture of fondness and regret. "That was Johnny, all right." Her face reddened. "I'm sorry. I guess you'd know that a lot better than I did."

"Do me a favor, Leanne, okay? Stop beating yourself up about Johnny. The only thing you did wrong was fall for his lines. You weren't the first girl to do that, you know."

"Thank you. And I hope you find what you're looking for and that everything goes well for you and your son."

Briar smiled again and turned back toward the door, trying not to let her suddenly energized legs break into a run as she headed out into the waning daylight.

It was after four when she pulled her Jeep out of the Pinter Construction parking lot. The drive back to Bitterwood would take more than three hours, an interminable amount of time when she was now almost certain where she'd find whatever it was that Johnny had stolen from Wayne Cortland.

It couldn't have been files, at least not the paper-and-ink sort of files, because there wasn't a Mason jar in her stash at home big enough to contain that sort of contraband. But maybe Johnny had taken photos of the files and stored them on a memory chip. Or even a flash drive. Either of those things would be small enough to store inside a jar of peach preserves or pickled okra. Store it inside a pill bottle or a small film canister, wrap it in a zippered plastic bag and shove it into a jar of canned vegetables or fruit, and almost nobody would think to look for it there. The plastic would protect it from the canned food, and the food would protect it from easy detection.

The only danger would have been if Briar had pulled that particular jar from the shelf and opened it. And since she had a particular system of storing things, oldest in front, newest in back, Johnny could easily have chosen the least likely jar to be opened right away.

All she had to do was go through the jars that would have been at the back of her stash at the time of Johnny's death and see which one held his secret.

Her phone trilled as she pulled out into traffic on the four-lane that led to the interstate highway, but when she tried to answer, she got a "low battery" message. "Damn it." She couldn't even see who had called.

There was a charger in the glove compartment. At the next traffic light, she pulled out the charger, hooked it to the cigarette lighter and plugged in her phone. The display came on and she saw that the missed call had been from Dana Massey. She called her back.

Dana answered on the first ring. "Briar? Where are you?"

"In Wytheville, Virginia," she answered. "Long story. What's up?"

"I've been trying to call Dalton for the last hour, and nobody's answering. Is he with you?"

Alarm rattled her nerves. "No. He should be at home. He's watching Logan for me."

Dana's silence raised her panic level by several notches.

"Maybe he's not answering any calls but mine," Briar ventured.

"That could be it." Dana sounded relieved by the thought. "Why don't you call him and see what's up? And then tell him to give me a call. I may have some information for him about a group of anarchists he's been trying to tie to Blake Culpepper. But I've been given the okay to talk only to Dalton."

"I'll tell him." She hung up and tried Dalton's cell phone. After five rings the phone went to voice mail. She left a message, then tried his home number.

She got a busy signal.

Maybe he didn't have call waiting, she told herself as she set the phone on the seat to continue charging.

But twenty minutes later when she tried the house phone again, she got another busy signal.

After a third try, she called Dana back. "There's something wrong," she told Dalton's sister. "And I'm three hours away."

"I'm still in Knoxville, but I'll call Nix and have him check on Dalton and Logan. I'll get there as soon as I can." Dana hung up the phone without saying goodbye.

Briar set the phone on the passenger seat, her heart starting to race as she pushed the Jeep's speed as high as she dared.

Chapter Thirteen

Someone was hammering outside the house. The sound droned on and on, setting off painful throbs in the middle of Dalton's forehead. He struggled to open his eyes, trying to stand up and cross to the door to yell at the offender to stop with all the noise.

But his eyelids seemed as heavy as boulders, and the hint of daylight that crept between the narrow openings felt like stiletto knives being rammed into his eyeballs. Nausea rolled through his gut in greasy waves, forcing him to be very still. For a second the hammering went silent, so silent that he feared for a moment that he'd been struck instantly deaf.

Then it started again, louder and more urgent than before.

Not hammering, he realized. Knocking.

Someone was knocking on his door.

He tried to sit up, but the world spun wildly around him, and he couldn't stop the nausea that time. The best he could do was direct his sickness away from the sofa onto the floor below.

"Dalton, it's Doyle. Are you in there?"

He couldn't move, except the helpless heaving that finished emptying his stomach onto the floor. What the hell was wrong with him?

He was home. He could tell that much from the smell of the place, the feel of the nubby sofa fabric against his cheek, the bits and pieces of decor he could see through the narrow slits of his eyelids. He tried to answer Doyle, but his aching throat felt dust dry.

A minute later he heard the door open. The sound of footsteps rushed toward him, stuttering to a stop a few feet away.

"Dalton!" Doyle said sharply.

Dalton managed a groan. He felt hands on his face. Warm, rough hands.

"Can you breathe?"

I am breathing, he thought, but he realized he wasn't. He concentrated on taking a breath, then another.

His head felt heavy and thick, but the air moving in and out of his lungs had a clarifying effect. Some of the dizzying pain in his head subsided, and the next time he tried to open his eyes, he was able to do it with minimal effort. "I don't feel good."

"I can see that." Doyle touched his fingertips to Dalton's throat. Checking his pulse, Dalton realized.

"What happened to me?" he asked.

"You tell me. What do you remember?"

Nothing, Dalton realized with a rush of panic. He remembered going to bed the night before and then...

Nothing.

"Where's Logan?" Doyle asked.

Dalton stared at his brother. "I don't know. Oh, God." He tried to get up from the sofa but the movement made his head spin again. He swallowed the nausea and tried to push up again.

"Sit still. I'll check." Doyle pulled his phone out of his pocket and headed out of the room. Going to search the downstairs, Dalton realized after a moment of confusion. Being thorough.

He stared down at the vomit on the floor. Not a lot, he saw. Mostly liquid. Had he eaten breakfast? He looked at his watch. Almost five. Morning or afternoon?

Afternoon, he decided, noting the western light. He'd lost nearly a whole day.

"Where's Briar?" he asked as Doyle came back through the living room, heading for the stairs.

"She's on her way back from Wytheville." Doyle paused on the stairs. "You don't remember her leaving?"

"I don't remember today," he answered, trying to stand up again. "I don't remember anything since going to bed last night. At least, I think it was last night."

The look Doyle shot his way scared the hell out of him. But his brother started back up the stairs quickly, not commenting.

He needed to clean up the mess on the floor, Dalton thought. He didn't want Logan or Briar to see the mess.

Staggering to the kitchen to grab a roll of paper towels, he returned to the sofa and tried to lever himself down far enough to mop up the mess. But even bending over made his head spin.

He did what he could, cleaning between bouts of dizziness. Finally, though the floor would need a good mopping, at least he was no longer staring down at his own stomach contents.

Doyle came down the stairs slowly, his expression grim. His gaze met Dalton's briefly, then skittered away. He pulled out his phone and made another call. "I need everyone available to meet me at Hale's place. 224 Maplewood Lane in Edgewood. We need to put out an Amber Alert. Logan Blackwood is missing."

Dalton felt sick all over again.

HE'S JUST HIDING. *He's hiding, and when he hears my voice, he'll come out and everything will be okay.*

Except Briar knew it wasn't true. Too much time had passed.

The call from Dana Massey had come somewhere around Bristol, Tennessee, while Briar was still more than two hours out of Bitterwood. The rest of the drive home had been a blur, driven at speeds that risked pursuit by the Tennessee Highway Patrol. She'd traded calls with Dana, Nix and even the chief himself during the drive, all apprising her of the latest information.

But no call from Dalton. Dalton, whom she'd trusted to protect her child while she was away.

Nobody had said much about Dalton.

The guard at the gatehouse had looked grim as he let her through into the subdivision. Flashing blue-and-red lights cut through the evening gloom, each swirling pulse a grim beacon, drawing her into her worst nightmare.

Nix stood sentry on the porch. He met her halfway up the walk, his hands closing over her arms. "We're going to get him back."

"I know that," she said shortly. "Where's Dalton?"

"Inside." The corners of Nix's mouth tightened.

"What aren't y'all telling me?" she asked as she walked with him up the porch steps.

He caught her hand in his, turning her to face him when they reached the door. "You know I'd be happy to blame him for everything, but we're pretty sure he was drugged somehow."

She looked up at him through narrowed eyes. "Drugged?"

"Paramedics came to look him over. He's coming down off whatever it was, but he has all the symptoms of some sort of drug ingestion. They got a blood sample to test.

They wanted to take him to the hospital, but he wouldn't budge until you got here."

The ache in the center of Briar's gut intensified. "What did he say happened?"

"That's just it. He doesn't remember." Nix's grip on her arm eased into a gentle caress. "Hopefully the test will tell us more, but given the memory loss and his other symptoms, I'm guessing it was something like GHB or Rohypnol."

Both date-rape drugs, Briar thought. GHB—gamma hydroxybutyrate—might be more likely, especially if her cousin Blake was behind what had happened. GHB could be cooked easily enough, and the Blue Ridge Infantry was all tangled up with mountain meth mechanics these days. "How did someone get close enough to drug him?"

"That's what we're trying to figure out. The TBI has been here an hour, going over the place with tweezers. If there's a clue to be found, they'll find it," Nix assured her.

"What about the gatekeeper?" she asked. "Nobody gets in or out of this subdivision without passing through the gate."

"We're trying to find the daytime guard. He went off duty around five—he was gone before we figured out we needed to talk to him, and nobody seems to know where he went. His replacement said he mentioned something about doing some nighttime crappie fishing. We're trying to track down where that might be, but he's not answering his cell phone."

"Do you think he could be in danger?"

"I don't know. Probably not."

"I need to talk to Dalton."

Nix squeezed her hand. "You're not going to be able to make him feel any worse than he already does."

She didn't want to make him feel worse, she realized. As

much as she was aching inside, aching like a bad tooth, she couldn't find it in her to vent that pain, or the rising anger filling her gut, on Dalton. She'd nearly lost her son right out of her own arms once, hadn't she? If Dalton hadn't intervened that night at the cabin, she didn't think she could have stopped those men from taking her son.

And one look at Dalton, sitting on his sofa with his head in his hands, was enough to drive away even the thought of blame.

He looked up at the sound of her footsteps, his face a road map of guilt and grief. "I'm so sorry."

She sat beside him, wrapping her arms around him. "Are you okay?"

He shrugged away from her grasp. "Don't, Briar."

She dropped her hands to her lap. "You can't remember anything?"

"I remember…last night."

She thought about the night before, how she'd sat on this very couch, anchoring Dalton's hips between her thighs as they'd strained toward some ephemeral promise of release. Just two people seeking pleasure in each other—as natural as breathing.

Profanely distant from this horrible moment some twenty-four hours later, she thought. "You don't remember waking me this morning to tell me you had to go see your father in the hospital?"

His gaze snapped up to meet hers. "My father's in the hospital?"

She could see the shock and fear in his eyes, as immediate and real as it had been early this morning when he'd awakened her to tell her he was on his way to the hospital.

"He's okay," she said quickly. "Just a panic attack. They transferred him back to the jail around lunchtime."

He looked as if she'd just punched him. "I don't remember."

"Nix says you were probably drugged."

He shook his head, stopping quickly. His face turned a sickly shade of gray, and for a moment Briar thought he was going to be sick. Color seeped back into his face after a moment. "I wouldn't have let anyone in. How could I be drugged?"

"Maybe they forced their way in?" she suggested, but even as the words left her mouth, she could see that while the room showed signs of having undergone a search by the crime scene unit, it showed no signs of a struggle.

"I don't think so," Dalton murmured. "They said I must have ingested whatever it was. That's how those kinds of drugs are usually administered."

"I guess the question now is, who would you have trusted to let into your house while Logan was here?"

He leaned back, resting his head on the sofa cushion behind him. "I've been wondering the same thing. It couldn't have been just anyone. I wouldn't have let just anyone in."

"Then think about it. Who would you trust enough?"

"My mother," he said immediately. "But there's no way she's involved."

"Okay. Who else?"

He rubbed his jaw, looking sick again. "Tom Bevill," he said. His boss at the county prosecutor's office. "Laney. Any Bitterwood cop, I guess."

That might be a problem, she thought, since they weren't yet certain that everyone on the force could be trusted. "Anyone else?"

He looked at her again. "Most of the attorneys at the office, if they were bringing files from work for some reason. My secretary. Maybe some of the clerks."

"What about Lydia?" she asked, thinking of the blonde she'd met in his office.

"No, not Lydia." He swallowed hard, his Adam's apple bobbing. "They still can't find George Applewood? The security guard at the gate?"

"He went fishing, they think. He's not answering his phone." At least, she hoped that was the situation. If he'd seen who'd come through that gate, he might be a witness.

And the people they were dealing with right now didn't seem the sort who'd care to leave witnesses.

"What are we going to do, Briar? What have I done?"

She rose from the sofa and sat on the coffee table in front of him, catching his face between her hands. A day's growth of beard scraped her palms as she forced him to look at her.

"I'm going to find Logan. That's what I'm going to do. And when I do, I'm gonna make whoever took him regret the sorry day they came mewlin' and squirmin' into this world."

Dalton's eyes were red-veined, his pupils a little dilated, but he found it within himself to meet and hold her gaze. "Don't leave me out of this, Briar. Please don't cut me off."

She dropped her hands to his shoulder. "You're in no condition to go lookin' for kidnappers in the mountains. You can't even see straight."

"So give me something. There's got to be a way to counteract this thing, right? Call the paramedics back here—they'll know what to do."

"I'm sure they already gave you something if there was something that could be done."

His brow furrowed, as if he were trying to remember.

"They said it's possible he vomited up a fair bit of the dose." Dana Massey had walked up behind her. She came around the coffee table and sat beside Dalton. "They tried to get him to go to the hospital for further treatment, but he refused to go."

"I had to talk to you first," Dalton told Briar. "I needed to tell you how sorry I am."

She put her hand on his knee. "You need time to let the rest of the drug get out of your system."

"We don't have time."

"Dalton—" Briar looked at Dana for support.

But Dana returned her look with hard determination. "He needs to be part of this. He's a lot more lucid than he was when I got here."

"Has anyone contacted you?" Dalton asked, making a visible effort to pull himself together.

"No," she answered, wondering why she hadn't even thought about getting a call from the kidnappers. That was the point of taking Logan from her, wasn't it? To get her to turn over whatever Johnny had taken.

At least now she had a pretty good idea where to look for his secrets.

She hadn't told the others, she realized. Why hadn't she?

Because they might try to stop you.

She was a police officer. She knew as well as anyone how the police would want to handle it. Stall for time to make a copy of whatever Johnny had stolen, assuming it was Wayne Cortland's secret books. Leave Logan in the grasp of men who were more than willing to risk his life for their own purposes. All in pursuit of a "greater good." As if there was a greater good than getting her son back.

Would Dalton feel the same way?

She studied his face, took in the shadows of fear in his eyes and the lines of desperation carving deep valleys in his handsome features. She wanted desperately to believe she could trust him.

But right now she didn't trust anyone. Not even Nix.

She barely even trusted herself.

To hell with letting the police call the shots this time. Her son was with people who had no trouble killing innocents. She'd seen what they'd done to Tommy Barnett. And a little boy like Logan would be so easy to harm, even if it wasn't their intention....

"I need to be alone." Her mind had already moved several steps ahead toward what needed to be done next. Now, before anyone tried to contact her. Before the clock truly started ticking.

Dalton's gaze narrowed. Just a tiny twitch, but she had come to know him well enough in the last couple of days to know what it meant.

He wondered what she was up to.

Digging deep, she found the core of steel it took to lie to his face. "I just need to be away from you for a little while."

He flinched almost as surely as if she'd slapped him with her hand instead of her words.

"Briar—" Dana looked shocked.

"My son is missing." Briar pushed to her feet, letting her voice rise with pent-up anguish. "I think that earns me the right to feel a little anger!"

She saw Doyle and Nix both turn their heads to look at her.

Now, she thought. *I have to move now.*

She strode toward the door, her jaw set with determination. If they tried to stop her, she'd make them get out of her way.

But Nix and Doyle stepped back, giving her unhindered access to the door. When Dana came up quickly behind her, Nix shook his head.

Dalton's voice rose from his place on the sofa. "Let her go. Give her what she needs."

The grief in his voice burned like fire in her ears, but she didn't let it stop her from walking out the door.

Outside, night had fallen completely, deepened by rain clouds scudding eastward toward the mountains. There would be no moon out tonight, she thought with satisfaction.

That was good. The darkness would make her approach to the cabin that much harder to detect.

They would be watching for her. She was certain of it. They must know by now she knew her son was missing. That she'd know who had taken him and why.

Maybe that's why they were waiting to contact her. Why risk it when all they had to do was wait at her cabin for her to make her move? They could swoop in, overpower her, and take what they wanted. No mess. No real risk.

But there was something she knew about the cabin that they didn't. Something nobody outside her family had known. Not even Johnny.

She knew a way to get into the cabin without being seen.

Chapter Fourteen

All the air seemed to rush from the room when Briar walked out. Dalton pushed up from the sofa and waited for another dizzy spell to hit, but it didn't materialize. He moved away from the door into the kitchen and stood there for a moment, looking around. Trying to remember.

There was a bowl on the table. The remains of chicken noodle soup. *Logan,* he thought, pain ripping through him like shrapnel. Had the boy been right here with him when someone had come to see him?

Why had he let anyone in? What had he been thinking?

He needed to get out of here. He needed to go out there and start looking for Logan. He didn't know where to start, but he couldn't just sit here and pretend that sweet child wasn't out there somewhere in desperate danger.

And if he couldn't do it, he realized, his gut knotting with a fresh new wave of anxiety, neither could Briar.

She hadn't left to get away from him. At least, that hadn't been her only reason.

"Briar's going to go off alone if we let her," he warned Dana as she walked up beside him and put her hand on his shoulder.

Dana looked at him in alarm. "You think she's going after Culpepper?"

"I don't know. I just know it's not like Briar to need

time alone. She'd stay here and say what she thought. She left because she wants to get away from here without anybody questioning her."

Dana looked across the room to where Doyle and Nix were talking quietly near the door. "They're not going to just let you walk out of here."

"There's a back door," he murmured.

"You can barely stand."

"I'm good. I'm feeling clearheaded now."

"You can't drive."

"You can."

She stared at him. "You want me to sneak you out of here? Lie to my brother and the man I love so you can wander off, drug-addled, after Briar?"

"If she goes alone, she could be in serious trouble."

"We tell Nix and Doyle or it doesn't happen," she said flatly.

Dalton grimaced. Neither man would be willing to let him go after Briar. Not without a long, time-eating argument.

"Okay, fine. We'll tell them. Convince them how important it is for us to go after her. Just let me go to the bathroom first and I'll come back. We'll tell them together."

He headed for the bathroom down a short hallway off the living room. But he bypassed that door and went straight out to the garage instead.

Going through the garage door would be faster, but the sound of the big door opening would bring Dana and the others running before he could get away. Instead, he grabbed the spare car key from the tool drawer where he kept it and went through the side door, hurrying around the garage.

To his surprise, Briar's Jeep was still parked in the driveway next to his car. She sat in the driver's seat, her head low, her white-knuckled hands gripping the steering wheel as if it were a lifeline.

He knocked on the passenger window, making her jump. Her gray eyes widened at the sight of him.

"I know you're going to go find Logan. Let me go with you," he said through the glass.

She continued looking at him, unblinking, for so long he almost forgot to breathe again. Then she reached over and unlocked the door.

He pulled himself into the passenger seat and turned to look at her. "I thought you'd already be gone."

"I thought I would be, too," she admitted.

"There are so many things I want to say to you. How sorry I am that I failed you and Logan. But in a minute Dana's going to realize I've been in the bathroom too long. A few minutes after that, they'll come looking for us. So if we're going, we need to go now."

She gazed solemnly at him for a few seconds longer, then put the Jeep in Neutral. The vehicle began to roll quietly backward down the gently sloping driveway. Wrestling with the wheel, she turned the Jeep onto the street and started the engine.

Dalton glanced back at the house. So far the front door remained closed. But it wouldn't stay that way for long. "They'll be coming after us."

"I know. I just need to get there first."

"To the cabin?" he asked.

"Yes. Although I should warn you—they'll have it staked out."

"The police? Or the kidnappers?"

"The kidnappers." She glanced at the rearview mirror and pulled suddenly down a side road.

"But we're going there? Just the two of us?" He grabbed the seat belt and wrapped it around him, even as she took another curve at a scary rate of speed, threatening to send him sliding into the floorboard. His stomach roiled at the thought of walking into an ambush. He was still feeling a little woozy, as much as he didn't want to admit it. Hardly in any condition to fight his way out of a mess.

"I think I know where Johnny hid what he stole from Cortland."

Dalton stopped in the middle of buckling the belt. "You know what he took? Was it Cortland's cooked books?"

"I didn't say I knew what he took. Only that I think I know where he hid it." She told him about her conversation with Leanne Dawson.

"He hid something in a jar of preserves?"

"Or pickles or stewed tomatoes. Something like that."

"Can't be physical files," Dalton said, trying to hide his sense of deflation.

"Could be photographs of files stored on a flash drive or a memory card," Briar said, making him feel like an idiot.

Of course, she was right. In fact, it made much more sense that Johnny Blackwood might make some sort of copy than try to steal the files themselves. If he'd taken the books, they'd have been missed. "Wouldn't putting them into something like preserves risk ruining the storage disk? I mean, I know he'd have stored them in something airtight, but—"

"I don't think he considered it to be a place of long-term storage," she said, whipping around another corner. He finished buckling his seat belt quickly, bracing his feet on the floorboard to keep from sliding into her. "I'm obsessive about using my canned goods by a certain date. So I know they haven't had a chance to go bad on us. He'd have put the disk in one of the newer jars, since I'd use them last. But he knew how I did things. He knew that if something happened, I'd open the jar within a year. Either to eat what was stored inside or to dispose of it."

"But what if you threw away the jar unopened?"

She shot him a look. "You don't throw away a jar. You sterilize it and use it again."

"Ah." He was beginning to understand the brilliance of using Briar's food stores as a hiding place. The average person wouldn't think to look inside a jar of pickles for a computer storage disk. But Briar would open the jar sooner or later because she wasn't the sort to waste anything. Resourceful woman, his Briar.

My Briar, he reiterated silently, a strange thrill running through his body like a jolt of electricity.

Mine.

"He probably thought he could keep rehiding the thing as long as he needed to," she said as they pulled onto Cherokee Road. "Of course, he didn't know I was planning to divorce him."

"So if the kidnappers have the cabin staked out, how are we going to get inside it to look for the file?"

Her lips curved upward at the corners. Not quite a smile, but it gave him hope to see something besides harsh lines of fear and anger on Briar's face. "You'll see."

DURING PROHIBITION in the 1920s and 1930s, liquor sales hadn't ended in the mountains any more than they had anywhere else in the country. They'd simply gone underground. Instead of the speakeasies and organized-crime control of liquor production and sales found in the bigger cities, bootleggers and moonshine stills had ruled the day in the mountains, even after the Twenty-First Amendment had ended Prohibition in the United States. After all, many of Tennessee's counties were still dry counties.

And people still liked to get hammered now and then.

For Briar's maternal great-grandfather, distilling moonshine had paid his bills and fed his kids long after 1933, when the rest of the country went back to drinking as usual. But the revenuers could be ruthless in their quest to shut down any distillery not putting money into the government coffers, so old Bartholomew Meade had come up with his own way of protecting his home-brew business from government scrutiny.

He'd learned, literally by accident, that his cabin was built very close to an underground cavern. His eldest son, Lamar, had fallen through an opening in the cave while hunting for rabbits in the woods about fifty yards from home. Unable to climb back up the hole, he'd followed the narrow cave to its exit deep in the mountains. When Bart Meade had realized he had a natural tunnel not fifty yards from his house, he saw the advantage it would give him over other moonshiners, who had to risk carrying their contraband over ground.

It had taken nearly two years of backbreaking labor for Bart and his three sons and two daughters to dig a tunnel between the root cellar beneath his cabin and the natural cave fifty yards away, but they'd done it, and the Meade family had thrived on their law-defying industry for several decades to come, until the 1960s, when Bitterwood had voted to allow the sale of liquor in hopes of drawing in tourists headed for the national park.

The still had been long gone by the time Briar's mother had deeded the cabin to her as a sort of dowry. But the tunnel was still there, mostly unused but still in good shape. And still a secret known only to descendants of Bartholomew Meade. Not even Johnny had known about the tunnel. Briar had never even thought to tell him about it.

Strange that she felt no qualms in telling Dalton about it now.

"It's called Smuggler's Cave by the Cherokee Cove locals," she told him as they made their way up the mountain toward the cave entrance. "My great-granddaddy made sure all the locals heard lurid tales about how the place was haunted. Fear of haints kept all but the most intrepid away. And the ones who didn't fall for the legend of Smuggler's Cave found themselves picking buckshot out of their backsides if they got too close to the place." She flashed him a wry grin.

"So your great-granddaddy was a moonshiner?" he asked as he followed her up the side of the mountain toward the cave entrance. A storm was brewing, lightning snapping and crackling on the western horizon. Clouds had begun to obscure the moon, making the last quarter mile of their trek up the mountain more difficult than Briar had hoped.

At least the hours that it had taken her to drive back from Virginia had helped dilute the effects of whatever drug Dalton had ingested. He was keeping up with her surprisingly well as they climbed the steep hillside.

"Technically," she reminded him, "yours was, too. On Tallie Cumberland's side. The Meades and the Cumberlands were bootlegging rivals back in the day."

"But wouldn't Blake know about this secret passageway already, since he's your cousin?"

"He's a cousin on my daddy's side. The Meades were my mama's people. Culpeppers and Meades were nearly as bitter rivals as the Meades and Cumberlands."

"Ah, a Romeo and Juliet story."

"Well, except my parents weren't fool enough to kill themselves over it," she said flatly. "Lucky for me."

It was strange to hear her own voice so calm and uninflected, considering the violent storm of terror ripping around inside her gut. The thought of Logan being held even for a moment in the rough and ruthless custody of her cousin Blake and his band of cutthroats had damned near paralyzed her earlier as she sat in her Jeep trying to figure out what to do next. If Dalton hadn't knocked on her window...

As if he sensed the turn of her thoughts, Dalton touched her arm as they neared the mouth of the cavern. "Briar, we're going to find Logan. I won't stop until we do."

She looked up at him. He was barely visible in the gloom, but the fierce determination in his eyes was impossible to miss, even in the dark. "I don't know what's going to happen once we get to the root cellar. They may have people already positioned inside the cabin. We could walk straight into an ambush."

"They're not going to hurt you as long as they think you can give them those files."

"I don't know why it hasn't occurred to them that I could have already made a dozen copies."

"I've been thinking about that," Dalton told her as he followed her through the dark mouth of the cavern. What little ambient light had illuminated their path outside disappeared, the darkness swallowing them completely.

Briar went still, just listening for a moment. She felt Dalton at her back, the heat of his body close and comforting. Quelling the urge to lean back into his solid warmth, she turned on the small flashlight she'd brought with her from the Jeep.

Damp stone walls continued for several yards ahead before twisting out of sight. She realized with a sudden flutter of alarm that she hadn't been in this tunnel for over a year. There could have been a cave-in she didn't know about. But the tunnel had remained solid and unshakable for decades. She had no reason to think it would fail on her now, did she? God knew, her day had already seen sufficient trouble without borrowing any more.

"You've been thinking about what?" she asked a moment later, when she was satisfied no pressing danger lurked ahead of them in the cavern tunnel.

"About why they don't care if we make a copy."

She looked back at him, shining the flashlight toward his face so she could read his expression. He squinted but didn't look away. "Why don't they care?" she asked.

"Because they don't have the information themselves. Cortland died in the blast. Merritt Cortland is almost certainly dead himself, whether we can find his body or not. I'm betting those two may have been the only people in the whole organization who knew all the connections. Blake Culpepper doesn't give a damn whether or not the police scoop up the people Cortland had working for him. He'd probably thank us for it."

"But he needs to know who they are. Who might turn state's evidence," Briar realized, following his thoughts. "Who to eliminate as a rival."

"It's a crash course in mountain crime," Dalton said. "If we want to understand how Cortland ran his crew, we need to get our hands on his files. Blake and I both want the same thing. For very different reasons."

Briar swung the flashlight toward the tunnel. "Then let's see what we can do to make that happen."

"I DON'T THINK we should drive right up to Briar's place," Walker Nix warned his boss as they neared the turnoff on the mountain road. Beside him, Dana's hands were clenched tight in her lap, her jaw as rigid as stone. Dalton had ditched her, and she was still smarting a little from the betrayal, even though she and her brother had both admitted, in response to Nix's confession, that like Nix, they'd probably have done the same thing if they'd been in Dalton's position.

"You think there are bears in the woods?" Doyle asked drily, slowing the truck's speed in response to Nix's warning. Nix knew he wasn't talking about real bears.

"It's what I'd do if I were Blake Culpepper. I've got her kid. Now she's going to make her move and find what she's going to have to give me if she wants Logan back. Everything in the world points to the answer being in Briar's cabin, but so far nobody's been able to find it."

"Do you think Briar's known what it is and where to find it all along?" Dana asked quietly.

"Not all along, no. But given the fact that she bailed on us, I think maybe she figured it out sometime today. I think she knows where to look, and she's not going to let us stop her from handing it over if she finds it."

"She's just going to hand over evidence to a criminal?"

Nix looked over Dana's head at her brother. "If I had to guess, she'd like to let things play out without having to give Blake anything he's asking for, but if it comes to a choice between the law and her son——"

"Of course she'll choose her son," Dana said flatly. "I'm pretty sure any one of us would do the same. *Will* do the same."

Nix couldn't argue with that statement. Apparently, neither could the chief. He went on past the turnoff, slanting a look toward Nix. "What now?"

"We park down the road and go on foot. Carefully."

THE CAVE CAME to an abrupt end, the twisting footpath running out at a solid stone wall. At least, Dalton thought it was solid until Briar pressed her fingers into a small rocky indentation on the left side of the wall and a dark seam appeared in the stone face.

It was a door, he saw, set into the rock by someone highly skilled and, apparently, deeply secretive. It swung open into the cave, revealing little more than darkness beyond.

Briar flicked on her flashlight, illuminating the dark space in front of them. Metal shelves tightly packed with jars of preserved food stood about two feet in front of the door, reflecting the flashlight beam back to them. "My stores," she whispered shortly, slipping into the tight space between the doorway and the shelves.

Dalton followed her down the narrow corridor between the shelves and the wall until they emerged in the center of a small densely packed cellar lined with the metal shelves of Mason jars on one side and large root bins on the other. Briar flipped a light switch and a bare bulb gave off a muted glow overhead, revealing more of the cellar.

To Dalton's left, a set of concrete block steps led up to a flat door that opened upward rather than out. "Where does that door go?"

"The side yard." Briar pointed out another, normal door at the top of a set of wooden stairs. "That door leads up to the house."

Dalton nodded toward the rows of Mason jars. "Is this where you think Johnny hid whatever he took from Cortland?"

She nodded. "I just have to figure out which jar."

"His last day driving the Travisville route for Davenport Trucking was August 15 of last year."

She nodded. "He died on the eighteenth. So it would have had to be in something I put away before the eighteenth but probably no further back than, say, June of last year." She looked at the jars. "Peach preserves, apples, pickles, peppers, squash, tomatoes—all summer crops.

Too late for strawberries, too early for the winter squashes and pears."

He looked at the rows of jars, feeling overwhelmed. "We have to open all of them?"

"Well, the most likely options would be the preserves. Most of the others are stored in brine or clear juice, but the preserves would be opaque. Better for hiding something." She crossed to a section of the shelves lined with jars of bright golden peach preserves. Dalton followed her, looking over her shoulder as she pointed to the label. "Here's the canning date. Look for anything between July and August 18 of last year."

He started culling jars with those dates. "Should we open them all?"

She looked up at him, frowning. "I realize this is going to sound strange from a woman who's terrified for the safety of her son, but these are his favorites, and I'd rather not ruin them if we can figure out which one is the right one." She turned the jar she held on its side and gave it a little shake. She set it to one side and started to do the same thing to the next jar in her stack. Dalton followed suit, trying to figure out if there was something besides peaches in each of the jars.

"Oh," Briar said a few minutes later, drawing Dalton's gaze. She was holding a jar up toward the overhead bulb. Pressing against the side of the jar, Dalton saw with a flutter of excitement, was the corner of a plastic bag.

Briar twisted off the band that held the vacuum-sealed lid on the jar. Pulling a small knife from her jeans pocket, she pried up the lid until it released with a soft pop. "Grab that bucket in the corner," she told Dalton. He brought it to her and she slowly poured out the sticky fruit contents of the jar until a small zip-sealed sandwich bag fell into the bucket.

She plucked it out with her thumb and forefinger, using the knife blade to scrape off as much of the peach preserves as she could.

Inside, wrapped in more clear plastic, was a small black flash drive.

Chapter Fifteen

Dalton didn't know what he'd expected Briar to do when she found Johnny's hidden secret, but dissolving into tears wasn't it. Big gulping sobs seemed to burst from her throat, beyond her ability to control, as she clutched the sticky bag to her chest and shook with tears. "I was so afraid," she said. "So afraid it wouldn't be here. I didn't know what I was going to do if it wasn't here."

He crossed to her side and put his arms around her, half expecting her to push him away. But she let him hold her, pressing her forehead against his shoulder and wetting his shirt with her tears. "I'm sorry," she said, her voice raw with emotion. "I'm sorry."

She'd been holding herself together by sheer will, he realized, despite her earlier show of composure. Pressing a kiss to her hair, he murmured soft words of comfort, not inclined to hurry her through this reaction to the stress and fear she'd been laboring under since Doyle had called her to break the news about Logan's disappearance.

But she finally gave herself a shake and pushed her damp curls away from her tearstained face, flashing him a wobbly smile. "That must have been a sight."

"I've felt like doing the same thing for the last three hours," he admitted. "I'm so sorry about losing Logan."

"Someone drugged you."

"Someone I let into my house," he said bluntly. "Why would I do such a thing with Logan in danger?" The question haunted him, not least because he could remember nothing. Not a hint of anything that had happened to him between bedtime the night before and waking on the sofa to Doyle's knock on the door.

"We'll figure it out later," she said firmly, closing her hands over his arms and giving him a little shake. "For now, we need to figure out what to do with this flash drive."

"I wonder why Blake hasn't already called you to make a trade."

She looked down at the sticky plastic bag, grimacing at the mess the preserves had made on the front of her jacket. "I'm not sure how Blake even knows this thing exists, unless Johnny told someone about it."

"Whom might he have told?"

"Nobody in his family. He didn't have much to do with his kin. I guess maybe somebody at the trucking company, maybe one of the other drivers."

Dalton frowned, trying to remember what he'd learned about Johnny's job at Davenport Trucking. "What if he mentioned something to Paul Bailey?"

Briar looked up at him. "If he did, no wonder he ended up dead. Bailey was completely in Wayne Cortland's pocket. But wouldn't Johnny have known that, if he was copying the files?"

"Maybe he tried warning someone else at Davenport about what Bailey was up to. Maybe someone he didn't know he couldn't trust, either."

Briar walked the plastic bag across the cramped little cellar to an ancient sink standing against one wall. She pulled a paper towel from the holder that hung above the sink and wet it with water from the tap, then went about scrubbing off the remainder of the preserves clinging to the plastic bag. "Johnny never did know who to trust."

"He should have told you. If this was really about stopping Cortland." He didn't want to ask the next question, but he forced the words from his mouth anyway. "Do you think he wanted to stop Cortland? Or was this about getting the information for his own purposes?"

She looked up sharply. "You mean blackmail?"

"That. Or even to set up his own network."

One corner of her mouth curved upward. "Definitely not that. Johnny wasn't that ambitious. I don't really see him as a blackmailer, either."

"So maybe he really did want to stop what Cortland was doing?"

"Maybe." She didn't sound very convinced of that option, either, he noticed. No matter what else he'd been, Johnny Blackwood had clearly been an idiot. He'd had Briar and Logan, and he'd been on the verge of throwing it all away because of his lies and infidelity.

If Dalton had been in his shoes...

You'd have done what, hotshot? Let some stranger into your house to pump you full of drugs and take the kid right out from under your nose?

"Johnny's old computer is upstairs in the bedroom." Briar's voice dragged him from an abyss of self-indictment. "I haven't turned it on in months, but it probably still works. Want to take a look at what's on the disk?"

THE POLICE HAD taken Johnny's computer not long after his death, hoping to discover some clue to the motive behind his murder. They'd returned it after the fruitless search, and Briar had put it on a table in her bedroom and mostly ignored it except to dust around it now and then.

She held her breath waiting for the system to boot up,

feeling the seconds ticking inexorably away from her. Why hadn't Blake made his move? What if Logan's kidnapping had nothing to do with this flash drive at all? What then?

Dalton's hand flattened against her back between her shoulder blades, as if he'd sensed she needed his grounding touch to keep herself from going off the rails. "Just breathe," he murmured.

The welcome screen popped up, and for an anxious moment Briar couldn't remember Johnny's password. Fingers fumbling on the keyboard, she typed in a couple of possible passwords before she remembered what had been important to her late husband. *PontiacFirebird92* got her into the system.

"Interesting password," Dalton said.

"Men and their cars," she said shortly, not wanting to dwell on the memories. One of the first things she'd had to do after Johnny's death was sell his beloved Firebird to pay off Johnny's debts and put a little savings away for the coming lean times. Going from two incomes to one, with very little in savings to pick up the slack, had been stressful on a lot of levels.

She inserted the memory stick into one of the USB ports and crossed her fingers that several months in a jar of peach preserves hadn't done any damage.

A message informed her the flash drive was loading its own software onto the computer, and a moment later the drive appeared on the list of drives. "Let's see what we have."

As she'd suspected, the flash drive was full of photographs. Over two hundred total. There was only one text file on the entire drive. It was titled "ForBR."

"This is for me," she said, surprised.

"Open it," Dalton said.

She double-clicked the file and held her breath. A short

note popped up. "Briar, if you ever find this, it means things went bad. I know you won't like what I've done, but I did it for Logan. He deserves more than we got growing up. But if you're reading this, I'm probably dead anyway. So do what you want with it."

Dalton's hand slid up to her neck, gently kneading the tight muscles bunched there. "Eloquent." His dry tone left little doubt about his assessment of Johnny's character.

Briar couldn't blame him, really. Johnny had been a very flawed man. She didn't try to defend him.

"You want to see what's on these files?" Dalton asked.

"Let's copy them to the computer first." She pulled up a second window, made a new folder she named JB and started the files copying to the hard drive. The computer was old and slow, and her attempt to access any of the files while they were copying led to nothing but annoyance, as the image program displayed not the expected photograph but a spinning digital hourglass that seemed to taunt Briar as the seconds ticked into minutes.

Giving in to her rising frustration, she stood and crossed impatiently to the window looking out on the small side yard, wondering if the faint glow of the computer had caught the attention of anyone who might be staking out the cabin. She pulled the curtain back a scant inch and peered into the darkness.

"See anyone?" Dalton asked.

"No, but they're out there." She let the curtain slide back in place and turned back to look at him. In the faint blue glow of the computer screen, he looked tired and troubled. She knew if she were in his place, the thought of being tricked into letting an enemy into her own home would have been a constant gnawing ache in her soul.

What she couldn't figure out was why she wasn't angrier at him. Thanks to his incautious moment, her son was missing and in grave danger, and most of the way home from Virginia, she'd cursed Dalton's name and planned ways to make him regret his mistake. But by the time she'd arrived at his house and walked through the door to see him sitting there on the sofa looking sick and broken, all her anger had changed course and flowed toward the nameless, faceless person who'd betrayed his trust and left him looking so crushed and heartbroken.

And toward Blake Culpepper, of course, whose wicked greed and ruthlessness had made Logan a target in the first place.

A soft thudding sound from the front of the house drew her attention away from Dalton's pale face. He turned in his chair, as well, his gaze going toward the bedroom door.

"Stay here. Keep that thing copying."

"It'll copy without me," he said, falling in step as she reached the hallway. "Are you armed?"

"Of course. You?"

"Of course not," he said with a grimace.

She stepped back into the bedroom and unlocked the closet door. The Mossberg shotgun felt like an old friend in her grip. She grabbed some shells off the top shelf of the closet and loaded both barrels.

Back in the hallway, she pulled the Glock from her holster and handed it to Dalton. "Don't shoot if you don't have to. But if you do, go for center mass."

She edged her way down the hall, stopping just short of the front room. Holding her breath, she dared a quick look around the corner.

The front door was open.

She reached back, her palm connecting with Dalton's hip. She gave a little squeeze, holding him in place. "They're already inside," she whispered, her voice barely more than a breath.

He tensed beneath her touch, but he didn't flinch or edge back. He was in this thing till the end, she realized. Warmth flooded her body, as if the knowledge that Dalton would have her back was enough to quell the anxiety of facing a darkened room full of God only knew how many ruthless, dangerous men Blake had sent to bring her in.

Blake can't win, she thought, and for a moment she believed it.

Then all hell broke loose.

THE TWO CAMOUFLAGE-CLAD men entered the cabin just as Nix, Dana and Doyle reached the edge of the tree line. Doyle and Dana both appeared inclined to rush in after them, but Nix caught them both by their arms. "Wait a minute."

"They've just committed a crime. We have cause to take them in," Doyle growled.

"Someone's already in there," he said quietly. He'd spotted the slightest twitch of a curtain in Briar's bedroom window, barely visible through the trees as they'd made a stealthy approach through the woods. There was also an odd glow to the room, as if someone had turned on a television or something like it inside.

"Who?"

"If I were a betting man, I'd say it's Briar. And your brother's probably with her, too."

"Her car isn't anywhere around," Dana protested.

"So she walked. Or she had another way of getting here." Nix couldn't give them a more concrete reason for what was essentially one of his infamous hunches. He'd been teased about his intuition for years, mostly by well-meaning folks on the police force who got a kick of having a real-life Cherokee "seer" among them.

There wasn't anything paranormal about his hunches,

of course. He just paid attention to things like twitching curtains and glowing rooms.

Before Doyle or Dana had a chance to respond, a flurried sound of movement drifted out of the open cabin door, and Nix could no more have stopped Dana and Doyle from rushing toward the cabin than he could stop himself.

Outracing his fiancée and her brother to the porch, he took a leap up the three shallow steps and hit the wooden slats of the porch just as a shotgun blasted from somewhere inside the house. He ducked and rolled toward the side of the porch, crouching in a tight ball. Doyle and Dana, he saw, scattered in opposite directions, away from the open door.

"Anybody moves again, this time I aim for flesh. Got me?"

That was Briar's voice, Nix realized with an emotion that fluttered between alarm and relief.

A male voice followed, deep and thick with a mountain accent that turned his string of curses into a profane sort of music. But the gist of his flood of expletives was that he understood her words and would do nothing to invite her further wrath.

Nix couldn't hold back a grin.

"BILLY HACKMORE AND Terry McDavid." A thick rime of contempt crusted Briar's voice as she looked down at the two men Walker Nix and Doyle Massey had just subdued and cuffed. Dalton wondered if she should put down the shotgun now, but he didn't want to be the one to ask her to do so.

"Boys, at the very least, we have you on breaking and entering. Plus, we're going to run your names, see if there are any outstanding warrants. And whether or not you have the right paperwork for these weapons." Doyle waved his hand toward the four pistols lying on the nearby kitchen table. "Seein' as how they all seem to have the serial numbers filed off, I'm thinkin' that might be an issue."

Dalton glanced at his brother. After just a few short months in Bitterwood, Doyle was already losing his flat-lander accent and beginning to pick up a mountain twang. His beach tan was also fading. He'd be a mountain man in no time.

Oddly, Dalton was starting to think of himself as a mountain man, as well. The thought of leaving these hills behind didn't hold nearly as much charm as it once had.

All the charms he could want in the world, he thought as he watched Briar lower her shotgun and shake her rowdy curls back from her face, seemed to be located right here in the Smoky Mountains.

"I'm thinking you don't have any reason to be loyal to Blake Culpepper beyond the money he tosses your way. Or maybe you're afraid of him?" At the flicker of fear in both men's eyes, Doyle leaned a little closer, taking advantage of his own power, both physical and legal, to keep the two captives off guard. "You should be afraid of me instead."

"Where is Blake?" Briar had apparently reached the end of her patience. She charged closer, making Terry McDavid, who sat nearest her, flinch away.

Dalton caught her arm. She whirled on him, and the ferocity of her gaze nearly made him recoil, as well. With obvious effort, she regained control of her anger.

"It's a good question," Doyle agreed far more calmly. "Where is Blake Culpepper? Where is he keeping Logan?"

"He'll kill us if we tell you," Billy Hackmore said.

"And I'll make you wish you were dead if you don't," Briar growled.

Doyle gave her a pointed look and she growled again but turned away, stalking out through the open front door.

Dalton followed her out, easing his arms around her. She quivered like a wild animal that had been cornered, but after a moment she gentled beneath his touch, leaning back against him. He tightened his embrace, burying his face in her curls. "They don't owe Culpepper any loyalty," he murmured. "Doyle will break one of them sooner or later."

"The longer Logan stays with Blake, the more likely something terrible will happen to him." A nervous ripple ran through her slender body, and he hugged her tighter. "And even if we find out where he is, what next? A SWAT raid? With my baby as a hostage?"

"We'll figure something out," he said, although he wasn't sure how to avoid just the scenario she imagined. Blake Culpepper was almost certainly well armed. Getting inside and getting Logan out wasn't going to be easy.

"I have to go alone," she murmured.

His body stiffened reflexively. "And give him two hostages?"

She turned in his arms, looking up at him in the glow spilling from inside the cabin. Dark shadows of anxiety bruised the flesh around her stormy eyes. "I'm not so easy to take hostage."

Her skin looked like velvet. He couldn't resist the urge to touch her cheek, to see if it was as soft as it looked. He brushed the pad of his thumb over her lips, and they parted, her soft breath warming his hand. "I want Logan back with us. More than anything. But I don't want to sacrifice you to make it happen. There's got to be a way that doesn't put you in that man's hands."

Her gaze met his, direct and unflinching. "I don't think there is. So I have to know—will you back me on this? Or do you plan to fight me?"

The thought of Briar going into Culpepper's lair, unarmed and alone, was unthinkable. And yet he knew she was asking him to not only think it but support her decision.

She wanted him to trust her instincts, to believe that she knew what she was doing and could bring her son home safely. And, God help him, he couldn't refuse anything she asked. Not even this.

"Okay. I'll back you. But I want to be there with you."

She shook her head sharply. "No."

"I won't go in with you. I'll let you play it however you want. But I'm going to be outside whatever lair your cousin's holed up in. No way in hell do I let you walk in there without backup. Are you going to back me on that? Or do you plan to fight me?"

She stared up at him, the look in her eyes a mixture of consternation and affection as she recognized her own words thrown back at her. "You're a lawyer, you know. You can't even shoot a rifle worth a damn."

"You're good for a man's self-esteem, Briar. Anyone ever tell you that?"

A bleak look passed over her face, and he realized he'd touched a nerve.

Tugging her closer, he bent and whispered in her ear. "You make me want to be a better man. You make me believe it's possible."

Her eyes flickered up to meet his as he backed away. One small work-roughened hand rose to his face, her thumb sliding over his lips the way he'd touched hers. "When this is over…"

He silenced her with a soft kiss.

The sound of a throat clearing drew them apart. They both looked toward the doorway, where Nix stood, his expression bemused. "We have a location."

Chapter Sixteen

"I wish we had time to wire you," Doyle grumbled as he looked from his brother to Briar. "But you're right. We need to move fast, before he's had time to wonder why his men aren't reporting back."

"What about those two?" Dalton nodded toward the two men in cuffs.

"Dana and Nix will stay with them. We're not going to call this in to the station until we have a chance to get Logan away from Culpepper," Doyle answered. Unspoken in his reply was the unsettling knowledge that they still weren't sure who in the police station could be trusted.

"There's a copy of this disk on the computer in my bedroom," Briar said quietly. "Maybe, if these files are what we think they are, they'll be able to tell you a lot more about who's a friend and who's not."

"I need a weapon," Dalton said.

Briar handed him the Glock he'd returned to her earlier at the house. She wasn't going to need it in the cabin on Smoky Ridge where Blake was holed up with her son. "Fifteen rounds, plus one in the chamber."

He nodded, looking both worried and determined. If she hadn't already been more than halfway in love with him, she'd have loved him a little just for backing her up on this risky plan. She knew she was asking a lot of him.

Of all of them. She was asking them to put their trust in her to handle herself in a battle of wills with one of the most dangerous men in the Smoky Mountains, with her son's life at stake.

"Dalton and I will come with you up to the cabin. Then we'll wait."

"We can't wire her up," Dalton murmured, "but what if we listen in through her cell phone?"

"He may take my phone as soon as I enter the cabin," she warned.

"And he may not. But even if he does, your phone display can go black even when a call is connected, right?"

She nodded, understanding his point. "And he may not think to check if it's on."

"Good idea," Doyle said. The look of pleasure on Dalton's face at his brother's approval would have been comical if it weren't so poignant. Briar had a feeling Tallie Cumberland's children were going to end up being a family after all.

Blake Culpepper's choice of hideouts was pretty brilliant, Briar had to concede as she led Dalton and Doyle through the thickening woods. The cabin was the old Cumberland homestead, abandoned years earlier when the inhabitants of Cherokee Cove had driven the accursed family from their midst after Tallie Cumberland's troubles with the Sutherlands and Hales. It was the one place in Cherokee Cove that nobody would ever think to go, for fear of the curse rubbing off on them.

The place was secluded but not particularly primitive. It had indoor plumbing and electricity. Briar assumed, as they came within sight of the mountain cabin, Blake had probably figured out a way to pirate the electricity that now lit up a room in the back of the small wooden structure. He was hardly a man who'd blink at such an easy bit of theft.

She paused and turned to her companions. Doyle was looking through narrowed eyes at the cabin, but Dalton's gaze was firmly on her. She felt an odd little thrill at being his singular focus at this peril-fraught moment.

"Be careful," he said, and there was a wealth of unspoken emotion behind his words. She felt an answering flood of feeling building like a fire in the center of her chest.

She pulled out her cell phone. "Your phone's on vibrate?"

He nodded.

She dialed his number. His cell phone buzzed. He swiped the screen and she lifted her phone to her ear, locking gazes with him as she spoke softly into the phone. "Let's bring Logan home."

His eyes glittered as he nodded. "Don't stop talking. If you stop talking, I might be tempted to come in and get you."

"If I stop talking, go in there and get my boy." She reached across the narrow space between them, touching her hand to his chest. "Promise me."

"I promise."

Doyle touched her shoulder. "We both promise. Take care." He nodded toward the cabin.

Her heart pounding like thunder, she walked slowly into the clearing.

Half expecting to be cut down by bullets before she reached the porch, she was surprised to make it all the way to the cabin's front door without incident. But she wasn't shocked when the door whipped open before she could lift her hand to knock and the double barrels of a shotgun greeted her.

Blake Culpepper stood behind the shotgun, his dark eyes narrow with suspicion. "Son of a bitch," he muttered with disgust. "I should have known not to send a couple of idiots to grab another Culpepper."

"I'm a Blackwood," she answered tartly, quelling the quiver of fear rattling through her. "That's really why you went after me, isn't it? Because of what Johnny took?"

He gave the shotgun a sideways twitch and backed up a few feet. Briar took the gesture as all the invitation she was going to get. Moving slowly, she entered the cabin, barely suppressing a flinch as the door shut behind her, slammed in place by one sharp kick of Blake's boot.

"Where is my son?" She lifted her chin and met her cousin's gaze.

His eyes glittered with almost indulgent amusement, as if he were watching a fluffy kitten show its tiny claws. *Good,* she thought. *Keep thinking I'm harmless.*

"Where are the files?" he countered.

She reached for the flash drive in the front pocket of her jeans. He jerked the barrel of the shotgun toward her. "Uh-uh."

Pressing her lips flat with revulsion, she stood still while he moved his hands over her body, looking for any sign of a weapon. She was clean, of course; she'd brought with her only her cell phone and the flash drive. Even her pocketknife was stashed in the pocket of Dalton's jacket.

As they'd hoped, Blake didn't bother checking to see if the phone was engaged. He shoved it back at her, and she slipped it back into the pocket of her windbreaker. He kept the flash drive, looking at it through narrowed eyes. For a moment the barrel of the shotgun dipped away from her, and she gauged her chance of overpowering him.

Not good, she decided. And too early. She couldn't be sure Blake had her son here in this cabin, despite the assurances of his henchmen back at her cabin. She needed to see Logan, make sure he was safe, before she took any risky chances.

"You have the files," she said. "Where is Logan?"

"I have a memory stick," he said bluntly, bringing up the barrel of the shotgun again. "Could be pictures of your Dollywood trip, for all I know."

"Never been to Dollywood," she answered. "Always wanted to, but money being short—"

He answered with another sideways twitch of the gun. "The kid's back here." He waited for her to move toward the doorway leading to the back of the cabin, then followed, the barrel of the shotgun flattening against her spine, right between her shoulder blades.

Right where her heart was hammering like a carpenter on speed.

"MAMA!" LOGAN'S VOICE, coming over the cell phone with tinny clarity, made Dalton's whole body rattle with relief. He looked up at Doyle, who grinned back at him as Briar's phone crooned endearments to her son. There was a soft swishing sound over the phone—Briar sweeping her little boy into her arms and hugging him tight?

It's what Dalton would have done in the same situation.

"Why don't you and your boy catch up while I take a look at these files?" Blake Culpepper's gravelly voice sounded sly through the phone. He was up to something, Dalton thought with a flutter of alarm. Could Briar hear it, too?

"Why don't we come up front with you instead?" she asked.

"You really don't take this shotgun seriously, do you?"

"I take it very seriously," she countered, sounding confident and calm. She was, Dalton thought, an utterly remarkable woman. He didn't deserve a woman like that in his life, but he'd be damned if he didn't try to keep her there anyway.

"Ah, hell. Why not? You've probably made copies of it already, haven't you?" Blake sounded more resigned than annoyed, making Dalton wonder if he had been right about why Blake wanted his hands on the files. If he planned to use them to eliminate his competition, it probably didn't matter much to him if the police brought in his foes and saved him some of the trouble.

"You think you can avoid capture, don't you?" Briar's tone sounded more conversational than confrontational.

"Ain't nobody knows these woods better than a Culpepper, darlin'. You know that better than most."

She didn't argue. Over the phone, Dalton heard the sound of footsteps as well as the soft murmur of Logan's little-boy voice saying something Dalton couldn't quite make out. Briar's answer was a soft shushing sound, a mother trying to keep her son from drawing unwanted attention.

"Stay right here, Logan. Stay close to Mama." Dalton heard the soft thud of feet shuffling on the floor. Had she set the little boy down? He wondered why she'd let him go instead of holding on tight.

He didn't like the answer that came to mind.

"Let's see what's on these files," Blake said. The faint sound of metal scraping metal drifted over the phone line. Dalton tried to picture what was happening in the cabin, but all his mind seemed able to focus on was why Briar had set her son down instead of holding him close.

What was she planning?

BRIAR SLOWLY BENT her knees, easing into a crouch next to her son as Blake pulled up a metal folding chair to the table where a laptop computer sat open, its screen dark.

He had settled himself where he could see her, but he'd leaned the shotgun against the wall beside him, as if he no longer considered her much of a threat.

Big mistake, she thought with rising confidence.

But she still had to be careful. Logan could easily get hurt if she tried to overpower Blake and take away the shotgun. She couldn't move yet. Not while Logan was in the room.

She hugged Logan close, nuzzling his neck. He was sweaty and a little grimy, but he still smelled like heaven to her. "How you doin', little man?" she murmured in his ear, glancing at Blake to see if he was listening.

His attention was focused on the files now opening on the laptop.

"He didn't hurt you, did he?"

Blake didn't react, but Logan answered, "He yells."

Blazing fury shot up her gullet and filled her throat with rage. She tamped it down and glanced at Blake again.

"Logan," she whispered, "when I say go, I want you to run out the door, okay? Just nod."

Logan nodded solemnly.

She glanced at Blake again. He was smiling at the laptop screen as he pulled up photo after photo. "Gotta hand it to Johnny," he said. "He was thorough."

"How did you know he had the files?" She pushed to a standing position and edged sideways, putting Logan firmly behind her.

Blake looked up at her briefly. "He tried to sell them to Merritt Cortland. He'd heard tell Merritt was trying to undercut old man Cortland. I guess he thought Merritt would be willing to shell out a few bucks to get his hands on the files."

Her heart sank a little. So much for Johnny's intentions being honorable. "Merritt wasn't buying?"

Blake shrugged, turning back to the computer. "Merritt made the mistake of thinking Johnny had the files on him. He stabbed first and asked questions later. Too much later."

Her blood ran cold. Blake was talking about Johnny's murder with as little feeling as if he'd been discussing putting poison on an anthill. Briar may have fallen out of love with her husband by the time he was murdered, but he'd been her first love and the father of her son. To hear his murder discussed with such heartless dispassion made her want to grab the shotgun and start shooting things.

She managed to remain motionless, her gaze firmly on Blake's profile. She studied him, looking for an opening.

He opened another file, and his eyes widened. He murmured a string of profanities, leaning closer to the computer.

Now, she thought.

She reached behind her and touched Logan's head. "Go!"

She heard his little feet pattering toward the door. Blake was slow to react, but when he realized what was happening, he reached for the shotgun.

She launched herself at him, her shoulder slamming into the barrel of the shotgun before it swung around to face her. With a deafening blast, the shotgun went off.

Two things happened in quick succession. First, the door of the cabin opened and Logan Blackwood came running out, his tiny legs churning.

And second, a shotgun blast split the silence of the deepening night.

Dalton and Doyle moved at the same time, brushing shoulders briefly as they ran. By the time they reached the cabin steps, Logan had made his way down them. With a glance at his brother, Dalton churned his way past the little boy and up the steps, leaving Doyle to scoop up the boy and run him back to safety.

Dalton faltered to a stop in the cabin doorway. Briar and Blake were standing upright but twisted around each other as they grappled, the shotgun perilously clutched between them. Though Blake was larger than Briar by at least seventy pounds and six inches, she had a mother's fierceness on her side, and she was close to taking him down to the ground.

But the shotgun was too close to her face. Only one blast had sounded, and the weapon had two barrels.

She'd told him to shoot for center mass, but her center mass was too damned close to Culpepper's. So he did the only thing he knew to do. He walked up boldly behind Blake and pressed the gun to the back of the man's neck. "I will kill you," he said in a tone so calm and emotionless that he almost didn't recognize his own voice.

Blake froze in place. But Briar didn't. Jerking the shotgun from his loosening grip, she slammed the butt of the gun right in her cousin's gut.

Air whooshed from Blake's chest, and he sagged backward, nearly toppling Dalton to the floor. Dalton braced his legs and kept the pistol pointed at the man's head as he struggled to keep Blake on his feet.

"Let him go," Briar demanded. She'd shifted the shotgun into shooting position, the barrel aimed squarely at her cousin's midsection.

"Put it down," Dalton said, alarm crawling up his spine at the look of sheer feral rage in her thundercloud eyes.

She shook her head, her gaze pinned to Blake's face. "Is Merritt Cortland still alive?" she asked through gritted teeth.

Blake made a groaning sound, still trying to suck in air.

"Is that bastard still alive?" Briar demanded, pushing the barrel of the shotgun right up to Blake's chest.

"Briar, put down the shotgun," Dalton said. "If you shoot him, you'll shoot me."

Her gaze flickered up to meet his, and some of the fire he saw burning behind her eyes cooled to just a flicker. She released a long, gusty breath, pain lining her features. "Merritt Cortland murdered Johnny."

"I know. I heard."

Her face started to crumple, and she backed away, lowering the shotgun barrel. With shaking hand, she pulled her cell phone from her pocket, pushed a couple of buttons and lifted the phone to her ear. "Chief? We could use a little help."

Chapter Seventeen

"This information is explosive." Tom Bevill's voice was usually enough to make Dalton snap to attention, but he couldn't seem to drag his gaze away from Briar's pale face. She sat across the police station foyer from him, rocking her sleeping son in her lap. Her gray-eyed gaze was distant and unfocused, making him wonder what she was thinking.

"Are you listening to me, Dalton?"

Dalton looked at his boss. "The files were all we hoped for?"

"And more. We have names, events—it's a treasure trove of actionable evidence as well as new threads for future investigations." Bevill's smile was almost wistful. "Makes me want to rethink my plans to retire."

"You should," Dalton said. "Rethink it, I mean."

Bevill's eyes narrowed. "You want me to run against you?"

"I'm not running," he said, giving voice to something he'd been thinking about off and on for the past couple of days.

Bevill looked stunned. "You've been planning to run for my job since you first signed on with the prosecutor's office. What happened?"

Dalton's gaze wandered back to Briar and her son. "I'm

thinking of making changes in my life. I don't need to add an election to that mix."

"I always figured you'd end up in the governor's office one day. Hell, maybe even the White House in time."

That would never happen, Dalton thought, thanks to his family's scandals. But he'd come to realize the dream of political service had always been more important to his father and grandfather than it had been to him. He liked being a prosecutor, finding justice for people who'd been wronged. And he hated politics. "I like the work I'm doing now."

Bevill's eyes narrowed, but he simply nodded. "I guess I should make an announcement canceling my plans for retirement. Maybe I'll announce it at this morning's press conference. You'll be there? Give me your support?"

"Sure." Dalton supposed there was no way to avoid politics altogether in his line of work.

"Good man." Bevill clapped his shoulder. "We'll be meeting in a couple of hours to plan the press conference about this bust. You'll be there, too?"

In any other circumstances, he'd say yes, despite feeling as if a whole beach's worth of sand had set up gritty shop in his eyes. But he had other matters he needed to deal with first. More important, even, than a press conference announcing a major arrest.

"The police want me to stick around a little while longer," he told his boss. At least, he hoped one particular police officer wanted him to stick around for a lot longer.

But his hope of talking to Briar alone anytime soon evaporated even as Tom Bevill headed off in search of a phone. Walker Nix had taken a seat next to Briar, his head close to hers in tense conversation.

Dalton crossed to where they sat. "Has something happened?"

Nix looked up. "We finally reached the gate guard who was on duty this morning. We've identified who visited you." The man's look of sympathy made Dalton's gut tighten.

"Who?" he asked.

Briar touched his arm. "It was Janet."

He stared at her a moment. "Janet Trainor? My secretary Janet?"

Nix nodded. "She signed in with a false name, but the gate guard's description was clear and detailed. On a hunch, Doyle called Laney and gave her the description. She said it sounded just like Janet Trainor."

Dalton felt sick. "Janet's been with me for years. She's a good woman. I would have trusted her with any of my secrets."

"She's been picked up for questioning. We're about to talk to her. If you'd like to observe the interview, we can arrange it."

He nodded. "I'd like to hear what she has to say."

He half hoped Briar would come with him, but while her hand tightened around his arm before he rose from his chair, she remained where she was. Swallowing a sigh of disappointment, he went with Nix through the detective's office and into Doyle's corner lair.

Doyle was there already, along with Laney and Dana. Sympathy shined in all three pairs of eyes. "Nix briefed you?" Doyle asked.

"Yeah. Who's doing the interview?"

"Delilah Brand," Doyle answered. "She and Janet were schoolmates back in the day."

They'd set up the chief's laptop computer to pick up the feed from the interview room. The picture was a little grainy, but the audio was clean. The tremble in Janet Trainor's voice came through loud and clear.

"You know, don't you?" she said before Delilah asked the first question.

"What do you think we know?" Delilah asked.

Janet began to cry, tears trickling down her pale cheeks. "Please, you have to understand—if they find out you know, they'll kill him."

Dalton leaned toward the screen.

"Kill who?" Dana murmured a second before Delilah asked the same thing in the interview room.

"Hunter," Janet answered in a soft whimper.

"Who's Hunter?" Doyle asked.

"Her brother," Dalton answered, the situation beginning to make a terrible sort of sense. "Hunter Bragg. Former Army infantry soldier. He was injured in an IED explosion in Afghanistan about a year ago. Army deemed him unfit for retention, and apparently he's pretty depressed about it."

"She's been worried about him," Laney said quietly. "Everybody knows how she worries about him."

"Who's going to kill him?" Delilah asked Janet in a gentle tone.

"Blake Culpepper." Janet took the tissue Delilah offered her, wiping her eyes. Her voice was a little stronger now, as if admitting her fear had given back the strength her secret had stolen. "I got a message this morning at the office. It was waiting for me in my chair. It said there was a bottle in my desk drawer. The one I keep locked. The note told me they'd been watching Hunter and that if I didn't do what they told me to do with the contents of that bottle, they would kill him before I could reach him. There was a photo—"

"Do you have the note and the photo?"

Janet nodded unhappily. "I locked it in the glove compartment of my car."

"Get me a search warrant for that car," Doyle said.

Nix nodded and headed out of the office.

"What did the photo show?" Delilah asked.

"Hunter. Tied up and gagged. They will kill him if they know I'm here."

Doyle gave Dalton a troubled look. "Blake Culpepper has already invoked his Fifth Amendment rights. He's lawyered up. He won't talk."

"Ask her for permission to see the photo. Tell her we have Culpepper in custody and we need to try to find her brother," Dalton said. "She'll cooperate."

Before Doyle could move, Delilah did just that. "We can get a search warrant for your car, but if you'll give us permission—"

"Of course," Janet said quickly. "Anything."

Dalton turned away from the computer screen, his gut roiling. Janet must have come by his house on some pretext. He'd have let her in, without a doubt. Maybe he'd made them some coffee and she'd slipped the GHB into his cup, as ordered.

Good God, he thought, *the poor woman.*

"I wanted to call the police," she was saying, her voice clear over the computer. "Please tell me that Dalton's okay. Please, please tell me that."

"He's okay," Delilah said.

No, Dalton thought as he walked out of the office, *he's not. Dalton is definitely not okay.*

BRIAR REALIZED SHE was being overly cautious, clinging to her son instead of letting someone find him a soft sofa somewhere in the cop shop to finish off his slumber. She just didn't want to let him go yet.

But when Dana came downstairs with news of a wrinkle

in their formerly wrapped-up case, she realized she had to put her cop hat back on and let someone else watch her son.

Blake wouldn't be coming after him now. There was nothing he needed from her anymore.

"Laney's agreed to watch him," Dana told her, the look in her green eyes full of apology. "I know it's too soon, but you and Nix know Cherokee Cove better than anyone else. He wants you in on this investigation. Time could be running out for Hunter Bragg."

Briar felt as if she'd been run over by a fleet of trucks, but one look at the photo Nix had found in Janet Trainor's car gave her a double shot of refreshed energy. The man in the photo still bore the scars of his war injury, along with new scrapes and bruises he'd no doubt earned during his more recent capture.

The thought of Blake Culpepper's band of ruthless thieves and killers using a war hero as leverage against a decent woman almost made her wish she'd blasted a hole in her cousin the way she'd wanted to back in his cabin.

She dragged her gaze away from the battered face and focused instead on the background of the photo, trying to figure out if anything looked familiar. "It looks like a cabin, not a house," she said after a moment. "There's something..." She paused, peering a little closer at the grainy out-of-focus background of the photograph. Her stomach gave a small lurch as she realized what it was. "See that black blur there, behind his shoulder?"

Dana nodded. "Can you tell what it is?"

She could be wrong, but if she was right—

If she was right, she realized with a sinking heart, then a whole lot of what she'd assumed about the world around her could be dead wrong.

"I think," she said finally, reluctantly, "it might be a black-bear skin."

"Does that mean anything?" Dana asked.

"I think it does." Her stomach knotting, she pushed to her feet. Logan shifted in her arms, clinging a little more tightly to her neck even in his sleep. The urge to keep him wrapped in her arms forever was so strong she almost sat back down. But the image of that bound and gagged soldier gave her the strength to keep going. She was beginning to believe she knew exactly where she'd seen that bearskin before, as much as she wanted to believe otherwise. And if she was right, Hunter Bragg was in a hell of a lot of danger.

They all were.

"Do you know where Dalton is?" she asked Dana as they hurried through the empty corridor toward the detectives' communal office.

"He was in Doyle's office with us watching the interview with Janet Trainor earlier," Dana answered. "You can imagine how shocked he was to learn who'd drugged him and took Logan."

"Is he still there?"

"No. He left the office after learning why Janet had drugged him. I don't even know if he's still here in the station."

Damn. She really wanted to see him before she left. Ask him, maybe, to stay with Laney and make sure Logan was okay. But she didn't have time to hunt him down. Hunter Bragg might be in a hell of a lot of trouble, even more than they thought.

"If you see Dalton, will you tell him where I went?" She wasn't sure he was in any hurry to talk to her, given how close she'd come to blowing him away along with her cousin earlier that night, but she needed to try, at least, to explain. To find out if it was possible to get past all of the craziness of the past few days and see if the attraction between them had any legs.

For her, she knew, it did. She'd been in love before. She knew what it felt like. And if she wasn't already there with Dalton, it wouldn't take much to get her to that point.

She just needed to know if she was fooling herself. Could he ever feel that way about her, too? Could they get past the obvious differences in their lives, in their pasts, and build something good and lasting for the future?

DALTON STARED AT his sister in dismay. "She's going on a raid?"

"Nix wanted her with him," she said flatly.

Nix, he thought with a grimace. "Your boyfriend does realize she's been awake for nearly twenty-four hours and she has a little boy who needs her with him?"

"She agreed to go," Dana answered, clearly trying not to bristle at his tone when he spoke of her fiancé. "She knows the area better than anyone but Nix. And there's a man's life at stake. A war hero, for God's sake."

Dalton rubbed his hand over his gritty eyes. "Have they located where he's being held?"

"Nix just called in with an affirmative. Doyle's about to send backup before they try to go in and get him."

"Who has him?"

"They haven't told me," she admitted. "I get the feeling it's a situational security thing. They don't want to be overheard."

Odd, he thought. Then again, the police station had been the locus of a recent not-quite-completed corruption investigation. "Have they left yet?"

Dana shook her head. "They're gearing up now. Why?"

Dalton started moving toward the police station's weapons-and-gear lockers, leaving her to catch up. "Because I'm going with them."

NIX'S DARK EYES bored into Briar's from the back corner of the mountain cabin. He nodded twice. The signal to go.

She was the only one not wearing protective gear, though her Glock was snugly tucked into a pancake holster snapped to the back of her jeans. She hadn't bothered freshening up before leaving the station. The more her weariness and strain showed, the better.

She rounded the corner of the cabin and climbed the porch steps, not bothering to be quiet. She wasn't there in stealth mode, after all.

She was the distraction.

The front door was made of solid pine slabs stained to a dark oak color. Knocking three times, she braced herself for whatever came next. It took a lot of control not to reach behind her to check on the presence of the Glock, but her job was to appear as normal and nonthreatening as a police officer could manage.

The door opened a few inches, making her nerves jangle all the way to her toes. She struggled not to show it, struggled not to react to the face she saw staring back at her in the open doorway, even though nausea rippled through her at the familiar sight.

"Good God, Blackwood," Thurman Gowdy growled, his voice gravelly with sleep. "Do you realize it's four in the morning?"

"Can I come in?" she asked.

Her patrol partner peered at her through narrowed eyes. His salt-and-pepper crew cut managed to look mussed despite its short, crisp length, as if he'd just rolled out of bed. Maybe he had, she thought. He had no reason to think his cabin was about to be raided. He probably didn't even know Blake was in custody yet.

"What's happened?" he asked.

"Logan was kidnapped," she answered, phrasing it so

she didn't give away whether or not he was still missing. Just in case she was wrong and he had already heard the news.

"I know. I'm so sorry." He looked so sincere, she thought, her stomach cramping with dismay. "I asked if I could be in on the hunt for him, but they said at the station they were trying to go low profile on it. Is there anything new on it?"

She wasn't sure if he didn't know or if he knew and was trying to trap her. Her weary mind couldn't figure out his meaning, so she just got to the point of her visit.

"Can I come in?" she repeated.

He hesitated, and the last of her doubts disappeared, leaving only disillusionment coiling like a snake in her chest. If Hunter Bragg weren't hidden somewhere in the cabin, her partner would have let her in without a thought.

"My brother's here, and he's a light sleeper," Thurman said. "Maybe I could meet you in a few minutes at Ledbetter's for some coffee and an early breakfast?" He glanced back toward the darkness behind him.

It gave her the distraction she needed.

She whipped the Glock from her holster. By the time he turned back around to face her, the pistol was pointed straight at his chest.

The shock on his face was real, she realized. "Good God, Blackwood, what are you doing?"

"Is there anyone in your cabin besides your prisoner?" she asked.

He feigned confusion. "Prisoner? What the hell are you talking about? Put down the gun, Blackwood. Have you lost your mind?"

She felt more than heard Nix coming up the porch steps behind her. "It's over, Gowdy. You made a mistake when you took that picture of Hunter Bragg. You forgot to move the bearskin off the wall behind him."

Thurman's expression shifted to dismay. Slowly, he raised his hands and twined them behind the back of his head. "I want a lawyer."

"Is there anyone in the cabin besides Bragg?" she asked.

Gowdy just stared at her, silent.

Nix led two deputies from the county sheriff's department's SWAT team into the cabin. Briar kept her weapon trained on Gowdy, lowering it only when Delilah Brand and another Ridge County deputy took him into custody. "Good work, Briar," Delilah said, sparing her a brief sympathetic smile.

She lowered her gun, trying to squelch the urge to sit in the nearby porch rocker and cry like a baby.

"He's here," Nix's voice called from the back of the cabin. "He's safe."

More deputies moved past her into the house. She didn't follow, instead trudging slowly down the porch steps and out toward the tree line at the edge of the yard. Sunrise was still at least a couple of hours away, but a faint lightening in the eastern sky over the mountains eased enough of the darkness for her to make out the shapes of trees and bushes in the mist-draped woods.

Suddenly, someone glided out of the gloom to stand in front of her. Dalton Hale, her mind registered with numb surprise. She blinked her eyes a couple of times, expecting the sight to disappear like the fatigue-induced fantasy it must surely be.

But he didn't disappear. He moved closer through the gray predawn light, his gaze locked with hers. "Are you okay?" he asked.

She wanted to tell him she was fine. But she couldn't push the words past her aching throat.

His eyes softening, he opened his arms and waited.

She didn't mean to run, but she must have, for one second he was a couple of yards away and the next she was pressed tightly against his body, wrapped up in a fierce, comforting embrace.

"I'm sorry," he said. "I would never have suspected Thurman Gowdy of being part of this mess."

She rubbed her face against his shirt. "It makes me wonder who to trust." She leaned back her head to look at him. "I heard about Janet."

"I suppose I should feel a little betrayed by what she did. I guess you must be angry at her."

She was, she had to admit. At first. But the more the image of Hunter Bragg's battered face had dug its claws into her thoughts, the less she could blame Janet Trainor for making the only choice she could bear to make. "I don't think I could have made a different choice in her position," she said.

He nodded toward the cabin, where Nix and the sheriff's deputies were leading Hunter Bragg from the cabin. The man was hunched and shivering beneath a thick quilt, but he was limping along under his own power, Briar saw with relief. She looked back at Dalton, who was still watching the scene through narrowed eyes. "They'll call it in to the station if they haven't already. Someone will let Janet know her brother is okay."

"I don't know what's going to happen to her. She kidnapped your son and turned him over to a criminal. I don't think we can just make the charges against her go away." He dragged his gaze back to hers, his grim look softening as he added, "I called Laney a few minutes ago to check on Logan. She said he's fine. Still asleep on the sofa in Doyle's office. She says Doyle's taking his sentry job very seriously."

She smiled, latching on to the one unadulterated bit of good news in her life at the moment. "I heard before I left that the county prosecutor was thrilled with getting his hands on that flash drive."

"He definitely was." Dalton smiled back at her, though there was a hint of reticence in his expression, as if there was something he wasn't looking forward to telling her.

Her own smile faded, and her stomach began to knot again, nearly as badly as it had before, while she was waiting for her partner to answer the cabin door and crush her last stubborn bit of hope that she was wrong about him. "What's wrong?"

He looked surprised by the question. "Nothing's wrong."

She wasn't convinced. "Did Bevill say something to worry you?"

His surprise faded into resignation. "No, it's not my boss I'm worried about."

"He's still going to back you as his replacement, isn't he?" she asked. She couldn't imagine the county prosecutor holding all that had happened to Dalton in the past few weeks against him. He was still the same smart, passionate prosecutor he'd been before the truth about his family came out. And he'd certainly proved his courage and determination during the past few tumultuous days while protecting her and Logan. "If he's giving you trouble, I can talk to him. I can tell him how amazing you've been—"

He smiled, though the worry in his eyes didn't quite disappear. "He's thinking about running again."

She looked at him in dismay. "He can't do that!"

"He can," Dalton assured her. "In fact, I encouraged him to do so."

"Are you crazy? Do you know how hard it'll be to beat a popular incumbent?"

"I'm dropping out of the race."

Now she knew he was crazy. "Why? You can't think people are going to hold what your father and grandfather did against you! People are smart enough to know you're blameless—"

"I never wanted to be a politician," he told her, curving his hands over her shoulders. His thumbs brushed lightly over her collarbone through her thin cotton T-shirt, making her shiver. "I just want to help people get a little justice in this world. I'm not cut out for politics."

She wanted to tell him he was cut out for anything he wanted, but she could see by the relief in his eyes that he'd already figured out what he wanted, and it didn't include running for office.

But did it include her?

She screwed up her courage and opened her mouth to breach the topic. But before she could speak, he lifted one hand to her cheek, his touch gentle and questing. "What I want," he murmured in a voice that made her blood spontaneously ignite, "is you. You and Logan. I want to go to my office and do what I can to help people, then come home to you and the little man and do what I can to make you feel happy and secure." A hint of doubt flickered in his eyes. "Do you think that's possible? I know the past few days have been nothing but crazy, but there's something between us, Briar. I feel it so strongly—it's like you're in my blood and there's nothing I could ever do to get you out. And I don't want to. I don't want to ever lose the feeling that you're part of me. That we're supposed to be like this. Am I crazy?"

Tears burned her eyes, but she wouldn't let them fall. She wanted to be clear-eyed and levelheaded. She wanted to talk about the problems and the struggles they'd have if they wanted to blend their lives together long-term.

But when she opened her mouth, what came out was

not what she'd intended. "Yes," she said, unable to tamp down a bubble of joy that burst into a smile. "Yes, you're crazy. And apparently I'm crazy, too."

He began to laugh, the sound just short of hysterical. His hand flexed convulsively against her face before wrapping around the back of her neck and pulling her into a hard, stake-claiming kiss.

Several breathless moments later, he drew back to catch his breath, his green eyes glittering with almost feral excitement. "I'm pretty sure I'm in love with you," he warned. "And I don't fall in love. So if you don't intend for this thing between us to be a long-term thing, better say so now."

Relief and a curious sort of triumph burned through her. She smiled up at him, her confidence soaring. "How long is long-term?"

He shrugged, his gaze mirroring her own growing boldness. His lips curved with satisfaction and just a hint of cocky masculinity. "I don't know. I was thinking this might lead to…forever? Think you can handle that?"

"I'm a mountain girl," she said, rising on tiptoes to wrap her arms around his neck. "I can handle anything."

* * * * *

Conner put a hand at the small of her back and led her inside the hotel. "I'll stay here tonight. In the lobby. That should give you a peaceful night's sleep."

Adrienne wasn't sure how to respond. She was so grateful for his offer. The thought of having a night of uninterrupted rest made her feel as if a huge weight had been lifted from her shoulders.

But she didn't want him in the lobby. She wanted him in her bed.

Adrienne smiled up at Conner shyly, and reached for his hand. "There's no need for you to stay down here."

He pressed the button for the elevator then stepped close enough to Adrienne that his lips were just inches away from hers.

"I think we both know if I stay up there, a peaceful night's sleep is not what's going to happen."

The elevator door opened but Conner didn't move. Finally Adrienne put a finger on his chest and pushed him back into the elevator and didn't stop until Conner's back was against the elevator's wall.

Casper put a hand at the small of her back and led her inside the hotel. "I'll stay here tonight, in the lobby. That should give you a peaceful night's sleep."

PRIMAL INSTINCT

BY
JANIE CROUCH

MILLS & BOON

Published in Great Britain 2014
by Mills & Boon, an imprint of Harlequin (UK) Limited,
Eton House, 18-24 Paradise Road, Richmond, Surrey, TW9 1SR

© 2014 Janie Crouch

ISBN: 978 0 263 91355 2

46-0414

Harlequin (UK) Limited's policy is to use papers that are natural, renewable and recyclable products and made from wood grown in sustainable forests. The logging and manufacturing processes conform to the legal environmental regulations of the country of origin.

Printed and bound in Spain
by Blackprint CPI, Barcelona

Janie Crouch loves to read—almost exclusively romance—and has been doing so since middle school. She learned to love Mills & Boon® romance novels when she lived in Wales, UK, for a few years as a pre-teen, then moved on to a passion for romantic suspense as an adult.

Janie lives with her husband and four children in southeastern Virginia. Her "day job" is teaching online public speaking and communication courses at a community college. When she's not listening to the voices in her head (and even when she is), Janie enjoys traveling, long-distance running, movie-watching, knitting and adventure/obstacle racing.

Janie tries to live by the anonymous quote "Life is not a journey to the grave with the intention of arriving safely in a pretty and well-preserved body, but rather to skid in broadside, thoroughly used up, totally worn-out and proclaiming, 'Wow, what a ride!'" You can find out more about her at www.janiecrouch.com.

To my mother,
the smartest and most well-read person I know.
I call you family because I have to,
but call you friend because I'm blessed.

Chapter One

FBI agent Conner Perigo knew throwing the file in his hand across the room would be childish and ultimately accomplish nothing except making a mess, but he was still tempted.

Ten months.

Ten months they had been on the trail of this psychopath. Ten months of being two steps behind and watching, helpless, as another woman was murdered. It wasn't in Conner's job description to attend the funerals of women he had never known. That hadn't stopped him from attending one last week. Or three weeks before that. Or a month and a half before that.

Each time he saw one of these women buried, it renewed Conner's determination to catch this bastard.

Five women dead in ten months. Most within a fifty-mile radius of San Francisco, which, of course, had the city in a panic.

"I'm not picking that up, so don't even think about throwing it," Conner's partner and friend, Seth Harrington, said without looking up from his desk.

Conner looked at the file in his hand, then set it down. Maybe flying papers would make him feel better momentarily, but it wasn't worth the aftermath. He sighed. "This case, Seth. I swear I'm about to lose it over this case."

"I hear you, man. It's messed up."

It wasn't just the murders, although those were bad enough. Now the perp was taunting them.

Yesterday the San Francisco FBI field office had received another package. It was the same thing every time. The outside was a box addressed with an innocuous label—like a care package. Of course, innocent-looking or not, each had gone through the extensive FBI bomb scannings and toxic screenings. There was nothing dangerous in any of the packages.

Every delivery was box after box, wrapped in plain brown paper, nested inside each other like one of those Russian dolls. Every time, inside the smallest box, Conner and his team had found a lock of a woman's hair.

And every time, the dead body matching the hair had been found a few days later.

The packages also contained a handwritten note, in third person, with the killer referring to himself as Simon. As if this was all a game of Simon Says.

"Simon says, the FBI is too slow."

"Simon says, you should try harder."

"Simon says, uh-oh, there goes another one."

They had kept all info about the packages from the public, knowing it would cause more of a panic. But around the San Francisco field office, the killer was known as "Simon Says."

There was no doubt about it: this pervert was calling the shots. The game was consistent. The FBI received a package—with zero helpful forensic evidence—then ran around for the next couple of days trying to figure out where the woman was being held with only the city in the return address to go on.

They were always too late. A body would be found somewhere; usually local law enforcement would call it in, and the Bureau would rush to the address. The crime scene, just like the packages, would hold zero helpful forensic evidence.

And then the game would start all over again.

Conner and Seth worked in the FBI's ViCAP division—Violent Criminal Apprehension Program—a subdivision of the Bureau's Behavioral Analysis Unit. Their job was to help law enforcement agencies apprehend violent criminals through investigative analysis. They were the best of the best.

But this killer was always one step ahead of them.

"Perigo, Harrington, my office."

Upon hearing his division chief's words, Conner rubbed his eyes wearily then glanced over to find Harrington looking at him, shaking his head. A trip to Division Chief Logan Kelly's office was never good. The two partners grabbed their notebooks and headed down the hall. The chief took his chair behind his desk and motioned for them to have a seat in the chairs across from him.

"I have spent the entire morning fielding calls. The governor. The deputy director. Even a city councilman. Everybody wants to know the same thing. Where are we on the Simon Says investigation?"

Conner and Seth didn't answer. Chief Kelly knew full well where they were in this investigation: nowhere.

"It's getting a little tiresome explaining over and over that we've got absolutely nothing on this psycho, despite our best efforts."

Conner couldn't agree more, although he didn't say so out loud.

The chief continued, "After talking with the deputy

director this morning, we've decided to pull in some independent contractors to help on the case."

Conner sat up a little straighter in his chair, as did Seth. "Independent contractors, sir? What type?" They had already brought in some outside help on the case—in particular, handwriting experts for the letters. What else could Chief Kelly have in mind?

"Actually we have just one specifically in mind. We want to bring in a...nontraditional profiling expert."

Conner glanced at Seth to find him looking as confused as Conner felt. Why would the department bring in an outsider for profiling? Despite what popular media suggested, there was no actual profiler position at the FBI. All agents were trained in profiling. But just like in all other training—hand-to-hand combat, weapons, languages—an agent could excel at profiling.

Conner and Seth were decent profilers, although both had other specialties. Rarely did the Bureau bring in outsiders unless it was for something very specific. They didn't know enough about Simon Says to bring in someone specific.

And what the hell did Kelly mean by "nontraditional"?

Conner leaned forward. "You and the deputy director have someone specific in mind, sir?"

"Yes, Perigo, we do. Have you ever heard of a profiling expert named Adrienne Jeffries?"

"No." Conner looked over at Seth, who shook his head.

"Perhaps you've heard of the Bloodhound?"

Now Seth spoke up. "Well, yeah, everybody has heard of her. She worked for the Bureau, what? Fifteen, twenty years ago? Had some sort of superpower or something. Could sense and track evil—I don't know. Something like that."

Conner barely refrained from rolling his eyes. Superpowers? Seriously? Didn't they have more important things to do than talk about FBI urban legends from decades ago?

"Adrienne Jeffries last worked for us eight years ago." Chief Kelly pushed a thin file across his desk toward Conner and Seth. "She was hands down the most gifted profiler any of us had ever seen. We want to bring her back in to help with the case."

Conner shrugged, grabbing the file and giving it to his partner without even looking at it. "No offense, Chief, but we have more important things to do than chase down a woman who has been out of the game for a decade."

Seth backed him up. "Yeah, Chief. If she's such a great profiler and can do everything the legend says, why isn't she still on the Bureau's payroll?"

"Ms. Jeffries cut ties with the FBI eight years ago after working with us for two years. During her tenure she was directly accredited with providing critical leads for thirty-seven criminal apprehensions. All over the country. Every team she worked with listed Jeffries as their number one asset and direct link to the arrests."

Seth whistled through his teeth. Conner had to agree. Thirty-seven cases solved in two years was unheard of. It also begged the question: With that success rate, why had she only worked for the FBI for such a short time?

"Why did she quit?" Conner asked.

The older man glanced away for a moment then looked back at Conner. "She decided working with the FBI was not what she wanted to do."

Conner reached over to grab the file Seth was hand-

ing to him. He opened it and took a brief glance. There
was no picture of Adrienne Jeffries, and half the file
was blacked out with thick black lines—making reading the information behind the lines impossible.

Someone very high in the FBI did not want much
known about the Bloodhound. Conner couldn't help but
be suspicious about so many black marks through a file.
Somebody wasn't telling the whole story.

"So for eight years nobody has brought the Bloodhound back in to assist in cases?" Seth asked. "It's been
so long, I think everyone just assumed she was dead or
too old or not even real to begin with."

"No, she's alive, definitely not too old and very real.
We've contacted her a few times over the years, to see
if she would resume her contract work, but have been
met with a resounding *no* as her answer." Chief Kelly's
eyes were cold.

"Why?" Conner looked down at the blacked-out file
again. Something was not right in this situation. Not that
Conner believed in any of the hocus-pocus junk that
surrounded the Bloodhound's reputation. In Conner's
opinion cases were solved by hard work and sometimes
a little bit of luck, not by superpowers.

"She says she's...not interested in renewing her
working agreement with the FBI."

Both Conner and Seth caught the slight hesitation in
the chief's statement, but neither said anything.

"Ms. Jeffries has been more interested in maintain-
ing her horse ranch near Lodi."

She was much closer than Conner anticipated. Lodi
was only about two hours east of San Francisco. Quite a
few vineyards out there and farms, too. And a whole lot
of empty space. Definitely a good place for a horse ranch.

"What makes you think she'll be interested in helping us now, if she hasn't been willing to help before?" Conner asked. Obviously the woman was pretty cold, if she was as good as they said she was, but refused to help. Another reason not to waste time on her in Conner's opinion.

"Her circumstances have changed in the past year."

"Does she need money?" Seth asked. Being broke caused many a change of heart.

"No. She hired a convicted felon as her ranch manager almost a year ago."

Conner leaned back in his chair, confused. "Are they doing something illegal?"

"No, nothing like that," the chief said. "Her ranch manager, Rick Vincent, was convicted in the mid-1970s for breaking and entering. Did three years, was released. Everything was fine. But he missed his last parole hearing for whatever reason. Warrant's been out for him since '79."

Conner frowned. "Sorry, Chief, but I don't understand what this has to do with anything. If Vincent hasn't been arrested since that incident in the '70s, never had any run-ins with the law at all since then, it doesn't seem like he would pose much threat to Ms. Jeffries now."

The chief tilted his head. "No, we're not worried about him being a threat to her. Reports indicate they are actually pretty friendly with each other."

Conner frowned over at Seth. *Reports indicate?* What was going on here?

Seth shrugged, obviously as confused as Conner.

"Reports, sir?" Conner asked. "Has she been under surveillance?"

"Not surveillance, exactly. Just attempts on our part, from time to time, to get her to return and provide profiling assistance." The chief looked down at his desk and began reorganizing papers, obviously not wanting to provide too much information about the reports or meetings with Ms. Jeffries.

It was damn strange, if anyone asked Conner. He waited for the chief to get to the point he was so long in coming to.

Chief Kelly finally looked up from his desk. "I want you to go out to Adrienne Jeffries's horse ranch and ask for her help with the case. And if she says no, then I want you to use the arrest of Rick Vincent as a threat to get her cooperation."

It was all Conner could do to keep from jumping out of his chair. He heard Seth make some sort of incredulous sound next to him. *"What?* Chief, that's pretty much blackmail."

The chief's eyes narrowed. "No, Perigo. It's doing your job. She has a criminal on her property, and you need to bring him in."

"A nonviolent criminal with a B&E rap from more than thirty years ago. No law enforcement agency would waste the gas out to Lodi to pick up Vincent!" Seth exclaimed. He didn't like this any more than Conner.

"Rick Vincent is not the primary objective here, obviously. Adrienne Jeffries's cooperation is."

"Chief…" Conner's cajoling tone was cut off before he could get a second word out.

"Perigo, I get it. You don't like the tactics. Fine, they're not my favorite, either. But how many more women are you willing to let die, when we have a known tool at our disposal? A tool proven to get results?"

Conner sat in silence. He didn't agree with Chief Kelly's orders. Hell, he didn't even believe Adrienne

Jeffries could possibly be as useful as everyone said. But regardless, if it meant catching Simon Says and saving even one woman's life, he was willing to try.

"All right, Chief. We'll go see her tomorrow morning."

A few hours later, long after the office began emptying and most of the other agents were gone, Conner and Seth sat at their desks. Conner reached into his bottom drawer and pulled out a toy baseball made of a foamy material. He leaned back in his chair and put his feet on the desk, tossing the ball up in the air and catching it on its way back down. Seth saw him and leaned back in his own chair.

They had spent every moment since leaving Chief Kelly's office going back over the details of the Simon Says case. They had read through the testimony of local law enforcement again, pored over the lives of the victims to see if they could find any commonalities once more, reviewed crime scene video footage and photos additionally, as well.

It had led to nothing.

Conner had hoped to find something—anything—that would keep them from having to bring in Adrienne Jeffries tomorrow. He wasn't interested in her help, and he wasn't comfortable with the means they were using to get it.

Conner tossed the ball over to Seth. "This whole Adrienne Jeffries thing just doesn't feel right, if you ask me."

Seth caught the ball easily. "Chief Kelly seems legitimately convinced that she can help us."

"Yeah."

"But you don't think so."

"I think this is a waste of time. I think this lady was probably hot back in the day, and maybe she and Kelly had a relationship or something."

"You think she snowed him." Seth tossed the ball back.

"Look, I'm really not trying to talk bad about anybody, but I don't believe in mind reading or telepathy or superheroes to solve cases."

And dragging some middle-aged woman from her *horse farm* in the middle of Nowhere, California, into a case of this magnitude was not Conner's idea of good situational management. Conner threw the ball to Seth.

"You know, there have been documented cases of nontraditional methods actually working."

Conner dragged a hand through his black hair making it even more scruffy-looking than usual. "I don't even want to hear it, Harrington. I'm pissed. I'm pissed that we're wasting time going all the way out there."

"As opposed to doing what?" Seth interjected. "Sitting around the office waiting for the perp to drop off another package?"

Conner leaned his head back and closed his eyes, sighing. Seth had a point. If this lady could help them break open the case in some way, Conner would take it. But he planned to be very careful about what info she was given. He wasn't sure if she had tricked Chief Kelly and the other agents in some way before, but she damn well wouldn't fool Conner.

"Fine," Conner said. "But I would just like it stated, for the record, that I am going there under direct orders. I do not believe this to be the most effective use of our time."

Seth nodded. "Duly noted, counselor." He tossed the ball back to Conner.

Conner laid the ball on his desk and picked up Adrienne Jeffries's ridiculously short and useless file. When he had tried to run her info in the Bureau's computer system, the same thing happened. Somebody pretty high up in the FBI—maybe even higher than Chief Kelly—was protecting her or hiding something. There was no picture, no physical description of the woman, no mention of her ability and definitely no use of the word *bloodhound*.

By looking at her file, she could've been one of thousands of contractors who had worked as support staff for the FBI. Everything from janitorial to catering, clerking to photographing, were hired out each year. Every single one of those people had a file at the Bureau.

The fact that so much was blacked out in Adrienne Jeffries's file was an immediate giveaway that she was no clerk or anything so benign. Basically her name and the years she'd worked for the Bureau were the only info the file provided.

It was what wasn't provided that concerned Conner. If she was such a gifted profiler, why wasn't Jeffries helping the FBI anymore? What type of person would turn their back on an ability like that, if it would save lives? A cold and uncaring one, to be sure.

And why the heck had she been under "not surveillance, exactly"? Contract workers quit the FBI all the time. Most were not being watched by the Bureau, as far as Conner knew. But this woman was, at least partially.

There was something not right about this situation and this woman. The one thing of which Conner was confident was that he did not have all the data. He loosened the top button of his shirt under his tie and grabbed the ball again, tossing it to Seth.

Conner did not like going into any situation blind. But it seemed like he didn't have much choice in this case. They would bring the woman in, as he had been ordered, glean any useful info, if any, and then would get back to real work.

This was a waste of his time.

Chapter Two

The next morning, as they arrived at Adrienne Jeffries's ranch, Conner was even more certain this trip was a waste of time. He could admit to himself that the ranch was picturesque among the rolling hills in Lodi but still resented having to come here. A modest-sized house sat in the middle of multiple corralled areas. A barn—at least the same size as the house, maybe even a bit bigger—sat a few hundred yards back from the house.

"Let's get this over with," Conner muttered.

They parked and walked up the three worn steps to the wraparound porch. Although the porch and its furniture was well kept, everything was obviously old and secondhand. Conner knocked on a door that could use another coat of paint. No one answered.

"Let's try the barn," Seth suggested, heading back down the steps.

That the barn was in a much better state than the house seemed to be immediately evident. Well maintained, organized, all repairs up-to-date. Evidently any money the horse ranch made went back into the barn first.

Conner could hear a man talking inside the barn, although couldn't make sense of what he was saying. Both Conner and Seth were immediately on alert.

"Hello in the barn! This is FBI Special Agents Conner Perigo and Seth Harrington," Conner called.

The talking immediately stopped, but there was no response.

"Sir? We're looking for a Ms. Adrienne Jeffries. We would like to come in the barn."

A muttered curse, then what sounded like chewing tobacco being spit. "Fine. Come on in," the man in the barn finally replied.

"Sir, is it just you in the barn?" Seth asked as he and Conner entered slowly.

"Yes."

"Are you sure? We heard you talking to someone."

"Yeah, I was talking to Willie Nelson, but I'm pretty sure he's not going to be talking back anytime soon."

Willie Nelson? Conner and Seth glanced at each other again as they walked farther in, both with hands near their weapons. As their eyes adjusted to the dimness of the barn, Conner saw the man was referring to a horse he was brushing inside a stall.

The man was in his mid-sixties, short and wiry. As he walked around the horse, Conner noticed he moved with a limp in his left leg. This had to be Rick Vincent.

"I'm Agent Perigo. This is Agent Harrington. We're from the FBI."

"Yeah, I heard you the first time." The older man was obviously not a big fan of law enforcement. "I'm busy."

"We're looking for Ms. Jeffries, sir. She owns this ranch, correct?" Seth asked, moving a couple steps to the left, subtly blocking the exit, should the older man try to run.

"Yeah, she owns it. She's not here right now."

"Not here on the ranch or not here in the barn?" Conner asked when the man didn't offer any more info.

"She's off riding one of the horses."

"And may we ask your name, sir?" Although they already knew.

"Vincent. Rick Vincent," the man offered after a hesitation. Conner could see he was trying to judge how much they knew about him.

"You work here, Mr. Vincent?" Conner asked.

"Just Vincent. Yeah, I work here. I'm the ranch manager."

"How long have you worked here?" Seth asked.

"Just about a year now."

"Ms. Jeffries owned the place the entire time?"

Conner let Seth ask the questions while Conner observed the man and the barn. They already knew the answers, but they could learn a lot by what someone was willing to lie about.

"Yeah."

"Just you and her working here?"

"Yeah. Although we get some kids from the 4-H Club who come in on weekends and stuff like that. And some horticultural students from the local community college every once in a while."

"May I get your address, Vincent? Just in case we need to talk to you again after we speak to Ms. Jeffries."

Vincent paused so long Conner thought he might not answer at all. "I live in the house here."

Conner glanced at Seth with an eyebrow raised. "So you live with Ms. Jeffries in the house?" *Interesting.*

"Yes."

"And it's just the two of you?"

"It's not like what you boys are thinking. We both

live in the house, but it's not like that." Vincent glared
at them both, then spat to the side again.

*Okay, maybe not romantic, but protective. Still in-
teresting.*

Seth seemed about to ask another question when a
female voice from outside the barn interrupted him.

"Vince! I officially love Ruby Tuesday! I so hope
the owners end up boarding her here. Maybe I should
offer a discount just so I can see this pretty girl all the
time." A burst of joyful laughter drew Conner's focus.

The woman's voice faded as she started talking to the
horse, obviously common practice around here.

A moment later a woman in her mid-twenties—
probably one of the college students Vincent had mentioned—led Ruby Tuesday into the barn. She stopped,
noticeably shocked when she saw Conner and Seth. She
looked at Vincent with concern then rubbed her head
and took a few steps back.

"You okay, kiddo?" Vincent asked.

The young woman looked almost panicked. Conner
stepped toward her with his arms held out in a soothing
manner. "We didn't mean to startle you, miss. My name
is Agent Perigo. This is Agent Harrington."

"You're FBI," she stammered out, still panicky. Did
everyone here have an aversion to the FBI?

Conner smiled and tried to reassure the young
woman. "Yes. We're actually looking for Adrienne Jeffries. Mr. Vincent said she was riding. Did you happen
to see her while you were out?"

The woman took a deep breath and rubbed her head
again. She looked at Vincent, then back at Conner. But
she didn't respond.

Seth decided to take a shot. "We can assure you Ms.

Jeffries isn't in any trouble. We were just hoping to talk to her for a bit."

The young woman took a couple of breaths and seemed to compose herself. "Okay."

Seth looked at Conner, who shrugged, then asked, "Okay, what?"

"Okay, I'm here. You can talk to me."

Conner could feel the shock rolling over him. This *could not* be the Adrienne Jeffries they were supposed to contact. She was too young, with her pixie-short hair and big brown eyes.

She was too damn beautiful.

"No." Conner denied it before he could help himself. "Your mom, maybe? Is there another Adrienne Jeffries at this address?"

The young woman sighed and shook her head. "Nope, just me." She led the horse over to Vincent and gave him the reins. "Let's go inside the house to talk. I think we'll be more comfortable."

"I'll come, too," Vincent was quick to interject.

Conner watched as Adrienne laid a gentle hand on the older man's arm. Obviously the protectiveness went both ways. He felt a little guilty that they were about to use that protectiveness against her.

"I'm fine, Vince, I promise." Adrienne smiled at Vincent then turned to look directly at Conner. "If they're FBI, I know why they're here."

There was definitely no smile when she said that. Vincent was obviously reluctant but agreed.

Adrienne Jeffries silently walked out of the barn, leaving Conner and Seth to follow, or just as obviously not to follow. They made their way behind her wordlessly. Conner couldn't help admiring how well she filled out her worn jeans as she walked ahead of them.

They obviously weren't designer jeans, but who the hell cared if she looked like that in them?

Seth reached over and nudged him with his elbow.

"What?" Conner whispered, reluctantly drawing his eyes away from Adrienne's jeans.

"I don't have a *hankie* so I'm offering you my sleeve."

"What the hell are you talking about?"

"To wipe the drool from your mouth, man. You missed some."

Conner thought just a moment about gut-punching his partner before reaching the house but decided it wasn't worth it. He wasn't *drooling,* for God's sake.

But his eyes were drawn back to her jeans one more time.

Adrienne Jeffries was definitely not some middle-aged woman who had worked for the Bureau a decade ago. Something was not adding up between what Chief Logan Kelly had told them and what Conner was seeing with his own eyes.

If she had been the Bloodhound for the FBI, then she would have been a teenager when it had happened. He knew that couldn't be right. Something did not fit in this situation.

Adrienne made her way through the back door, not gesturing for the men to follow, but at least not slamming the door behind her. Conner and Seth followed her and found themselves in the kitchen. The room, like everything else they'd seen on the ranch—the front porch, the steps, the barn, *her jeans*—Conner quickly pushed that thought away—was clean but worn.

Adrienne crossed over to the sink, filled a glass with water and drank it down without stopping. Only afterward did she place the glass on the counter and turn to face them.

"Have a seat." She gestured to the four chairs at the kitchen table. Conner took one and Seth took the one across from him.

Adrienne stayed where she was with her back against the sink counter. She didn't offer them a drink or any food. Nor did she offer them any information. She didn't exactly glare, but her gaze definitely wasn't inviting. Conner reclined in his chair and returned the almost hostile look.

If this was the way she wanted to play it, that's how he would play it.

Seth noticed Conner's angry expression and sighed. They had played Good Cop–Bad Cop many times over the years, but it was usually Conner who was the good cop. He had a way of putting people at ease when he wanted to. But looking at the woman staring at him so haughtily, Conner had no desire to play good cop today.

"Ms. Jeffries," Seth took over, "we'd like to ask you a few questions about your…contract work for the FBI."

"What about it?" Adrienne spoke to Seth but continued to glare at Conner. Conner glared back.

Seth sighed again. "Can you tell us the nature of the work you did for the Bureau?"

Adrienne finally looked over at Seth, her stance softening a bit. "Why don't you tell me what you know, and I'll fill in some gaps."

Conner cut in. "How old are you?"

The glare was back at him now. "Didn't your mother ever teach you that is a rude question? Besides, I'm sure you have a fancy FBI file on me with that sort of information."

Seth smiled engagingly. "You'd be surprised at how sparse your file is."

Some of the heat left Adrienne's eyes. "I'm twenty-eight."

Conner shook his head. That could not be right. "Are you sure?" he demanded more gruffly than he intended. He heard Seth sigh again.

"Am I sure?" All the hostility was back. "Am I sure how old I am? Wait, let me get out all my fingers and toes so I'm sure I haven't miscounted."

"I didn't mean that. I just mean, now is not the time to lie about your age for vanity's sake or some such nonsense."

"I am quite sure of how old I am and have no need to lie about it. Twenty-eight."

Seth jumped in, obviously trying to instill some reason into the situation. "I think what my partner means, Ms. Jeffries, is that, if you are twenty-eight years old and worked for the FBI ten years ago, that would've made you pretty young."

Adrienne looked away but not before Conner saw shadows looming in her eyes. "Let's just say the FBI made a special exception in my case." She walked over and got her wallet from a purse hanging on a wall hook. She took out her driver's license and threw it down on top of the table.

"Twenty-eight." Seth glanced at it then slid the license over to Conner.

She wasn't lying. He supposed the ID could be forged, but it didn't seem like there was much purpose to it.

That meant she had been *eighteen years old* when she'd been the Bloodhound for the FBI. No wonder all the information was blacked out in that damn file.

"Still rude to ask," Adrienne muttered under her breath from back at her perch at the sink.

Conner knew he should apologize but couldn't bring himself to do it. Twenty-eight or not, this woman was getting under his skin.

Seth attempted to start again. "Obviously there's a lot we don't know, Ms. Jeffries. If you would be willing to help us fill in the holes, this would probably be a lot easier on all of us."

"Please, call me Adrienne, Agent Harrington." The invitation was very obviously not extended to Conner.

"Thanks, Adrienne. And you're welcome to call me Seth." She smiled sweetly at Seth, and Conner thought he might have to jump out of his chair and stand between the two of them. Neither of them seemed to notice his strange behavior, thank God. He needed to calm the hell down.

"Could you tell us what you did for the FBI?" Seth asked her with a smile that had Conner ready to jump up again.

Calm. Down. What in the world was the matter with him?

"I'm sure you've heard rumors. I have a special talent. I can profile evil very well."

Seth nodded. "Exactly how did you use your talent to help the Bureau?"

"The closer I am to a person with malicious intent, the more clearly I can sense what the person is thinking. And I don't have to be near the actual person. I can be around something he or she has touched or been near and be able to 'read' the evil."

"Bloodhound," Conner muttered under his breath, shaking his head. He still didn't believe any of it.

"Yes, it's an accurate description, I suppose." Adrienne's smile was rueful. "Although I was glad nobody ever called me that to my face. Teenage girls don't respond well to being told they're like a dog."

Conner still did not like this teenager talk. He planned to have a discussion about Adrienne with Chief Kelly as soon as possible.

"So you're a psychic? Or an empath or something like that?" Harrington asked gently, although his doubts crept into his tone.

"No, not really. I don't have superpowers. I can't read people's minds or anything. I don't feel what other people are feeling. Like, if you were sad right now, I wouldn't feel your sadness. Really it's just evil I feel, malicious intent. It's kind of like they draw me into their thoughts."

"Why? How?" Conner didn't attempt to hide his incredulity at all.

"I don't know. Some people are terribly sensitive to heat or light. My brain is just sensitive to negative energy."

"Do you feel it about everybody?"

"No. Most people aren't menacing. They can be catty and rude, but usually it's due to their own insecurity rather than actual malevolence."

"So how do you 'sense' it? Do you see images? Have visions?" Seth asked.

"Hear little voices in your head?" Conner tagged on.

Adrienne ignored Conner. "The closer I am to the person—in terms of physical proximity—the clearer I can sense everything. From far away it's like seeing and hearing through multiple panes of glass—difficult to make out the details. If I am close, it's like being inside someone's head. I can see and hear everything."

Conner didn't believe any of this. "So what if I want you to demonstrate your 'powers'? Can you do that?"

Adrienne's irritated gaze swung around to Conner again. "Not really."

"Well, that's pretty convenient, isn't it?" Conner snapped.

More glaring was shared between Adrienne and Conner. "It's not a dog and pony show, Special Agent Jackass."

That got a snicker from Seth.

"And no offense, but I don't owe you anything."

Conner stood up before he was even aware of what he was doing and took a step toward Adrienne. What was it about this one tiny woman that made him feel like he was about to jump out of his own skin?

Fortunately Seth waylaid him before he had a chance to… Conner had no idea what he would've done when he reached Adrienne.

"Adrienne, can you excuse us for a moment? I need to discuss a text I just received with Agent Perigo out on the porch."

Seth grabbed Conner's arm—hard—and began pushing him through the small living room and out the front door.

"What?" Conner barked at him the moment the door was closed.

"You're asking *me* what?" There was obviously no text Seth wanted to show him. "I was just wondering if you wanted to arrest her. Maybe you've got her fingered as our killer."

"What?" Conner felt like a parrot.

"Well, the way you've been treating her, Agent *Jackass,* is like she's a perp, or at the very least some sort of hostile witness."

Conner rubbed his hand over his face wearily. Everything Harrington was saying was true.

"I don't know what the hell's the matter with me, Seth."

"I don't know either, but you've got to get yourself under control. She's not the bad guy here."

"I know."

"You think this is a waste of time, Con, I get that. And to be honest, I don't know what to believe, either. But if what she's saying—what Chief Kelly said—is true…"

"Then it could really be the break in the case we've been hoping for," Conner finished for him.

"You don't like her, for whatever reason. Fine. But let's see what she can do."

Conner almost corrected Seth but stopped. It wasn't that he didn't like Adrienne Jeffries—he hadn't made up his mind whether he liked the little spitfire or not. But liking or disliking didn't really seem to matter. He was *affected* by her. And it made him damn uncomfortable.

"All right, I'll behave."

Seth looked relieved. "Good."

They walked back through the door and into the kitchen.

"Saving the world one text at a time?" Adrienne asked with one brow cocked. She had taken a seat at the table in the chair farthest away from where Conner had been sitting.

"Something like that." Seth smiled.

Conner didn't say anything. He figured opening his mouth would just get him in trouble.

"You two must be on some pretty big case for the FBI to put you at my doorstep after all these years."

"We are. It's gruesome," Seth informed her.

"And you were told I could help."

Both men nodded.

Adrienne continued. "And when they sent you out here to bring me back, did they warn you I would tell you to go screw yourselves?"

Chapter Three

Adrienne could not believe it was all happening again.

She would not let the FBI just walk in and take over her life. She was older now, wiser. And she knew the toll using her gift to help the FBI would take. She had lived through it before.

Barely.

She knew Special Agent Friendly and his sidekick Special Agent Hot-But-Annoying sitting at her kitchen table really had no idea what her gifts were or what her life had been like ten years ago when she had worked for the Bureau.

Worked. Adrienne barely restrained a bark of laughter. More like *duped and manipulated.*

She knew Agent Hot, *excuse me,* Agent *Perigo* was particularly skeptical. Adrienne wasn't offended by that. But there was something about him that made her slightly crazy. She had spent the past twenty minutes itching to slap the alternating smug and hostile looks off his face. Either that or jump his bones.

Adrienne had been downright shocked when she had returned Ruby Tuesday to the barn and found the two men standing there with Vincent. Whenever someone unfamiliar was around, Adrienne could always sense it.

Unless they had some sort of malevolent side, she couldn't see their thoughts, but everyone—good or bad—gave off some sort of buzz that she picked up on in her brain. With familiar people she had learned to ignore it, the way someone ignores the slight sound a computer or TV makes when it's on but has no volume. Just the slightest buzz. The more people that were around, the louder the buzz.

But Adrienne had heard nothing when she had walked into the barn. That's why she had been so shocked to see the agents—she hadn't heard their buzz.

Nothing. As a matter of fact, she still couldn't hear it.

But they were here, and they wanted her help. She couldn't afford to help them. The best thing she could do, she knew, was be cold and turn them away. But looking at Agent Perigo, she knew turning them away would not be easy.

"Guys, I appreciate that you've come all the way out here. But Chief Kelly shouldn't have sent you. Whatever your case is, I can't help you."

"Adrienne…" Agent Harrington began in a cajoling tone.

"Can't or won't?" Perigo interrupted Harrington and got right to the point.

The urge to slap Perigo was itching its way through Adrienne's palm again. "I have responsibilities here."

"The FBI would more than compensate you for your time. Plus, don't you have Vincent to run things for you if you're gone?" Perigo continued.

"It's not just that," Adrienne backpedaled.

"Then what is it, Adrienne?" Seth asked in a concerned voice. He sounded completely sincere. Adrienne wondered for a moment if he practiced that voice.

"There's a discomfort that comes with using my

gift." That was putting it ridiculously mildly. "Plus, like I said, I can't—or am not willing to—uproot my life. I'm needed here."

Adrienne watched as the two men looked at each other across the table, communicating without speaking. Obviously there was a plan B, although it looked as though both of them found the thought of it distasteful.

"Adrienne, we were sent here by our superiors with a directive to obtain your cooperation in our case." Agent Harrington paused, but she knew his statement wasn't finished. She didn't have long to wait. "By any means available to us."

Adrienne looked at Harrington, then Agent Perigo, confused. "'Any means available?' Are you planning on making me leave the ranch at gunpoint?"

"No. Nothing so drastic, I assure you," Harrington responded with a smile. "But our instructions are to either bring you back with us or bring in your ranch manager, Mr. Vincent."

"Why Vince? What does he have to do with this?"

Agent Perigo interjected, "Do you make a practice of hiring and cohabiting with convicted felons or fugitives on your ranch?"

"What?" Adrienne expressed her shock before she could help herself. Not a good logistical move.

"So you're unaware of Mr. Vincent's past history and that he is currently wanted in the state of Nevada for parole violation?"

Adrienne shook her head. "I knew he had some trouble with the law a while ago. But he never offered much information about it, and I never asked."

Harrington leaned toward her. "Isn't it dangerous to work and live with a man you know so little about?"

Adrienne smiled grimly. She had never been concerned about her safety with Vince—she had known from the beginning he meant her no harm. That was one of the few good things about her gift. "Let's just say that my talent makes me an excellent judge of character. Vince would never harm me."

Agent Perigo sighed. "Regardless. Our instructions are clear. We're either to bring you in or bring Rick Vincent in. You choose."

Adrienne could feel temper rising up through her body. Obviously nobody in the FBI had changed in the past decade. They still didn't care who they used—or used up—to get what they wanted.

"Common blackmail? Is that what the FBI has resorted to?" It was all she could do to keep her fist from banging down on the table.

Harrington reached a hand out toward her, but she jerked back in her seat. "Ms. Jeffries."

At least he had the sense to revert to last names if they were going to use blackmail.

"We have to uphold the law. There is a warrant out for Mr. Vincent's arrest."

"That you will conveniently overlook if I agree to help the FBI on the case."

Agent Harrington cleared his throat. "Let's just say, if we had your help on the case, we would probably be so busy, we may totally forget we even saw Rick Vincent here."

Adrienne was too angry to say anything. She did not want to be forced back into helping the FBI but couldn't stand the thought of Vincent going to prison. The older man had no evil in him whatsoever. Whatever crime he had committed, it was in a past far behind him. Now he was kind and helpful and wonderful with the horses, if a little gruff with people.

They sat in silence for long moments. Adrienne had no idea what the FBI agents were thinking, but they wisely did not give voice to their thoughts. She glanced at Harrington first but found him looking down at his hands. She then glanced over at Agent Perigo with hesitation, unsure of what she would find.

He met her eyes directly. Instead of the hostility she had expected to see, she found sincerity and the slightest hint of compassion. No matter what he thought of her abilities, or her personally, he obviously found this stalemate distasteful.

And he had the most gorgeous green eyes she had ever seen. Just the slightest hint of gold in them. For the first time Adrienne wished she had met Agent Perigo under different circumstances. Wished he didn't work for an organization that was sure to leave her broken by the time this was all over.

Adrienne looked away from Agent Perigo's piercing eyes and down at her kitchen table. She couldn't see any way out of this. She wasn't going to let anything happen to Vincent, as long as there were any other options. Plus she was older now, wiser, more able to protect herself from the FBI. Because she had no doubt that what had happened before, ten years ago, would happen again if she wasn't careful. The solution was making sure it didn't repeat itself.

Of course she had no idea how to do that.

She looked up from the scarred kitchen table, hoping she didn't resemble it by the time this was all over.

"Okay, fine. I'll help you."

An hour later, just before lunch, Adrienne watched Agents Perigo and Harrington drive away. She had been given instructions about where and when to report tomorrow, and had assured them she would be there.

Then, just before leaving, Agent Perigo made a special trip out to the barn to say goodbye to Vincent. All for Adrienne's benefit.

Jackass. Obviously, she had been mistaken about any compassion she had seen in him.

Vince immediately knew something was up.

"That FBI agent came out to the barn to say goodbye to me," the older man stated as he washed his hands for lunch. "Seemed a mite odd."

Adrienne rolled her eyes. "Yeah, I know. If it helps, I think it was a gesture meant for me, not you."

"We never really talked much about you working for the FBI."

Adrienne began making each of them a sandwich. "I worked for them briefly years ago. It wasn't a pleasant experience. Not something I discuss much."

"I've found, in my general experience, that anything having to do with law enforcement is not a pleasant experience."

Adrienne smiled at that. Although her and Vince's experiences with law enforcement were different, the resulting feelings were the same.

"And now they want you to come back and work for them again?" the older man asked.

Adrienne slapped mustard onto the sandwich and rubbed it around with more force than necessary. "That pretty much sums it up."

"But you don't want to go back to work for them."

"My life is here. My responsibilities are here." More mustard was slapped on the other piece of bread.

"Well now, you know I can handle everything around here if you needed to go off somewhere. This place isn't so big that one person can't hold down the fort for a while. You did it for long enough before I came along."

"I know you can handle it, Vince. I'm not sure what I would've done without you for the past year." She smiled gently at him.

The older man blushed and looked away. Nothing thrilled Vince less than talking about feelings, Adrienne knew.

"Vince, I know you had trouble with the law in your past, but I've known from the beginning that you were someone I could trust. Whatever happened in the past isn't important to me. You've been a godsend." She handed him a sandwich.

"Well, you know that goes both ways." Vince took a big bite of his sandwich and chewed thoughtfully. "Why do I get the feeling all of this conversation has to do with those FBI agents?"

Adrienne sighed. "It looks like I'm going to need you to keep things afloat for me here for a little bit."

"While you go help the FBI."

"Yeah."

"What exactly do you, or did you do, for them?"

Adrienne pushed her sandwich around on her plate. How was she supposed to explain this? "I guess I was kind of a profiler for them."

Vince grunted in agreement the way he often did. He didn't look at all surprised. "I figured it was something like that, given your…" He waved his hand in circles above his head.

Adrienne was shocked. She had no idea Vince was aware of her gift. They had never talked about it. "You knew?"

"Not at first. As a matter of fact, when you initially hired me, I thought you were a little reckless. What woman hires someone completely unknown, then invites him a few weeks later to move into the house with her?"

"Vince, you were sleeping out in the barn!"

"I know, I know. Don't get me wrong. I am grateful for your invite. But I could've been dangerous." Vince shook his head.

"I knew you weren't."

Vince grunted in agreement again. "Then I saw over the next few months how patient you were with almost everybody. Even some of the brattiest or angriest kids who came out here to work. You were always kind and gentle, when I wanted to throw some of them out on their ears."

Vince put down his sandwich and looked Adrienne right in the eye. "Then that blond guy showed up last July. He seemed polite and charming. All the college girls were sighing over him and his good looks. You came out of the house, glanced at him for five seconds, and asked him to leave and never come back."

Adrienne remembered very clearly the appearance of the young man, probably twenty or twenty-one years old. Like Vince said, he had blond hair, blue eyes—all-American good looks. Seemed amiable and charismatic, at least on the outside.

But the thoughts in his mind were utterly sinister. A malevolence that only Adrienne could pick up on had permeated the air around the young man. The things he thought of doing to the female students who had worked at Adrienne's ranch—to Adrienne herself, once he had seen her—made Adrienne's stomach churn. She had immediately made him leave, much to the girls' dismay, telling him there were no more internships available.

Then had promptly gone back inside and vomited the entire contents of her stomach.

The next day Adrienne had gone into town to check with the sheriff's office to see if there were any warrants out for the man or any reported attacks on women in the area. There were none. Adrienne decided to leave it alone—after all, she had no idea if he would ever act on any of those evil instincts floating around in his brain. Perhaps not. But either way she did not want him around her ranch or the young people she had working there. Thankfully they never saw him again.

Adrienne looked at Vince. "Yeah. I remember him."

"I don't know why you sent him away. I don't know why you made him—a good, clean-cut-looking kid— leave when you had hired some of the roughest-looking tattooed hoodlums multiple times. Hell, I'd seen you *make* jobs for people when we didn't need another soul."

"He just wasn't a good fit for our ranch."

"It's your ranch, and you can certainly hire or not hire anyone you see fit. But you not even giving that kid a chance—that kind of caught my attention."

Vince stood and walked his plate over to the sink, then continued. "I watched you after that when you were around people—especially new folk. It took a while, but I realized you have a sort of insight into people that most don't have."

Adrienne sat in silence as Vince rinsed his plate off, then turned to look at her. "It's probably more than just an insight if the FBI wants your help."

"A little. Especially when it comes to anyone who has some sort of sinister intent. I can kind of hear their thoughts." Adrienne was worried that she may be freaking Vince out, but he seemed to take it all in stride.

"Hmm. And you helped the FBI before?"

"Yes."

"You must have been pretty young."

"Barely eighteen."

Vince's eyes narrowed at that. "Hmm. And working with them wasn't a pleasant experience?"

"That's putting it mildly."

Vince nodded. "But you're going back to work for them?"

Adrienne looked away; she didn't want Vince to know he was the reason she was returning to work for the FBI. "Yeah."

"Even though you don't want to." It wasn't a question.

"Pretty much."

"And you told them you're not interested in helping?"

"I tried."

"But they didn't listen?"

"Evidently they need my help in a pretty big way. 'No' wasn't a possibility for an answer."

"Seems to me, living in this free country of ours, no is always a possibility in a situation like this."

Adrienne finished her sandwich and brought her plate to the sink so she wouldn't have to look at Vince. "Well, let's just say they made me an offer I couldn't refuse."

There was silence for long moments, and Adrienne made the mistake of looking over at the older man.

"If I told you," Vince began with a grimace, "I had missed my last few meetings with my parole officer after I left prison, and that there's a warrant out for my arrest, would this be new information to you?"

Adrienne looked back down at the plate she was washing. "I already told you, Vince. I don't care what happened in the past. I just know I can trust you now," she sidestepped.

Vince nodded. "But that's not what I asked you."

Adrienne sighed. "No, that info isn't new to me."

"Did you know this before today?"

Adrienne turned and looked the older man in the eye. "No. Agents Perigo and Harrington told me."

"And that's how they're getting you to come back, right? By using me?"

"Vince..." Adrienne reached toward him but he leaned back in his chair away from her.

"I won't let you do it, you understand? I'm not going to let you be forced into something because of me!"

"Vince, it's all right. I'm going to do this one thing for them, and that will be the end of it. And before I do, I'll get their assurance that the warrant for you will be canceled or whatever. I promise. It's not a big deal."

"I still don't like this," Vince muttered.

"Don't worry. I'm going to be fine. Maybe I'll find that the FBI has become a little better at playing with others in the past ten years."

Vince took a sip of his drink and sat back in the chair. "I wouldn't hold your breath."

Chapter Four

Hours later Conner lay sprawled in his bed looking up at the ceiling. After leaving Adrienne Jeffries's house, he had been pretty much useless for the rest of the day. They had gone back to the office for a couple of hours, briefly reporting to Chief Kelly about their success with getting Adrienne's agreement to help. Seth, well aware of Conner's black mood, had talked Conner out of questioning the chief about Adrienne's history with the FBI.

There were so many things about Adrienne Jeffries's history that didn't add up that Conner didn't know where to even begin his questioning. Definitely better to leave his questions until he was in a better— or at least more respectful—frame of mind. Maybe he would just talk to her and leave the chief out of it altogether. Less chance of Conner getting fired that way.

Adrienne definitely had not been what he was expecting. For one, her age. Certainly not the middle-aged woman he had been anticipating. But that wasn't even what caught him off guard so much. Conner ran his hands through his hair, staring up at the ceiling from his bed. He had never had such an instant reaction to a woman before. Adrienne Jeffries had affected him on every level.

She was five feet four of pure dynamite, it seemed. Conner normally preferred taller, more athletically built women—and with long blond hair. Adrienne Jeffries was slender, but short, and her hair definitely wasn't long and blond. Rather pixie-short and brown, with little chunks of copper in it. But Conner found his fingers itching to run through it.

He knew his behavior earlier today had been unprofessional and may have seemed borderline psychotic to Adrienne. Harrington had let Conner have it more than once on their way back to San Francisco from Lodi. Conner knew, whatever he was feeling, he had to get it under control before he saw her again in just a few short hours.

No matter what confusion Conner may have over his attraction to Adrienne, he had no confusion over his feelings about her so-called "abilities." Obviously years ago she had somehow convinced the Bureau she could track criminals like some supersleuth. Conner had no reason to believe she could do all that the FBI urban legends about her suggested she could do.

As far as he was concerned, she would come in, they would get all the insight from her that they could—if any—and then they would send her on her way. It shouldn't take more than a day. His boss would be appeased, and he and Harrington could get on with real law enforcement work and catch Simon Says as soon as possible.

And maybe, after Simon Says was apprehended, Conner would head back out to a certain horse ranch in Lodi and see Adrienne Jeffries again under very different circumstances.

But until then, Adrienne—and her abilities—were just a distraction. Something to draw his focus away from what he knew needed to be done to catch the killer. Conner couldn't allow that to happen. No matter how much he may want it to.

Conner decided to get up and get dressed since dawn was about to break anyway. He may as well go into the office and make an early start of what surely would be a long day. He wouldn't be surprised if Seth was there early, also.

FORTIFIED WITH MULTIPLE cups of coffee, Adrienne drove herself into San Francisco the next day. She needed the coffee after being awake most of the night—first packing and preparing for the trip, and then worrying about the toll it would take on her. The drive was relatively uneventful, but she found herself getting more and more uptight as she got closer to the city. Already she missed her little ranch and the serenity it offered.

And she hadn't even put herself in the clutches of the FBI yet.

She turned the radio up in her old Corolla as she crossed the Bay Bridge and entered the city. She forced herself to sing along to some familiar song by an '80s hair band. Singing helped her not to think too much and to ignore any buzzing she might start to hear in her head. With a population of nearly a million, Adrienne knew there would be people around the San Francisco area with malicious thoughts. There was nothing Adrienne could do about them, so she knew it was better to try not to hear them at all.

Adrienne navigated the hills and multiple one-way streets San Fran was famous for and finally parked at the FBI field office's parking garage. As she shut off her car, Adrienne braced herself to be bombarded by other people's thoughts in her head or to at least hear a dull roar of competing voices. She was pleasantly surprised to find just the slightest buzz—almost nothing.

Adrienne smiled. Evidently everybody in San Francisco must be having a good day or something. She didn't mind, less of a headache—literally—for her.

Upon entering the building, she was escorted up to the Violent Criminal Apprehension Program offices. She saw Conner Perigo as soon as she entered the main area. Dammit. The man looked just as good as he had yesterday. She had hoped she had imagined the thick black hair and gorgeous green eyes. But evidently not.

Those green eyes were fixed on her as Agent Perigo's partner, Seth, came over to meet her in the doorway.

"Ms. Jeffries, we're so glad you made it," Seth said as he led her over to an interrogation room. The two agents sat in the pair of seats on one side of the table and motioned for her to sit in a chair across from them.

Teams had obviously been drawn, and she wasn't on theirs.

"Not that I had much choice," Adrienne muttered. "But it's still okay to call me Adrienne."

She could feel Conner Perigo's eyes on her. Adrienne resisted the urge to fidget in her chair.

Agent Harrington smiled. "That's good. Please, like I said yesterday, call me Seth." He pointed at Agent Perigo. "And you can call him Conner. He promises to be on his best behavior today."

Somehow Adrienne doubted it.

"Okay, Seth, Conner it is, then." Adrienne decided she should try to make the best of the situation—not antagonize the agents, especially Conner. "But before we get started, I want your assurances that all charges or warrants or whatever against Rick Vincent will be dropped once I help you."

Conner spoke to her for the first time. "That won't be a problem, Adrienne. Neither of us were thrilled with how that went down."

Adrienne looked at Conner, and he nodded. She believed him. Whoever's idea it had been to use Vince as leverage, it definitely hadn't been Conner's. But that still didn't mean he liked or trusted her.

"Okay, Adrienne," Seth said. "We'd like to get started right away. But to be honest, we're not exactly sure how to proceed. Maybe you can provide us a little insight."

Adrienne took a deep breath. Might as well just get this over with. She had already made sure her purse contained a full bottle of ibuprofen. She would need most of it over the next few days.

"What can you tell me about the case?"

She watched as Conner and Seth—now in full FBI agent mode—looked at one another. Obviously until she proved herself and her abilities, they were loath to provide her with too much information.

"We have a serial killer on our hands. The victims are all women—five in the past ten months," Conner told her.

Adrienne waited to see if there would be further information, but evidently that was all they felt comfortable sharing with her.

"Okay, well, do you have anything from the crime scenes? Particularly anything the killer may have touched."

Seth responded this time. "There was no forensic evidence found at any of the scenes. Whoever the killer is, he's very careful."

No forensic evidence made it more difficult for Adrienne to get any sort of clear bearings about the killer, but not impossible.

"Do you have anything the killer might have touched, even with gloves on?"

Conner and Seth looked at each other once again. She saw Conner give a slight negative shake of his head.

Seth handed her an envelope that had been lying on the table. "We have some pictures of the crime scene. Will that help?"

Adrienne nodded and took the pictures. She braced herself as she opened the envelope. Death scenes were always jarring. She took out the first set of pictures, slowly looking at each one. The dead woman in the picture had been left in what looked like an abandoned warehouse of some sort. Multiple stab wounds covered her body. Different pictures showed the poor woman at various angles.

Three or four pictures in, Adrienne realized that, while she was horrified at what she was seeing, none of it was causing her any pain. Which was great, except for the fact that she also was not getting any insights or feelings from the pictures whatsoever.

Adrienne went through the entire set of crime scene photos for the woman in the warehouse. She then looked through them all again to be sure.

She felt nothing.

Adrienne looked up to find Conner and Seth watching her intently. She didn't know what to say—nothing like this had happened before when she had helped the FBI in the past. What was wrong with her?

"Do you have pictures of any of the other cases?" Adrienne finally asked.

"Yes. The ones you were just looking at is the first victim," Conner replied as Seth got out another set to show her.

First victim. Adrienne relaxed for a moment. Maybe

the reason she couldn't get any feelings from those pictures was because of the length of time that had passed between then and now. That had never happened to her before, but it seemed plausible.

Adrienne tried to clear all thoughts from her head as she took the next set of photos. Another stabbing scene with a young woman. This time it seemed she had been left under a highway overpass bridge.

Again Adrienne was horrified by the violence but felt nothing in terms of the killer's thoughts, plans or motivations.

This continued for the next hour as Adrienne pored over the photos again and again. Nothing. Her insight wasn't working at all. Although the agents across from her never said anything, she could tell their frustration was growing.

"I'm sorry," Adrienne said, handing the photos back across the table. "I'm not getting anything from any of these."

Conner Perigo didn't look a bit surprised. "Do pictures not work for you?"

"They did in the past. The glimpses I would get from crime scene photos weren't as clear as actually being at the crime scene or touching something the perpetrator touched, but there was always something."

"I see." Perigo's smug tone grated on Adrienne's nerves. Obviously her lack of ability to perform here was just confirming what he had suspected all along— she was a fake.

Adrienne sat back in her chair and rubbed her eyes with both hands. On one hand she was happy her gifts weren't working—it definitely saved her a literal headache—but on the other hand she desperately wanted to show Conner Perigo he was wrong.

Adrienne crossed her arms on the table and laid her forehead on her arms, taking a few deep breaths. She needed to center herself. She needed to block out all the buzzing around her and focus.

That's when Adrienne realized there was no buzzing going on inside her head at all. It was completely silent.

Even if she wasn't getting any reading from the pictures, she should still be hearing some sort of low murmur just by the very nature of being in a large building filled with people. Everyone gave off static. The more people around, the louder it was to her. That was why she chose to live in a relatively isolated area—so she wouldn't have to put up with the white noise all the time.

As long as there was no one with malice in their thoughts, then everything stayed at a low static— annoying, but bearable. But sinister intent would instantly throw pictures into Adrienne's mind. Along with searing pain. When she touched something that had been handled by someone malicious, she also could usually get some sort of picture of what had been going through the mind of that person.

She should have been able to do that with the crime scene photos, but she couldn't. Right now not only was she not getting any pictures in her head, she wasn't even getting any static. That had never happened before.

The silence was so unusual to her it was eerie. But not unwelcome.

She had no idea how long the silence would last. But the way the agents across the table were looking at her—especially Conner—they were not willing to wait long to see. Maybe she would get out of this after all. But then she thought of Vince back at the ranch. She wanted to get rid of whatever guillotine blade that the FBI had hanging over him.

If only for Vince's sake, she wanted her gifts to work, just this one time. Although, if she were honest, Adrienne knew she also wanted to show Conner Perigo what she was capable of.

She watched Conner and Seth look at each other. Seth finally broke the awkward silence that had been building. "Look, it's early. Maybe I can get you a cup of coffee or something and that will help."

Adrienne nodded, grateful for the reprieve. "Yeah, coffee would be great. I didn't get a whole lot of sleep last night. I'm not sure exactly what's going on. Maybe I've just been out of the game for a little too long and need to ease my way back in."

"No problem," Seth said. "You stay here and look through the pictures a little more. Conner will stay, too. I'll get coffee and be back soon. Anything in particular in it?"

"No, just black, thanks."

Seth stood. "I'll run down to the coffee shop in the lobby and get it. If you drink what's in our office, you're liable to have to be chained up in the next full moon."

Conner looked over at Seth. "If you're going down there, I'll have the usual."

Seth rolled his eyes and snickered, walking out the door without responding.

"What's 'the usual'?" Adrienne asked Conner, her curiosity piqued by Seth's response. In the long silence that followed, Adrienne wasn't sure he was going to tell her.

"Skinny vanilla chai tea latte with no foam and sugar-free vanilla," Conner finally said. "I get ragged pretty hard from the guys."

Adrienne couldn't help it; she broke out into a smile. The thought of this big tough-looking agent whose shirt seemed to be perpetually slightly wrinkled and whose tie was probably one of a dozen stuffed in his glove compartment, using the words *skinny* and *latte* when referring to his coffee was downright hilarious.

Conner smiled back, looking sheepish. "I know. It doesn't exactly fit the tough-guy image."

The way he cocked his head to the side caused his black hair to fall onto his forehead. Before she could stop herself, Adrienne's fingers reached up to tuck the hair into place. Halfway to his head she realized what she was about to do and immediately lowered her hand back to the table. She studied the photos again intently, hoping he hadn't noticed her…

Her *what?* Desire to touch him? Inexplicable need to be closer to him? Complete lack of control of her own hands?

Adrienne stared down at the pictures for a long time without looking up, grateful for the distraction, although she still wasn't getting any helpful info from them.

"Are you sure these are all the work of the same killer?" she finally asked.

"Yes." There was no doubt in Conner's voice. "He has a signature that makes it clear they are all the same killer." He didn't offer any information about what that signature was. Adrienne didn't ask, knowing he wouldn't tell her anyway.

Adrienne was tired of looking at these poor dead women. It was so frustrating to review them without any understanding as to what and how it had happened. She pushed the pictures back toward Conner's side of the table.

"I need a break. I can't look at them anymore right now."

She gazed at Conner, expecting to find more of

yesterday's hostile and condescending tone from him. Instead, he looked attentive, even the slightest bit sympathetic.

"You know, it's okay," Conner said gently. "Whatever's going on here, whatever reason you're not able to help us, it really is okay."

Adrienne couldn't help but respond to his gentleness. "This has never happened to me. The…nothing. I've always been able to hear or see or feel *something* before."

"It's been a long time since you've done anything like this, right? Maybe you just need to ease yourself back into it, like you said." The gentleness was still there but Adrienne could hear the disbelief that colored his tone.

"You don't understand. I always hear something when I'm around people, no matter what. It's like a buzz. But right now I don't hear anything."

"Maybe it's the pressure of the situation. Or maybe the pictures are too old or something."

"Yeah, maybe."

"Look, Adrienne. I want to give you this chance, while we're here alone, to tell me if there's something you want to tell me. You know, about your abilities or about when you worked for the FBI before."

"I don't understand." Adrienne was honestly puzzled.

"I mean, if you were in some way exaggerating what you could do—in terms of profiling and working for the FBI—either then or now. Or, hell, even if you had completely tricked the Bureau before, you can tell me, and I'll make sure nothing happens to you."

"What?"

"I'm just telling you, I'll protect you from any repercussions. We'll come up with some reason why you can't help us that everyone will buy. I'll even make sure Rick Vincent is taken care of and won't be arrested."

He had the nerve to sit there with his gorgeous green eyes and say this to her.

Adrienne struggled to keep her temper from boiling over. "So let me make sure I understand this. You think I deceived the FBI ten years ago when I worked for them and that I'm back again, lying now. Wasting my time and yours."

She could see Conner attempting damage control in his mind. But she never gave him a chance to speak.

"And you, very magnanimously I might add, are offering to protect me if I just come clean now and, what, admit this was all a hoax?"

"Adrienne, calm down."

Adrienne raised her eyebrows at that—no man should ever tell an upset woman to *calm down*—but she kept quiet.

"I'm just trying to offer you an out if you need it."

"Well, thank you, Agent Perigo." She saw him grimace. "But despite you thinking I'm a liar and a cheat, not to mention some sort of juvenile attention-seeker, I don't need an out!"

"Listen, I'm not trying to offend you. But I've been an agent a long time, and I've never seen anything that suggested a gift such as yours is real. As a matter of fact, the exact opposite is true. When someone comes forth and claims to be 'psychic' and know something about a case, almost always he or she is involved in some way."

Adrienne took a deep breath. Conner was skeptical. She had dealt with skepticism before, even considered it healthy. No one should blindly believe someone else without reason. Why did she feel the need to prove herself to him when she never had felt that way about anyone else?

"I'm not a psychic," Adrienne said quietly.

"Whatever you want to call it. Good, smart detective work is what solves cases, not hocus-pocus."

"It's not magic, Perigo. It's just the way my brain works. Some people are geniuses with musical instruments. Some are whizzes when it comes to math. My brain is just wired differently than most people."

"Then why isn't your gift working now?"

Temper threatened again. "I don't know!"

Seth chose that moment to come in with the coffee. He put the cup carrier down, looking back and forth between Adrienne and Conner, noticing the obvious tension between them.

"Here you go, Adrienne. Coffee, black. And here's your froufrou, princess," he said as he handed Conner his drink. "You owe me $4.50."

"How come I have to pay, but she doesn't?"

"Because her drink didn't involve an embarrassing list of words to order." Seth sat down in his chair. "Anything come to you while I was gone?"

"Nothing, Seth, I'm sorry."

"Don't worry, we've got time."

Adrienne hoped time would help.

Chapter Five

Six hours later Adrienne still had not experienced anything helpful to the case. Conner and Seth had left her alone in the interrogation room but stood just a few feet away on the other side of two-way glass. They could see Adrienne, but she couldn't see them.

All day Conner had watched Adrienne pore over the pictures again and again. He had watched her try different methods, studying each picture one at time, spreading as many out on the table as could fit, flipping through them all quickly. Everything she tried ended with that same blended look of frustration and confusion.

He had to give it to her; if she was pulling some sort of scam, she was definitely tenacious about it.

They hadn't talked again about his get-out-of-jail-free offer. She seemed legitimately offended by it, so he didn't bring it back up. Conner shrugged. He was just trying to provide her an escape if she needed it—not all those things she had accused him of doing.

He and Seth had tried to help her any way they could. They encouraged her to take breaks, walked her outside to get fresh air and took her on a lengthy lunch to get her away from all of it for a while. Nothing seemed to help. Now, watching her, she just looked exhausted.

Conner would be angry at Adrienne, but Adrienne was so frustrated with herself that he couldn't bring himself to be mad. But he was definitely concerned that they had wasted an entire day doing something that had provided zero results. Conner had stayed with her the whole day—he could admit it was at least partially because he didn't trust her out of his sight—and watched her get more frustrated and disheartened as the day went along.

"I guess this is a bust, huh?" Seth broke into Conner's thoughts as they both watched Adrienne. "Looks like you were right."

"About what?" Conner asked, breaking his gaze from Adrienne to look at his partner.

"That this was all bogus and a waste of time. She's done nothing to help us."

"Yeah, I guess, but you definitely can't say she didn't try. I almost want her to get a feeling or reading or whatever, just so she won't have that look on her face anymore."

"Yeah, she looks pretty upset. I told Chief Kelly that we weren't having much luck with her. He wanted to know if we thought she was withholding information on purpose."

Conner shook his head. "I don't think so. If she is, she's one hell of an actress. What do you think?"

Seth gazed through the two-way glass again. "Who knows? But it doesn't seem like she found something and isn't telling. The chief wanted to know if we wanted him to come in and talk to her since she had worked with him before. I told him no. That okay?"

"Yeah. The way she spoke about Chief Kelly before,

I don't think seeing him would help any. What are we supposed to do? Call her a failure and send her home?" Conner asked.

"The chief wants us to consider letting her see the packages Simon Says sent. The hair locks."

Conner's eyebrows shot up. "I'm not ready to do that yet. I don't want to give away anything that detailed about the case."

"I told the chief that. Bureau's going to pay to put her up in a hotel room at least for tonight. See where we are by the end of tomorrow. Maybe she just needs a good night's sleep."

"All right. But look at her, she's exhausted. How about I'll drive with her in her car to the hotel, and you follow and give me a ride back."

Seth nodded and headed out of the door. "Sure. Let me shut down my computer, and I'll be ready to go. I'll meet you at her hotel."

Conner walked over to the interrogation room. Adrienne was still poring over the pictures. She didn't even look up when he entered.

"Hey, you about ready to call it a day?" Conner asked as he sat down across from her.

"Conner, I still don't have anything. *Nothing.* These women...they died so horribly, and I can't seem to help them in any way."

"Well, if it helps, Seth and I have been feeling that exact same frustration for weeks."

Adrienne shook her head. "I don't know how you do it."

"You just do the best you can with what you have."

"Well, right now, it looks like I have absolutely nothing."

Conner reached over and took the pictures from her.

"That's enough for the day. You need a break. We're going to put you up at a hotel, and we'll start fresh in the morning after a good night's sleep."

As Conner put each of the pictures back in their respective envelopes, he watched Adrienne put her elbows on the table and rest her head in her hands. She looked fragile, breakable. Conner was overwhelmed by the urge to protect her.

And kiss her.

Of course that still didn't mean he trusted her or believed what she said she could do.

When he finished putting away the photos, Adrienne stood with him. He held the door open for her as they walked into the hallway. His other hand hovered near the small of her back.

"I'm going to drive you in your car to the hotel. Seth will pick me up and bring me back here."

"I'm okay to drive," Adrienne insisted, stopping.

"I know you'd probably be fine, but San Fran streets can be crazy even for those of us who drive them every day. Just let me do this for you, okay?"

She looked at him for a long moment.

"What?" Conner finally asked.

"You're kind of being nice to me. Not sure what to do with that."

Conner wanted to reach out and stroke her cheek but, instead, squeezed her shoulder in a friendly manner. "Well, how about I'll go back to being mean to you tomorrow? After we both get some sleep."

Her smiled transfixed her whole face—an impish grin that suited her features perfectly. It took Conner's breath away. And definitely brought back the urge to kiss her.

She stuck out her hand, and they shook on it. "Okay, a truce, then. At least for today."

Conner tried to find a neutral topic as they headed to her car in the parking garage. "Neutral" wasn't exactly simple for them, considering they couldn't talk about his work or her work or his background or her background or the city, or most other topics lest it bring them back to why they were here.

"We've had some really great weather here lately," Conner finally said.

Adrienne looked at him as if he were crazy. It was San Francisco. The weather here rarely strayed from the averages.

Conner shrugged and grinned. "Just trying to make conversation that doesn't break the truce."

"You don't have to pander to me, Perigo. I don't mind you being skeptical about what I can do. It's your petty comments I can live without."

All five foot four of her was glaring up at him. He swallowed the laughter he knew would just get him in more trouble.

"Yes, ma'am."

"How long have you worked for the Bureau?" Adrienne asked as they entered the garage. Adrienne directed them to her car, and Conner opened her door for her.

"Twelve years. I was at Quantico for about four years, as part of CIRG—Critical Incident Response Group. I liked that and kind of naturally morphed into ViCAP."

Adrienne rolled her eyes. "The FBI loves its acronyms. So how did you end up out here from Virginia?"

"Natural progression, mostly. My family is all on the

West Coast. My grandmother lived here in San Francisco, and I stayed with her for a while when a ViCAP position opened. Worked out for everyone."

As they drove, Conner answered Adrienne's questions about his time at the FBI. He had arrived at the San Francisco office not long after she had left eight years ago but had always been in a different section of the Bureau office. If she had stayed just a year longer, they might have crossed paths.

Conner parked the car at the hotel and got Adrienne's bag out of the trunk and walked her into the lobby, allowing her to get checked in.

She turned and offered her hand for him to shake and to take her bag. "Thanks for getting me here, Conner. I guess we'll just pick up tomorrow?"

Conner found he wasn't ready to let her go just yet. He took her outstretched hand, but turned it in his palm. "I'll walk you to your room. That okay?"

Adrienne gave him a shy smile and pulled her hand away. "Sure. Thanks."

They strolled to the elevator and went up to her floor. At her room's door she slid by him and opened it with her key card.

They walked in, and Conner placed her bag on the bed. Out of habit he checked the closet and bathroom to make sure both were empty. When he came back into the room, Adrienne stood looking at him with an eyebrow raised. "Everything clear?"

"Sorry—habit. Look, before I go, let me give you my number, just in case you need anything."

Adrienne tried to find a pen and paper so he could write it down but didn't see any. She tossed him her phone. "Just program it straight in."

Conner punched in his number and handed it back to her. "I guess I'll see you in the morning. I'll come by and get you around nine o'clock?"

"Sure."

Conner watched as a pinched look came over her face, and Adrienne's gaze dropped to the ground. "Listen, I just want to say I'm sorry I was so useless today. I'm sure tomorrow will be better. It has to be."

Conner put a finger under her chin, tilting her head up. "Hey, you tried your best. That's all anybody could ask."

"Yeah? Well, my best didn't accomplish squat today." Frustration fairly oozed out of her.

"I've certainly had those types of days myself. You just have to recalibrate yourself for tomorrow."

Adrienne nodded. That she seemed to understand. "Thanks, Conner." She smiled softly.

That soft smile was his undoing. Almost without meaning to, he bent down and kissed her. He meant the kiss to be brief, comforting. Conner was surprised when Adrienne, in turn, deepened the kiss. He felt her hands grab the lapel of his jacket and pull him closer, and she stood up on tiptoe.

Conner's armed snaked around her waist as her mouth opened and her tongue ran along his lips. He was pulling her even closer when a brisk knock came from the door that wasn't completely closed. They shot apart as Seth walked in.

"Hey, Conner, you ready?" Seth looked from Adrienne to Conner and recognition flared in his eyes. "Oh, sorry. I'm leaving now."

"No, hang on, Seth. I'm coming." Conner looked at Adrienne, who seemed as shaken up as he felt. "I'll see you in the morning, okay? We'll start completely over with everything."

Adrienne smiled. "Fresh start sounds good. With everything."

THE FIRST THOUGHT that invaded Adrienne's consciousness when she awoke the next morning was that the static was back. She sat up in her hotel bed, holding herself still to be sure. Yes, it was definitely back—the buzz she got from being around people. Adrienne grinned. It was annoying, but she was thrilled.

Another noise joined the slight static—her stomach growling. She was starving. Last night she had had no interest in food. The combination of the day she had had and the sleepless night before had caught up with her. All she had wanted to do was curl up and go to sleep, even though it had been early in the evening.

Once Conner had left, Adrienne had taken a shower trying to wash away the pictures of those women—all dead—and her failure to help them. After she had dried off, she had grabbed an oversize T-shirt out of her suitcase and had fallen into bed, asleep as soon as her head hit the pillow.

Now it was early in the morning; the sun was barely up. Adrienne wandered into the bathroom and began brushing her teeth. She didn't mind waking up at an hour beginning with five. Living on a ranch had turned her into an early riser.

She brushed her hair and picked some clothes out of her suitcase. She put on khaki pants and a blue button-down blouse. The rest of her clothes she hung in the closet or put in a drawer; the slight buzzing sound in her head hopefully meant she would be staying longer, able to help Conner and Seth find the killer of those women.

Adrienne wasn't sure exactly when she had completely committed herself to helping the FBI. But she knew it was sometime yesterday when she had looked through all those pictures of the murdered women, helpless to do anything. Conner and Seth sitting across from her, hopeful she could provide information that would give them a lead, and her able to do nothing. She had always considered her gift a nuisance at the very best, and often downright painful and debilitating; but yesterday, when she couldn't use it, she knew she wanted it back.

And now it looked like it was.

A few minutes later Adrienne was ready to leave the hotel. It was still too early to meet Conner and head to the Bureau's office. She decided she would spend an hour or so at a local coffee shop within walking distance, then would call Conner and tell him that she would meet him at the field office earlier than 9:00 a.m. She wanted to be there as early as possible so she could get a look at those pictures again. Provide some sort of insight and hopefully help crack open the case.

Adrienne knew she also wanted to see Conner's face when she was able to provide intel he totally wasn't expecting. Certainly Conner had become more kind as yesterday had progressed, and that kiss had been unexpected and magical. But Adrienne knew Conner still didn't believe her or trust her.

Adrienne smiled. For once she was almost looking forward to the physical discomfort that came from using her gift. It would be worth it.

Adrienne walked up one of San Francisco's famous hills to get to the nearest coffee shop. She breathed in the crisp morning air, grateful for exercise and being outside, however briefly. She knew today was going to be another long day.

Adrienne entered the coffee shop, surprised at the number of people already there, despite the early hour. The static inside her mind became quite a bit louder. Adrienne got in line, hoping a cup of coffee would ward off the headache forming.

She smiled, thinking of Conner's froufrou drink order. Skinny vanilla chai latte... Adrienne couldn't even remember the rest.

After ordering and paying for her drink, Adrienne made her way over to one of the few empty tables by the window. She was a step away from a chair when the screaming began in her head. The sound was deafening, as if someone had put headphones over her ears, then turned up the volume as loud as possible. The pain immediately blinded her and she stumbled toward the table, blindly grasping for its edge with her free hand. She tumbled into the seat trying to keep hold of her consciousness.

I will kill her! I will kill them both!

The general rage clouded everything, but that one thought filtered through her mind over and over.

She was crushing the foam cup of coffee still clutched in her hand. The scalding liquid spilled out, but she couldn't force her muscles to relax their locked grip of the cup. She felt the burn almost distantly, secondary to the pain in her head that seemed to shoot daggers into her eyes.

I will kill them both!

The scream was getting louder now, and closer. Adrienne forced her eyes to open slightly, although the agony from the effort nearly caused her to black out.

She looked around the coffee shop trying to find the two people the screaming voice referred to. She spotted them in the opposite corner—a man and woman, both in their mid-twenties, huddled close together. Their hands were linked, and they smiled and spoke softly to one another.

There was no doubt this was who the voice was referring to. Adrienne had no idea how far the man with the voice was from the coffee shop. She could see him storming up a hill—his anger growing with every step—but she couldn't tell how far he was. Given the loudness of his thoughts, Adrienne didn't think it would be very long before he arrived.

And when he did, the young couple would die.

Suddenly the volume of the enraged man lowered, and Adrienne could see him walking in through a double set of doors in a coffeehouse. Adrienne whirled her head around to see if it was this one he was entering and wilted back into her chair in relief when she saw it wasn't.

He was in another location of this same chain, somewhere nearby. But there was one on every corner, so she had no idea how far away he was. His screaming thoughts had subsided a bit as he concentrated on looking for the couple, not yet knowing he was in the wrong shop.

Adrienne knew she had to act now. Whether the enraged man found the correct coffee shop in a few moments or twenty minutes, he would still eventually find it. She had to get help and warn the couple.

She forced herself to loosen the grip on the ruined coffee cup and reached into her purse for her phone. She stared at it in her hand for a long moment, trying to decide what she would say to 9-1-1 when she called. She wasn't sure she could get out a coherent sentence. Then she remembered Conner had programmed his number into her phone last night. He may not trust her, but he would at least not ignore her.

She pressed Send on her phone, praying his was still the last number called, knowing that looking through a contact list now would be impossible. His sleepy voice answered on the second ring.

"Hello?"

"Conner." The one word was all she could manage. Her voice was weak and shaky.

"Adrienne? What's wrong? Are you okay?"

"I need help." Her voice was barely more than a whisper now.

"Where are you? At the hotel?"

"No. I'm at the coffee shop. Up the hill." She took a breath between each sentence. The white dots were floating in front of her eyes now, but she fought to hold on to consciousness.

"Okay. Hang on for just a second." She could hear him saying something to someone else. She leaned her head against the cool glass of the wall next to her table.

"Adrienne? Listen, Seth is already near the office, he should be there in five minutes. I'm on my way, too. Should I call 9-1-1?" The urgency in Conner's voice made it through to her subconscious. He believed her that something was wrong; she felt profound relief.

"Conner..." she started weakly.

"Yes? What is it?"

"Hurry. He's going to kill..." Adrienne was unable to finish the sentence. The man's voice screaming inside her head hit her so hard that the phone flew out of her hand as she brought her hands up to keep her skull from splitting.

He was looking for them again, the intent to kill at the forefront on his mind, rage that he couldn't find them a close second. And he was getting nearer.

Adrienne knew Conner had Seth coming to help her, but even five minutes would be too late. She had to warn the couple sitting across the coffee shop. Get them to leave. Bar the door. Do *something*.

Or people would die.

Adrienne attempted to stand up, but her legs wouldn't seem to support her. She took her hands from her head and put them on the table to use as leverage to get up, vaguely aware of the concerned looks she was getting from the people around her.

I will kill them both!

The pain seared through her head with each of his thoughts. His feelings were beyond just a jealous rage. It was a malicious desire to see them both suffer, to watch them cower in fear. And he didn't care if he had to kill others to achieve that goal.

Adrienne finally hoisted herself up from her seat, leaning heavily against the table. She looked down and saw a drop of blood on the table and realized her nose must be bleeding. She wiped it with the back of her hand as she took her first unsteady steps toward the couple in the corner across the way.

The trip seemed to take forever. Adrienne concentrated on putting one foot in front of the other. She was losing her peripheral vision, could feel blackness closing in around her, but fought it back. He was getting closer, Adrienne knew.

She finally reached the table where the couple sat, still gazing at each other, oblivious to Adrienne's agony.

They looked up in alarm when she finally stumbled into their table.

"Excuse me…" the boyfriend started in a perturbed tone.

"Oh, my gosh, are you all right? Your nose is bleeding," the woman asked. Both she and the boyfriend stood to help steady Adrienne.

Adrienne couldn't think straight. How could she get them to leave?

"A man," she finally said, her breath sawing in and out of her chest as if she were running a marathon. "Coming. Hurt you."

Adrienne could tell they didn't understand, had no idea of the danger they were in. She knew they were out of time, could feel the man getting closer. What could she do? She had to make them leave. Maybe if she could just get the woman out.

Adrienne turned to the younger woman and grabbed her upper arms, trying to keep herself upright. She took a deep breath and focused desperately on the words she needed to say.

"Can you, please." *Breathe.* "Go get me." *Breathe.* "A wet paper towel." *Breathe.* "From bathroom."

The woman looked very confused, but finally nodded. "Sure. Just hang on. Do we need to call a doctor?"

"No, not yet," Adrienne answered. She slid into the woman's vacated chair with relief as Adrienne watched her cross to the bathroom. Hopefully it would be enough.

The boyfriend looked at Adrienne with a blend of concern and apprehension. Adrienne didn't blame him for either.

The door slammed open behind her. He never said

a word, but at this close proximity, Adrienne could see every malicious thought the man had. He was sure they were here. He looked around at all the tables and eventually got to where Adrienne and the boyfriend were sitting. He didn't even pause to glance twice at them. The woman he searched for was not there; Adrienne had sent her to the bathroom.

A rage overwhelmed the man once again that he had not found his prey. Adrienne whimpered, the pain consuming her, but nobody heard. The man turned to walk back out the door.

"Here, miss, is this enough? Your nose is bleeding more." The woman rushed across the coffee shop with paper towels in her hands.

Adrienne felt the absolute glee the man experienced when he heard the woman's voice. He would not be denied his vengeance after all.

He was only a few feet behind where Adrienne sat. Adrienne knew he was about to reach for the gun he had hidden in his pocket. Using the remainder of her strength, she got out of the chair and hefted herself toward the man, knocking into him. He pushed her off easily and Adrienne slid to the floor.

By now the woman had recognized the enraged man, and was pulling her lover away and around the back of the coffee bar. The man began to draw his gun out of his pocket. Adrienne tried to get up but couldn't make her body respond.

"Sir, I am an agent for the Federal Bureau of Investigation." A voice rang out from near the back door. "I need you to lay down your weapon and put your hands on your head." It was Seth Harrington. Conner had gotten him here in time.

Adrienne felt the rage briefly overtake the man

before he resigned himself to the fact that he had been caught. Sirens could be heard pulling up outside the coffee shop. The man slowly put the gun on the ground and his hands behind his head.

Over the next few minutes, organized panic ensued. Uniformed officers filed into the coffee shop, taking statements and making sure no one was hurt. Someone helped Adrienne up into a chair since she was still unsteady on her feet. The attacker was handcuffed and placed in the back of squad car just outside the door.

Although he was no longer in the coffee shop, his proximity, combined with his continued malevolence, continued to cause jagged pains to shoot through Adrienne's head. She could still hear everything he would've done to them if he had just been given the chance. She could feel bile pooling in her stomach, and she wasn't sure how much longer she could hold on.

Adrienne stood, prepared to stumble her way to the bathroom if she was going to lose the contents of her stomach, when all of a sudden the pain and noise in her head completely stopped.

Caught off guard by the blessed silence, Adrienne looked around in confusion. Then she saw him.

Conner.

He had pulled up in his vehicle, double-parked and was rushing inside. Straight toward her. She could see myriad emotions crossing his face: confusion, concern, relief. He didn't stop until he was standing right in front of her.

"Conner…" Adrienne reached for him and found she couldn't hold on any longer.

Her last thought was hoping Conner would catch her, then she slipped unconscious to the floor.

Chapter Six

Conner caught Adrienne as she dropped to the floor, unconscious.

As he had pulled up in his vehicle—he didn't even want to think of all the traffic laws he had broken getting here from his house in record time—he had seen Adrienne inside the coffee shop. At first he was overwhelmed with relief just to see she was okay. But as he had rushed closer to Adrienne, he had realized she definitely was not okay.

There was zero color in her face, except for the dried blood that had trickled from her nose. Against her unnatural paleness, the blood stood out with jarring brightness. She was on her feet but looked none too steady. As he came through the door, some sort of shocked look passed over her features; she took a step toward him and said his name.

Then promptly collapsed.

Conner grabbed her as she fell and gently lowered her to the ground. "Seth!" he yelled out to his partner, who was talking to a witness over by the coffee bar. "I need help here."

When Seth saw Conner holding Adrienne, he quickly made his way to them.

"Is she okay? What happened?"

"I wanted to ask you that. I walked in and basically caught her as she collapsed." Conner brushed a stray strand of hair that had fallen onto her forehead. Adrienne sighed and moved a little toward his hand. Although her movement reassured Conner, the absolute lack of color in her face did not. "Did the perp hurt her?"

"There were no reports of him doing anything. He was pulling the gun as I walked in. Didn't resist arrest or put up any fight." Seth shrugged.

"So what happened to her?"

"I don't know. She was sitting on the ground when I got here but then was at the table when I looked over at her again. She didn't seem hurt."

Conner didn't like it. "Why is her nose bleeding? Did she get hit?" He couldn't see any bruising or swelling around her face, so couldn't figure out what the blood was from.

"Not from any reports I've gotten. As a matter of fact, the only one who seemed to be acting odd—before the perp pulled the gun, that is—was Adrienne. More than one person has said she looked sick or drunk or something."

Conner looked down at the woman lying against his arm. She was stirring more, and he knew she would be regaining consciousness soon. "Did you talk to her at all?"

"No. I was too busy making sure our psycho wouldn't open fire on anyone."

Conner felt more movement from Adrienne and watched as her beautiful hazel eyes opened. She looked at him with confusion.

"Hey." He smiled at her gently. "Don't try to move too much. You passed out."

Adrienne brought a hand up to her head. "The man was going to attack the woman."

"I don't know exactly what was going to happen, but Seth stopped him. He's been taken into custody."

Adrienne nodded. "Good. That's good. Can you help me up?"

Conner noticed some of the color was returning to her face. That was a good sign. He and Seth reached down on either side of her to get her into the chair a few feet away.

"What happened to you?" Conner asked as she sat down. "Did you get hit or something? You have dried blood under your nose."

Adrienne brought her hand self-consciously to her face. "No. Sometimes that just happens. I'm okay."

Conner noticed the raised red marks on her wrist. He took her hand away from her face to look at it more closely. Her entire hand was covered by the angry welts, and on some parts there was even blistering.

"What the hell happened to your hand?" Conner asked, careful not to touch what were obviously burns.

Adrienne looked down at her arm and hand. "I think I spilled my coffee on myself."

"Doesn't it hurt?"

Adrienne nodded. "Yes. But up until a few minutes ago, my head hurt much worse, and I kind of forgot about my hand."

Seth whistled through his teeth. "I'll get you a cold compress to put on it."

Conner looked at her hand, then her face. "I should take you to the hospital."

"No!" Adrienne's response was vehement. "I'm okay.

It hurts, but putting something cold on it will help. I don't need a hospital. I promise."

Conner was torn but decided not to push it. The burns, although painful-looking, were mostly first degree. Even the blisters were clear, suggesting superficial scalding—not anything that would require prolonged medical attention.

Seth returned in a moment with a bowl of water and a clean washcloth. He then excused himself to go help some uniformed officers finish up with the witnesses.

Conner took the washcloth and dipped it in the water. It was cold. "Do you mind if I help?"

Adrienne laid her arm out on the table between them. "Thanks."

She sucked in her breath as the wet cloth touched her skin—the water was chilled but not icy, helping to lessen the pain and cease any further burning.

"Sorry." Conner grimaced. "I know it has to hurt."

"No, the cold feels good. Thanks." She smiled at him, and Conner was glad to see even more of her color was coming back into her face. She looked almost normal.

"How did you spill your coffee?"

"I could…hear the man's thoughts and they…startled me."

Conner noticed her hesitations. Obviously she expected some sort of argument from him about her gifts.

To be honest he didn't know how he felt about her special skills. When he had gotten her phone call a little while ago, he could tell immediately that something was wrong. Dangerously wrong.

As soon as she had said she needed help, he had gotten Seth on the other line. Conner hadn't questioned, hadn't hesitated—just knew she needed him and had responded.

He could admit to himself that his instantaneous response in coming to her aid without knowing details was pretty odd behavior, especially since he had all but called her a phony and a liar over the past couple of days.

But he had known—*known*—when she had called today that the situation was dire from the very beginning. She had needed him to help her, but he couldn't get there quickly enough, so he had sent Seth, who had been closer.

And thank God, if the perp had been drawing a weapon when Seth had arrived.

Conner took the washcloth gently away from Adrienne's hand and wrist, and dipped it in the cold water again. Wringing it out, he placed it back on her arm.

"So you knew he was going to kill her?" Conner asked.

"Yes. That's what I was certain about most of all. He was definitely planning to kill her and the man she was with."

Conner nodded but didn't say anything else. She had obviously been through a lot already today. He didn't want to say anything that would come across as combative.

"You could hear what he was thinking?"

Adrienne nodded gingerly. "It was like he was screaming his thoughts right in my ears. And I could see what he was seeing."

"You could actually see him?"

"Not see him, exactly. More like see things through his eyes."

Conner nodded to encourage her.

"I know he went into some other coffee shops looking for them before coming here."

Conner made a mental note to check into that. Maybe somebody would remember seeing the guy.

"When he couldn't find them," Adrienne continued, "he got more and more furious."

"When did you call me?"

"As soon as I realized he was going to make it here to this coffeehouse soon. I wasn't sure how long I had before he did, but I knew it wouldn't be very long."

She looked away, over toward the table where the couple had been sitting.

"I called you while the guy was having a momentarily sane period, when he walked into another coffeehouse. He had to put his rage and malice aside, and concentrate on seeing if she was there. That's what allowed me to pull it together long enough to call. I'm glad your number was in my phone, or I never would've gotten through to anyone."

"Why didn't you call 9-1-1?"

Adrienne gave a quiet bark of unamused laughter. "And told them what? That there was a man coming up the street, and I knew he planned to kill someone?"

No, that probably would not have gone over well with the 9-1-1 dispatcher. A city the size of San Francisco got a variety of prank calls every day. Even though they would've sent out a patrol unit as standard procedure, it would not have been a priority and wouldn't have been quick.

"Nine-one-one would still have sent a squad car. Or you could've lied and said he was already here."

Adrienne nodded. "Yeah, but I wasn't thinking too clearly at the time. Just trying to engage in normal functions, like breathing and staying upright, was taking all my concentration."

Conner remembered the terrified tenor of Adrienne's voice when she had called. The hesitation and breathlessness in how she'd talked. He realized now how difficult even their very short conversation had been for her.

"I'm glad you called me." Conner reached over and stroked her elbow far from the area affected by the burn.

Adrienne smiled tiredly at him. "I'm glad you believed me."

Conner shrugged. He wasn't sure he believed, exactly, but he had acted.

"Losing you in the middle of a sentence like that scared me. What happened?"

"The guy was furious when he realized the woman was not in the coffee shop down the block. He was so intent on hurting her—it was like a bomb went off in my head."

"Is that when your nose started bleeding?"

Adrienne brought a corner of the washcloth on her arm up to her nose, wiping the dried blood. "I guess so. I know that's when I decided I had to get over to the couple and try to get them out."

"So you went to talk to them?"

"Talk? I'm not sure that *talk* is the right word. I stumbled over to their table, literally. I couldn't figure out what to say—my brain felt like mush." Adrienne looked up at him with panic in her eyes. "Finally they noticed my nose was bleeding, and the lady got me a wet paper towel from the bathroom. She had just disappeared out of sight when the guy walked in."

Conner saw Adrienne shudder. Whatever she was remembering about this guy, she definitely didn't like it.

"I thought we were going to make it," Adrienne said

in a low voice. "But then she exited the bathroom, and he saw her."

Conner took the wet cloth off her arm again—the burn was looking better, although still angry—and waited for her to continue.

"I tried to get over to the guy to stop him myself. But his thoughts..." Adrienne closed her eyes. "They were so *loud*. So unbearably loud." She cringed again, and Conner found himself cringing with her.

"I tried to get to him, but he basically just brushed me off, and I fell and couldn't seem to get up even though I wasn't hurt. I didn't have any more strength." Adrienne looked at Conner with distress in her eyes. "I just knew he was going to kill them, Conner. I *knew* it."

"But he didn't," Conner reminded her.

"Thanks to Seth. He got here literally in the nick of time."

"You know, this is all going to be really iffy in court. His lawyer will argue the guy basically had a gun and made a bad judgment about when it was okay to take it out of his pocket. He didn't actually threaten anybody with it. We have no proof of any intent to harm the woman or the other man. At best the gunman will probably get charged with illegal possession of a firearm."

Adrienne nodded. "I know. I don't stand up well as a witness in court, I'm sure. But the important thing is, nobody was hurt today."

Conner gestured down at her burnt arm. "Not exactly."

"I'll be fine." Adrienne took the washcloth from him.

Conner took her hand in his. He rubbed his fingers gently on the part of her hand that wasn't burned. "I'm still sorry."

Adrienne smiled shyly, then withdrew her hand. Conner looked around him. Things were wrapping up. The man had already been taken away by the local police. Conner motioned to Seth, and Seth made his way over to them.

"Everything almost done here?" Conner asked him, standing up.

"Yeah. Seems like the perp was the ex-husband of the lady. Although they've been separated for over a year, he totally freaked out when he discovered she was dating someone else."

"He tell you that?" Conner asked.

"No, the lady. Evidently he's been calling her non-stop for the past couple of weeks—wouldn't get the hint. She finally changed her phone number, and he started showing up at her work."

Conner shook his head, not surprised. Domestic violence often escalated like this.

"She told him about the new boyfriend yesterday, thinking that would get him to move on. But evidently not," Seth continued. "She knew as soon as she saw him here this morning, he meant her physical harm."

Adrienne looked up at Seth from where she sat. "I'm glad you got here when you did, Seth. I really think he planned to shoot her. Shoot them both."

Seth grimaced. "Well, that's going to be hard to prove. But no matter what, she at least knows to be aware of her ex and keep away from him."

Conner walked over to help Adrienne out of her chair. He kept a hand at the small of her back in case she started to keel over again. "Are you ready to go?"

"Sure. Are we headed straight to the Bureau office?"

Conner looked down at Adrienne's clothes, splattered with coffee stains. "Do you want to go to your hotel first? Change clothes?"

"Yeah, that would be great." Adrienne smiled with relief.

"Do you want me to drive you or do you think you can walk? I'll walk with you. It's a couple of blocks, right?"

"Yeah, I should be fine to walk. Usually fresh air makes my head feel better."

"Usually?"

"Well, it just doesn't seem to hurt much at all now."

Conner noticed her confused look. "That's a good thing, right?"

"Yes, yes, I'm thankful," Adrienne responded quickly. "It has never…not hurt before. In a situation like this."

"Have you had many situations like this?" Seth asked her.

Adrienne looked away. "Enough. Not as many over the past few years."

Conner met Seth's eyes. They had a lot to talk about when Adrienne wasn't around. Not the least of which was what had happened here in this coffeehouse this morning. Adrienne obviously wasn't faking her physical reactions, and she had known that the perp meant harm to that woman.

It was looking more and more as though maybe she could do some of the stuff they'd heard she could do.

"All right, I'll take her to the hotel and let her change clothes, and then we'll meet you at the office, Seth." Conner looked at Adrienne's burnt arm. "Are you sure you're up for coming into the office today?"

Adrienne nodded. "I'll be fine."

"We'll stop at the drugstore on the way and get some gauze to protect the worst part of your burns."

Conner and Adrienne began walking toward the door. Seth told him that he would see them in a little while.

"Thank you," she said intently, grabbing his hand with her uninjured one.

"For what?"

"Believing me. For not asking for details and explanations I couldn't give at the time. For *acting* rather than allowing your natural doubts to cloud your instincts and demand more information."

Conner was stunned. That statement exactly summarized what had happened. The *instinct* had been to get her the assistance she needed immediately. He had almost let his doubt overshadow that gut reaction but didn't. And because of that, nobody had died today. Not the woman or her boyfriend or maybe even Adrienne.

Conner still wasn't sure what he believed Adrienne could or could not do in terms of "seeing" evil. But he was at least now willing to give her a chance.

Conner squeezed her hand. There were many things that probably could be said right now, but he wasn't sure which would be best or which might lead to an argument. So he said the only thing he could.

"You're welcome."

CONNER WAITED IN the lobby for Adrienne as she went up to her room and changed out of her coffee-soaked clothing. They had stopped at a corner drugstore to get Adrienne some ointment and gauze for the worst of her injuries.

The red blisters on her arm bothered Conner but on some level reassured him. Adrienne had obviously been in the grips of something…strange to be burned like that and not notice. And it was too extreme a measure for someone to act out in order to prove they weren't faking something. Adrienne had no reason to go that far, had nothing to gain by it.

Conner's phone buzzed in his pocket. It was Seth.

"Hey. You back at the office?" Conner asked, sitting on the armrest of one of the couches in the lobby.

"Yeah. Where are you guys?"

"We're at the hotel. Adrienne is up changing clothes. Finish everything okay on your end?"

"Yeah. Turned the ex over to the locals, and the lady is filing for a restraining order even as we speak."

Conner nodded. "Well, that's good." He and Seth both knew that a restraining order would not stop an ex-husband intent on doing the woman harm, but it was a start and at least made everything official.

"Her new boyfriend looked pretty spooked by the whole thing. Not sure how long that's going to last."

"Don't blame him." Conner chuckled ruefully.

"So it ends up that the coffeehouse had some closed-circuit video."

Conner stood up and walked outside, away from the few people in the lobby. "What did the CC feed show?"

"Mostly it was pointing at the counter and register, away from the action this morning. Didn't get the ex at all. But it caught Adrienne a couple times."

"And?"

Seth knew what Conner meant without explanation. "It was scary, man. Seriously. The people who described her as drunk? That's pretty accurate. And the coffee spill on her hand? That was spooky."

"I was just thinking about her burns, Seth. Burns

like that? Nobody does that to themselves on purpose to continue some stupid facade."

"You've got to see this footage. It was like something took over her body. She crushed that cup in her hand with a death grip. Didn't drop the cup or anything when it spilled on her. It was like she *couldn't* release it."

Conner rubbed his forehead and began pacing up the sidewalk. "What do you think, Seth? Does this mean she's legit? That she can really...whatever?"

"Con, all I know is that something happened to her in that restaurant this morning. You can literally see it overwhelm her. And it's not pretty. Damn scary."

Conner stopped his pacing. "But what does it mean?"

"I don't know. But she had no reason to fake it and no reason to know we would be watching. It leads me to believe she may be telling the truth, man."

Conner had never seen anything to make him think "gifts" like Adrienne's were possible.

He turned back toward the hotel and saw Adrienne walking out the lobby door. "Okay, I've got to go. Did you bring a copy of the CC footage back with you?"

Seth snorted. "Do you really have to ask? Of course. See you in a bit."

Conner hung up and walked toward Adrienne. She had changed into a khaki skirt and a white sleeveless blouse. Her short hair was a little damp from the shower she must have taken. Color had returned to her cheeks. She smiled, crossing to him.

She was breathtaking.

If only Conner knew that he could truly trust her.

Chapter Seven

Three hours later she was back in that same FBI interrogation room from yesterday. Adrienne sat, sure she was only minutes away from becoming a serial killer herself.

Nothing. She had absolutely nothing.

Staring at these pictures for the past hour and a half had brought not one single thought, feeling or insight. Just like yesterday. Like her gift had switched itself off. Again.

Although they didn't say anything, Adrienne knew Seth and Conner had to be at their wits' end with her. They had sat with her for the first hour as she went through the pictures. They had gotten her lunch but that didn't help. Then they had left; she assumed to do something more productive—which, let's face it, would be *anything* else.

She looked down at the crime scene pictures again. A dead woman, stabbed and left in a warehouse.

Nothing.

Adrienne stood from her chair in the interrogation room and leaned onto the table to stretch her back. The movement caused pain to shoot up her arm from the burns. It was a reminder that her gift had certainly worked well enough this morning. Why wasn't it working now?

A brisk knock on the door had Adrienne looking up from the table.

"Yes?"

In strolled Division Chief Logan Kelly. Adrienne recognized him right away. He had not changed much in the eight years since she had seen him last.

"Ms. Jeffries. It's good to see you again."

"Chief Kelly." Adrienne shook his outstretched hand but kept her greeting short.

That Adrienne didn't return the sentiment wasn't lost on the chief. He raised one eyebrow but said nothing.

"I understand you're having some difficulty using your profiling gift for this case."

"For some reason I can't seem to get insights on anything that has been shown to me so far."

The chief's eyebrow raised again. "Perhaps you just aren't trying hard enough." He sat down in the chair across the table from her.

Adrienne barely refrained from rolling her eyes and sat down herself. "I assure you, it is not for lack of effort."

"It seems like you never had this sort of problem when you worked for us before. It all came quite easily."

"Easily?" Adrienne gave a quiet cough of joyless laughter. "Although I may not have had this much difficulty in the past, there was never anything easy about what I did for the FBI."

Adrienne noticed rather smugly that her statement seemed to quiet Chief Kelly for the moment. She watched as he looked down at the pictures.

"Quite gruesome, aren't they?" he asked after a moment.

There was nothing Adrienne could do but agree. "Yes. Horrible."

"Don't you want to help stop whoever is doing this from killing more women, or do you just not care at all?"

Adrienne knew better than to be taken aback by the chief's abrupt tone but found herself feeling defensive anyway. "Chief Kelly, I'm not playing any games here. For whatever reason I'm just not able to get any insight into this case."

"Perhaps I should remind you that it is not you who has much at stake here, but your ranch manager, Rick Vincent."

Adrienne's eyes narrowed. "Yes, Chief. I am well aware of why I am here and what's at stake. And as much as I'd like to tell you to go to hell, I won't."

The chief sat back looking smug, but before he could respond, Adrienne continued in an angry tone. "And although you think you have some sort of hold over me now, Kelly, you don't. I may have been here yesterday because of what you think you can do to Rick Vincent if I don't cooperate. But I'm here right now because I want to help these women."

Adrienne stood and began sorting the pictures back into the correct files. Chief Kelly stood also and walked over to the interrogation room door.

Adrienne stopped him before he could leave. "But I want to make sure you understand this—I am not back to work for you. This is a one-shot deal, and I'm done. I'm older now, and I won't allow what happened to me before to happen again."

Chief Kelly surprised her by looking apologetic.

"Adrienne, we wouldn't let anything like that happen again. We could put measures in place to prevent it, to look out for your well-being."

"I thought that was true when I was eighteen years old—too young to know better. Now I know who I can trust. Myself," Adrienne all but scoffed.

Chief Kelly seemed about to respond when the door to the interrogation room burst open. Conner gave a momentary look at Adrienne, then turned to Chief Kelly.

"Chief, we just got a call. There's another victim."

Whatever Chief Kelly had been about to say to Adrienne was completely forgotten. "Simon?" the chief asked quietly.

Conner glanced at Adrienne, then turned back to the chief, nodding curtly.

"Did we receive another package?"

Conner glimpsed at her again and then away. Adrienne couldn't help but notice the way Conner posed himself with his back to her, which made it obvious that Adrienne was not a welcome part of this conversation.

"No, sir. Harrington and I are ready to proceed to the scene immediately."

"Okay, keep me posted." The chief excused himself quickly, and Conner turned to her.

"Seth and I have to leave for a little while."

"I understand."

"Do you want me to get someone to give you a ride back to the hotel?"

"No, I'll just stay, if that's okay."

Conner shifted uncomfortably. "That's fine. But I'll need you to stay in this room. If you have to leave, use the phone on the table to call the offices and someone will escort you."

"Don't want me wandering around on my own, huh?"

"Adrienne…" Conner took a step toward her.

Adrienne held her arm out to stop him. "No, it's fine. I'm not trustworthy. I get it. I haven't been of any use to you yet, anyway."

Conner sighed. "Adrienne, nobody's mad at you. It's okay if you can't…"

Adrienne cut him off. "I know you have to go. That's fine. I don't need to be placated. I'm just going to look over the pictures some more."

"Okay." Conner looked relieved as he walked to the door. "If it looks like we're going to be too long, I'll call and let you know so you're not just stuck here…"

Doing nothing.

Conner didn't say the words out loud, but Adrienne could hear them as sure as if he had spoken them.

He gave an apologetic shrug and walked out the door.

"Doing nothing" aptly described what Adrienne had accomplished here over the past day and a half. She glanced down at the pictures again. She didn't want to look at the brutal slayings anymore. Maybe she should just give it up, and head back to Vince and the horses.

Whatever Adrienne had been able to do for the FBI a decade ago, she was beginning to think she couldn't do it anymore.

She should be glad. Seeing Chief Kelly had reminded her of the pain she had gone through working for the FBI before. Just thinking of it now made her head begin to throb a little. Not being able to use her gift meant Adrienne wouldn't have to go through agony like the scene this morning at the coffee shop.

Adrienne sat and looked at the picture in her hands. It also meant she wouldn't be able to help catch the psycho who had horrifically murdered this beautiful young woman. Or stop him from killing anyone else.

Was it worth the pain—although calling it *pain* was really like calling a sumo wrestler chubby—if she knew she could help? That's what had kept her going for those two years, long past when any reasonable person could be expected to keep going. Knowing she could help.

Of course it looked like the decision was being made for her. She didn't seem to be able to help whether she wanted to or not.

And great, now *not* being able to help was starting to give her a headache.

Adrienne reached into her purse to grab a bottle of aspirin and then picked up one of the crime scene photos that had fallen to the floor. She glanced at it as she set it down on the table.

And all the images came screaming into her head.

The killer, with his knife, taunting the victims. Cutting locks of their hair to mail. His absolute glee at their terror. Knowing he had the power.

Adrienne put her hands up to her head, trying to hold it together and keep it from splitting into thousands of jagged pieces. As she looked at more pictures, thoughts from the killer became clearer.

He didn't kill them at the locations where they were found. He was much too smart for that. And the FBI agents were so stupid. It took them so long to catch on, he had to finally start sending them gifts. Bless their hearts.

Adrienne used all her concentration to block out the killer's feelings, instead trying to concentrate on useful information: a location, a time, thoughts about his appearance.

She could see a building with beams in the ceiling. Maybe a warehouse? A large cellar? There were no windows. This is where he brought them and where he kept them for a few hours before he killed them.

It was so hard to wait. He was in charge. He had the power. He tried to wait so the good feeling would last longer. Simon says, wait. But it was so hard.

It was like listening to a child whine. Adrienne tried to hold on to that. His thoughts were very childlike.

But holding on to anything with all the noise in her head was nearly impossible. The killer's malevolent thoughts were at the forefront, the loudest and most demanding. But pushing against her consciousness were other noises—other menacing forces, blurry ones with no distinct voices or sights—like someone was screaming at her in a different language. She knew she should be able to figure out what the noises meant, but it was too hard.

Adrienne persisted as long as she could, tried to gather as much information as possible in the screaming recesses of her mind. But eventually it overwhelmed her. She crawled over to the trash can—walking was impossible—and vomited the entire contents of the lunch she had eaten a little while before.

She dragged herself back to the table, pushing the pictures as far away from her as she could. She laid her head down on her arms on the table, closing her eyes. She just focused on breathing in and out, on trying to empty her mind of the noise and images.

This was what she remembered most about working with the FBI ten years before: the concentration it often took just to survive the next moment. Because trying to think about more than that was impossible.

Adrienne wasn't sure how long she lay with her head on the table. She thought it was hours, but she had been wrong before about that. She gingerly opened her eyes, delighted when the light didn't shoot agony into her head. She sat up slowly, expecting at any time for the images and sounds—and pain—to return, and was surprised when they didn't. Previously the only way to escape had been to physically remove herself from the area and any people.

Adrienne glanced at her phone. Conner had been gone for just over three hours. She wasn't sure when he was coming back, but she wanted to share what had happened as soon as she could. Some of it would help, surely.

She hoped so. She hated to think she had gone through that for nothing.

Although she had to admit she felt much better than she ever had before when she had worked for the FBI. Instead of the splitting headache and nausea she had expected, she just felt a little tired.

She wasn't brave enough to pick up the pictures that lay scattered all over the table and chair in case it instigated another physical onslaught. But she knew she had to remove the trash can where she had lost the contents of her stomach earlier. It wouldn't take much longer before the smell of that would overpower the tiny interrogation room.

Double-bagging and tying the small garbage sack, Adrienne headed out the door to look for a larger trash can. Despite the icky contents of the bag, the farther she got from the interrogation room, the better she felt. She saw a large trash can at the end of the hallway and headed to it.

She had just thrown away the bag when the elevator doors opened, and Conner and Seth exited, both looking annoyed and harried.

"What are you doing out here?" Conner snapped. "I thought I told you to stay in the interrogation room."

Adrienne was taken aback by his abrupt tone. "I needed to throw something away, so I stepped out for a few seconds."

Conner looked at her suspiciously. "Isn't there a trash can in the room?"

All the eagerness Adrienne had felt at sharing what she had discovered about Simon now disappeared with Conner's annoyance and disapproval. "Yes, there was, but the trash smelled bad so I took it out."

Adrienne didn't wait to hear Conner's response, just turned and headed back down the hallway.

He called after her anyway. "You're not supposed to leave the interrogation room without an escort!"

Adrienne ignored him. Jackass. After what she had been through this afternoon, she really didn't feel like putting up with him.

She made it all the way back to the interrogation room door before he caught up with her, grabbing her arm, but she noticed he was careful not to touch her burns.

"Did you hear me? I said you're not supposed to leave the interrogation room without somebody with you."

He had her at a distinct disadvantage—he towered a good ten inches over her five-foot-four frame. Adrienne had no doubt Conner Perigo knew exactly how to use his size to his advantage in intimidating others. But Adrienne wasn't going to let him bully her. She looked him dead in the eye.

"The. Trash. Smelled. Bad." She stood on tiptoe and accentuated each word with a poke to his chest. "So I took it out. It's the only time I've left the room for the entire time you've been gone."

Conner glowered down at her. "When you're in this building and I tell you to do something…"

"Ahem, excuse me, kids," Seth interrupted, sticking his head around Conner's shoulder. "Is everything okay here?"

Adrienne and Conner continued to scowl at each other.

"Any luck while we were gone, Adrienne?" Seth continued.

Adrienne smirked at Conner then turned to Seth. "Actually, Seth, yes. As soon as you guys left, my abilities started working. I think I may have a lot of information for you about Simon Says."

CONNER TOOK A step back when he heard the words *Simon Says* come out of Adrienne's mouth. Dammit, he *knew* they shouldn't have left her here alone, unsupervised. He didn't know how she'd done it, but somehow she had gotten pertinent information about the case. Information she shouldn't have known. Maybe she had chatted it out of some agents, or maybe she had gotten access to a file she shouldn't have been privy to.

Either way she now had information she shouldn't have.

Conner completely released Adrienne's arm. She immediately turned and went into the interrogation room. Seth began to follow her in. Conner didn't move.

"You coming?"

"In a minute. I need to get something from my desk. Don't start without me."

Conner could feel the anger building up inside him. He had to admit it was not all leveled at Adrienne. The crime scene they had just returned from had been an utter farce. When the call had come in that another woman's body had been found, he and Seth had hoped this was the break they were looking for. Finally a crime scene before they had gotten a package from Simon Says. But upon arrival at the location, it hadn't taken them long to figure out that this had not been Simon at all, but some sort of copycat. Too many differences, too much disorganization for it to be Simon.

Another waste of their time.

And then, as soon as they had returned, Conner finds Adrienne wandering all over the office, looking for a trash can? Seemed highly unlikely. And then she conveniently notifies them she has something to tell about the Simon Says case. A name she never could've known unless someone or something at this office had clued her in.

Conner walked over to his desk and grabbed a pen and ledger of paper. He and Seth would listen to what Adrienne had to say, but then they would send her back to her ranch. He didn't care what the chief said anymore. Conner was tired of being jerked around by dead ends.

Conner headed back to the interrogation room. He had wanted to believe Adrienne and her "abilities," especially after this morning. But he was tired of wasting time.

The smell hit him as he walked into the interrogation room. "Holy cow, what is that?"

Adrienne rolled her eyes at him. "I told you the trash smelled bad. That was why I was taking it out. You'll get used to it in a second."

Conner realized Seth was gone. "Where's Seth?"

"He went to get a can of air freshener."

"Thank God. What was in the trash?"

"I got sick to my stomach while you were gone."

Conner felt bad and let go of a little of his anger. "Oh, I'm sorry you got sick. Are you feeling better?"

"Yes. Surprisingly I feel pretty great."

Conner looked down at the photographs scattered all over the table. "Did you have a temper tantrum?" He gestured at them with his hand.

"No." Adrienne glared at him. "But I didn't want to touch them again, just in case."

"In case what?"

"In case I had the same reaction as I did the last time I looked at them."

Seth walked in and began spraying the room with freshener until it was difficult to breathe. But at least it smelled better.

Conner and Seth picked up the photos and sat across the table from Adrienne. He watched as Adrienne sat up straight in her chair and folded her hands lightly in her lap. She closed her eyes and took a deep breath.

Conner realized he was watching a ritual. She had done this before. Perhaps many times.

"Part of him thinks of this as a game," Adrienne began in a serious tone and then opened her eyes. "And he thinks you—the FBI—are stupid."

Conner and Seth looked at each other. They knew what Adrienne was saying was true. It was obvious from the mocking tone of the notes Simon had sent with the locks of hair.

Conner grimaced. If Adrienne knew this, it meant she had somehow accessed the files. That was more information than he wanted available to her.

"Go on," Seth encouraged.

"He's alternating between gleeful and whiny—like a young child. He likes to be in control, to terrify the women and prove he has power over them. He takes absolute delight in sending you the locks of hair."

Conner stayed still, but Seth sat back and whistled through his teeth. He obviously believed this was coming from Adrienne's "visions" rather than her accessing information while they were gone.

"No offense," Conner interrupted, "but you're not telling us anything that is not already in a file here. A file that perhaps got shown to you while we were gone."

That seemed better than accusing her of breaking into a desk.

"Agent Perigo."

Uh-oh, they were back to last names.

"Why would I do that? There's no point to it."

"I don't know, Ms. Jeffries. You tell me."

Conner felt Seth nudge him under the table. "Ignore him, Adrienne. Continue, please," Seth entreated.

"He keeps a separate lock of hair for himself. A trophy."

That was new. Of course, conveniently, there was no way to know if it was accurate.

"He places all the women at the locations where they are found, but he doesn't kill them there."

They knew this too—no blood had ever been found at any of the crime scenes.

"He kills them all at the same place—some sort of cellar or large empty room. It has a basement that's almost hidden. It's unusual. But there are no windows, and it has a ceiling with high dark rafters."

Conner now sat up straighter in his chair and saw Seth do the same out of the corner of his eye. This was something that they had never heard. It could potentially break open the case.

If they were willing to believe her.

"Can you remember anything else about the place?" Seth asked Adrienne.

She shook her head. "No, I'm sorry. I can only see this room. For some reason I can't see when he comes in or out of it, which would give us more to go on."

"Can you usually see stuff like that?" Conner asked.

Adrienne rubbed her forehead. "Usually. I'm sorry."

"What else can you tell us?"

Adrienne reached out to gather the five files of the dead women, where Conner and Seth had returned all the pictures. The files were blank on the front except for each woman's first name. Adrienne took the files and laid them out on the table.

"I know this was the order they were killed in," Adrienne told them without looking up from the files. Then she took a pen and proceeded to write the last name of the women on each of their files. "I know their names, also."

This was too much for Conner. Whatever she was doing, he was done playing her game. He stood up and grabbed the files from the table.

"You know what? I think that's just about enough." Conner was livid. "I don't know exactly what you're playing at here, but I don't have time for it. You obviously didn't stay in this room while we were gone today. I don't know which agent helped you or if you just broke into a desk. But I am done with this."

Adrienne stood with her hands leaning on the table, obviously upset. "Can I remind you, Agent Perigo, that *you* came to *me* and asked for my help? Oh, scratch that, I mean *blackmailed* me into helping. What possible reason could I have for making this stuff up?"

Conner mirrored Adrienne's stance on the table. "I have no idea, and I don't care anymore. Maybe you just want attention. Maybe you need to feel important. But the only way you could possibly know these things is if you got your hands on the case file or talked to someone else who did."

Adrienne slammed her small fist down on the table. "Unless—although I'm sure this is an unbearable thought for you to consider—I'm telling the truth!"

"Do you know that this room is equipped with video and audio recording equipment, Ms. Jeffries? It automatically starts digitally recording whenever someone is in here."

"So?" She continued to glare at him from across the table.

"So? It will certainly show any time you left this room or anyone who came to see you while we were gone. And anything that was said."

Conner wasn't sure exactly what he expected Adrienne to do with this information. Change her story maybe. Start crying. Try to make up some excuse for the information she had.

He definitely didn't expect how she actually responded.

"Well, I guess I know how you'll be spending your next three hours, Special Agent Jackass. But I'm leaving."

She reached down to get her purse—he saw her wince when her burned arm scraped the chair—then stormed out of the room, slamming the door.

Conner stared at the closed door for a long time. Beside him, he heard Seth begin to chuckle. Conner muttered something unrepeatable under his breath and headed out the door to look at the recorded footage of Adrienne. But he suddenly didn't feel as sure as he had just a few minutes before.

Chapter Eight

The great thing about San Francisco was all the parks, Adrienne thought as she walked around in one of them. You couldn't walk half a block without running into some little grassy area or square. And the weather hovered around sixty degrees all year long in San Fran. Gorgeous.

The bad thing about San Francisco? All the jerky FBI agents who made her want to tear her hair out. Either that or jump across the table and kiss him until neither of them could breathe.

Adrienne smiled. At least if she kissed Conner, she wouldn't have to listen to any of the asinine statements that seemed to pour endlessly from his mouth.

Adrienne sat down on a bench. The buzzing was back. She wasn't sure exactly when it had started up again, but it was there. And a headache was coming on—pressure surrounding the back of her skull. Annoying but bearable.

This was the headache she was used to having when she was around people. The constant distant buzzing. Nothing bad; nothing to see or hear. Just light static. She had found over the years that most people were not evil. They may be tired or cranky or just plain mean.

But most did not walk around with sinister intentions, so Adrienne never had any clear idea of their thoughts. Just low static.

Usually being outside helped a bit—fewer people than were cooped up in buildings—but now it seemed worse than when she had been in the FBI field office.

Maybe being annoyed at Conner Perigo had helped her forget about her headache. But when she thought about it, she realized, no, she hadn't really had any sort of headache—or any pain at all—since she had taken the trash out of the interrogation room. That was so unusual.

But the pain was making its way back now, that was for sure. Adrienne reached into her purse and got out aspirin from the bottle she always kept with her. This would help keep the headache in check, to a degree.

Adrienne sat in the sun for a little while then decided to take a walk down to the Embarcadero—San Francisco's waterfront area. It had a beautiful view—the Golden Gate Bridge and Alcatraz—but Adrienne barely noticed it.

Why was she so angry at Conner Perigo? It wasn't as if she hadn't had to prove herself before. Nobody believed what she could do at first. She had always accepted that as reasonable. What sane person would believe her without proof?

And her gift had been so sketchy over the past couple of days. Why should she expect Conner to just believe what she could do out of hand? And more than that, Adrienne had *never* cared who had believed her in the past. Why was she starting to now?

There was something about Conner Perigo that was different. Adrienne didn't know really what it was, but she knew she hadn't been able to stop thinking about him from the first moment she had seen him in the barn two days ago. And the kiss at the hotel last night. She had thought they had turned some sort of corner then.

But evidently Agent Perigo didn't actually have to trust or believe her in order to act on his attraction to her. The kiss obviously hadn't implied he had feelings for her, because feelings were based on trust, and Perigo most definitely didn't trust her.

Of course Adrienne could also admit to herself that whatever she felt for Conner didn't come wrapped up in a nice little bow, either. She seemed to spend most of the time she was around him fighting the urge to slap the smug look off his face. But she definitely had to admit that he affected her. She wasn't sure what she was going to do about that.

Adrienne knew he would watch the footage from the interrogation room and know she was telling the truth. Where things would go from there—professionally and personally—she had no idea. She wasn't sure what she wanted.

It wasn't long before Adrienne realized coming down to the Embarcadero hadn't been a good idea. It was much more crowded. The buzzing was becoming louder and her headache worse. Adrienne bought a pretzel from a vendor—to replace the lunch she had lost before, and hopefully to ward off some nausea now—and decided to begin walking back toward the FBI building.

She stopped at another park and nibbled on her pretzel for a few moments before giving up. Her headache was definitely worse, and she doubted she'd be able to keep any food down long. Adrienne put her hand up to her forehead to try to shade her eyes and give her head some relief from the pain the sunlight was causing, even though it wasn't a particularly bright day out.

This was what she remembered from her years with the FBI. The constant bombardment. Even when she was out of the office with no one asking her to look at some crime scene photo or touch some artifact, she still had never been able to get any quiet in her head. When she was eighteen and nineteen, she had thought she could just push through the pain and the noise and keep going.

She had been wrong.

It hadn't seemed so bad earlier today, but now Adrienne just felt like hell. She would go back to the office, tell Conner and Seth that she was heading to the hotel. Maybe she'd even drive back to Lodi tonight. At least there she knew she'd have some peace. But she definitely needed to get away and give her body a chance to rest and heal. She couldn't keep this up for long.

That she knew from experience.

Plus, if her gifts were only going to work every once in a while, then she really wasn't going to be much help to the FBI at all. So she might as well go.

From where she sat on the park bench, she heard the car pull up to the curb—tires slightly squealing—and saw it at the same time. She watched as Conner Perigo got out of the car and strode with determination straight toward her bench.

Adrienne looked down at her watch. She'd been gone about forty-five minutes. That was quicker than she had thought. She'd figured it would take him longer to go through the footage.

"How did you find me?" Adrienne picked at her pretzel some more as he sat down beside her without saying anything.

Conner cleared his throat in an embarrassed fashion. "I had them track your phone's GPS."

"Special Agent Perigo, I'm shocked. Isn't that a misuse of taxpayers' money?"

"Probably. I thought you were already gone, maybe headed back to Lodi. If I had known you were only a few blocks away, I wouldn't have driven."

"So you found me." Adrienne put another small piece of pretzel in her mouth. "I would've thought it would take longer to go through all that footage of me in the interrogation room. They must have a fast forward switch, huh?"

Conner shifted uncomfortably on the bench. "Look, Adrienne…"

Adrienne took that as a yes. He trailed off, obviously waiting for Adrienne to say something, but she wasn't about to make this easy for him. "Yes?"

"I'm sorry, okay? I was wrong."

"You saw the footage?"

"Yes, some of it."

Adrienne cocked an eyebrow at him. Only some?

"Okay, most of it. Enough to know you were obviously telling the truth. You didn't leave and nobody came in."

"Where's Seth?"

Conner looked away sheepishly. "He stayed to watch the rest of the footage, just in case."

Adrienne shook her head. "You have real trust issues, you know that?"

"Occupational hazard, I guess."

They sat in silence for a moment before Conner spoke again. "I lost my temper, and I was wrong. When we left today, we rushed to that crime scene thinking it was a big break in the case only to find out it wasn't Simon at all. A copycat. When I got back I was in a bad mood already. Then when I saw you in the hall-way, I just lost it."

Adrienne peeked over at him, turning toward him slightly. She wasn't ready to let him off the hook yet, but she could at least understand how the copycat killer would've put him on edge.

Conner slid a little closer to Adrienne. When she didn't move away, he put his arm along the back of the bench, touching her shoulders.

"That still doesn't excuse how I behaved. What I said. I *am* a jackass. I'm sorry."

"You know, it's okay to be incredulous. Usually I'm not offended by skepticism." Adrienne broke off another piece of her pretzel and began to eat it, realizing she was now starving.

"I want you to know, it's not you personally I'm critical of." Conner hesitated as he seemed to try to find the right words. "It's just that I have no script for what you can do. No way to categorize it and hardly know how to process it."

Adrienne nodded as she chewed. Not being able to categorize her gift was something she understood.

"This is hard for me," Conner continued. "But after what happened to you this morning and this afternoon, I can't doubt you anymore. But I don't know how to explain what you can do or how you can do it."

"Sometimes there doesn't have to be an explanation. It just is what it is," Adrienne said softly.

Conner turned toward Adrienne on the bench. "Your abilities fly in the face of normal reason. It goes against everything I've learned in all my years of law enforcement," he said in a tone gentler than she would've thought him capable of when discussing this topic.

"I'm sure that's not as true as you think," Adrienne

assured him. "Haven't you ever followed a hunch and found it to be valid? My abilities aren't so different than that. Just more well developed."

"Yeah, but yours are a little more hocus-pocus."

Adrienne smiled, unoffended. "It's not like my mother slept with Thor or that gypsies cursed my family or something. I just have a talent."

Conner snorted. "I heard what you said today. Things you saw and know? It's quite a bit more than a talent."

"My brain just works differently than most people. Like how some kids taught themselves how to play the violin when they were five years old and had never heard the instrument before. I'm kind of a prodigy, but I'm not a freak."

Freak was a sensitive word for her. It was why she had always hated the nickname Bloodhound. Too close to freak.

Conner reached over and ran the backs of his fingers down her cheek. "Not a freak. Never. Your brain is different and can do special things."

"I'm a terrible speller," Adrienne said softly.

"You can't spell?"

Conner was still stroking her cheek. Adrienne smiled. "No, not at all. I have to think about the difference between *there, they're* and *their* for five minutes before I figure out which is correct."

"Okay, maybe a little bit of a freak." Conner smiled and closed the distance between them, cupping the back of her head with his hand.

His lips were firm but gentle, and Adrienne was immediately swept up in the kiss. She felt Conner's other hand come up to frame her face as she leaned closer to him, her hands tracing his arms from his elbows up to his shoulders.

Adrienne gave herself over to the kiss, drowning in it. It was like yesterday's kiss—overwhelming. All she could feel was Conner. There was no buzzing, no static in her head, only Conner.

Adrienne's eyes flew open.

No buzzing. No headache. Silence.

Nothing.

Adrienne jumped off the bench, out of Conner's arms, ignoring his shocked gaze. She shook her head as if to clear it and concentrated hard, trying to pick up on the buzz that she should hear from the other people in the park—the static. She looked around; there were at least a dozen people. She should hear them.

Her eyes spun back to Conner.

She watched wariness enter his gorgeous green eyes. "You're not going to start calling me Agent Jackass again, are you? That's starting to get around the office."

"What did you do to me?"

"I...kissed you?"

Adrienne could tell Conner wasn't sure how to handle her strange reaction. She didn't blame him. She knew she was acting abnormally, but something was wrong here.

"You've done something to me." Adrienne shook her head again, as if to unclog something.

"Well, my kisses have been known to cause a commotion in many a lady," Conner joked.

"It's you. You're the problem." Adrienne threw herself back down on the bench looking at him with wide eyes.

"What?" Conner obviously had no idea what she was talking about.

"Wait. I have to think." Fortunately thinking was much easier without the noise and headache.

When she had worked with the FBI before, the pain from her gift had been a constant. Only when she could physically remove herself from people had she had any relief from the noise and discomfort. But since she had come back to help Conner and Seth, she'd experienced some pain, but not constantly. And her abilities had worked, but not constantly.

Adrienne looked down at the burn on her arm. Her gift had worked this morning at the coffeehouse—she remembered the excruciating pain in her head. She had even gotten a nose bleed. Then she had passed out and felt better when she woke up. No headache at all, just the pain from the burn.

Conner had been there with her when she had woken up.

And at the field office today, nothing seemed to work when she was looking at the pictures of the murders, until Conner and Seth had been called away. Once they were gone, it had completely overwhelmed her. Images, sounds, the thoughts of the killer. And the agony that came with them.

All gone away again once Conner was back.

Adrienne remembered when she had first laid eyes on Conner two days ago. She had walked into the barn and was absolutely shocked to see someone standing in there besides Vince. Vince's buzz was a constant that she was so used to she totally didn't notice it anymore. But other people's should've been evident. Adrienne remembered how taken aback she had been at the silence, although it hadn't been long before Conner had made her so angry she hadn't even noticed the quiet.

Conner. It kept coming back to Conner.

He was looking at her expectantly, although she had to give him credit, he had waited quietly like she had asked him to. Adrienne reached over and grabbed his hand in hers.

"Do I need to apologize for kissing you?" he asked warily.

Adrienne smiled shyly. "No."

"Good, because I don't think I can. You want to fill me in with what's going on?"

"I think I know what's wrong with me."

"What are you talking about? I already told you, there's nothing wrong with you."

Adrienne shook her head. "I mean, what's wrong with my abilities. Why they didn't work yesterday but are working today. Sometimes."

"I don't understand. What did you figure out?"

"It's just a theory." Adrienne hesitated. She could be wrong, and she didn't want to make him mad. She should find out for sure first, before she said anything to him.

Adrienne looked down at her hand that rested on his. Hers looked so small and frail compared to his big capable hands.

"It's okay, just tell me."

Adrienne gripped his hand harder. "I need you to do something for me."

"Sure. What?"

Adrienne reached up and put her hands on either side of his cheeks. She leaned over and kissed him. She meant it to be just a quick peck, but her plans to distract him evaporated as soon as her lips touched his. She felt his arms come around her and draw her closer. She sighed and gave herself over to the kiss.

Her lips opened when she felt his tongue, and she slanted her head to give him more access. Her fingers slid up into his hair as she pulled him closer. It was Conner who broke away after a few moments.

"Um, Adrienne, we're in a park, baby. And I'll probably lose my job if I get arrested for public indecency."

Adrienne giggled softly. "Sorry."

Conner brushed his lips with hers again softly. "A giggle. Quite the beautiful sound."

"I'm not much of a giggler."

Conner's lips brushed hers again. "Maybe you should consider becoming one."

"Maybe."

"So, Ms. Jeffries, what's your theory? What do you need me to do?"

Adrienne took a deep breath and put her forehead against Conner's.

"I need you to get away from me. As soon as possible."

Conner pulled back from her immediately. "What?"

"I just need you to go away from me for a little bit while I check a couple things out," Adrienne responded as gently as she could.

"Why can't I come with you? Where am I supposed to go?"

"This is something I have to do alone to test my theory. And you can go wherever you want. Go to your house or my hotel or Golden Gate Park. Wherever. I just need you to not be near me for a while."

Adrienne could tell Conner didn't understand and was struggling with her request. She knew he wanted to demand more answers and appreciated his restraint.

"Please, Conner. Just for a little while. Call Seth and have him meet me in the lobby of the field office. It won't take me long to figure it out."

Conner shook his head and stood up. "Okay, fine. But I don't like this."

Adrienne stood up onto her tiptoes and kissed him on the cheek. "I know." She smiled at him. "But thank you for doing it anyway."

Conner ran his fingers down Adrienne's cheek. "I'll do it as long as you promise to explain to me what's going on as soon as you can."

Adrienne nodded. "I promise."

Conner turned and began walking to his car. "I'm going to head to my house since I left there before six this morning. A shower would probably do me good."

"Thank you, Conner," Adrienne called out to him.

"Call me soon." Conner opened the driver's-side door but didn't get in. Instead, he looked at her over the roof of his car. Adrienne was entranced by his intent stare. "And, Ms. Jeffries? No matter what your theory is, we're going to finish what got started here this afternoon. And when we do, it won't be in a park."

Adrienne couldn't think of anything to say to that. Lord, she hoped they did get a chance.

"Seth will be waiting for you in the lobby," Conner called out to her as he got in his car and pulled away.

Adrienne quickly began walking back to the FBI field office. The sooner she got this done, the sooner she could take Agent Perigo up on his offer.

Chapter Nine

Adrienne found Seth waiting for her when she walked into the FBI office a few minutes later. She could already feel tension building up in her head, but told herself that it didn't prove anything definitively.

"Hey." Seth smiled at her. "Glad you didn't leave for good."

"No. I was just trying to get some air."

"Conner called but didn't give me very much detail about what we're doing right now."

"I know. That's because I didn't give him much detail. Let's just say I'm testing a theory." She cocked her head toward the elevators, and they began walking.

"Theory about what?"

"My abilities."

Seth hit the button for the elevator. "Okay. Anything particular about them?"

"Why they seem to be a little hit-or-miss lately. They've never been that way before."

The elevator door opened, and they walked inside. Seth pushed the number for the floor their offices were on. "So, what's the plan?"

Adrienne turned and looked straight at Seth. "I'm

going to ask you to do something you might not want to do. But it's kind of important."

"What's that?"

The elevator chimed, and the doors opened. Adrienne stepped out and began walking down the hallway. She could already hear the buzzing, and her headache was definitely back. "I need you to show me one of Simon's packages."

"Okay."

Adrienne was a bit taken aback. She had expected more resistance from Seth. "Just like that?"

"Yep."

"Do you think Conner will be mad when he finds out?" Adrienne wondered aloud.

"Nope. He's the one who told me to give you access to whatever you need."

Adrienne stopped midstride. "Really?"

Seth half smiled at her. "Yep. Do you think he's been abducted by aliens?"

"Probably." Adrienne snickered. But she was so pleased. This was a huge step for Conner, she knew. She began walking again.

"Where do you want to go? Back to the interrogation room again?" Seth asked.

The buzzing was getting worse and taking on more definite form, like there were whispers coming from within the walls all vying for her attention. This building was, of course, a place where evil was investigated every day. Definitely no lack of menacing and threatening people here. The images and sounds seemed to want to jump from the rooms and throw themselves into Adrienne's mind.

Adrienne rubbed her forehead and concentrated just

on walking. "Yeah, let's go back there. At least I'm familiar with that room."

Seth told her that he would meet her there in minute, and Adrienne went inside. The room had been cleaned out since she had left earlier that afternoon. She sat down at the now-empty table. She could still hear all the whispers, see vague visions of violence as she waited for Seth to return.

Adrienne breathed in through her nose and out through her mouth to try to keep herself focused, a practice she had learned in a yoga class. It didn't really help, but at least it gave her something to do.

Seth walked in holding a box. He set it on the table in front of her. It was a small brown box, about half the size of a shoe box. Plain. Unassuming. It looked so benign, like millions of packages that get mailed daily all over the world.

Adrienne was terrified to touch it, but she knew there was no point in waiting.

Touching as little of the box as she could, she pulled back the flaps on the top. Inside was a small jeweler's box that a necklace might come in. Adrienne flinched as she reached in and pulled the smaller box out of the package.

She could feel her breath sawing in and out of her lungs. She forced herself to open the jeweler's box. Inside it was a lock of hair. She reached down and touched it gently.

Every muscle in her body tightened unbearably. The force of what she was feeling threw her back into the chair. She still had some of the lock of hair caught between her fingers.

Adrienne began sobbing as all of the killer's thoughts overwhelmed her mind. She could tell Seth was trying to say something to her, felt him touching her arm and shaking her, but he seemed so far away—outside the impenetrable wall of the killer's ominous thoughts.

All the killer's feelings piled on top of each other in a hideous cacophony within Adrienne's head. She focused her energy on trying to sort through them, to pick out useful information, but the effort was too great. It was like the killer was in the room with them, his presence was so strong.

Adrienne forced her fingers to release the lock of hair, but that gave her only the slightest reprieve. She brought her hands up to her head, pressing her palms hard into her eyes.

Adrienne knew she should touch the hair again; should keep going. After all, this was what she had been hoping for, right? For her abilities to work? But this was different—the intensity was so much greater than before.

Adrienne touched the hair again, trying to brace herself against the mental anguish, but it didn't help. The noise in her head sky-rocketed. She fell against the table and could feel blood begin to drip from her nose. She let go of the hair, but it didn't seem to help at all.

Adrienne couldn't take this anymore; she had to get away—just for a while. She would mentally refortify then come back. But for right now she had to get away. She looked over for Seth but found he was gone. In the back of her mind, Adrienne knew there was something she was trying to do but remembering was too much effort.

She had to get out of this building. Where was Seth? She couldn't take time to look for him. The elevator was just a few yards down the hall. Surely she could make it there and then outside. Away from this package and this killer.

Away from this evil.

Adrienne hoisted herself out of the chair and walked unsteadily to the door. It took her a few moments to remember how to turn a doorknob. She pulled the door with as much strength as she could muster, but the opening was so small she could barely slide through.

The hallway was a twisted carnival fun house, seeming to stretch on endlessly. Leaning heavily on the wall, Adrienne concentrated on putting one foot in front of the other. She could hear sounds, words, but she didn't know if it was actual people talking to her or the evil in her head, so she ignored them.

Just making it to the elevator used all Adrienne's strength. She pressed the button on the wall and sobbed with relief when the elevator doors opened immediately. She heard shouting and saw Seth's concerned face just as the doors closed.

Strength gone, Adrienne leaned her back against the elevator wall and slid to the ground heavily. She reached up and pressed the lowest button without looking, hoping it would take her to the ground floor. From there she would crawl out if necessary.

As soon as the elevator started moving, Adrienne felt better. She was going to make it. The noise and pain were already lessening. The dimness that had threatened her vision was receding.

The elevator dinged, and the door opened. There stood Conner, tension outlining every muscle in his body. He dropped down next to her immediately.

"Conner..." Adrienne reached for him.

For the second time that day, Adrienne fell unconscious into his arms.

THIS WAS BECOMING a pattern. Conner caught Adrienne before she fell to the ground. Seth's panicked call to him a few minutes ago had Conner racing back into town, breaking all sorts of traffic laws—just like this morning—to get back to Adrienne.

By the looks of Adrienne, Seth hadn't been exaggerating. She looked like absolute hell. She had no color whatsoever and seemed to be shivering uncontrollably even though it wasn't cold in the building.

The elevator started protesting at having the door opened too long, so Conner let it close. He brushed back a couple errant strands of short hair that had fallen over her forehead. Adrienne murmured and started to move.

"Hey, sweetheart," Conner whispered. "You ready to wake up?"

Just a few moments later her big hazel eyes opened.

"It's you." She hesitated for a few moments then smiled at him.

"Yep, it's me."

"No, I mean it is you who affects me this way. The pain is gone. And the noise."

Adrienne began to get up from her place on the elevator floor. Conner reached down to help her. "Are you sure you're okay to get up? It's fine to rest longer if you need to."

She smiled at him again. "No, I feel fine. So much better than I did a few minutes ago. Seth is probably worried about me. We should go see him."

Conner pressed the button on the elevator, and they began to go up again. When the doors opened, Seth was there, concern radiating from him.

"Oh, thank God. Are you all right, Adrienne? You looked like absolute, god-awful death when you stumbled into that elevator."

Adrienne rolled her eyes. "Thanks."

"I'm serious. I think I aged ten years watching what just happened to you. Are you okay? You do look much better now, I have to admit. What happened?"

Adrienne stuck her thumb out toward Conner. "He happened."

Conner looked down at her, confused. "That's the second time you've alluded to me. What are you talking about?"

Conner led her down the hall, away from the interrogation room. Instead they went into the main section of offices. He sat Adrienne in his desk chair and perched on the corner of his desk. Seth pulled up another chair near them.

"I noticed it earlier this afternoon," Adrienne explained, huddling back in the chair.

"What exactly?" Conner asked.

"Whenever I'm around you, my abilities don't work."

Conner was taken aback. "What? Why? Why would you think that?"

Adrienne shrugged. "I don't know why. Think about it—every time you've been around me I haven't been able to do anything to help with the case."

Conner glanced over at Seth. He shrugged.

"And whenever you aren't around me, everything does work—like at the coffeehouse this morning."

Conner wasn't convinced. "That still doesn't mean..."

"And this afternoon, it was only after you guys had gone to the crime scene and were away from this building that I got anything from looking at the pictures."

Conner wasn't sure how to feel about this information. Adrienne reached over and touched his hand. "I can't hear or sense anything when you're around. Like right now, there's silence—no buzzing, no static, no voices or images pushing at me. No pain. And in this building, with all the case files and evidence, that's pretty unbelievable."

"But bad." Conner frowned.

She squeezed his hand. "Not for me." She smiled softly at him.

He squeezed her hand in return. "But what does this mean?"

"I don't know." She let go of his hand and sat back in the chair. "But I'm grateful I'm not vomiting and throwing back pain relievers like candy."

Conner still wasn't sure what all this meant or the ramifications if what Adrienne suggested was true. He decided to focus on what he did know. "Tell me what happened while I was gone earlier. Were you able to pick up anything?"

Adrienne nodded.

"I showed her the package from Josie Paton."

Josie Paton, the most recent victim, found in an abandoned building two weeks ago. Married, age thirty-one.

Conner looked at Adrienne. "Did you get anything when you saw the package?"

She flinched and drew in her breath. "He was mad at her because she refused to be scared. She couldn't fight, because he had her restrained, but she would curse at him and call him names."

Adrienne stopped, but Conner knew there was more. "You can tell us, Adrienne. Just go ahead and say it."

Conner listened for a long time as Adrienne told them details of the murder and the abduction. Things she would have no possible way of knowing without her abilities to understand the killer's mind and his reasoning.

"I still can't get a good picture of where he's taking them when he first grabs them. I don't know why that is."

"Why is he choosing these particular women?" Conner asked. Their physical size seemed to be the only similarity. He and Seth had checked and double checked to see if there were any other ties between the women: where they shopped, ate, worked, exercised. They couldn't find anything.

Adrienne rubbed her forehead wearily. "They remind him of someone—a woman he knew. But I'm not sure who that person is to him. It seems to float in and out of his mind, and I can't get a hold on it."

Adrienne shifted uncomfortably in her chair, and Conner really looked at her. She seemed exhausted, on the verge of utter collapse. Conner wasn't surprised; it had been a long, physically difficult day for her. She needed a break.

"Hey, why don't we give it rest for a little while? There's a couch in the conference room where you can lie down. I just need to go over a few things with Seth, then I'll take you back to the hotel."

Adrienne smiled up at him gratefully. Conner offered both hands out to her which she took to help herself out of the chair. He grabbed his jacket from the back of it and led Adrienne to the conference room. She immediately sank heavily onto the couch.

Conner squatted down and draped his jacked over her. She smiled, snuggling into it.

"I'm just going to rest for a few minutes," she said as her eyes began to close.

Conner couldn't stop himself from reaching over to stroke her cheek. "That's fine, sweetheart. No one will disturb you here."

By the depth of her breathing, he doubted she even heard him.

Two hours later Conner and Seth had thoroughly re-vetted the Josie Paton file, adding and cross-referencing all the information Adrienne had provided. Although it didn't give them any immediate leads, it did provide a better overall understanding of who—and what—they were dealing with.

For the first time in ten months Conner felt a sense of hope. They were going to catch this psycho. Adrienne's help was going to be key.

After going through the file, Seth showed Conner the video footage of Adrienne opening Simon's package. Conner watched in barely concealed horror at the physical reaction the package had on Adrienne. There was no way something like that could be faked. He looked on as her muscles seemed to lock up. All color left her face. Touching the lock of hair in Simon's package seemed to almost hurl her across the room.

Conner watched as Adrienne tried to control it, closing her eyes and breathing.

He looked over at Seth who studied the screen, blankly shaking his head. "She scared the hell out of me, man. I am not kidding. I couldn't get her to come out of it. That's when I called you."

Conner turned back to the screen as Adrienne fought with what she was seeing and feeling for a long time to determine who would get control. It was almost as if she were in a trance. Then her eyes jerked open, and she started walking for the door.

If walking is what you could call it. It was more like dragging her own body.

"That's when she headed for the elevator," Seth whispered.

They both watched in horror as it took her minutes to figure out what a three-year-old child could do in two seconds: turn the handle of the door. She opened it as far as she seemed able, then squeezed through. And out of the sight of the camera.

Seth and Conner both sat back in their chairs, exhausted from just having viewed that. Neither spoke. What could be said?

Conner knew he had to get her out of this building. Whether he blocked—he mentally scoffed at that term—her abilities or not, he did not want her here one more minute.

He turned to Seth. "I'm taking her back to the hotel. I can't stand the thought of her here anymore."

"I totally agree. I'll see you tomorrow."

Conner went back into the conference room where Adrienne still slept. She had curled both legs under his jacket and had one arm tucked under her cheek on the armrest. Dark circles still framed her eyes. Conner hated to wake her up but knew she would be more comfortable sleeping back at the hotel.

"Hey, Sleeping Beauty, ready to wake up?" He touched her shoulder gently.

Her eyes fluttered open, then she sat straight up on the couch. Conner could tell she was trying to get her bearings. She brought her hands to her head, almost as a reflex, then slowly lowered them.

"How long have I been asleep?" she finally asked.

"A couple hours. Not long. I'm done here for the day and thought I would take you to the hotel."

Adrienne stood and stretched. "Okay, that sounds good. I don't usually fall asleep in busy places—too much buzzing. But I'm still tired anyway."

They returned to the interrogation room to grab Adrienne's purse and were soon in the parking garage, getting into Conner's car.

"I've been thinking about me blocking your abilities," Conner started as they pulled out of the garage.

"I'd be more comfortable if you'd call them my freakishly awesome crime-fighting superpowers. But please continue."

Conner chuckled. If Adrienne was back to wisecracking, then she was feeling much better. "Why do you think *I* block your superpowers? Does that happen often?"

It took Adrienne so long to answer, Conner wasn't sure she was going to. "Honestly, I don't know why you block them. The only other time this has happened is with my sisters..." She faded off.

"You have sisters?"

"Yes. One older, one younger. But I don't see them very often."

"Why not?"

"Our parents died when I was twelve. There wasn't any other family to take us in, and we ended up in the foster system. Trying to find a family to take three traumatized preteen girls with special needs became impossible. So we wound up in different homes." Adrienne shrugged.

Conner grimaced. First she'd lost her parents, then her sisters. Not easy. But he caught an interesting turn of phrase.

"Special needs? As in 'freakishly awesome crime-fighting superpowers' special needs?"

"Sort of."

"Do they have abilities like you do?"

"Yeah, but not exactly the same."

Conner waited for Adrienne to say more, but it became apparent that discussing her sisters' special needs/ freakishly awesome abilities was not on the table. "But they block your ability, too?"

"Yes, when the three of us are together, we block each other out. But we don't really know why."

Adrienne obviously didn't want to talk about her sisters, so Conner changed the subject. "Was using your superpowers always this painful when you worked for the FBI before? Seth showed me the footage from this afternoon when you opened the package."

"Well, I have to admit, I'm out of practice. I was mentally tougher back then, better able to focus and protect myself. But I'm not sure that anything could've prepared me for that package today. The evil was so *immediate.* So close." Adrienne shuddered. "But, yeah, it always hurt."

Conner shook his head. "Why didn't you tell someone about the physical pain? You were a teenager, for heaven's sake. Somebody could've helped you. Done something."

"Conner, I did tell people. Including Chief Kelly. It's not like I could hide it. Half the time I was vomiting my guts out or walking around with a bloody nose."

Conner ground his teeth. How could Chief Kelly— hell, how could anybody at the Bureau—allow a teenager to be abused in such a way?

"The FBI weren't monsters. I realize that now," Adrienne responded as if Conner had spoken the thought aloud. "There just was always a critical case. Always *one more case* that needed the abilities of the Blood-hound, before I took a break."

Conner grimaced. He didn't like it, but he at least understood. How much pain would he be willing to allow someone to go through if it meant saving the lives of the women Simon Says was killing?

Even worse, what if you were the one who had to choose how much agony you would endure in order to help people in dire situations? How did an eighteen-year-old make a decision like that?

"So you quit?" Conner asked. He didn't blame her.

"No, I finally had a complete breakdown and ended up in the hospital for six weeks. Then I quit."

Yep, that would do it. Conner drove in silence as Adrienne stared out the window.

"I just couldn't take it anymore after that," Adrienne whispered. "I was afraid working for the Bureau would end up killing me."

Conner could hear the regret in her voice; she obviously considered herself a coward for the choice she had made. He reached over and linked his fingers with hers.

"Hey, no one could blame you for making the choice you did. It doesn't do any good to have you help others if you barely live through it yourself."

She looked down at their linked hands then smiled sadly at him. "Maybe." Her voice was still small.

Conner pulled into a parking spot at her hotel. He turned off the engine but didn't get out of the car. He released his seat belt and turned toward her.

"Adrienne, you were so young. Someone—Chief Kelly, or, hell, any of the agents—should've seen what was happening to you and done something about it."

Adrienne shrugged and looked away. Conner let go

of her hand and put his hands on either side of her cheeks, drawing her gaze back to him.

"After what I saw with you today, I would not blame you if you never set foot in a Bureau office again. Nobody would. You're not a coward, Adrienne. The fact that you're still here helping us proves that."

She was stronger than she knew and more beautiful than he could stand. He bent his head down to hers and kissed her. The kiss was soft and almost sweet at first, but as Conner felt her respond, he deepened the kiss. Her hands slid up to his chest, and he pulled her closer.

They had kissed before, but this time Conner was aware of how fragile Adrienne really was. How tiny she was in his arms. When the tip of Conner's tongue outlined Adrienne's lips, she sighed very softly. The sound sent a shiver through him. Conner felt Adrienne's fingers curling into his shirt and cursed the restricting confines of the car. Conner didn't want to leave Adrienne's lips even for the little time it would take to walk inside and up to her room.

The sudden ringing of Adrienne's phone was jarring in the relative silence of the car. Breathing heavy, Conner pulled away from her lips slowly. Adrienne had a slightly dazed look.

"I think that's your phone," Conner finally said after the third ring.

Adrienne fished the phone out of the bag. "It's Vince at the ranch. I have to take this. I'm sorry." She answered the phone and told Vince to hold on for a moment.

Conner ran his fingers down Adrienne's cheek. "It's been a long day for us both. I'll just see you tomorrow. I'll come by and pick you up for breakfast."

Adrienne turned her head to the side and kissed his

palm then smiled and got out of the car. Conner watched until she was safely inside the hotel, then started the ignition and pulled away. It really had been a long day for both of them.

And Conner had a feeling the long days were just getting started.

Chapter Ten

The next morning Conner picked Adrienne up at the hotel, they had breakfast and went into work. As soon as they got in the Bureau office, Conner could tell something had happened. It didn't take them long to find out what.

Another package had arrived from Simon Says.

It had already been vetted by security and held no threats to the FBI team in terms of its physical contents. All that was left to do now was open it.

Conner and Seth met in the conference room as well as Chief Kelly and a couple other agents working the case. Adrienne came in, too, but stayed as far away from the box as she could and yet still be in the room.

Donning latex gloves, Conner and Seth wasted no time in carefully opening the package. The outer packaging, as always, held nothing but the jeweler's box. Conner pulled the box out and set it on the table. Seth took the lid off the box.

It was all so horribly familiar. A single lock of hair. A typed note on a folded sheet of plain paper. No one spoke as Conner unfolded the paper and read it.

Simon says, you're still too slow.

There was no response. Everyone in the room knew

that the note meant another woman was dead. It would just be a matter of time until the body was discovered. Sometimes it was hours; sometimes it was days.

The packages were almost anticlimactic at this point. But still frustrating as hell.

Stepping back from the box, he realized everyone was looking at Adrienne. Only a select few were aware of the affect Conner had on Adrienne's abilities, so they obviously expected her to shed some sort of light on this newest arrival.

"Can I talk with you by my desk for a minute?" Conner asked Adrienne. She followed him out of the room. Seth wasn't far behind.

"I guess I'm going to go get some coffee." Conner grimaced. He knew he had to get away from the office in order for Adrienne to work. But he didn't like it.

Seth sighed dramatically. "Good. That should buy us some time. Since it takes twenty minutes for you to get out all the words in your order."

Conner ignored him as Adrienne put her hand on his arm. "I'm sorry. I know this has to be hard for you."

"I can take it as long as we catch this guy soon."

"You will." She squeezed his arm gently. "Don't go to the coffee shop in the lobby. You're still too close."

Conner rolled his eyes. "I know when I'm not wanted. I'm going. I'm going."

Adrienne released his arm. "But don't go far. I have a bad feeling about this one."

Conner nodded and left. Once outside he was overwhelmed with frustration again. There had to be something more he could do. Is this really what he had been reduced to at this point in his career—coffee boy?

This feeling of uselessness sucked. It went against everything in Conner's nature to sit on the sidelines while someone—*anyone*—else did the hard work. And knowing it was Adrienne suffering, and that he could stop it, left a bitter taste in his mouth. His every instinct was to protect her.

So, yes, Conner was pissed that he was four blocks away from his building getting coffee when Adrienne was back at the office fighting for her mental survival.

Conner gave his order to the cashier and paid. Yes, sugar-free vanilla in his latte. He couldn't tell if the ladies behind him were smirking at his order or not. Why did everyone find his drink choice so amusing?

Conner walked back outside. No matter how useless he felt, he was still glad he was able to help Adrienne. He didn't know why he blocked her powers, and he didn't care. He had no idea how she had survived her work with the FBI before.

Conner felt the phone buzz in his pocket, signaling a text message. It was too soon to hear from Seth or Adrienne; he'd only been gone about ten minutes. But the text was from Seth.

Come now.

Conner frowned at the phone. Another text appeared.

Hurry!

The exclamation point had Conner dropping his drink in the nearby trash can and taking off at a dead run. If Seth was telling him to hurry, something was wrong.

Within minutes Conner was back at the building. The elevator was too slow in arriving so he bolted up the stairs, fear burning through his brain.

Conner tore into the conference room. Adrienne was lying on the ground, unconscious, blood dripping from both nostrils.

"What the hell? Seth, what happened?" Conner dropped on his knees beside her.

"Con, I have no idea. You left, and she got that pinched look like she always does. Then we came in here. She touched the box and went really still for a minute—that's not unusual. She said something about a hotel. Then she reached for the note, and it was like she had been electrocuted. She couldn't even get any words out. It looked like she was trying to scream, but there was no sound."

Conner checked Adrienne's pulse. It was thready and weak. There was no color to her face at all, causing the blood from her nose to stand out in the most garish way.

Seth continued, shaking his head. "Then she fell to the ground. It was like she was having some sort of seizure. I texted you immediately. Thank God you weren't far, man."

Conner continued to stare at Adrienne. Her breathing was not quite so shallow any longer, but she still wasn't waking up. He stroked her cheek gently.

"I think we should take her to the hospital," Conner said, looking up at Seth for the first time. Seth nodded.

"No," Adrienne's weak voice responded, and Conner jerked his gaze back to her. Her eyes didn't open. "I'll be okay in a minute. Just don't leave me." She felt blindly for Conner's hand with hers. Conner grabbed it and laced his fingers through hers.

"No, sweetheart. I won't leave you."

Seth ushered out the other people in the room and closed the door behind them. It seemed to Conner that some of Adrienne's color was returning. He felt her pulse again at her wrist. Stronger.

Seth came over with a tissue and handed it to Conner. Conner gently wiped the blood from her nose and applied a bit of pressure to stop the rest of the bleeding.

"Thanks," Adrienne whispered, opening her eyes.

"Hey." Conner smiled at her. "You know, if you want me to come back sooner, just ask. You don't have to go to all this drama."

Adrienne smiled at him. "Busted."

"You want to try to sit up or do you prefer lying down?"

"I think I'm okay to sit up. I'm feeling better."

Conner helped her, and they scooted over until they were leaning back against the couch with their legs stretched out in front of them. Seth sat in a chair at the table.

"So, that was not awesome," Adrienne finally said.

"What the hell happened, Adrienne?" Seth asked. "That was worse than anything I've seen."

"Believe me, it was worse than anything I've *felt*." Conner was close enough to feel her shudder. "The feeling was so strong. It was like he was in the room with us. He was laughing this horrible mocking laugh."

Adrienne drew her knees up to her chest and wrapped her arms around her legs. "And then he reached out to touch me, and I just lost it. I felt like my body was burning. I was screaming."

"It looked like you were trying to scream," Seth corrected her. "But no sound came out of your mouth."

"I don't know why I had such a huge reaction. Maybe because he touched it so recently? I don't know. Maybe that's why the feelings are so strong."

There was a brief knock on the conference room door. An agent stuck his head in.

"There's been a call, guys. Woman's body found at

a hotel on Harrison Street. Locals called it in. Pretty sure it's Simon."

Seth looked at Adrienne. "You said something about a hotel before you fell."

Adrienne nodded and looked up sadly. "Yes. It's definitely her. Simon's latest victim."

ADRIENNE WAS EXHAUSTED. Riding in the backseat of the car with Conner and Seth on the way to the crime scene, she could admit the exhaustion to herself, even if she didn't want to admit it to anyone else.

She knew the guys weren't exactly happy she was with them, but what else could they do? Either Conner had to stay at the field office with her—and there was no way in hell that was happening—or she had to come with him. Adrienne didn't really want to see the crime scene. After what had happened this morning, she just wanted to get far away from all of humanity, go to bed, pull the covers over her head and sleep for a week.

This morning had scared her. The only time she'd ever had a reaction that strong was when the perpetrator had been in close proximity and had turned his malice toward her. It was like Simon had *known* she was there. But Adrienne knew that couldn't be right, because she would've felt him long before touching the letter.

There was something not normal about this serial killer. Adrienne just didn't know what it was yet. *A not-normal serial killer. Go figure.* Adrienne barely refrained from scoffing at herself out loud.

They pulled up outside the motel where the body had been found. This was definitely the place she had seen in her vision.

"Do you want us to clear the scene so you can go in first?" Conner asked.

She knew how hard that question was for him. Clearing the scene would include clearing him also. She couldn't imagine that option sat well with him.

"No. If it's okay with you guys, I just want to sit here for a while. The other people being in there won't make any difference for me." She saw relief flutter across Conner's face before he hurried out of the car.

She watched all the activity for a long while—a crime scene was a busy place. Technicians, photographers, local law enforcement buzzed around everywhere. It wouldn't be long before the press was here, and the bystanders. Local officers were already roping off a good area of the scene so it wouldn't be disturbed. Adrienne watched it all with interest. It was actually the first crime scene she had been at where she could just observe like a normal person. Until Conner left, Adrienne's abilities wouldn't work. Blessed silence.

The entire place would be photographed then fingerprinted. The room and body would be scoured for forensic evidence. Adrienne doubted they would find any. Simon had proved to be quite fastidious so far about not leaving any evidence behind.

Eventually, a tall, lanky man, camera clutched in his hand, came up to the car. He tapped on Adrienne's window and smiled. Adrienne opened her door.

"Hi, Ms. Jeffries. I'm Victor Faraday, FBI photographer. It's nice to meet you." The man spoke rapidly, in a much higher pitch than Adrienne would expect from someone his size. "Can I get you anything? Are you okay?"

The photographer—she'd already forgotten his name—was definitely odd, but seemed sincere in wanting to assist Adrienne. She smiled distractedly at him. "I'm fine. Thanks. Just waiting."

"Okay. Agent Perigo sent me to tell you that you can come in. We're done with photography, and I believe the forensics team is finished also."

Adrienne thanked the man and got out of the car. She walked slowly up to the hotel room door. Looking at the photos over the past few days had been bad enough; she was not looking forward to seeing the crime scene live.

Conner saw her and came over.

"Already in here? I thought you were going to wait for me to get you. You okay?"

Adrienne ignored his comment about not waiting for him. She had waited until he'd sent Victor out, right? She hugged her arms around herself. "Not really. I have to be honest. I'm not looking forward to this."

Conner reached over and rubbed her upper arms and hands. Adrienne couldn't help but lean a little toward his strength. "Give me about five minutes, and I'll get out of here."

Adrienne nodded. Might as well get it over with. She glanced around the room, purposely avoiding looking at the body on the bed, and waited. It wasn't long before Conner returned.

"Seth and I have worked out a plan. I'm going to go a couple blocks away in the car, so I can get back here immediately if needed. I'll be on the phone the entire time with Seth, so as soon as I'm far enough for you to start getting clear feelings, let him know."

Adrienne was touched that they had taken time to figure out how to best balance the needs of the case with her well-being. She smiled at Conner then stood on tiptoe quickly and kissed his cheek.

"Thank you."

Conner winked at her and strode out the door. A

few moments later she heard the car starting and pulling away.

It didn't take long for Conner to be far enough away for Adrienne's abilities to work.

"Tell him to go just a little farther, Seth, then stop. I'm getting stuff now."

Seth relayed the message to Conner on his phone then turned back to Adrienne. "Are you okay? My heart cannot stand another repeat of this morning."

Adrienne took deep calming breaths to focus herself. "I think I'm okay. I'm just going to take it slow."

For the first time Adrienne looked over at the dead woman lying on the bed. She walked over to her. Obviously, like the other victims, this woman had been stabbed to death. Adrienne touched her ankle featherlight.

Boring. This one was not nearly as fun as the others. She just cried quietly. Killing the last one had brought such a high because she had been so bossy and bad. Killing her had been fun. But this one was pathetic.

As soon as Adrienne removed her hand from the woman's leg, the killer's thoughts stopped. She looked over at Seth, who was furiously writing in his notebook.

"Anything else?" he asked.

"Was I saying that out loud?"

"Yeah. About him being bored and stuff. I'm just trying to get it all down." He pointed to the phone, now on speaker-mode, on the table next to him. "Conner is listening, also."

Adrienne touched the dead woman's ankle lightly again. She didn't want to go anywhere near the stab wounds at the top of the woman's body.

She couldn't breathe right, so of course she couldn't scream. The screaming was what made it fun.

Adrienne let go of the woman's ankle. She knew what happened next. He killed her. Adrienne didn't want to see that.

She looked over at Seth. "She had asthma or something. She couldn't scream, so it wasn't as fulfilling for him."

Seth nodded. "Anything else?"

Adrienne walked around the room but couldn't seem to get any reading. She decided to experiment. "Tell Conner to drive away a little farther. I can't hear anything right now except from the body. Maybe if he's not so close, I'll be able to get something else."

Seth relayed the message to Conner, and Adrienne walked around the room some more. But still nothing. "He's very careful, methodical, when he's placing the bodies. Not angry. It's difficult for me to get any information."

The general buzzing got louder, and Adrienne's head began pounding, and her stomach rolled, so she knew Conner was far enough away not to affect her. She touched different pieces of furniture in the room, hoping to pick up something from them, but had no luck. She was giving up and about to leave when the image came to her.

"Seth! He was standing right over here in this corner." Adrienne rushed over there and placed herself where she saw the killer. "Watching. Almost like he was watching while you were in here processing the scene. He knew or envisioned or *something* what it would be like when you all got here and found the body."

Adrienne followed the actions of the killer in her mind. "He laughed to think of you here, unable to figure anything out. Then he turned and walked out the door."

Adrienne followed the same path outside, knowing

Seth was right behind her. "He turned and walked down this block to where his car was parked. He knew not to park it in front of the hotel. He had to hurry. There was something he wanted to see, to make sure he didn't miss."

"Miss what?" Seth asked.

"I don't know. He keeps thinking of it as 'the show.'"

Adrienne stopped and looked down. "He dropped his keys here, and he was mad. He was going to miss the show if he didn't hurry."

Adrienne stopped and looked around, confused.

"What happened then?" Seth asked.

"I don't know. He just disappeared."

"You mean he got into his car?"

"No. He reached down to get his keys. And then I couldn't see him anymore." Adrienne rubbed her forehead. Why had she lost him like that? There were no other people around, nothing to confuse her. She shouldn't have lost him like that.

"He was just gone," Adrienne explained to Seth. "I don't know why. It doesn't happen like that."

She looked around but didn't pick up any other images from the killer. "Conner didn't come back, did he?" But she knew he hadn't, because her head still hurt and she could hear all the buzzing. So what was the problem?

Seth was about to double check with Conner when Adrienne interrupted him. "Never mind. You can tell him to come back. I can't see anything else here."

Adrienne walked back to the crime scene, frustrated. She was frustrated with herself, with what had happened, with why she couldn't get a clear, full glimpse into the killer's mind. Was it her that was the problem? Was it Conner?

It brought her back to her thought from earlier today: she was dealing with something *not normal*. Well, she better figure out what that *not normal* was before another woman died.

Conner returned a few minutes later and walked directly over to Adrienne. "You okay?"

"Yes. Just tired. This is all so strange, so different from other cases I've worked. I'm frustrated."

"I know you are. Let Seth and I finish up here, and I'll take you back to the hotel."

Adrienne nodded and got back into Conner's car to wait for them to process the scene. A lot of work, a lot of people to manage and, as the agents in charge, everyone kept coming to Conner and Seth for answers and instructions. Adrienne didn't mind waiting in the relatively peaceful cocoon of the car. At some point one of the local police officers even brought her a sandwich, which she ate gratefully.

Eventually everything wrapped up, and Conner and Seth were ready to leave the scene. She saw them chat for a moment before Conner came to the car and Seth headed in the other direction.

"Seth is going to get a ride back to the office so I can take you straight to the hotel. I know you're exhausted. Sorry it took so long." Conner started the car and pulled out into the street.

"That's all right. It was interesting watching everyone work."

"Yeah, the locals have been pretty great about working with us in this case. That doesn't always happen. Cops can get pretty territorial about their cases. I think we all just want to catch this son of a bitch."

"Me, too." Adrienne sighed.

Conner reached over and took her hand. "You're

doing your best, Adrienne. Seth told me about today. You can't let that upset you. Everything you've done has helped, and we're all grateful."

"But it hasn't been enough!" Adrienne's frustration burst from her.

"It will be. We'll get ahead of him."

Exhaustion poured over Adrienne. She was tired of killers and dead bodies and voices and visions of evil in her head. She just wanted one night of good solid sleep with no buzzing or static to keep waking her.

They pulled up to her hotel. Conner parked the car and came around to open her door. "You're dead on your feet." He trailed a finger down her cheek. Adrienne could feel the warmth it left behind. "These days are rough on you, I know."

"The nights aren't great, either."

Conner grimaced. "No wonder you're tired all the time. Trouble sleeping?"

"Every night. Seems to be getting worse."

Conner put a hand at the small of her back and led her inside the hotel. "I'll stay here tonight. In the lobby. That should give you a peaceful night's sleep."

Adrienne wasn't sure how to respond. She was so grateful for his offer. The thought of having a night of uninterrupted rest made her feel like a huge weight had been lifted from her shoulders.

But she didn't want him in the lobby. She wanted him in her bed.

Adrienne smiled up at Conner shyly and reached for his hand. "There's no need for you to stay down here."

He pressed the button for the elevator then stepped close enough to Adrienne that his lips were just inches away from hers.

"I think we both know if I stay up there, a peaceful night's sleep is not what's going to happen."

The elevator door opened, but Conner didn't move. Finally Adrienne put a finger on his chest and pushed him into the elevator and didn't stop until Conner's back was against the elevator's wall. The doors closed behind them.

"Sleeping is overrated." Adrienne reached up and threaded her hands through his hair, bringing his lips down to hers.

She pulled Conner's lips to hers in a fierce kiss. She could feel a moment's hesitation before he gave himself fully over to the passion between them. Adrienne gasped as Conner spun her around so her back was against the wall. He wrapped his arms around her hips and lifted her so they were eye to eye.

Heat pooled in her belly as he pressed up against her. She hooked one elbow around the back of his neck to pull him closer, deepening the kiss. He groaned, rocking against her, setting off sparks of electricity up and down her spine.

Adrienne vaguely heard the elevator door *bing* and open—she couldn't remember either of them even pushing her floor's button. Conner groaned and slid her slowly down his body and onto her feet. Then trailed his hands up from her hips past her waist to her shoulders, then cupped her cheeks.

He grabbed her hand and led her from the elevator to her room. Adrienne found the card key in her purse and handed it to Conner, who unlocked the door. He jerked her to him as he opened the door, and Adrienne giggled. Her giggling stopped when his mouth captured hers again, closing the door behind him with his foot.

After a moment, Adrienne eased away from Conner

and turned to put her purse on the table, flipping on the light. Her breath came in a shocked gasp as she turned and looked around her.

Her hotel room was in shambles. Someone had destroyed nearly everything in it.

Chapter Eleven

When Conner heard Adrienne's shocked gasp he immediately threw her behind his body and drew his weapon. The room was completely destroyed. He checked under the bed, in the closet and bathroom, cursing himself for not securing the room when he had first walked in, but found nothing.

Conner saw Adrienne still looking around with huge eyes, trying to take it all in. An envelope on the pillow—the one area of the room not destroyed—caught her attention. Before he could stop her, she walked over to the bed to read the note.

When she saw what it said, her hands began to shake.

"Conner?" Her voice came out as a hoarse whisper. He was immediately at her side and took the note from her.

Simon says, don't worry, it's almost your turn.

Conner lowered Adrienne's shaking form to the bed. He immediately called Seth.

"Seth. I'm at the hotel with Adrienne. Simon Says has been here. He ransacked the room, left a note on her bed." Conner glanced over at Adrienne, glad she couldn't hear the expletives that came out of Seth's mouth when he understood the full ramifications of the situation. "I need you to get the full team up here right away."

Conner turned back to where Adrienne still sat on the bed. She didn't seem to have moved from where he had placed her. The letter was still gripped in her shaking hands, but she wasn't looking at it. Her eyes were unfocused, staring at some faraway place only she could see.

"Hey, sweetheart," Conner said gently, kneeling in front of her perch on the bed. "Adrienne?"

She finally focused in on him. His heart broke as big tears filled her eyes then spilled onto her cheeks.

"He was here, Conner. In my room."

Conner caught her tears with his fingers. "I know, baby."

"How long ago? How did he get in here? How did he know where to find me? And what could he be looking for?" She stood up as her panic built. Conner stood with her. She grabbed the front of his shirt. "Do you think he's still around here?"

Conner was reminded that Adrienne wasn't a trained FBI agent. Just a young woman who had seen way too much violence in her lifetime. Now the psychopath had turned his madness toward her. She was rightfully panicked.

He covered the hand that gripped his shirt and rubbed it gently. "Adrienne, no, he's not here. I already checked the room and the hallway. There's nobody around."

She nodded up at him weakly.

"Seth and the team are on their way. We should try not to touch anything until they process the scene."

Adrienne released his shirt and stood. She looked around the room like she'd never seen it before, then turned back to him. "Maybe you should leave and I'll… see what I can see."

Conner immediately closed the space between them. He gripped her upper arms. "There is no way in hell I'm leaving you here alone. You got that? Don't even say it." He would not leave her now.

"But…"

Conner put his hands on both sides of her face and stroked her cheeks with this thumbs. "Baby, no. I'm not leaving you."

Intense relief flashed through Adrienne's eyes. She had been willing to try, Conner realized—and appreciated—but she would've paid a high price for it.

Conner led Adrienne out of the room and down to the lobby. He explained to the night manager that there had been a break-in and that an FBI team was coming to process the scene. Finding out that the room next to Adrienne's was available, he asked for the keys to it. Adrienne could stay there while they processed her room.

Conner would not leave Adrienne alone in this hotel. In any hotel. Not now. He would take her home with him. She would stay there until they caught Simon Says.

It wasn't long before Seth and the rest of the team arrived. Adrienne still had that exhausted, pinched look about her and gave no fight when Conner suggested she stay in the room next door. Conner posted one of the agents as a guard at the door, just to be safe.

Seth looked as ticked as Conner when he saw the room and the note. Conner's anger increased even more as he saw how Adrienne's clothes had been ripped into pieces and thrown all over the room.

Deliberate, ugly violence.

"Thank God you were with her, man," Seth said through clenched teeth.

Conner could barely stand to think about the alternative. "What if I hadn't been, Seth? What if I had just dropped her off, and she had discovered this alone?"

Something like this would be scary enough for any woman to walk in on. But who knows how it would've affected Adrienne. Simon having been in her room? Having touched everything around her? A note directed especially to her?

Conner remembered Adrienne's reaction this morning to Simon's latest package. It had knocked her out cold. Almost had them taking her to the hospital.

What would've happened to her if Conner wasn't around to block it and there was no one there to help her get out of the room?

Conner didn't even want to think about it. He was filled with the overwhelming urge to get Adrienne out of here—away from the violence that had bombarded her all day.

"Seth, Adrienne can't deal with anything right now. I'm taking her to my place. Bag everything, and she'll look at it when she's ready."

Seth nodded, and Conner was grateful not to get any flak from his partner. Conner went to the next room to get Adrienne and found her in the same seat where he'd left her, looking off into space.

He walked up to her slowly, careful not to startle her. He sat down in the chair beside her and gently touched her arm. She blinked and looked over at him.

"Hey," she whispered.

"You ready to go?"

Adrienne nodded and stood up.

"I'm going to take you to my place. I have a town house in Daly City, not too far from here."

Adrienne nodded again, then rubbed her hands up and down her arms as if to warm herself.

"Cold?"

"Yeah. But my jacket was…" She swallowed hard and shrugged.

Conner took off his blazer, slipped it around her shoulders and watched her snuggle into its warmth. Not having his jacket meant his holster and weapon showed, but Conner didn't care. He got Adrienne downstairs and bundled into his car. Her huge eyes peering at him still looked overwhelmed.

The drive to Daly City—a suburb of San Francisco—didn't take long at this time of the evening. Conner tried to talk to Adrienne about neutral things, like his family, who lived in Nevada, and how he had inherited this town house from his grandmother, the only way he could possibly afford a place like this anywhere near San Fran on his salary.

Adrienne didn't say much, but she seemed to listen.

They parked at the town house, and Conner helped her out of his car and in his front door. Her eyes still held that somewhat vacant look. He wished she would cry or yell or anything but keep what she was feeling buried inside her.

"How about some hot tea?" he asked as he herded her into the kitchen and sat her down by the table.

"Chai tea?"

"If that's what you want. Sure."

"Only if it's sugar-free vanilla and has no foam." A ghost of a smile passed her lips.

Conner was relieved to see even that tiny smile. "Smart aleck."

"So this is where you live?"

"Yep. For about six years now."

"Always been just you?"

"Is that a more subtle way of asking if I've ever been married?" Conner chuckled when Adrienne blushed. "I lived here with my grandmother for a couple years before she died. But since then, it's just been me."

"Mind if I look around?"

Conner was glad some life was returning to Adrienne. "Sure, be my guest. But please excuse any mess. I wasn't expecting company."

Adrienne wandered around looking at his pictures and knickknacks. A lot of it was decorations from before his grandmother had passed away. Conner had just never changed it.

"How about you?" he asked as he finished making their tea. "Ever married?"

"No. After my work with the FBI before, I just needed to totally be away from people for a while. Then I never found the right guy, I guess."

"Not a whole lot of guys in Lodi. How'd you end up there?"

"That's where my foster mother's family was from. She had passed away and left me some money, plus I saved a lot while I worked for the Bureau, since I never had any free time. It ended up being enough for the down payment on the horse ranch."

"You love horses?"

"I love how they don't put any voices or thoughts into my head, mostly. But I've grown to love them, yeah."

Conner smiled and walked over, handing Adrienne the mug of tea.

"How did you end up working with the Bureau anyway?" Conner sat down in his normal recliner across from the couch. But Adrienne seemed more interested in walking around, looking at things: his pictures, his books, his DVDs.

"I was eighteen. After my foster mother—really the only person I called family—died, I had to go into San Francisco for some business with her will at the courthouse. As you can imagine, a courthouse is not the best place for me to be with my gift."

Conner could imagine.

"Plus I was used to living in a small town," Adrienne continued, still wandering around his living room looking at things. "I was a mess, hardly able to function. I literally ran into Chief Kelly, knocking all the papers out of his briefcase. I went to hand a photo back to him—it was a picture of one of the Bureau's 'most wanted' criminals—and got a clear image of exactly where the guy was right at that moment. Which happened to be just a couple blocks away as he was about to rob a convenience store."

Adrienne came and sat down on the couch across from Conner's chair.

"And?"

She smiled. "Well, I told him what I saw. I have to give Chief Kelly credit—he didn't laugh or scoff or arrest me. He called it in, and they caught him. Right where I said he'd be.

"After careful vetting and making sure I wasn't that guy's accomplice, Kelly offered me a job as a 'consultant.'" She sighed. "I was eighteen and had nobody. I wanted to do something important. To make a difference."

"You did make a difference, Adrienne. You still are making a difference."

Adrienne shrugged. "I guess. Part of me always felt

like I was a coward for quitting. Even though I honestly had no alternative at the time. It was too much."

Conner came and sat next to Adrienne on the couch. "I've seen the price you pay for using your talents, Adrienne. Nobody should've expected you to keep paying that price. It couldn't be done. And you were a *teenager*, for heaven's sake."

Adrienne leaned her head back against the top of the couch. "My perspective on that time has changed, thanks to you."

"What do you mean?"

"I now understand what my job with the FBI could've been like, if it had been done right. You've shown me how much more I can handle if I can just get some sort of rest and reprieve in between."

Conner sighed. "I don't know how true that is. You're still exhausted and in pain a lot of the time."

"Yeah, but I know there is a time coming every day when I won't be in pain. When there won't be noise. That's thanks to you."

"I wish I could've been around ten years ago."

"That would've been ideal." Adrienne turned her face toward him and grinned without lifting her head from the couch. "But I realize now, if I had just demanded time off in between cases to recuperate—that would've made a huge difference. And I needed to get a place out of town so I wasn't always bombarded by noise in my time off."

"You were eighteen. Most eighteen-year-olds are trying to figure out which English class to take at college or how to get beer without being carded."

Adrienne shrugged. "Yeah? Is that what you were like at eighteen?"

"Pretty much. I always knew I wanted to be in law

enforcement, so I stayed pretty clean. Went into the Bureau right out of college."

"Never married?"

"No. Engaged once, back East. But she really wasn't interested in the hours an agent has to put in. Glad we figured it out before we got married. No harm, no foul."

Adrienne reached for his mug and took it along with hers back to the kitchen. Conner could hear the water running as she rinsed them out.

"It's still pretty early," he called out to her. "Want to watch some TV?"

Adrienne returned from the kitchen and stopped right in front of Conner on the couch. "No, actually what I was hoping is that you might kiss me some more, and we could eventually work our way to you showing me your bedroom."

ADRIENNE WASN'T SURE she had ever wanted anyone as much as she wanted Conner Perigo right now. Glancing down at him, she could see myriad emotions cross his face: concern, hesitation, passion. He was worried about her vulnerable state. He didn't want to take advantage. She truly appreciated that he was the type of man who would consider these things and want to do what was right.

But she wasn't going to allow it to get in her way tonight.

Adrienne could admit she had been shaken earlier. What she saw in her hotel room had frightened her. Deeply. And she knew she was going to have to deal with it and process it—but not right now. Here in this house, enveloped by all the items Conner held dear—pictures, knickknacks, items of the past and the present—Adrienne felt safe. This was a house centered in love and security. Adrienne could feel herself drawing strength from it.

They had right now. Adrienne wasn't going to waste it. Vicious psycho on their radar or not, nobody ever knew how many tomorrows they had.

Conner still hadn't responded. He was eyeing her warily, as if he couldn't quite decide the best way to talk her down from this particular ledge.

Obviously he was going to need a little help getting over his nobility.

Adrienne crossed the few remaining steps to him. She leaned down to where he sat on the couch and put her hands on his knees. She smiled at him.

"Adrienne…"

Adrienne leaned the rest of the way and kissed him. Lightly. She put her hands on his shoulders. He didn't pull away, but he didn't pull her to him, either.

"I'm not sure this is a good idea." Conner rested his forehead against hers.

"You may be right," Adrienne said, smiling again. "But I don't think we have enough data collected yet to be sure."

Not giving him a chance to respond, Adrienne straddled her legs on either side of his on the couch and lowered herself the rest of the way onto his lap. She took his face between her hands and kissed him.

Adrienne kissed him with all the passion she'd felt for him since the moment she'd met him.

It didn't take long for Conner to give up the fight. She heard him sigh as his arms hooked around her hips, pulling her closer to him. Everything about them seemed to explode. The hot, needful pressure of his mouth made her dizzy. Her hands locked in fistfuls of his hair as he released her lips and began kissing his way along her jaw to her throat. His mouth slid to the soft hollow beneath her ear, placing a not-too-gentle bite on that side of her neck.

Adrienne felt the heat inside her intensify. She whispered his name and dragged his mouth back to hers, drowning in the kiss. She reached between them and unbuttoned his shirt, loving the feel of his chest against her palms. She felt him reach for the hem of her T-shirt and broke their kiss long enough for him to peel it over her head.

Conner's lips returned to her neck, nipping with just enough force to drive her absolutely crazy. His hands unhooked and removed her bra, then cupped her breasts.

"You're beautiful."

Adrienne could hear the reverence in Conner's tone as he kissed her again. She wrapped her fingers in his hair and held him to her.

Abruptly Conner pried her off him and stood, wasting no time getting the rest of her clothes off her. He made quick work of his own, then reached under her hips with both arms and lifted her again. She wrapped her arms around his neck and her legs around his waist. He carried her up the stairs.

"You mentioned something about wanting to see my bedroom?" He raised one eyebrow.

Adrienne giggled. "So considerate of you to give me the tour."

"We aim to please."

His bedroom was decidedly masculine with heavy wooden furniture. A plain cream-colored duvet was thrown haphazardly across the bed—as if he had attempted to make it up this morning, but hadn't been willing to give it more than thirty seconds' worth of effort. Conner tossed the cover to the side and eased

Adrienne onto the bed and followed down right on top of her.

His lips found hers again, and Adrienne gave herself over to the feeling of being utterly surrounded by Conner. Being held against him felt good. His incredible body heat felt good. Everything about this felt good. With every touch he aroused another wave of sensation.

For the first time ever, Adrienne gave herself over to passion without holding back, knowing without a doubt she was safe.

THE NEXT MORNING Conner looked over at Adrienne asleep in his bed. She was curled around a pillow, tucked up in a tiny ball. Her deep, even breathing suggested she was a long way from waking up. Good, she needed sleep. Last night had been wonderful, but it definitely had not helped her get any rest. Conner couldn't bring himself to be sorry about that.

He had wanted her like he'd never wanted another woman. It was all he could do now to just leave her alone.

Conner eased himself from the bed, careful not to disturb her. He grabbed some sweatpants from out of a drawer and put them on as he headed downstairs to the coffeemaker.

Yeah, Conner was glad Adrienne was asleep. She was going to need it now that it seemed Simon Says had turned his sights on her.

The thought made Conner break out in a cold sweat. Simon knew who Adrienne was, had known where she was staying. And they still knew next to nothing about him.

Conner made coffee—a full pot; he was going to

need it—and sat down at his kitchen table. His phone chirped from the counter. A text from Seth.

You up?

Conner texted him back, Yeah.

There in five. Bringing breakfast.

Conner was always up for a delivered meal but was especially glad Seth was coming over. It would give them a chance to talk through the thought that had come to Conner sometime in the night.

Simon Says was an FBI agent. Or a cop. Or some sort of law enforcement.

It was the only way he could've known who Adrienne was or that she was working with them.

It hadn't occurred to Conner while they were processing Adrienne's room at the hotel, probably because he had been too caught up with getting Adrienne out of there as soon as possible. But now that he had thought about it, it was the only thing that made sense.

There was a tap on the door, and Conner got up to answer it. Seth walked through, thrusting a bag of breakfast sandwiches at Conner.

"Simon Says is a cop," Seth said with no preamble.

Conner didn't need one. "I agree. I was just thinking that myself. A cop or agent. Some sort of law enforcement."

They sat down at the kitchen table and opened the sandwiches. "We've worked with a lot of people over the past six months. It could be any of them." Seth looked at the sandwich he got and traded it with Conner. "But it at least gives us a place to start looking. A way to narrow things down."

Conner took a bite of his breakfast. "It can't be someone at the Bureau office. Adrienne would be totally incapacitated just by him being around."

"Unless you're there blocking everything," Seth pointed out.

"Yeah, but how could he know that? We haven't told anybody. That would be taking an awfully big risk."

"Well, obviously this guy doesn't have a problem taking risks."

"I want her with one of us all the time, Seth. Or at least always in the Bureau office." Conner set his sandwich down and sat back in his chair shaking his head. "If Simon got her alone— You've seen what she's like after accessing evidence. Could you imagine how helpless she'd be if Simon actually got his hands on her?"

Conner was determined not to let that happen.

"We could get a protection detail on her."

Conner shook his head. "No. Not until we know for sure who we can trust. It could be anyone."

"Who could be anyone?" Adrienne's voice came softly from behind them over at the stairs.

Conner turned to her and was immediately stunned at how beautiful she was despite being in one of his T-shirts and a pair of his shorts. Or maybe she was so gorgeous because she was in them, even though they were huge on her.

Whichever. He had it bad.

"Good morning." Conner smiled at her. "Want some coffee?"

"Yeah, I'll get it. Hi, Seth."

"Morning, Adrienne."

Adrienne walked into the kitchen. Conner turned

back in his seat to find Seth looking at him with one eyebrow cocked.

"Shut up. I don't want to hear it," Conner muttered.

"And to think I was just about to comment on how gentlemanly of you it was to have taken the couch and let her sleep in your bed."

"Things just worked out differently."

"I'm just kidding you, man. The way you two have been from the very beginning, I'm surprised it has taken this long."

Adrienne walked back in, saving Conner from needing to reply. She came to stand next to him and he looped his arm around her waist, pulling her down into his lap. Without any thought to Seth whatsoever, he kissed her thoroughly.

"Good morning to you, too," Adrienne said, blushing, when Conner finally released her mouth. "What are you guys talking about?"

Conner was loath to bring it up but knew Adrienne should know. They explained their theory about Simon Says being in law enforcement. Listening, Adrienne got more and more tense in his lap.

"We want one of us to be with you, or you to be at the Bureau office all the time," Conner concluded.

Adrienne stood up. "That's not going to work. I'm going to need to go back to the ranch soon, at least for a few days. Vince can't run everything there alone forever."

Conner shook his head again. "No, Adrienne, you can't go back there right now. Not until we've caught Simon."

"But that could take months!"

Conner could feel his frustration building. She could not leave—he wouldn't allow it. He wouldn't let anything compromise her safety. "It won't take months. Not with you helping us." Conner reached out to Adrienne, but she stepped back from his grasp. Conner looked over at Seth, but found his partner was looking down at his hands, unwilling to get involved.

"Conner, I will take normal, reasonable precautions. Of course I don't want Simon to get ahold of me. But my abilities allow me to know if he's nearby, so I don't have to worry about that."

Conner couldn't think of a logical argument against what Adrienne was saying. "Three days. Give us three days to narrow down the pool of suspects. During that time, you stay with one of us or in the middle of the Bureau office. After three days we can reevaluate."

Conner watched as Adrienne considered his offer. She didn't like to be boxed into a decision, he could tell. Finally she nodded her head. He reached out for her again, and she took his extended hand.

"Okay. Three days."

Chapter Twelve

The three days were tough. Conner watched as Adrienne worked herself into exhaustion trying to help them. She fleshed out details about Simon Says—his thoughts, his motives—and the crimes. Based on comparing how tall the victims were with what angle Simon held his head while looking at them, Adrienne determined roughly how tall the killer was—around five foot ten.

She worked with an artist to provide a rendering of the room where the women were killed. And went through file after file, package after package, to see what insight she could gather. With the information Adrienne provided, both Conner and Seth knew they would eventually gain the upper hand on Simon.

What Adrienne could do—her freakishly awesome crime-fighting superpowers—was truly amazing. And the price she paid for it was hideous. Of course Conner always saw both secondhand. He had pretty much been banned from the office while Adrienne was working. He spent a lot of time around the city, going back over crime scenes, reinterviewing different parties, trying to piece together anything they may have missed the first time. He didn't like being away from Adrienne—not when Simon could be anyone at the Bureau.

But in order for them to get ahead in the case Conner had to stay away. Each afternoon he would return to the office and watch the footage of what happened with Adrienne while he was gone. He watched as she pored over any item they had associated with the murder and gleaned whatever information she could. And the cost she paid to do it.

Watching Adrienne go through such mental torture on a daily basis—knowing he could stop it at any time—was destroying Conner. He was torn between wanting to catch a sadistic killer and protecting the woman he loved.

The woman he loved?

Where exactly had that come from? Conner shrugged, didn't fight it. In the short time he had known Adrienne, she had eased her way into his heart. And he wanted her there. The moment he'd seen her walking into that barn last week, talking about some crazy horse, that had been it for him.

Of course, he had no idea how Adrienne felt. And he couldn't imagine why she would ever want to stay in San Francisco or ever be a part of the Bureau. The price she paid was too high.

Conner tried to be a buffer for her as much as possible, but it wasn't easy. Not only did she have the Simon Says case to work on, but soon word had gotten out around the building that the Bloodhound was real, not an urban legend. That she was back. That she was here. Everybody wanted to meet her or shake her hand or just ask for a moment's worth of help.

It was like Adrienne could spin straw into gold, and everyone wanted to bring their little bit of straw to her.

Not that any of the other agents meant any harm. At worst, they were just overly curious. At best, they wanted insight on a case or two so they could help justice prevail.

Not unlike him and Seth.

The problem was, nobody realized the price Adrienne paid for the help she gave. The violence and malice she was exposed to whenever she touched something new to help someone's case. The pain and exhaustion that often overwhelmed her.

Because Adrienne never told anyone it hurt. Someone would ask for her help, and she would do it. They would have all sorts of curious questions about her abilities, and she would answer with some light joke—putting them at ease. As far as he could tell from the footage he had watched, her favorite responses for when she was asked how she got her abilities were radioactive spider bite, bombardment of cosmic rays and gamma-radiation accident—all comic book characters' plights if Conner wasn't mistaken.

Conner wasn't sure how she functioned so efficiently or how she was able to keep such an upbeat personality when she was pelted all day by malice of the worst kind. But somehow she did.

The nights were better. Adrienne had moved in with him for all intents and purposes. Only Conner, Seth and Chief Kelly knew Adrienne's location. Until they discovered who Simon was, Conner intended to keep it that way.

They spent their evenings together with quiet dinners and walks around the city. He loved how the tension that surrounded her when he arrived at the office each afternoon was gone by the end of the evening. He was glad to offer her peace and quiet. And relieved to have her in his bed every night, knowing she was safe and not in any pain.

But having to be away from the office—away from the action—during the day was frustrating as hell.

Conner was gone now as Adrienne prepared to go through her own ruined clothes from the hotel. Simon had shredded most of them into pieces. Because it was her own stuff, this would probably be worse for Adrienne. So Conner didn't want to go far. In the past few days they had worked out exactly how many blocks away he needed to be in order for Adrienne's abilities to work.

One of the FBI photographers, Victor Faraday, had seemed to figure out what was going on with Conner and Adrienne, or at least that Conner was never in the room when Adrienne was using her abilities, and had shown Conner how to set up a video chat on his phone so he could see what was happening, even if he wasn't there. They were trying that now.

That made it easier, but not much.

"Okay, Seth, I'm far enough out, I think," Conner told Seth, looking into his phone.

"Okay. Faraday is going to hold the camera so I can help Adrienne if she needs it. She's opening the first of the crime scene bags now." The camera zoomed in on Adrienne and the bags.

Conner didn't like how pale she already was. Before even touching her clothes.

Adrienne cut open one of the crime scene bags and reached inside for what looked like had once been a sweater. He saw Adrienne tense as she touched it, but she didn't say anything.

"Adrienne?" Seth placed his hand on her arm. Adrienne shook her head but didn't answer. Instead she reached for a different bag, pulling out its contents. She spread her fingers wide over them so she could touch as much as possible.

"Seth, am I missing something? What's going on? Faraday, do we have audio?" Conner asked.

Victor Faraday was the one who answered. "Ms. Jeffries isn't saying anything, Agent Perigo. The audio is fine."

Adrienne tore a third evidence bag open more quickly than she had the first two. She pulled out their contents, careful to touch every piece. But still she said nothing. Conner waited as she did the same to the other three bags.

"Conner?" Adrienne finally looked over at the camera Faraday was holding.

"What, sweetheart?" The endearment was out before he could catch it. Conner supposed it didn't matter—Seth already knew, and Faraday wasn't high enough on the Bureau food chain to really matter. Although hopefully he wouldn't say anything.

"There's nothing, Conner," Adrienne responded.

"Do you think I'm too close? Is that it?"

"No. I can feel Simon on the clothes. He definitely had some sort of plan and was in the room. But when he did all this damage, he was not in any rage. At least none that I would be able to feel."

"What do you think that means?"

He saw Adrienne shake her head. "I don't know. He wasn't menacing in any way while he was destroying the room. So it's really hard for me to get any reading from any of this."

"Are you positive it was Simon?" Seth asked.

"Definitely. He just wasn't angry when he did this.

Had no malicious intent toward me or anyone. It's like he was doing a job, calmly and methodically."

Conner's eyes narrowed. "Calmly and methodically" scared him almost more than "murderous rage."

"I can't see anything else. I'm sorry." Adrienne sighed.

"Don't worry about it. I'm coming back."

ADRIENNE WASN'T SURE what to make of this. It all just wasn't right—as if Simon knew the weakness in her visions and was exploiting them. Without malicious intent on the killer's part, she really couldn't see anything clearly.

But only someone who knew the type of work she did for the FBI would know that. Adrienne was becoming more and more convinced of Conner's theory that whoever Simon was, he had some sort of link to law enforcement in this area.

From where she sat at Conner's desk, Adrienne looked around. There were people everywhere in this building—agents, suspects, witnesses. Most of them she didn't know at all.

Any of them could be the killer.

Adrienne shook her head and chased away that thought. No, Simon Says couldn't be in this building. If he was, Adrienne would know it. Even now she could hear the buzz of everyone around her and feel some of the malevolent thoughts and artifacts pushing their way toward her. There was no way a killer could slip by her unnoticed.

She could see the conference room down the hall from where she sat. Seth was putting her destroyed clothes back into the evidence bags. Adrienne knew Conner would return soon.

Conner had agreed to drive her back to Lodi this afternoon so she could check on Vince and the horses. Adrienne knew it would do her good to get out of the city and away from the FBI for a little bit. They had planned to stay the night and come back tomorrow morning. But now Adrienne had a new plan, and she didn't think Conner was going to like it at all.

Adrienne looked down at the files on the desk and opened one in particular—the one she had worked on with the artist to try to pinpoint the location of where Simon Says was taking and killing the women. She knew she was missing something about this place. Something important. But she could never seem to find time to focus on it. Here at the FBI field office, or really anywhere in the city, there was too much outside interference. The only time she had quiet was when Conner was around.

She was so incredibly grateful for Conner. He had made this all bearable. Not just because of how he negated her abilities and gave her blessed silence. Adrienne had come to depend on him in other ways as well, and couldn't wait to go home with him each night.

Adrienne looked up just in time to see him walk into the conference room where Seth was still working. From the door he paused and turned in her direction. Seeing her watching him, he smiled and winked at her. Then turned and walked the rest of the way into the conference room.

Adrienne could feel her heart puddle at her feet. There was no doubt she was falling in love with that man. Everything about him fit her perfectly.

Adrienne giggled to herself, thinking about last night. Yes, *everything* about him fit her perfectly.

Closing the file and attempting to get her wayward

thoughts in check, Adrienne walked to the conference room. She knew what she needed to do. But she also knew Conner was not going to like it. Seth and Conner looked up from repacking the evidence bags as she entered.

"I've been thinking about Lodi," Adrienne stated from the doorway.

"Do you still want to go?" Conner asked.

"Yes. I need to. But, Conner, I don't think you should come with me."

Conner stopped the work he was doing and looked directly at her. "What?"

Adrienne held up the file in her hand. "I've been thinking about the place where Simon Says is killing the women. I feel like there's more about this that I can figure out."

"Okay. That would be great."

"But I can't do it with you around."

Conner shrugged. "Fine. Then do it here, and I'll leave again for a while."

Adrienne walked over to Conner and put her hand on his arm. "No. I don't want you to have to leave again. This is *your* office."

Conner began to protest, but Adrienne cut him off. "Besides, it's too mentally loud in this building. There are so many things trying to pull me away from focusing. And not just here in the building—in this entire city. I need some quiet. I want to take some of the photos with me to Lodi."

"And you can't do your magic if I'm there."

Adrienne ran her fingers down his arm and grasped his hand. "Yes. I'm sorry. But I know I'm missing something with these. Being alone where it's quiet might give me more insight."

"Alone? No way. Simon knows who you are. There's no reason to think he doesn't know where you live."

"Conner, I'll be able to know if Simon is around. He can't sneak up on me."

"That's fine. But if he somehow did get close to you, you would be totally helpless. I've seen what happens to you when you're just around things he's touched. What would you be like around him in person?" His expression hardened, determination glittering in his eyes. "There is no way in hell you're going by yourself."

"I'll take her," Seth chirped in. "We'll leave this afternoon and come back in the morning, just like you planned to do."

Adrienne could tell Conner didn't like it. Adrienne didn't much like the thought of being away from him, either. But there wasn't much way around it.

"I won't let her out of my sight, Scout's honor." Seth held up two fingers in some sort of incorrect scout salute. "I'll even sleep in the bed with her if she'll let me."

Conner rolled his eyes and put his arm around Adrienne. "Don't push it, Harrington." But Conner nodded. "I guess I should get caught up on some of the three hundred pounds of paperwork I have here."

Adrienne cringed. He hadn't been able to do any of his normal work in the past few days so that she could work here in safety.

"I'm sorry." Adrienne looked up at Conner. "I've pretty much kicked you out of your own office."

Conner kissed her quickly on the lips. "I would give up my office anytime if it meant you were safe. Plus, I like that at the Starbucks they know my order now as soon as I walk in. I am no longer mocked by the masses when ordering my drink of choice."

Seth smirked. "Happy for you, princess. You ready to go, Adrienne?"

"Sure. My stuff is by Conner's desk." She didn't have much since all of her clothes had been destroyed by Simon three days ago.

"Okay, I'll grab it and meet you at my car."

Conner walked with Adrienne out to the parking garage. "Stay with Seth the entire time. Don't even go to the barn without him. And definitely no riding."

Adrienne smiled. "I promise."

"I don't like you not being with me. I trust Seth with my life, but I wish I could be with you." He gently grabbed both sides of the collar of her shirt and pulled her up on her tiptoes. "I'll see you tomorrow."

Adrienne kissed him. "Yes, you will. And hopefully with more answers than I have right now."

Conner kissed her again. "I don't care about answers as much as I care about you getting back to me."

Adrienne could feel heat flood her center. "Me either," she said with a smile.

THE DRIVE TO the ranch was uneventful. Adrienne was relieved to see Vince and the horses—all in excellent shape. Vince truly was able to handle everything without her and even seemed a little disappointed to see her back. He immediately cheered when he found she would only be staying for the night.

Adrienne walked with Vince out to the barn. "You sure you've been doing okay?"

"Never better, Missy. You know I like it best when it's just me and the horses. No offense. Real question is, are *you* okay?"

Adrienne nodded. "It hasn't been as bad as I thought it might be, Vince. As a matter of fact, some of it has been downright nice. Maybe FBI agents aren't as bad as you and I made them out to be."

Vince grimaced. "I don't know about that. But I'm glad they're looking out for you."

"They're looking out for you, too, Vince. I don't think anyone is going to be bothering you about a missed parole anytime soon."

The older man looked decidedly relieved. Adrienne reached over and hugged him. He hugged her back in his stiff way. Adrienne left him alone in the barn and went back to the house.

Seth was a very active guard. All evening, he constantly checked windows and walked around the house. Perhaps that was because Conner called every hour for an update. Finally at 10:00 p.m. Conner switched to texts so he wouldn't disturb anyone else, but he evidently had no qualms about disturbing Seth. Adrienne wasn't worried about Simon Says at all.

Adrienne was glad to have the relative quiet of the ranch. She could hear the slight buzz of Vince and Seth, but that was easily ignored. It gave her the chance to study the pictures she had brought with her.

The pain was a constant as she looked at them, but she forced it aside. Although she had seen these images before—both the photos and the disjointed flashes of insight in her mind—they were still jarring. She focused on the building, the location where Simon Says was taking the women, and let everything else slide out of her mind.

Why couldn't she see the outside of the building? Always before she had been able to see a suspect entering or leaving their dwelling; that was one of the reasons she had been so helpful to the FBI—her ability to pinpoint location. *Bloodhound.*

But not now. Why?

It was too fuzzy for her. She could feel Simon's presence outside the building but couldn't see anything clearly. Just like when she had been touching her own clothes that Simon had destroyed.

Adrienne released the pictures and thought about that for a second. She had determined that Simon had been calm and methodical when he had destroyed her hotel room, not in any sort of vicious rage. So maybe Simon was calm and methodical when he brought the women to this place. Maybe he didn't have any desire to hurt them.

But that didn't make any sense. Why would he bring them there if he didn't have a desire to hurt them?

Then a thought occurred to Adrienne: was it possible Simon had a partner? Someone helping him bring the women into the building, but who had no desire to hurt them? Someone so meek and unassuming that Simon's personality all but overwhelmed the artifacts and pictures Adrienne had touched so she never felt the second person at all?

Adrienne went back through every picture again, one by one, searching for the presence of a second person, however minute. She could sense something different sometimes, but not always, and Simon's presence overshadowed whatever the lesser presence was.

Frustrated, Adrienne gave up on that line of thought. There was nothing in any of the evidence that had ever suggested Simon Says had a partner. He was too egotistical to share his control with someone else. Too sure of his own importance to leave details to someone else.

Exhausted, Adrienne decided to take a break. Simon having a partner was out of the question.

Adrienne wandered into the kitchen and found Seth making a pot of coffee.

"Planning to be up all night?"

Seth rubbed his face wearily. "Yeah. Someone's overprotective boyfriend keeps texting me every hour."

Adrienne winced. "Sorry."

"Don't worry about it. He was a pain in my butt long before you were around. Any luck with the pictures?"

Adrienne explained her theory about Simon having a possible partner, then all the reasons she had discarded it.

"It's worth keeping in consideration. Anything on location?"

"Nothing yet. I'm going to give it one more try in my room before I go to bed." Adrienne smiled at him. "I hope you get some sleep tonight."

She heard Seth mutter something under his breath but decided it was probably better not to ask him to repeat it.

In her bedroom, Adrienne changed into her pajamas and spread the pictures out on her bed. Once again she looked through each picture individually. It was all the same images as before. Nothing. Adrienne decided to look through them one last time and then give it a break. Maybe tomorrow would bring more clarity.

Even concentrating as hard as she was, she almost missed it.

She was studying the pictures of Josie Paton, the woman who had made Simon so angry because she refused to be scared. At first he had wanted to kill her quickly so he wouldn't have to hear her anymore. But he knew that would take all the pleasure out of it, so he decided to wait.

To calm himself down, he went for a walk. For just a

split second, as he went outside, she could see it. Some sort of old white mission-style church. Then Simon was having some sort of problem with vertigo, and it was all gone.

Adrienne went through the pictures with Josie Paton again just to be sure, but there was nothing else. But Simon having vertigo and a white church? Maybe those could be helpful. She would definitely tell Seth first thing in the morning. Right now she just wanted to get some sleep.

But lying in bed a few minutes later, Adrienne found sleep wouldn't come. She missed Conner. She'd only been without him for one night, but it felt like much longer. What was she going to do without him after they caught Simon? Adrienne didn't want to think about it. She closed her eyes and pushed the thought away.

Chapter Thirteen

Adrienne went from fast asleep to completely awake in an instant. She sat up in bed immediately alert. Had she heard something? What had woken her? Something definitely didn't seem right, but she couldn't figure out what it was.

Adrienne looked around, then stilled herself to listen. Nothing. It was still dark outside. She glanced at the clock—3:45 a.m.

Dressed in her pajama pants and T-shirt, she slipped out of her bedroom. Was Seth still in the living room or had he gone to sleep? Adrienne didn't know. She quietly made her way past the bathroom and down the hall. There was no need to wake anyone else up if there was nothing wrong.

But something felt wrong. Sort of. Nothing was hurting in her head, nor was she seeing any visions. But there was almost a residual evil presence. Like what Adrienne had been thinking about last night when she'd considered Simon Says might have a partner.

Adrienne entered the living room and saw Seth wasn't there. She had thought he might still be awake, but maybe Conner had finally given Seth some peace and quit texting, allowing Seth to sleep. Adrienne headed to the house's third bedroom, which had been converted into an office. Although the desk took up most of the space in the room, there was also a couch. Adrienne had left a pillow and blanket there for Seth in case he wanted them.

The door was cracked, so Adrienne peeked in. There on the couch lay the pillow and the blankets, still neatly folded. Seth had definitely not been here.

"Seth?" Adrienne called out. Something wasn't right. Adrienne no longer cared if she woke anybody else up. She rushed from the back bedroom to the kitchen, but found Seth wasn't there, either.

"Seth?" Adrienne called louder.

"What's going on?" Vince came out of his bedroom already dressed in his shirt and jeans but still looking sleepy.

"I'm looking for Seth. Agent Harrington. He wasn't in the living room or the office."

Adrienne didn't want to panic, but she didn't think Seth would've left her here without telling her.

"Maybe he ran out to his car to grab something."

That would make sense. But Adrienne hesitated to open the door and look. Instead she grabbed her cell phone from the table.

She called Conner.

"Are you okay?" he answered without greeting.

"I'm fine. Have you talked to Seth recently?"

"What time is it?" Adrienne could hear the sleepiness in Conner's voice.

"Almost four o'clock."

"I haven't talked to him in a couple of hours. Where is he?"

Adrienne was really getting frightened now. "I don't know, Conner. He was on the couch when I went to bed a few hours ago, but now he's not here. Seth wouldn't just *leave*."

Adrienne looked over at Vince, who was watching with concern. He shrugged.

Out of the corner of her eye she saw it then—in the window that faced the barn. Some weird orange glow in the darkness just past the house.

Adrienne walked over to the window to get a closer look. A chill overtook her as she realized what the orange glow was.

The barn was on fire!

Vince realized it at the same time and ran out the door as fast as he could with his limp. Almost forgetting about the phone in her hand, Adrienne was right behind him.

"Adrienne! What the hell is going on?"

"The barn is on fire, Conner!" Adrienne yelled to him as she ran.

"Adrienne, listen to me, you need to stay in the house. If Seth is gone, this could be Simon Says."

"I can't, Conner! I have to help Vince get the horses out!"

She could hear them now, their high-pitched screaming. Bucking as they tried to get out of their stalls and away from the fire that terrified them.

"Adrienne!" Conner roared from the phone. Adrienne stopped running at the urgency in his tone.

"Conner, I cannot do nothing while the horses are trapped. I just can't!"

"I know, baby. But listen to me. Do you have any weapons in the house? A handgun?"

"No, only a rifle."

"That's too big. Do you have any pepper spray or anything like that?"

"Yes."

"Get it and keep it with you. Or grab a kitchen knife if you have to. But be aware, Adrienne. Help Vince, but be mindful that Simon may be out there somewhere. I'll get locals on their way to you."

Adrienne couldn't hear anything else over the horses, so she ended the call. She spun and started running back toward the house. Conner was right. Although she couldn't feel him now, Simon could easily be out there somewhere, waiting for her. She had to help the horses, but she also had to protect herself.

In the kitchen, Adrienne grabbed the can of pepper spray in a drawer. She decided not to bring a knife; she would probably only cut herself. She headed in a dead sprint out to the barn.

The fire was quickly spreading, and the horses were becoming more panicked. Adrienne tried to remember what Conner said about Simon Says and awareness, but it was hard in all the chaos. She had to get the horses to safety.

Vince was making his way back out to the main barn door, dragging something. At first it looked to Adrienne like a huge bag of feed. She felt nausea pit in her stomach when she realized it was a person Vince was trying to drag out.

Seth.

Adrienne rushed over to help Vince.

"The FBI agent," Vince yelled. Adrienne grabbed one of Seth's arms, shuddering as she looked at the blood from an obvious head wound dripping down his face.

"Is he dead, Vince?" Adrienne couldn't bear the thought.

"No. Still breathing. We've got to get him away from here, then get in to help the horses."

They dragged Seth far enough away to be in no danger from the fire. He was still unconscious. Vince immediately returned to the barn, but Adrienne hesitated. She hated leaving Seth there alone, unprotected, but the horses were working their way into a complete frenzy. She had to go help Vince or all of them would die.

Adrienne turned back to the barn. The flames were climbing higher. From over to her right, she could see the flashing lights of emergency vehicles making their way, but they were still off in the distance. They wouldn't get there in time to help the horses. Only she and Vince could do that.

Adrienne dashed the rest of the way to the barn, the smoke getting thicker with every step she took. When she entered, she found she couldn't see anything because of the smoke. The horses, screaming and bucking in their terror, desperate to get out of the barn, made hearing impossible, too. She grabbed a nearby towel, dipped it in water from a bucket by the door and wrapped it around her head. She began looking for Vince but couldn't find him anywhere.

Unable to locate Vince, Adrienne decided to follow the sound of the horses. The first panicked one she found was Willie Nelson. Adrienne opened his stall and slowly walked toward the frightened animal, grabbing the halter and lead rope from the wall.

Although generally gentle by nature, Willie Nelson was beyond reason now. He nipped at Adrienne and kicked at the barn walls with his hind legs. Adrienne knew if she couldn't get the halter on him in the next few seconds, she would have to leave him behind and go for another horse. Seconds were precious.

From out of nowhere a hand grabbed Adrienne's shoulder. Terror shot through her. She reached for the pepper spray, but it was deep in her pocket and she couldn't quite get it out. She let out a high-pitched scream as the hand roughly spun her around.

It was Vince.

Adrienne almost sagged in relief, seeing the older man. He didn't seem to notice any of her strange behavior.

"The only way to get them out of the barn is to blindfold them and then put on the halter," he yelled over the horses' screams and the sound of the fire. He threw a few short towels at Adrienne and ran back out of the stall.

Adrienne approached Willie Nelson again, towel in hand. After a couple of tries, Adrienne was able to get the towel over his head. Unable to see, he immediately calmed. Adrienne quickly led him from the barn and into a nearby fenced corral, far enough from the fire to keep the horses from panicking. Two other horses were already there.

That meant there were five more left in the barn.

Adrienne sprinted back, coughing as she entered the barn's barrage of black smoke again. Everything hurt: her lungs, her throat, her head, her eyes—but she knew she couldn't stop.

Adrienne found another horse and followed the same procedure as she had with Willie Nelson. It was getting harder to breathe, and the heat was now beginning to truly become a factor. Adrienne knew she wouldn't be able to make many more trips before the fire would overwhelm the barn completely.

As she made it to the barn door, she looked up, shocked to see Seth stumbling unsteadily toward her.

"Give me the horse. I can get it to the corral."

Adrienne coughed and looked at the blood dripping down his face. "Are you sure?"

Seth didn't try to answer, just took the lead from Adrienne and slowly began walking the horse away from the barn. As Adrienne turned to go back inside she saw some movement on the front porch of the house. In the dark it was difficult to tell, but it looked like someone was sitting in one of the rocking chairs on her front porch.

Simon Says.

Adrienne knew it was him. Could feel the pounding in her head clearly now. Could feel his glee at the chaos he had caused.

Adrienne deliberately turned away and went back inside the barn. Let the bastard watch. She was going to get every single one of her horses out. She wouldn't let Simon win this sick little game. She didn't think he was going to harm her; it looked like he was more interested in watching from the sidelines.

But she made sure the pepper spray was easily reachable in her pocket just to be sure.

Five minutes later she and Vince had gotten all the horses out. Thanks to Seth's help, all the horses were safe, if very spooked, in the corral. When Adrienne looked up at the porch again, it was empty. And her head no longer hurt.

Simon was gone.

Not long afterward, the fire department arrived. Adrienne, Seth and Vince sat exhausted on the back steps of the house and watched as they put out the fire and saved what was left of the barn.

Adrienne was relieved that they were all safe and relatively unharmed. A paramedic had looked at Seth's head wound and announced he probably had a concussion and should go to the local hospital. Adrienne and Vince had been given oxygen and told they suffered from smoke inhalation and should also go.

But none of them did. Instead they sat on the back steps almost too exhausted to move. They would live.

The sun began to work its way up over the landscape. The rising sun somehow made everything seem a little better. The sound of a vehicle squealing into the driveway made things even better for Adrienne.

Conner was here. One hour and twenty-six minutes after she had called him. She would bet he had broken quite a few traffic laws to get here this quickly.

She watched as he walked toward the barn. She would've called out to him but knew her voice would never carry in the state it was in. She saw him notice where they sat. He turned midstride and quickly made his way over to them, eyes only on Adrienne.

Adrienne was too tired to even stand and hug him. Not that he would want her to hug him—she must look and smell like a chimney.

Conner sat down on the step right next to her. He reached over, picked her up and deposited her in his lap. His arms came around her in a crushing hug.

"Thank God."

Adrienne could barely breathe from the force of his hug but didn't care.

"I knew I should've never let you come to Lodi without me."

"Conner." Adrienne wiggled until she could get her arms out from under his and put them around him. "I'm okay. It's all okay."

She was here with him now, safe in his arms. Eventually he loosened his grasp to a more reasonable level.

He studied her face intently then reached down and touched her just over her lip.

"Simon was here."

Startled, Adrienne peeked up at him. "Yes, he was. How did you know?"

"Your nose was bleeding."

Out of habit Adrienne tried to wipe it with the back of her hand. She was sure that just got more soot on her face.

"I saw him, Conner. He was sitting on the other side of the house on the front porch. He was in a rocking chair watching us get the horses out."

"Could you see him well enough to make out any features?" Conner asked.

"No, it was too dark. I guess I could probably feel him there more than I could actually see him."

She couldn't make out features, but she knew she had seen someone in one of the rocking chairs.

"But he didn't try to hurt you?"

"No. Clocked Seth cold, though," Adrienne told him.

Conner looked over at Seth, who nodded his head gingerly. "Yeah, I thought I saw a light in the barn and I went to check it out. Stupid. Didn't find anything so was on my way back inside when he caught me on the steps. Dragged me back to the barn."

Adrienne sighed. "That must be what woke me up. I thought I heard something, but maybe I just felt Simon when he was that close to the house."

Seth grimaced. "Maybe. Whatever it was, I'm glad you woke up when you did. He definitely intended for me to die in that barn. If Vince hadn't gotten there when he did…"

Seth trailed off. Adrienne didn't blame him.

"Could you feel Simon Says while you were getting the horses out of the barn?" Conner asked.

"Yeah. But everything was loud and chaotic and painful, so I didn't let it stop me."

Two uniformed police officers walked around the side of the house. Conner set Adrienne down on the step beside him and stood up to talk to them. Seth joined them. She saw them both show the officers their FBI credentials.

Vince looked over at her. "Guess you and that FBI officer don't hate each other so much now."

Adrienne was not so exhausted that she couldn't flush. Hopefully the soot hid it. "Yeah. He ended up not being so bad after all."

Vince chuckled. It was the first time Adrienne remembered the sound coming from the older man. "I've decided to like him," Vince finally said.

Adrienne was shocked. She didn't think Vince would like an agent for any reason. "Oh, yeah? Why?"

"He just picked you up and plopped you down right on top of him—and no offense, girly, but you look and smell terrible—without any concern for his clothes whatsoever. That's a man who's got his priorities straight."

Adrienne smiled. She thought so, too.

After a few minutes of talking to the officers, Conner and Seth made their way back to the steps where Vince and Adrienne waited, still too tired to move. Both Seth and Conner looked grim. Conner had some sort of paper in his hand.

Conner sat back down next to Adrienne. "It was definitely Simon you saw on the porch."

Adrienne didn't have any doubt of that. "Did you find something?"

Conner held up an envelope. Adrienne immediately recognized it. She had seen ones just like it multiple times. Simon's literal calling card.

Conner opened it and read the note.

Simon says, thanks for the show!

So Adrienne had been right. He had been there, watching, reveling in their frantic attempts to save the livestock. Maybe his initial intent had been to harm Adrienne, but he had gotten caught up in watching their efforts in the chaos he had created.

Nobody said anything for a long while. It was finally Vince who broke the silence as he stood up. "I don't know who this 'Simon' character is, but I don't care for him much. He and I are going to have words if he ever sets foot on this property again. But right now I'm going to see if I can get some of this burnt barn smell off me, before it drives the womenfolk mad with desire."

Both men chuckled, and Adrienne grinned.

Conner bent his head and kissed her. "You did a good job, you know."

Adrienne slumped exhaustedly against his arm. "We all did. All the horses survived. We all survived. Simon didn't win this time."

But they knew Simon wouldn't stop trying until he had.

Chapter Fourteen

It took days before Adrienne was able to get back to San Francisco. She had to find temporary boarding situations for all the horses, complete an endless number of insurance forms and find contractors to begin rebuilding the barn. It was tedious work.

Conner stayed by her side the entire time.

Seth headed back to San Francisco the day after the fire, once he and Conner had finished processing the scene—what was left of it, anyway.

Simon Says had very definitely started the barn fire. He'd made no attempt to hide where his arson was initiated—in one of the far stalls where no horses were housed, thank God—or his use of accelerants to help the flames along.

All in all, the arson detective said it was a miracle no people or animals had been killed.

Having her own FBI agent able to explain the nature of the foul play to the insurance inspectors made the process much more streamlined. Adrienne was thankful to have Conner around every day. And every night.

Conner was always by her side. Always watchful in case Simon struck again. Somehow Simon had made it through Adrienne's mental warning system before, although Adrienne blamed it on sleep rather than on Simon being far away in the barn. But Conner was still very vigilant.

Four days after the fire, Adrienne was finally able to get the ranch and rebuilding of the barn to a state where she could leave. Vince was overseeing the construction, and the horses were all gone—there wasn't much at the ranch she was needed for. So she and Conner decided to return to the city.

Although he had never said anything outright, Adrienne could tell Conner was anxious to get back to the office where he could work. He wanted to protect her. She knew the best way he could do that was to catch Simon Says. Conner's very personality demanded he be more active in that pursuit, not reactive, waiting with her.

Adrienne knew as soon as they entered the ViCAP office areas later that morning that something had happened. She and Conner headed directly for Conner's and Seth's desks amid the buzz.

"What's going on?" Conner asked.

"Another package from Simon arrived a little bit ago," Seth said. "I was waiting for you guys to get here to open it."

Conner grimaced. "Okay, I'll get out of here."

"You're not going to stay and open it?" Adrienne touched Conner lightly on the arm.

"No. I might as well just let you do your thing from the get-go. Seth will catch anything I would see." Conner shifted away from Adrienne, not overtly rejecting her touch, but definitely not welcoming it. Adrienne understood his frustration but was still hurt.

"Conner, I'm sorry." Adrienne couldn't stand the distance between them, the tension.

"No, don't you apologize." Conner didn't move any closer to her, but his eyes warmed. "This is me—my problem. I have to learn to deal with it."

"I'm still sorry." Adrienne ached for him.

Now Conner did move closer to her. "You're too tenderhearted to do this." He ran a finger down her cheek. "I don't know how you've survived this long with all your emotions still functional."

Adrienne smiled, but the truth was, sometimes neither did she.

Conner stepped back, putting a more appropriate workplace distance between them. "I'll just be a few blocks down. Seth's going to stream it live to my phone again."

Seth called from the conference room. They were ready to open the package. Adrienne turned toward the room, but Conner caught her waist and jerked her back to him.

His lips fell heavily on hers, stealing her breath. Before she could say or do anything, he moved away, pushing her gently toward the conference room. "Go do your thing, sweetheart. Let's catch this guy." Conner grabbed his jacket.

Adrienne started walking but turned back. Being back in the office had reminded her. "After this, make sure I show you what I found before the fire. It's in the file. I might have some details about Simon's hideout, although right now they're pretty useless."

Conner smiled. "I'll look it over with you when I get back."

It made Adrienne feel better knowing Conner was watching from his phone. It wouldn't stop her physical discomfort, but emotionally it helped her gear up. It was good having Conner as close as possible.

Adrienne stood in the corner of the conference room as Seth opened the outer package. She could hear the buzzing getting louder, so she knew Conner was out of the building. One of the other agents—Adrienne vaguely remembered seeing him around—was holding the camera so Conner would be able to see what was going on.

It was the same as all the others. A lock of hair and a note.

Simon says, hurry.

Decidedly less mocking than the other notes Simon had sent. But yet, not helpful in any way. All the people in the room—mostly agents, but a couple photographers and even an analyst—looked disappointed at the content of the box. What were they expecting exactly? Adrienne had no idea.

Seth wasted no time shooing them out of the conference room so Adrienne wouldn't have an audience while she worked. After last time, that was important to her. The less noise and distractions around, the better.

"Ready?" Seth asked. Only he and the agent holding the camera remained. Adrienne nodded and took a deep breath.

Knowing that touching the lock of hair would show her the murder and wanting to put that off for as long as possible, Adrienne reached out for the note. The notes always told her more about Simon anyway. The hair was too enmeshed with the victim—her fears and feelings. The note was solely Simon.

Unlike before, this time Adrienne immediately could envision a place. A theater, complete with a stage and props and lighting.

All the world's a stage, And all the men and women

merely players. They have their exits and their en-
trances; and one man in his time plays many parts...

Simon standing on this stage quoting Shakespeare to an invisible audience. So sure of his own importance and intellect. Adrienne couldn't see his face but could hear his voice.

His voice didn't match what he thought of himself in his head. He believed himself to be powerful and potent, but his voice was high and whiny, and would never demand respect.

Adrienne wished she could tell him this to his face. But she knew he'd kill her for it. An image—memory— flashed through the killer's mind and Adrienne understood why he had picked the women he had.

Not because of their appearance or because they'd all shopped or visited the same locations. He had picked them because they reminded him of a woman from his past, from his childhood. Simon just thought of the woman as "her."

Adrienne didn't know exactly who *this woman* was to Simon, but she had made him feel weak and powerless. She had mocked and ridiculed him. Especially his voice—so high-pitched, as if he had never become a man. Would never become a man. A whiny little girl, she had called him. He hated her. His hatred of her overshadowed everything about him.

It wasn't their looks that caused him to choose his victims. It was their *voices*.

His memory of *her* was soon pushed away by Simon. He took a bow before his invisible audience, then looked up toward the spotlight and waved. He jumped down from the stage and walked straight down the aisle out the front entrance to the street outside.

Then, in an almost deliberate motion, he turned and looked up at the sign.

"The Eureka Theater." Adrienne said the name out loud. She let go of the letter and looked over at Seth. "Did you get that?"

"Yes. Eureka Theater. It's across town. We're calling locals now. Conner's on his way back."

"No. Tell him to wait a minute. Seth, there's something not right here."

"What?"

"I don't know. Let me touch the hair. Something's different."

Seth relayed the message to Conner over the phone. Adrienne could hear Conner's curses even from where she stood. But she knew she had to do this to figure out what was going on.

Taking a deep breath again, she reached her fingers out and touched just the tiniest part. She braced herself, prepared for the worst.

But she had not prepared herself for this. She reached down and clutched the entire lock of hair in her fist, to be sure.

Adrienne couldn't help herself, she began sobbing. Seth tried to talk to her, but she couldn't stop. Seth put his phone up to Adrienne's ear, so she could hear Conner.

"Adrienne, baby, I know it's hard. But I need you to tell us what you see."

"Conner…she's alive. She's still alive!"

Everything was a blur after that moment. Conner was back in the building within two minutes. He and Seth wanted to know every detail of what she had seen. Was Adrienne sure the woman was still alive? Yes. Was Adrienne sure she was at the Eureka Theater? Yes.

Was Adrienne sure this was a trap? Yes.

She couldn't seem to make them understand. Conner rushed past her to get to his desk and Adrienne followed. "Conner, there's something else. I can't quite figure it out. Everything about this screams 'trap.' You have to be careful."

Conner put his hands on either side of Adrienne's neck and rubbed her cheeks with his thumbs. "We will be careful. I promise."

Adrienne grasped his wrists. "I want to come with you."

She could feel him stiffen. "No. No way in hell. You just said this was a trap. You're not a trained agent. And after the fire— You being at the crime scene unprotected? No, that's just what he wants. Stay here where you're safe."

"I want to help."

"It helps me knowing you're here, safe."

"What if you need me? My abilities?"

Conner reached down and kissed her lightly. "We'll get someone to bring you if we need you. I promise. Just stay here and be safe."

He was out of her arms and running down the hall with Seth before she could even respond.

THIS WAS THE break they had been waiting for. The excitement was palpable in the area outside the Eureka Theater. The local police had been the first to arrive but had waited—as ordered—for the FBI. They had secured all entrances and exits, making sure no one had come in or out.

Conner had no idea why the girl was still alive— if the package had just arrived earlier than Simon expected or if something had gone wrong. Regardless he did not take Adrienne's warning lightly. If she suspected this may be a trap, they would treat it as such.

The bomb squad had pulled in just ahead of Seth and Conner, and were now inspecting the doors for explosives. Conner watched with barely restrained anxiety. Was there a woman in there suffering while they were taking so long out here? Could she possibly be bleeding out even now, and they would be too late to help her?

Could Simon still be inside the building?

They had to be cautious, Conner understood, but everything in him screamed to get inside that theater as soon as possible. The minutes it took for the bomb squad to determine the front door safe seemed like hours. Once the front door was opened, the bomb dogs were allowed inside to sniff out any explosives.

It wasn't long before they found something.

In a breakaway door, just under the stage, a grouping of explosives had been set. Some sort of remote detonation device was attached to it. The bomb squad was able to disarm and remove it without anyone being harmed.

Adrienne had been right—it had been a trap. If the local police or FBI had rushed into the theater without the bomb squad, many more lives would've been lost. Her gift had saved untold lives today.

After another thorough sweep of the building by the dogs, it was deemed safe—at least from explosives—to enter. Conner and Seth were the first inside, weapons drawn. Certainly bombs weren't the only danger Simon Says could've laid out for them.

They cautiously made their way through the theater, calling out for anyone who might be in there, but received no response. Conner and Seth, along with the other officers, began systematically checking through the aisles for anyone who might be on the ground, out of sight. They checked the stage with even more caution but found nothing. Discouragement began to sink in. Perhaps the woman wasn't really here at all.

Conner stood on the stage looking out where law enforcement of all different types were searching through all the seats of the theater for anything—or anybody—who may be hidden there. There were others behind him, searching through the stage and the backstage area, but so far had come up empty.

Seth came over to Conner. "Think this is a bust?"

"I don't want to think so, but…" Conner shrugged. The frustration in both of them was close to boiling over. And standing in the damn spotlights aimed at the stage was causing them to sweat.

"'All the world's a stage…'" Conner said it out loud, remembering watching from his phone as the words had come out of Adrienne's mouth an hour ago. Not her words, but Simon's. Well, actually Shakespeare's, from *As You Like It,* if Conner remembered his college literature class correctly.

"Yeah, Simon obviously thinks of himself as the playwright in this ridiculous scene." Seth grimaced.

Conner went over everything Adrienne had said in his head. Then looked up at the spotlight. Although all the house lights had been turned on when they had entered the building, none of the other stage lights were burning. Why were these?

"Seth, Adrienne said Simon looked up at the spotlight and waved, right before he jumped off the stage and ran down the aisle to the front door. He had to have been standing right here when he did that."

"Damn, Con. Why is that light even on? It wouldn't have been on the house lights switch."

They both sprinted to the metal ladder leading up

to the theater's catwalk. They quickly made their way to where the spotlight stood attached to a lighting batten. Sure enough, there lay a young woman, bound and gagged.

But very much alive.

"We found her! We need a medic up here," Seth yelled out, as Conner reached down to remove the gag wrapped around the woman's head. She immediately began sobbing.

"Are you all right?" Conner asked her, helping her sit up. "Are you injured in any way?"

The woman shook her head. "No, I'm f-fine…" The medic rushed over the catwalk to where Conner knelt beside the woman. Conner stood to give him room. He wanted to ask the woman questions, but it could wait the few minutes until she was checked out. Conner watched as the medic cut away the zip-tie that tied her hands and feet, and checked over her body for broken bones or injury. When he got to her back, the medic stopped. Frowning, he unpinned something that was attached to the woman's clothing.

"Special Agent Perigo?" The medic looked over at Conner.

"Yes?" Conner frowned at Seth then looked over at the medic. How did the medic know his name?

"I think this is for you." He handed Conner a note with his name on the front. Seth rushed over as Conner opened it.

Simon says, never mind. I found someone better.

WAITING AT CONNER'S desk back at the field office, Adrienne thought she might go out of her mind. They hadn't heard anything from the crime scene—that was good news. If anything catastrophic had happened, they would've heard about it.

That still didn't stop her from worrying. Had they found the woman? Was she alive? Had Simon Says tried anything to hurt them?

Adrienne ran her hands over her face wearily. Being here in this office was painful without Conner. Too much buzzing, too many voices and images trying to push their way through to her mind. She had to constantly battle to keep them out. It was exhausting.

Adrienne looked down at the file she had brought in with her—the picture of Josie Paton still on top. Maybe she could start searching for this church she had seen. But there were hundreds of churches in San Francisco. Adrienne had no idea where to begin.

Or maybe she should focus on Simon's vertigo. Was that something requiring medical treatment? Could the FBI find a record of him through that? And why had Simon seemed so happy about his vertigo?

Adrienne did a quick search of vertigo on the computer to get an understanding of exactly what it was. *A feeling of motion when one is stationary.* It seemed like a dead end, not something likely to require long-term medical treatment or records.

Adrienne spotted it as she was about to turn the computer off.

Vertigo. Vertigo with a capital *V.* The famous Alfred Hitchcock movie.

As soon as she read it, everything clicked into place. Simon didn't have vertigo. He was thinking of the famous scene from *Vertigo* while he stood outside San Francisco's Mission Dolores Basilica. Simon was proud he was right in the middle of the most upper crust of San

Francisco, and no one was any the wiser. That was why he was so gleeful when he thought of the word *vertigo*.

Adrienne printed out a map of Dolores Street and the surrounding areas. Based on Simon's thoughts about the church, and the inside of the building she had seen, there were only a few places where his hideout could be. Adrienne marked them carefully on the map. As soon as Conner and Seth got back, she would take them there.

She briefly considered going there herself, but deemed it too stupid to act on. Wasn't that always how people got killed in movies—by doing something brash and alone like that? But she definitely wanted to take Conner and Seth to check it out as soon as they could.

"Ms. Jeffries?" One of the FBI photographers rushed up to where she sat at Conner's desk. What was his name? Adrienne had seen him around but couldn't remember.

"Yes? I'm sorry I've forgotten your name."

The man smiled, but Adrienne could tell the smile didn't reach his eyes. "I'm Victor Faraday, a photographer. A report just came in from the scene everyone is at."

Adrienne stood up. "Yes?"

"Evidently there was a woman dead by the time they got there."

Adrienne was crushed. She was so sure the woman had been alive. Maybe they had been too late.

"There's no cell phone coverage in the theater, so Special Agent Perigo couldn't call you. But he had someone radio in and wants you out there as soon as possible."

Adrienne took a deep breath. Another crime scene. She wasn't looking forward to it. "Sure, I'm ready whenever."

"Okay, I'll give you a ride, if you want. I've got to go out there, too."

Adrienne hesitated for just a second. She had seen Victor around, but she didn't really know him. But she knew if he had any malicious intent toward her she would sense it, since Conner wasn't around. "That would be great, Victor. Thanks so much."

They walked together down to the parking lot and got into Victor's SUV. Adrienne was overwhelmed again with sadness that the woman was dead. The last time Simon Says had seen her, she had been alive, that much Adrienne knew from touching the lock of hair he had sent. Something must have happened to her between the time Simon had left and when the FBI had gotten to the theater.

Adrienne didn't know where the theater was, so she was glad Victor was driving. As they got farther away from the FBI building Adrienne noticed the visions and voices pressing in on her were getting more insistent rather than less. Usually outside the FBI office, the noise got a little softer—there weren't so many suspects and so much evidence trying to tell its story to her.

But something in this vehicle was demanding her attention. She looked over at Victor—it wasn't him. She looked around and noticed how dark all the windows were tinted.

"Your windows are really dark."

Victor nodded at her. "Yes, I had to get a special permit for the tinting. It keeps sun off my equipment. Also helps prevent theft."

Maybe that was it. Theft. Maybe someone had tried to break into this SUV recently, and that was what Adrienne was picking up on. Whatever it was, it was getting worse.

Adrienne rubbed her head. She reached into her purse for some aspirin.

"Head hurt?" Victor asked.

"Yeah. I'm not sure what's going on."

"I hope it feels better soon."

Adrienne looked over at Victor sharply. Was she imagining things or did his voice just change a little bit? Become a little higher. And a little more whiny.

Just like the voice she had heard in her head earlier when she had opened Simon's note.

The SUV pulled up to a curb and stopped. But they weren't at the Eureka Theater. They were in front of the building Adrienne had been scoping out and researching this morning. The building where Simon was killing his victims.

Adrienne turned to Victor to get a good look at him and watched as everything about his demeanor changed before her eyes. He went from an unassuming, softspoken photographer to a furious, violent killer Adrienne had never seen.

Without warning everything in Adrienne's head exploded as the malice radiating from Victor hit her. She felt her nose begin bleeding, and she barely held on to consciousness under the onslaught.

"Victor?"

A high-pitched voice—not Victor's—responded in a whiny tone. "Sorry, Victor's not here right now. I'm Simon. And I'm going to need a little piece of your hair."

Chapter Fifteen

Conner and Seth arrived back at the FBI field office a few hours later, happy they had gotten to the woman and the trap had been avoided. This entire situation definitely had been a departure from Simon's usual course of action. What Conner couldn't figure out was the why of it all. If it wasn't for Adrienne's description and explanation of the scene and the note found with the woman, Conner wouldn't have believed it was Simon at all.

After answering what questions she could—and there weren't very many she could answer since she had not seen or heard much of anything that could give them a lead on Simon—the woman had been taken to the hospital. She was dehydrated and scared out of her mind, but otherwise unharmed. Conner planned to take Adrienne to see her as soon as possible, and take Adrienne to the Eureka Theater, to see if she could pick up anything.

He had been trying to call Adrienne since they had found the woman alive. He knew Adrienne would want to know, that it would perhaps lift some of the burden she carried. But Adrienne wasn't picking up her cell. Conner knew the field office was a difficult and mentally loud place for her to be without him, so he wasn't surprised she wasn't paying attention to her phone. He was excited to be able to tell her face-to-face.

Conner was also anxious for Adrienne to provide her insight on what the newest note meant. *Simon says, never mind. I found someone better.* Upon reading that note, Conner's first thought had been concern for Adrienne. But he had believed Adrienne when she had said she would see Simon coming—he couldn't sneak up on her. In order for Simon to take her, he would have to use brute force, which wasn't going to happen with Adrienne in the middle of an FBI office.

Conner tried Adrienne's cell again as he walked into the office from the garage. Things should be quieter in her head now he was back. But there was still no answer.

"Dammit," Conner muttered.

"Still can't get a hold of Adrienne?"

"No. I can understand why she didn't answer while we were at the crime scene. But I thought she'd answer now."

There was more urgency to both their steps as they headed from the elevator down the hall to their desks. Conner scanned the area for Adrienne but didn't see her. Maybe she was in the conference room. The office seemed to be buzzing with activity. Conner understood why a moment later when Victor Faraday came up to him with a package in his hands.

"Agent Perigo?" Faraday said. "This came in a few minutes ago. I was already coming through the security area, so they asked me to bring it to you."

Conner frowned. Another package had arrived from Simon Says? He and Seth looked at each other without saying anything. Two packages in one day? Something was definitely not right.

"Has it already been scanned and vetted?" Seth asked.

Faraday nodded enthusiastically. "Yes, sir. It was cleared to bring up here. This one was different. It was left by the door, not mailed."

"Thanks." Conner took the package from Faraday. Faraday nodded again and gave Conner a weird smile. The man was acting odd, but, hell, they all acted odd every time a package came in.

Chief Kelly met them at their desks. "That the new package?"

"Yeah, we just got it," Seth responded. "We haven't opened it. This one is different—it wasn't mailed."

"Has it been scanned?" the chief asked. After the close call with the explosives earlier today, they weren't going to take any chances.

"Yes, came through clean," Conner told him. He looked for Faraday to reconfirm, but the photographer was gone.

Chief Kelly looked down at the package. "Okay, let's not waste any time. Get Adrienne and let's open it."

Conner felt something in his gut tighten. "Adrienne's not already in the conference room?"

"No. She was here earlier, waiting for you guys. You haven't seen her since you got back?"

Conner already had his phone out of his pocket and was dialing her number again. It went straight to voice mail.

"Con, don't panic," Seth told him. "She didn't know how long we were going to be gone. Maybe she's down at the coffee shop or out at one of the parks. You know how this building can become too much for her."

Conner took a deep breath. What Seth said made sense. But something was not sitting right with Conner.

"Perigo, we need to get this package opened," Chief Kelly told him. "If Simon Says is changing his pattern, this may be our best opportunity to catch him. Adrienne will show up soon."

Conner nodded, and they walked into the conference room where the new package sat. After donning gloves, they opened the outer box. It once again held a jewelry case, like always, and light enough only to hold a lock of hair. They opened it and found a lock—but instead of blond, as it had always been, the lock of hair was brown.

Brown with reddish tones. Conner knew the hair perfectly. He looked over at Seth who seemed to have lost all color. Conner took the note from Seth's nerveless fingers.

Simon says, it's not so easy without your little cheater, is it?

It took a moment for the facts to truly sink in. However impossible it seemed, Simon had Adrienne.

Conner heard shocked responses from around the room but couldn't quite make out what they were saying. The panic seized Conner in such a way that he could barely function. That psycho had Adrienne.

Was she already dead?

Conner pushed that thought completely from his mind. There was no way he would be able to function if he even allowed that thought to enter his head. Adrienne was not dead.

"Perigo!" Conner finally heard the chief who had evidently called his name more than once.

"Chief?"

"Keep it together, Perigo. We're going to find her."

Conner tamped down the panic deep inside. Chief Kelly was right. He had to keep it together if he wanted to be any help to Adrienne at all. He turned away from the package.

Thinking about what had happened today, Conner could see it was a perfect setup. Simon had gotten them away from Adrienne with the only possible thing that assured they would leave—live bait. Adrienne had sensed it was a trap from the beginning—and it had been, just for her, not for them.

Simon had even planted those explosives at the scene to draw them off the scent of his real plan. And it had worked beautifully. Caught up in all the prospective danger at the crime scene, Conner had hardly been worried about Adrienne at all.

Conner turned to Seth. "The woman we rescued this morning was never one of Simon's intended victims. Adrienne had always been the next target. We played right into his hands."

"Chief," Seth asked. "Did you see Adrienne here while we were gone?"

"Yeah. I saw her. She was talking to that photographer Victor Faraday when I saw her last."

"I'll go find him and see if he saw anything," Seth offered.

"I'm going to see if I can track her phone. Worked before." Conner headed to his desk to access the Bureau's network. Not long after putting in her phone's information, it came up with a location.

A spark of hope grew in Conner's chest until he saw the address. Her phone was somewhere inside the FBI field office.

Conner slammed his fist down on his desk. A few moments later Seth came rushing up.

"Faraday's gone, Conner. I went out and checked the garage myself and found this." Seth held out a phone. Conner slid the power button to On and saw the last seven missed calls were from him. This was definitely Adrienne's phone.

Chief Kelly walked up to their desks. The way he sighed, Conner knew the news was not good. "We pulled the camera footage from the parking garage camera. She definitely left with Faraday earlier today, about two hours before you guys got back."

The confusion that coursed through Conner quickly gave way to rage. Victor Faraday was Simon Says? How was that even possible? They had worked with the man for years.

And that bastard had been right here next to him, just a few minutes ago. Had the nerve to hand Conner a package, and *smile* at him, after he had already taken Adrienne.

The murderous rage was almost as incapacitating as the gut-wrenching fear Conner had felt when they had opened Simon's package. It also had to be pushed away so Conner could function.

"I've already checked with security. No second package came in today. Faraday must have brought it in himself and said it was found outside the door," the chief told them.

"We need every bit of information we have on Faraday. Right now." Conner announced, eyes hardening.

It turned out every bit of information they had on Victor Faraday was not a great deal. He had worked for the San Francisco field office for two years, having transferred from the Austin, Texas, field office. A search through the Bureau's systems confirmed a rash of unsolved murders had occurred in the Austin area around the same time Faraday had lived there. Once he had transferred here, the murders there had stopped.

"Hell if I can remember anything specific about him at all," Seth said with disgust, throwing Faraday's file on his desk. "Two years of working with him and I could barely pick him out of a lineup."

"He's played us from the start." Conner sighed roughly. "It's part of the reason Simon was always a step ahead of us."

"How do you think he got around Adrienne's abilities?" Seth asked.

"That's what I can't figure out. She should've been able to sense him coming. Hell, she should've sensed him the first time she was in the building. Or at least whenever I wasn't around. I don't understand it. She never had any specific insight to Simon at all. Except…"

Conner couldn't believe he had forgotten it. This morning Adrienne had come in all excited about a possible location where Simon—Faraday—might be keeping the women before he killed them. In the excitement of a new package and a live victim, her discovery had been pushed aside.

But she had given him a file, put it on his desk. Conner quickly tore through the papers on his desk. He found it and pulled out the map and information she had written. Mission Delores Basilica. She had highlighted the few places she thought could be Simon's hideout.

Conner was almost giddy with relief.

"Seth, I forgot until now. This is a map Adrienne left me. She mentioned something this morning. It's where she thought Simon Says was taking and killing the women."

Both men stood. It wasn't much, but it was better

than sitting here looking at files on Victor Faraday. Within moments, both men were sprinting for the car.

ADRIENNE WOKE UP to the screaming in her head. The noise and pain made her thoughts work slowly. She couldn't figure out where she was or how she had gotten there. She took deep breaths, trying to calm herself and focus.

She realized she was lying on the ground and her arms were restrained in front of her. The floor was hard, uncarpeted. She turned her body as gently as she could, so she could look around the room. High ceilings with dark rafters. A stairway that led to a thick door. No windows. It was an oversize cellar.

Through the fog of her brain Adrienne realized she had seen this place before. In her visions about Simon Says. It all came back to her then. Victor Faraday had brought her here. Victor Faraday was Simon Says.

"There you are. I thought you were never going to wake up. I tied you up while I was gone, but it looks like I don't really need to, do I?" A high-pitched giggle caused Adrienne to cringe in pain. Her fog-permeated brain could not figure out where the voice was coming from.

She knew she had to keep Simon talking. She could feel his malice—the terrible things he planned to do to her.

He had no plans for her to be alive in the next hour.

The agony of remaining conscious was almost more than Adrienne could bear. But she forced herself to focus. She could see Simon now. He was sitting on a wooden crate just a few feet from her.

"Where did you go?"

"Had to drop off the package to the FBI, of course.

I couldn't mail it. That would take too long. I wanted them to know I had you today. Right now." That high-pitched giggle again. Adrienne was sure her head would explode. "Victor just waltzed right in and handed it to your boyfriend."

So Conner had made it back from the other crime scene. That was good. He would figure it out and come for her, Adrienne knew that. They were at the place Adrienne had noted down and left for Conner in the file.

But would he remember it in the midst of everything going on? Would he get here in time?

Adrienne had to give Conner as much time as she could. She had to keep Simon talking.

"So Victor just walked in?"

"Yep. They didn't suspect a thing. I was sad he couldn't stick around and see Agent Perigo's face when he read the letter." Simon walked around her as she lay on the floor. Adrienne flinched away from him no matter where he was. She didn't want him to touch her, even by accident.

"You know," Simon said in his grating, singsongy voice, "I'm not surprised you and Conner fell in love with one another. It was fate."

Just keep him talking. "Oh, yeah. Why is that?"

"I like to look up what people's names mean. *Simon* means 'to be heard.' Don't you think that's perfect for me? I have always known I was meant to be heard." The giggle again. "Do you know what *Conner* means?"

Adrienne didn't want to talk about Conner with this sick bastard. "What?" she muttered through teeth gritted in pain and annoyance.

"*Conner* means lover of hounds." Simon clapped his hands like an enthusiastic second grader. "Don't you get it? *Conner* means lover of *hounds*. Like *bloodhounds*.

And you are known as 'the Bloodhound.' So apropos! Just perfect in every way."

Adrienne smiled just a bit through the pain. Conner probably wouldn't like knowing that's what his name meant. Too much like getting her name and picture tattooed on his skin.

But, "lover of hounds"? Somehow the nickname she had hated so much all those years ago didn't seem so terrible anymore. Not if it linked her with Conner.

Adrienne knew she was getting loopy. She needed to concentrate.

But it was so hard to think clearly with Simon so close. The pain was overwhelming.

"But not all names are correct," Simon continued as sadly now as he was delighted a moment ago. "*Victor* means champion. And that couldn't be further from the truth."

"But you're not Victor."

"That snively little bastard? No."

"Can I talk to Victor right now?"

Adrienne could feel his anger before he even stood. She cringed away from him but couldn't get far, lying on the floor with her hands tied. Simon walked over to her, anger suffusing his face. He grabbed her hair and brought his nose inches from hers. Adrienne fought to hold on to consciousness. Having him near was bad enough. Him touching her was unbearable.

"Do you think I'm stupid? That idiot could never do what needs to be done. He never could." Simon jerked her head away from him and released her in disgust.

Adrienne knew she was on dangerous ground. The wrong words said to Simon would send him into a murderous rage.

"Victor couldn't do things right like protect you from *her?*"

Adrienne could feel hesitation in Simon, along with bitterness and fear. He turned from Adrienne and walked back to his perch on the box.

"Auntie always ignored us, and when she wasn't ignoring us, she hurt us," Simon whispered. "We were never good enough for her. She had to be punished."

"But you know those women aren't her, right?"

"But they sound like her and act like her. They hurt and ignore people, like Auntie. They needed to be punished."

"Did the women hurt you?"

"No, but they ignored me when I tried to talk to them, just like Auntie. They mocked me and hated me, just like Auntie."

Adrienne wanted to keep Simon talking as long as possible. "The women made fun of you?"

"Not out loud. But I could tell they were laughing at me inside their heads!"

Adrienne could feel the rage emanating from Simon at the thought of these women mocking and laughing at him.

"But how could you tell, Simon? Did they say mean things to you?"

"No," he scoffed. "They didn't have to. I would try to talk to them and they would just ignore me. But I could see in their eyes that they were laughing at me. All of them."

Adrienne knew trying to further convince Simon of the women's innocence would be futile at best, and possibly deadly for her. She sat silently. You couldn't reason with madness.

"I had to punish them!" Simon continued. "So they

wouldn't hurt other people—just like Auntie. I had to stop them. It was good for me to stop them."

Simon paced back and forth, muttering under his breath. His mind began to calm; evidently he found peace in thinking he was ridding the world of these women.

Adrienne took advantage of the lack of pain and attention from Simon to test the tightness of the rope that tied her hands. Not as tight as she had feared—perhaps she would be able to get them off if she worked at them. But she'd never be able to walk away with the agony of Simon's thoughts filling her head. It was all she could do to stay conscious right now.

But Adrienne still kept working at the bonds—even if she had to crawl away, she could do that.

"Mostly, you're not like them, though. Although you are a little bit because you couldn't even remember Victor's name."

Adrienne could feel Simon's thoughts grow darker.

"I know you're not really like them, but you have to be punished, too, because you're a cheater."

"Didn't you punish me enough when you burnt down my barn?"

The maniacal giggling came again. "That was so much fun! You all looked so inane running around trying to save the silly horses. It was the best entertainment I'd had in a week!"

"I saw you on the porch in the rocking chair," Adrienne muttered through gritted teeth.

"I thought you might have! I'm so glad. You should've come over. We could've chatted."

But Adrienne could see what he would've done to her if she had tried to confront him that night. She defi-

nitely would not be alive now. Adrienne shuddered, bile
growing in her throat.

"I did mean to kill Agent Harrington," Simon continued. "I must admit I was quite upset he made it out
of the barn alive. That was *your* fault."

His rage was back and targeted at her. Adrienne
knew she had to do something—right now—but thinking was so hard she couldn't figure out what.

Simon paced back and forth, rubbing his hands together as if he was in deep thought. "Just wanted your
opinion on something. I was thinking I would kill you
and leave you at the hotel where you first stayed here in
San Francisco. Kind of a full circle, don't you agree?"
That hideous giggle erupted once more.

Adrienne knew time was running out.

"I think it would be poetic justice for Agent Perigo
to find you there, don't you agree?"

"They know who you are now, Simon," Adrienne
managed to get out around the pain. "They know what
Victor looks like. The FBI has files on him."

Simon stomped his foot like a petulant toddler. "I
know! That's so unfair! Now I won't be able to watch
as they find you!"

Simon walked toward her and, crouching down,
whispered conspiratorially, "That was my favorite part,
you know. Watching the FBI process the scenes. Watching them appreciate my handiwork. Knowing they were
too stupid to figure out it was me."

Adrienne eased farther away from him. "But they
know what you look like. You're going to have to stop.
Maybe if you turned yourself in now, they could help
you. Maybe you wouldn't even have to go to jail."

Adrienne didn't care what lies she told if it bought

her more time. She knew that was what Conner would want her to do.

Simon wasn't buying it. "No, they don't want to help me. They just want me to stop."

Simon stood and walked across the room to another table. Adrienne watched in terror as he picked up one of the knives on it. He had made his decision; he was going to kill her now. Adrienne knew her time had run out.

She had made some progress getting her wrists loosened, but it didn't matter—the first time he touched her, she would be totally helpless. Her thought process was difficult enough now, and he was across the room.

Whimpering, Adrienne began dragging herself across the floor away from Simon. She heard him laugh and knew he would soon be coming after her. Adrienne tried to stand but collapsed on the floor without even making it to her knees. She began to scoot slowly across the floor again; her limbs were too heavy to move any quicker.

She turned and saw Simon watching her from the table, a knife shining in his hand, smiling with evil glee. "Cheaters never win," he said in his singsongy voice.

It happened so gradually, Adrienne didn't really feel it at first. But instead of being overwhelmed by Simon's thoughts, Adrienne found she could think a little clearer. Looking around her, she saw the door for the first time. She knew that was where she had to get to. She started dragging her body in that direction.

This time when she tried to crawl, her body obeyed. Soon she was able to stumble up onto her feet. She looked over at Simon and could see his surprise that she was able to stand. He was expecting her to fall again.

But Adrienne was able to balance and stay on her feet as she made her way toward the door. She could see the door and Simon clearly. The noise and the pain were leaving.

It came to her then. *Conner.* It had to be Conner. He must be somewhere nearby, blocking her abilities and therefore getting Simon out of her head. She just needed to stay alive for a few more minutes, and Conner would find her.

But Simon didn't look like he was willing to give her a few more minutes. He ran at Adrienne, knife raised in his hand. Adrienne forced herself to stay calm and stepped out of the way as Simon brought the knife down right where she had been standing. She kept her back to the wall and scooted away quickly as Simon advanced on her again.

She could hear a pounding on the door and knew it had to be Conner and Seth.

"Conner!" Adrienne yelled as loudly as she could.

"Adrienne?" she could hear Conner's muffled response before the pounding on the door became more intense. They were trying to break it down.

Adrienne could see the murder in Simon's eyes. Conner and Seth would be too late to help her. She would have to save herself.

Adrienne saw the piece of wood lying on the ground just as Simon rushed her again. When he swung the knife toward her head, she ducked and grabbed the board. As she rose, she swung with all her might, cracking him in the jaw. Simon crumbled at her feet.

A few seconds later the door gave in and Conner and Seth stormed into the building with their weapons raised, obviously ready to take down Simon.

Adrienne could only see Conner. Using the last of her reserves, she stumbled over to him.

"What took you guys so long?" she managed to say as, for the third time in a few days, Adrienne collapsed in Conner's arms.

Chapter Sixteen

"Multiple personality disorder. Unbelievable," Conner muttered. He and Adrienne were back at Conner's town house much later that night. Simon/Victor had been treated for a concussion and broken jaw—thanks to Adrienne—and arrested. Conner and Adrienne had provided statements and had been debriefed, with the promise to be back at the ViCAP offices first thing tomorrow morning.

But multiple personality disorder? Seriously? Well, it certainly explained why Simon/Victor had been able to slip past Adrienne's abilities unnoticed. Evidently Victor had no ill intent toward the women Simon had killed. And the personalities were so separate that Victor had no real knowledge of what Simon was doing.

So he had been around Adrienne all the time but had never given off any ill thoughts to attract Adrienne's abilities. Every once in a while Simon had made his presence known, and those were the times that had hit her the worst and really scared them all.

Conner wasn't certain he believed any of the MPD stuff. He just hoped it didn't end up being the basis for an insanity plea that got Simon off the hook. Too many

women had died at the hands of Simon or Victor or whoever you wanted to call him.

And Adrienne had almost been another of his victims.

Conner would never forget those hours of absolute
panic when he'd known Simon had Adrienne in his
clutches. And those final minutes, trying to get into
the building, when he was afraid they weren't going
to make it in time. When they got the door open just
to see Adrienne crumple to the ground right in front
of him, Conner had watched his own world lying broken at his feet.

In that moment it had been crystal clear to him: nothing in his life had any purpose without Adrienne in it.

She sat across from him now, eating a burger they
had picked up from a local fast-food place. She looked
exhausted—still had dirt on her cheek and some sort of
plaster or something in her hair and every bit of makeup
had long since worn off.

She was the most beautiful thing he had ever seen.

"I love you." The words were out of his mouth before he had even finished the thought.

Her eyes rounded, and her throat began working up
and down. He thought for a second she might be chok-
ing and stood up in case she needed help.

"Are you okay?"

Adrienne nodded and finally managed to swallow
her food. Conner sat down again. He wasn't expecting
the little fist that darted out and punched him in the
shoulder. Hard.

"Hey! What was that all about?" Conner complained.

"You're going to make me remember this terrible cheeseburger forever! You're not supposed to say

something like that when a girl has a mouthful of greasy food!"

Conner smiled. "Sorry."

"You should be sorry. And I love you, too, Agent Jackass."

"And I want you to marry me."

Adrienne's eyes were wide open again, but this time she didn't have any food in her mouth. Conner knew that less than two weeks wasn't long to know someone. But he had felt more for Adrienne, felt deeper for Adrienne, than he had for anyone in his whole life. He wanted to be with her, to laugh with her, to protect her, to give her the silence she needed whenever she required it.

"Our lives are different," Adrienne finally managed to say.

"But not unblendable. We'll just have to figure out the right balance as we go along. But I want you to know that I don't expect you to come back and work for the Bureau."

Adrienne reached out and stroked his cheek. "I want to help. With you around, I finally think I can." She sighed and pulled away. "But I feel like you give me more than I give you. That it's unequal."

Conner leaned forward and gazed at her intently. "Well, I feel like you give me everything that's important in my life, and I can't live without you. So I'm not sure how we can be unequal."

Adrienne smiled and walked over to his chair. She pushed her finger against his chest until he leaned back, then hiked her legs over his hips so she was sitting astride him. She wrapped her arms around his neck.

"Everything that's important, huh?" she asked. He settled his arms around her hips.

"Every. Single. Thing." Between the words he kissed her, each successive touch of his lips becoming a little deeper, lingering a little longer.

"Well, then, I guess we better get married."

Conner stood up with Adrienne in his arms. "I thought you'd never ask."

* * * * *

A sneaky peek at next month...

INTRIGUE...

BREATHTAKING ROMANTIC SUSPENSE

My wish list for next month's titles...

In stores from 18th April 2014:

❏ Sawyer – Delores Fossen

& The District – Carol Ericson

❏ Scene of the Crime: Return to Mystic Lake
   – Carla Cassidy

& Navy SEAL Surrender – Angi Morgan

❏ Lawless – HelenKay Dimon

& The Bodyguard – Lena Diaz

Romantic Suspense

❏ Cavanaugh Undercover – Marie Ferrarella

Available at WHSmith, Tesco, Asda, Eason, Amazon and Apple

Just can't wait?

When five o'clock hits, what happens after hours...?

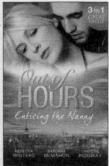

Feel the sizzle and anticipation of falling in love across the boardroom table with these seductive workplace romances!

**Now available at
www.millsandboon.co.uk**

Join the Mills & Boon Book Club

Want to read more **Intrigue** books?
We're offering you **2 more** absolutely **FREE!**

We'll also treat you to these fabulous extras:

- 🌹 **Exclusive offers and much more!**
- 🌹 **FREE home delivery**
- 🌹 **FREE books and gifts with our special rewards scheme**

Get your free books now!

visit www.millsandboon.co.uk/bookclub

or call Customer Relations on 020 8288 2888

The World of Mills & Boon®

There's a Mills & Boon® series that's perfect for you. We publish ten series and, with new titles every month, you never have to wait long for your favourite to come along.

By Request
Relive the romance with the best of the best
12 stories every month

Cherish™
Experience the ultimate rush of falling in love
12 new stories every month

Desire™
Passionate and dramatic love stories
6 new stories every month

n o c t u r n e™
An exhilarating underworld of dark desires
Up to 3 new stories every month

For exclusive member offers go to
millsandboon.co.uk/subscribe

M&B/WORLD4a

Discover more romance at

www.millsandboon.co.uk

❤ WIN great prizes in our exclusive competitions

❤ BUY new titles before they hit the shops

❤ BROWSE new books and REVIEW your favourites

❤ SAVE on new books with the Mills & Boon® Bookclub™

❤ DISCOVER new authors

PLUS, to chat about your favourite reads, get the latest news and find special offers:

🔗 Find us on facebook.com/millsandboon

🐦 Follow us on twitter.com/millsandboonuk

❤ Sign up to our newsletter at millsandboon.co.uk